Thieves

Thieves

VALERIE WERDER

FENCE BOOKS

New York

FENCE MODERN PRIZE IN PROSE

PUBLISHED IN THE UNITED STATES BY

FENCE BOOKS
36-09 28TH AVENUE, APT. 3R
ASTORIA, NY 11103-4518

WWW.FENCEPORTAL.ORG

THIS BOOK WAS PRINTED BY VERSA PRESS
DISTRIBUTED BY SMALL PRESS DISTRIBUTION
AND CONSORTIUM BOOK SALES AND DISTRIBUTION

COVER CONCEPT BY LEONA CHRISTIE
EXECUTION BY COLIN PACKARD
COVER AND INTERIOR DESIGN BY REBECCA WOLFF

LIBRARY OF CONGRESS CONTROL NUMBER: 2023941389
ISBN 13: 978-1-9443802-1-2

FIRST EDITION
10 9 8 7 6 5 4 3 2

For Christopher

Table of Contents

I.

TAKING SOME TIME OFF

1

Valerie often played a game. Because the game had no other players, she didn't feel obliged to give it a name or a straightforward set of rules. The goal was this: to gut herself of her usual contents—by taking the subway to an unfamiliar station and wandering its vicinity in concentric circles, no thoughts in her head, or by sitting through a matinée at the theatre on Sixth Avenue and draining herself of language until she was, at most, a mass of buzzing static in a creaking seat—and become another thing entirely.

She didn't fully trust the game. The problem wasn't its premise: likely depriving a body of its context and contents *would* transform it into something other than it was. No, the problem was much more practical: the game was, at the end of the day, impossible to play for real. Valerie couldn't scoop out her insides or turn herself placeless. Whatever she was, she couldn't get rid of her body.

She didn't remember how it started. Maybe in response to a phrase encountered on a motivational poster in her high-school girls' locker room, or as an epigraph to a softcover self-help book in her analyst's foyer. *Wherever you go, there you are*, or *there's no escaping yourself*. Likely she'd lodged complaints against the poster while pulling on ankle socks or straining to overhear her analyst analyze the preceding patient. Likely she'd interrogated the poster or book on who its addressee, that slippery *you*, actually was.

Most games begin innocently enough. Valerie found herself gradually forced to up the no-context game's stakes to reap its rewards. The last time she'd played had also been the most serious. She sat at her desk at work, tracking the receptionist, Sylvie, on the art gallery's surveillance-footage software. It was, by all metrics, a normal workday: Valerie assembling strings of words meant to sell objects, Sylvie orchestrating deliveries and recognizing recognizable faces at the front desk. At 2:00 P.M., the swarm of pixels that spelled *Sylvie* stepped outside for a smoke break and Valerie hurried downstairs to join her. The two walked in diagonals around each other to ward off the late winter cold, amusing themselves by comparing stories.

Sylvie: *I have to research and order at least twelve different brands of espresso from five different countries because the Japanese collector was offended that Emilio only had Ethiopian when he came to look at the Basquiat.*

Valerie: *Did you hear that Nick had to fly to Milan yesterday to pick up the catalogues for the opening? Out of the blue. They didn't even let him go home to change. And he didn't have time to leave the airport once he got there. The printer met him outside Terminal 1 with a box, and he caught the redeye back an hour later.*

Sylvie: *FedEx couldn't ship the catalogs here in time?*

Valerie: *They're big books, really heavy. Flying him out was cheaper. They're at my desk, if you want to come take a look.*

Sylvie: *Fuck. I wish I'd known. I would have asked him to get some coffee from the Duty Free while he was at it. Bet the Japanese don't mind Italian espresso.* She stopped and took a drag to finesse her joke. *Ah, shit. Never mind. Italian espresso could've been grown anywhere, huh?*

Valerie: *Yeah, anywhere except Italy.*

Valerie returned to her desk and stared at the catalogs in their mute brown boxes, sealed with shiny packing tape and stamped in two languages from international travel. She had written these books, the catalog texts, the introduction by the gallery owner and the neatly laid-out and illustrated chronology charting the artist's life. The main essay by the famous academic, a former professor of hers who told her that he was *busy, much too busy to compile my notes into a proper text, but perhaps you'd like to take a stab at it.* She took a stab at it, scrapping his notes and inventing anew, and he thanked her for *being a wonderful copy editor* and *barely touching my words at all*, and she sealed the envelope containing his $7,000 fee and instructed the designer as to how large, precisely, the byline should be. She paid for image rights, checked captions and citations, organized the material in chronological order, situated the story she'd created into the larger story, the better story, the story of art. She wrote the press release, made up quotes about how pleased the gallery was, *so pleased*, to represent the artist, and how thrilled the estate was, *so thrilled*, to work with the gallery. She drafted sales pitches and highlights lists, conducted interviews from the gallery owner's email address with reporters who addressed her by the gallery owner's name. *Dear Helene.* The exhibition would be good. The work would sell. Valerie hadn't seen the paintings in person. She hadn't needed to—the language wrote itself.

The catalogs stared back at her, stupid lumps. It wasn't necessary to open the boxes to look at the books. They would look like all the other books she'd edited for the gallery: printed and bound in Milan by a man named Massimo, front cover dedicated to a detail of the show's most expensive painting, the essay wearing her professor's name careful to emphasize (and she remembered him quoting the phrase when she ran into him at the bar earlier that week, remembered their horrible fight) that the work *playfully subverted the rigid codes of body, identity, and representation.*

In that moment, she knew. She'd made up this story as she'd made up any other. Though the books had the look and feel of seriousness, they'd been chauffeured here for the opening only to be displayed in a stack and then given, gratis, to collectors who'd take them home and throw them out or else set them on their Sarfatti side tables, spines uncracked, simulations of artworks decorating living rooms while the collectors phoned their accountants and consulted advisors to move around funds, inquire about markets, take the requisite steps to buy the real thing, to ship it to the freeport and allow it to sit in storage, mutely absorbing that year's taxes.

Razor-calm, Valerie gathered her belongings, avoiding the gaze of the boxes, not telling Sylvie or her manager or anyone. She left in the middle of the workday. The afternoon was cold and bright. She walked to a nearby bookstore and browsed the aisles with clear, unhurried intent. Books organized according to profit reports and Amazon ratings, names extolling other names stamped on each cover. The sales game, again, here.

Ted said there was a fundamental difference between winning a game and beating it. Those who wanted to win agreed with the game's terms, molding themselves to its rules. Those who wanted to beat a game, though, were playing at something much greater. They were troubling the perimeter of the knowable world. Valerie toyed with a blue-and-green paperback, its cover declaring it *wild, exhilarating, fresh*. According to Ted, winning would be having the money to buy the book, the brains to read it, and the well-appointed apartment in which to display it. Neither a *wild* nor an *exhilarating* future for the book, Valerie thought. Surely it deserved a life adequate to its own promise. She selected a book whose hard cover was patterned in geometric pink and orange and—casually, casually, angling herself just so—dropped it into her bag. Still not as smooth as Ted, she knew, but Ted, who was tall and dexterous and almost comically handsome in his cowboy boots and worker's overshirt, had advantages. He was the most skilled shoplifter she'd ever met and, though she hadn't met many, she'd wager he was the best in all of New York, at a minimum, if only because of his grace.

In the early days of their relationship—if it could be called that—Valerie and Ted were walking down Bleecker Street when a man, lumbering and pockmarked, stopped them, calling out an old nickname more to some invisible witness than to Ted himself. *Hey-o, Sneak Attack, is that you? Sneak-Attack Smith?* Hands bloated and sweating, he grabbed Ted's shoulder, shaking him, telling him that his high-school wrestling pictures were still on their old gymnasium's walls. *Can't believe you're in the Big Apple, too,* he said, before admitting he was there only on a family vacation. *Can't believe you made it out of that place alive.* When they got home, Ted stripped his pants, laughing, to reveal blood trickling down his legs. Big glistening stains on his thighs. Drips crossing his shins in deep red webs. He walked to the bathroom to shower and Valerie watched it run down his ankles and hit the floor in small dark drops. He'd stuffed dozens of dainty and disk-shaped steaks, raw, down his jeans at the Gristedes on Ninth before meeting up with her. *I felt it happen when that guy hugged me*, he said, mopping lines of steak juice with his palm. *He squeezed so hard, the wrappers broke.*

Ted moved not like a wrestler but like a modern dancer, a Martha Graham trainee, his gestures precisely attuned to every interlocutor, every situation. Were he at the bookstore with Valerie now, he might have picked off a shelf of books in full view of the security camera, all the while chatting up a salesperson in the next aisle. Valerie shifted her bag, considerably heavier now, and rearranged the shelf. She didn't want any of these books. She'd taken the pink-and-orange bestseller only as a token, a reminder that being sold something doesn't necessarily mean you have to buy it.

The getting game, as she and Ted called it, did have a few rules, based more in the cosmic laws of the universe, karma and all that, than in human norms and standards. For example: if you steal for any reason besides really needing what you take, you have to either a) buy something small as an offering to the economic system you're cheating, or b) give away another stolen object to a person who doesn't know how you obtained it. Of course, the rule's conditional term—*really needing* what you take—allowed ample room for interpretation, and Ted rarely followed his invented rules, anyway, though he attributed every misfortune or close call to their trespass. Ted was the sort of person who seriously believed that he was at the mercy of hidden forces greater than himself: not in a New Age-y, ayahuasca-retreat-in-Peru way, but in the desperate manner of bums and wanderers who have to stake their bets on something, being unable to stake them on a bank account, a job, a stable group of age-appropriate friends.

Valerie was the sort of person who followed rules. She browsed her way to the bookstore's café and bought an apple, 75¢, which she took to the ladies' room. Offering in hand, she sat pants-down on the toilet as a barrage of messages and emails from the gallery came through: *Urgently need sales packet for Richter viewing. Helene looking for you. Where have you gone? Where are you now?*

Where had she gone, and where was she now? Why here, and not somewhere else? Why herself, and not anyone else?

hey, you hiding inside the Turrell? Sylvie texted. The gallery's March show (as Valerie described it in the press release) *interrogated the conceptual and spatial poetics of the void.* A corner of the second floor had been partitioned by James Turrell's assistants to create an enveloping dark space cut by two thin, violet lines. Sylvie had taken to climbing inside the installation at least twice a day, *for power naps,* she said.

Nope, went for a walk, Valerie replied, and then, *I think I'm going to quit.*

right now? what for? Sylvie responded. *who is gonna finish the Richter packet?*

Valerie had neither a reason nor a backup copywriter in mind. *I'm fed up.*

yr gonna get a job at another gallery?

No, I guess not.

so u will finish the packet today? The ellipses beside Sylvie's name paused, disappeared, reappeared, and then a longer text came in. *u should ask for a sabbatical. say its for health reasons. I heard they paid Françoise to go to a spa in the black forest for three months last year to heal some sort of liver imbalance.*

Valerie sent the conversation careening back into its speech-bubble icon and clicked the envelope on her screen, making it vibrate and bounce before releasing it to compose an email. Subject line: *Sabbatical request.*

She'd been constipated but now, as she wrote, her swollen bowels moved. Valerie recalled that the dying often defecate in the moment of passing from life to death. She might take this as a sign: lumps heavy in the bowl indicating a transition, a new act in her narrative arc; the body announcing itself in its expulsions, collusions with bacteria and fungi, harbingers of the hidden.

Valerie picked up her bag, book secured inside, and flushed the toilet. She couldn't convince herself that her shit meant anything at all.

2

The newly unemployed, Ted said, report that the first few unoc-cupied days are the most difficult. Without a constant influx of externally imposed tasks, former workers quickly lapse into sloth or depression. Time runs differently. Disorientation abounds. Ted had never experienced this because he'd never held a job long enough for its rhythms to become routine. Valerie remembered how he looked when he said this, his wiry frame settled comfort-ably against a cheap metal chair, gaze restless above his pretty mouth. After their conversation, she poked around on the Internet reading first-person accounts of the recently laid off. If she ever lost her job, she'd be prepared. She'd have a list of things to do with her time. She wouldn't wander around, aimless.

When her sabbatical was approved, Valerie spent the first week hiding one hour under the next, moving purposefully into and out of home-goods stores, bodegas plastered with Virgins of Guadalupe and lottery numbers, plant nurseries like fishbowls of tropical humidity in New York's February freeze. As she walked, she thought she might untangle the architecture of the world, peer between beams and chip away plaster scenery to find traces of its production, how it had come together just so. Upon her return to her apartment in the evening, she created a document organized chronologically, the kind of report with steps and symptoms that her mother had taught her to take to the doctor when she was sick. *Doctors don't trust women,* Susan reported to a fourteen-year-old Val-erie, who had complained of cramps in her side. *Much less teenage girls. You've got to track the aches and pains; write out a list of symptoms; add it up. Go to them with evidence, and you're much more likely to get a diagnosis.* Narrative, Valerie was given to understand, had power.

3

At Valerie's request, Susan packaged the childhood diaries in a brown paper bag and then a padded mailing envelope, swaddling them as if they were seriously precious, and mailed them to her daughter's Queens address.

Why a sabbatical? Susan asked when Valerie called her from the plant store. *You've only been working at the gallery for two years. What'll they think? And what about money?*

Valerie gave a vague response about identity shifting with emplacement, needing to feel herself become someone else. She'd go back to her job after a short break. But first, she wanted to feel the world without a workday. She wanted to understand who she might be without a series of tasks. Susan sighed, shook her head, opted for diplomacy. Sure, she'd send the childhood journals. *Just don't be away from your job for too long. And count your blessings that you've got a boss who'll write the check for a useless vacation.*

It's an unpaid sabbatical, Valerie replied, but her mother didn't respond.

When the journals arrived, Valerie read them alone in her apartment, feeling divorced from the girl who wrote them years before, not even a hint of kindness or nostalgia for her. She wanted to read the diaries because of the Lent conversation. Holy Week, a time for abstinence, but Valerie and Ted met up with Virginia at their favorite Ethiopian café. Virginia arrived late, shedding an old-fashioned fur coat and squeezing Valerie on the shoulder as she maneuvered herself into a barstool. She promptly took over the ordering: two beers, $3 special, a glass of house red for herself, a vegetarian platter to split.

When I was little, Virginia said, *I'd pick a single thing to give up for Lent. No one forced me to do it. My mom wasn't religious. I don't think I'd ever set foot in a church. I wanted to be pious, though. Self-denial seemed like a real statement. 'I can voluntarily forgo this thing I love. I can weather forty days and nights.' And it was great because, after I gave up the whatever, I felt I deserved it that much more.*

The café had recently hired a perky blonde bartender, small and tattooed, who refilled their waters, smiling at Ted before bouncing away. *Café must be doing pretty well,* he said, indicating the girl. *The American Dream.*

Now it seems like total bullshit, Virginia continued, ignoring him. *Because even though my mom couldn't afford fancy groceries or nice clothes, we could still walk into the stores. Little plastic clamshells of arugula and baby lettuce. Baby lettuce! Do you know how rich you have to be to look at a bunch of leaves and think, "Oh yeah, there's the baby lettuce"?*

You sound like Valerie, Ted said. *Or nineties-era Moby. Blah, blah, capitalism, everything is wrong.*

No, but it's true, and you know it, and I know it, and that's the thing. Even though I know it's ridiculous to give up candy or fried foods for a few months while everything else in my life remains exactly the same, it still feels good. On a symbolic level. Deludes me into thinking I'm in control.

Sounds like a habit, Ted said. *A habit that hardened into an identity.*

How do you think that works? Valerie asked. She liked to ask the obvious questions, disguising her absolute lack of agency as a sort of naïve objectivity. *I am a studious alien,* she thought as Ted smiled, indulgent, pushing their plates toward precarity with a stray elbow.

I think it's called memory, he replied, teasing.

Although Virginia and Ted were nearly a decade Valerie's senior, they agreed: each felt a grand sense of continuity with their childhood self. Virginia, wine glass in hand, pointed to a faint scar crossing her upper lip. *Remember when I showed you the picture of this one, Ted? I was running down a hill too fast, and I tripped and fell, split my face in two. I must have been four years old. My mom wouldn't take me to the hospital. She put some glue on my busted-up face. Liquid stitches, I think she called it.*

But, besides scars, how's your actual grown-up body connected to your past? Valerie protested. Ted and Virginia exchanged an annoyed look. This conversation again.

Valerie picked at a mole on her elbow. *Memories are just stories. Me, here, this thing*—and she gestured loosely, tipsy, at her torso—*it's not connected to the other versions of a self I've been.*

Deep reds saturated Ted's skin, the edges of his face dissolving into the dim bar light. *Sure it is. Physically.*

Valerie opened her mouth to speak, but found nothing inside. She wasn't certain she could say anything, know anything, really, about the physical world, a series of scenes and images she screened to herself through the day.

And that's how memory works, added Virginia. *Memories are stored in your body. It's all held together by the same, uh, substance.*

You know, liquid stitches. Ted grinned.

Valerie didn't know, and Virginia and Ted didn't want to know. They wanted to play games. *I'm being stupid. Forget it*, she said, blood prickling her cheeks. She knew that her body was distinct from herself, her life. She, Valerie, was compressed into language. This body, though (she pictured herself gesticulating, even as her limbs remained still), couldn't quite be understood.

And so, the Lent conversation now as neatly packaged as any other story, Valerie sat on her thin mattress, diaries beside her. Orange streetlight insisted its way through plastic blinds. The finished diaries, unremarkable both in form and content, had sat for years in Valerie's childhood closet. One had a flexible black plastic cover, green ink scrawled across blank pages, wear and tear from frequent flipping and rereading. Another was hard and substantial, scribbles of imaginary characters on its mustard-yellow cover. Valerie had decorated the sixth-grade diary with a pink feather boa, matted and dusty from storage. Year after year, the entries revealed only formulaic plots and confused attempts to shape their writer into a recognizable image, a self to wear on her skin as a face.

Sitting with the diaries, laptop open, she performed a sociological examination. Page upon frantic diary page was filled with adolescent accounts of products—the urgency of differentiating herself from her sister by means of a lip-gloss flavor, the absolute necessity of a particular brand of jeans in a game of middle school seduction. Occasionally, Valerie addressed the diary directly: *Dear Diary*, or a parenthetical, *I know* you *understand me.* The young writer advertising herself: was it here that she'd begun accumulating dense layers of abstraction, ceaselessly, in her wake?

> Feb. 26, 2003—Who is Valerie, really? At this point, I want answers. My life seems so surreal. These are the questions I'm trying to answer: Why is everyone who they are? Am I important? Why do my parents always get the final answer? Why don't I know what to do with my life? Who is this narrator, prodding me on from inside my head?
>
> (Valerie had been told *the world was her oyster* and she could *do anything she set her mind to.* She would set her mind to the usual things: going to high school and then college and then graduate school, accumulating tremendous debt, pursuing several failed relationships, moving to the big city and getting a grown-up job.)

Valerie opened a new Microsoft Word document, flipped open one of the diaries, and watched her own face lit by the glowing blue screen as she wrote:

> How can I create a coherent character from these episodic banalities, these transcribed formulas who have all, to some degree (and they know it), taken a deep breath, plugged their noses and closed their eyes, and plunged deep into the pool of appearances?

4

Absent any audience for woozy philosophizing, she typed questions into her phone.

What can I do if words don't have meaning? They don't connect to a hidden reality. You can do anything with words. You can make them say whatever you want, she wrote in a desperate message to her sister.

To Google: *How can you detect a lie?* Trust actions, not words, said the first instructional article on a therapist's website. *But what about when words are the only way of knowing,* she wrote, pressing enter. A famous philosopher shared her concern in a video lecture posted in 2014. Valerie pinched her red comforter's plasticky care label between thumb and forefinger, rubbing its undersides together until the thing made a satisfying scratching sound. *Utopia Bedding,* the label announced, and then, a few lines down, *3D hollow siliconized.* The line defining its country of origin had faded in the wash; only the peaks of an *M* and the remains of a lowercase *g* remained legible. *Garment labels trustworthy?* Valerie typed and deleted, writing instead, *possibility of knowing truth about material world once and for all.* Google didn't understand this as a question. She was confronted with an assortment of badly written articles, blog posts, links to spiritual advice sites, and courses at the University of Metaphysics. She could become an expert in such matters for a few thousand dollars.

Con artists capable of telling the truth? she revised the sentiment, getting straight to the heart of the matter. *No, con artists not capable of truth-telling, nor of love,* Google wrote back, pessimistic. *All you can know is yourself,* said Google.

Who do you think you are, Valerie shot back, *the Oracle of Delphi or something?* Google turned up some ancient links to a PBS.org educational effort for kids, pre-Java programming.

As a child, Valerie had assumed that life's mysteries would progressively open out in front of her, a kind of mystical scroll preparing her way. By her death, she'd have done it all, attained the totality of knowledge, experienced complete immersion. To better enable herself to handle such immensity, she locked herself in her and her sister's shared bathroom to read the unpronounceables on Suave shea butter moisturizers and hydrogen peroxide bottles, dose herself with Advil to see if she could open up new layers of consciousness. (This wouldn't work. Knowledge would be progressive and cumulative.)

What are you doing in there? eleven-year-old Julie demanded, thwacking a palm at the bathroom door.

I'm getting ready, Valerie called back to her sister from across the divide.

But we're not going anywhere, Julie protested. *And I have to pee.*

Some products had the loveliest names. *Ravishing, Ivory, Shanghai Express.* The bathroom was not equipped with a dictio nary or encyclopedia, so Valerie invented meanings for the words (meanings that, inevitably, had to do with her own life).

Well. Nearly a fifth of that life and two university degrees had passed, and no mysteries had unfolded before her. The objects in her medicine cabinet were more stubbornly inert than ever, calling out to her only when she'd soon need to buy or steal more. She had learned—with great effort and embarrassment—that *ravishment* wasn't lovely, and that *ivory* came at the cost of a living thing's death.

Valerie collected her limbs and willed herself into the kitchen, phone in hand. There were condiments in the cupboards, toiletries in the linen closet: plenty of products to check against their labels. She consulted a red-and-yellow tin's ingredients—*celery salt, paprika, black pepper, cinnamon, ginger, other spices*—and entered "other spices" into Google, receiving a catalog of common seeds and roots sorted in alphabetical order, a culinary magazine's quick-and-dirty guide, a link to Spice Islands's inventory. *"Other spices" meaning*, she tried, but the search returned more of the same. Adding preceding ingredients—*black pepper, cinnamon, ginger*—brought a biography of a bearded, sword-wielding and crimson-tights-wearing man— *His Lordship, the Terrible*—who'd circumnavigated Africa with the two-pronged mission of spreading misery and stuffing ships with seasonings. *Other spices* hid only violence and dispossession. Valerie sighed, turned, and walked the few steps to the hallway closet: neatly folded towels, a half-empty bag of Epsom salt, an eight-pack of Ivory Soap on the top shelf. *Ivory!* She grasped hold of the shelf's edge, jumping with a strategic pull. On her third attempt, she sent the soaps scattering across the floor. Surely this Ivory, cheap and inoffensive as it was, would be innocent of death. *Ingredients/Ingrédients/Ingredientes*, she read. *Sodium tallowate and/or et/ou y/o sodium palmate.*

Palmate, she Googled. *Botany*, her phone suggested. *The sodium salt of a palm leaf.*

Tallowate, she tried. *The fatty tissue of sheep or cattle.*

Dammit. Valerie considered the phrase again, its sneaky *and/or*. *Ivory* wouldn't even reveal to her whether or not it had killed anything. She lamely threw her phone against the wall where it bounced and, as if on cue, glowed the carpet blue with a halfhearted hum. A message from Julie. *The only thing u can do is take all the words and figure out what they say to u. Theres no getting out of it. Sry I cant help more.*

5

Three days into her sabbatical, standing at the kitchen counter (vaguely pinkish in the still-nighttime light), soles of her feet pocked with pebbles and grime, Valerie discovered another layer to the no-context game. If she emptied her attention of words and images and stared, still or swaying, at a spot of cupboard or a sliver of outside between window blinds, she could trigger a shudder in her body, or else her mind, transporting her body or mind—herself—about in time. She had previously experienced her memories as a story happening in language, a garment neatly ironed and laid out to dry. This was different: not remembering, but carving her habitual self out of her body and allowing something to fill her up, something that came from without while being incanted inside. It would perhaps become part of her.

She set her sight upon an eggshell sheen on the cupboard door, air around her recomposing itself in lungs and on skin, and found herself small, in the backyard of her childhood home, living-room windows open. Radio sounds filtered through mesh screens and thin walls, penetrating the membrane of Valerie's skin, becoming atmospheric. Spring air, too, filled the house. The cold would feel fresh and wild in her lungs when she returned inside later. Valerie looked down at her feet: stark white knockoff Keds on wet grass. She sensed herself as a *thing*, a cohesive and discrete *thing*, and she sensed it from a certain distance. She became whole from that distance: red jumpsuit with delicate flower print, mosquito-bitten legs covered in downy hair, white sneakers, thick bangs.

I wonder if she's watching me. She craned her neck to look for her mom. Was Susan standing at the window, keeping an eye on her? She was not. Valerie looked around, feeling acutely seen, but there was no one in sight.

Later that day (and now a memory in language, thought and not felt), Valerie gathered weeds and arranged them on the porch, a feudal peasant in Flanders, or maybe an imperial handmaiden in the Chinese court. She felt the gaze again, this time originating from somewhere a few feet above her head and to the left. Or, to be more precise, she became the gaze: she saw not what her own eyes were looking at, but instead a vision of herself as if a film character, from above. She realized that no one was watching her. She was watching herself. She went on playing, adjusting the game of categorizing and sorting weeds according to the viewing pleasure of the gaze that lived within, monitoring her.

6

Sometimes, when I have a thought, she typed, *I have it so quickly that it's not in words. It happens all at once. And then I repeat it back to myself, but this time in language. Sometimes I do this just to slow down the thinking, but also maybe to make sense of the thought, to try to register it in the storehouse of my memory.*
Valerie.doc

In the third person, Valerie is a sociologist of herself.

She is critical. She operates at a distance. The third
person allows her to do away with any idea that Valerie
might be special: she tells her story simply because it
is the only one she knows. She presents a case study
of Valerie, that generic form, that mishmash of a self
stuffed into the contours of a body. Any sense of interiority to be found within a third-person narrative will
be impersonal and banal. Valerie is nothing more than
an observable social phenomenon.

You write about yourself in the third person, she wrote, *when the
story has passed*.

Like that time you looked through an old photo album
with your mom. She pointed to your small, careful
face in a blurred group of grinning kindergarteners.
She smiled and spoke about you, and for her—she's
watched you your entire life—you're a discrete entity,
but you could tell she was talking about something
that was gone. What she was talking about was you,
but also not. You stole the photograph, wedged it in
the mirror in your college dormitory, looked at your
nineteen-year-old reflection alongside the kindergar-
ten school photo, which you situated below a picture
of your toddler self wearing a Burger King crown and
hiding under a picnic table, above your sixth-grade
self in braces and a bulky blue sweater. The photographed faces made sense alongside the mirror face,
but they didn't seem to be directly related. You didn't
know where these girls had gone, but they weren't
you, and they weren't there. And you knew that you'd
soon be not there, either. Sure, cells shifted chronologically; a body grew and changed over time. You knew
that. But the idea that the self you were at any given
moment, in any given snapshot—the idea that this

[16   ]

person was *you*, and that *you* stably persisted through time despite your morphing, mysterious flesh—

And who was this *you* emerging on the page? Why so quiet, the sociologist's voice? *Against itself*, she wrote, *the third person collapses toward the first by means of the direct address, the selves speaking to each other from a distance.*

> It's in the direct address, the voice aimed at a particular interlocutor—a friend or stranger, an authority, a future self seconds away, too close for *she* but too far for *I*—that language navigates between one body and the next. *You* infects both speakers, performs a transplant. The direct address is the mode of orientation, beginning in the precise and personal, extending outward and reaching its target only to ricochet back, resituating the first *you*, now, as something else. You often find yourself speaking to Valerie in your mind as *you*—a split within, a voice coming to address the thing that operates as its twin, narrated in third-person, *Valerie*.

> The first person claims some slim space for my voice, rejoins language with body. Voice comes from throat, material when spoken, material when written, a force shaped by fascia and synapses and nerves. The voice makes no claim at abstraction or objectivity, knowing that these are, strictly speaking, impossible. *I* admits this, begins from its own location. My voice represents nothing but its origins in my body, my body's points of contact with the outside, its existence as a compilation of things. The singular *I* gathers these together, expels them forth.

There's no reason to choose one mode of address for these notes, Valerie wrote. She was working, feverish, against the idea that any of this might cohere into a meaning, a story. The only coherence to be had, she understood, would be had in writing.

II.

BUYING

1

The summer Julie turned eleven, we started playing the game. It was her idea. You could say it was her fault.

While our mom deposited paychecks at the HSBC across the parking lot, we hid in the CVS lobby, flipping through coupon booklets and licking our fingers to taste newspaper ink and salt. Julie motioned for me to stand with her beneath the fisheye surveillance mirror, out of range of the parking-lot cameras and invisible to the stoner girl at checkout (occupying herself with a thorough examination of the gunk beneath her fingernails, anyway). Even our mom, fiddling with the bank's drive-thru ATM, couldn't see us. It was the perfect spot.

I'm going to get a L'Oréal eyeshadow palette, gold sparkle, Julie said. *What are you getting?*

I don't have any money, Jules.

Me neither, said Julie. *But what are you going to get?* She pulled out the elastic waistband of her shorts as though to reveal something small and hard and plastic nestled against her left hip.

Seriously?

That's how I got a Revlon shimmer powder last time we were here. Put it right in my pants. You didn't see. She cupped the immaterial compact in her left hand and feigned bringing it close to her nose, dabbing a thin layer of invisibility on each cheek.

You don't look any different.

I know. That's not the point.

What's the point, then?

Julie screwed up the muscles around her eyes. I saw that particles of shimmer were caught in the fine hairs covering her cheeks, matting out her freckles. She wasn't lying: she'd taken the powder and used it at home. *You'll see.*

See what?

But Julie just snapped her waistband and walked into the store. The automatic doors closed behind her.

For weeks, I had wanted a three-pack of Bonne Bell Lip

Smackers. *Tropical Punch, Razzle Raspberry, Smooth Vanilla.* $2.99 or, by some magical equivalence, three-quarters of an hour's worth of babysitting for the four-year-old up the street. I took a last look at the coupon booklet. Store-brand batteries were on sale that week.

By the time I ventured in, Julie had made her way across the store to Cosmetics. I snuck down the Greeting Cards aisle and wove back up Snacks and Soft Drinks, plotting my sharp diagonal toward Bonne Bell. *Make it look casual,* Julie had told me. I slowed down, picked up a Butterfinger, put it down. I was an average shopper. I was browsing.

I watched Julie's reflection in the mirrored ceiling above Cosmetics. She was right. Although the cheek shimmer was imperceptible, it had somehow transformed her into the kind of girl who should be pausing before the L'Oréal display, considering a Ravishing Red, turning it around in her hand. I tried the same gesture with a Milky Way bar, clumsy and self-aware.

How far, how unbearably far, Cosmetics was from Snacks and Soft Drinks. How impossible it would be to cross from Aisle 4 to Aisle 6, to pass by the darkroom attendants and pharmacists, risk being apprehended by a stocking associate, cornered, questioned. *Can I help you find anything?* No help for me, thank you, suffering before chocolates and sour gummies and Pepperidge Farm cookies, $4.99.

The cookies had a certain round elegance, or else their image did, printed on matte white plastic. Little melty treasures shrouded from view, lined up row by row, package after package, each one stamped with an orange sticker: $4.99. How many cookies in a package? *Serving size, three cookies. Servings per container, about five.* How much did a single wafer cost? I hadn't yet mastered mental arithmetic.

Milk chocolate shavings curled beneath stacks of cookies, *Actual size*, on the package's front. *Milano*, read the text. Where was that? Europe, I decided, having no idea what that meant. A place where Julie could be ravishing and I could eat milk chocolate. I'd tell her I had decided against Bonne Bell on purpose. The cookies,

I'd say, were for us to share. I stood still, stiller, hovering my hand above the package, sure I could sense something stirring deep inside. Something warm and soft and evil, for me and only me.

The package was too large. It wouldn't do. I cursed the wafers, hated them. To their left, though, glimmered packets of peppermint patties, almond bars, peanut-butter cups, heaped in a metal-wire bin. 99¢ each, or five for $4.

Who knew how long I'd been standing in Snacks and Soft Drinks. The things on the shelf were greedy: they stole time from me, shut down sound and perception, cordoned off sight like blinders affixed to my temples. I looked again for Julie in the mirrors dotting the ceiling, but couldn't find her. Who could be my guide? I squinted at an Almond Joy. *Tell me what you want from me.* I haunted my hand above the stash, asking the contents to speak through their plastic wrappers, beyond their labels, images, nutritional information. If one wanted to be taken, it would say so.

Blood pulsed and pooled in my fingertips, twitchy, and, hawklike, I grabbed. I hardly knew what I'd selected. It didn't matter. I had been hailed by a larger force, more powerful than my little life, than the CVS and its anesthetized cashiers. The words stamped into the candy wrapper had loosened from the plastic and were coursing through the air, reciting litanies to me. Who was I to ignore a calling? I looked up and down the aisle, leaned forward as if examining family packs of Reese's on the top shelf, and tucked whatever I had grabbed into my pocket.

It was safe. I was not. I felt myself again, a sweating body in a drugstore scene, teetering on tiptoe into the candy display. The surveillance cameras were directly to my right, making returning the loot to its shelf impossible. The checkout girl, clever watchman, only feigned interest in her fingernails. She had a direct line to the security guards. They were monitoring my every move.

I watched myself as did the camera; the image it transmitted to the cashier and security guards, I saw clearly, was that of a vaguely pathetic middle-school girl with an inoffensive haircut, too-long arms, googly eyes. The camera certainly couldn't detect that I was in the throes of a desperate struggle. *A struggle for what?* My breath came in shallow fits past Health and Medicine. *For self-preservation*, I replied. *But preservation of yourself, or of the thing in your pocket?* Strange: in that brief sliver of time between grab and exit, there was no difference between its life and mine. *This must be how a mother bear feels about her cubs*, I thought. (Julie and I had watched a *National Geographic* the night before.)

There, in Household Products, was Julie, lurking in front of bags of cat litter. Checking in with her would only be a waste of time. My legs propelled me toward the exit, perception lagging seconds behind. *Casually*, I told myself. *Casual.* I held my breath through the first set of doors and then the second, sweaty hand in pocket (back, left, my baggiest jeans). The film in my head played a voice-over, a phalanx of checkout girls speaking into Walkie-talkies. *She's leaving through the Greeting Cards aisle. She's praying the motion sensor won't stick over the tacky gray carpet; she's betting the doors will release her to the parking lot.* Escape. The multiplying, conspiring checkout girls dissolved and my usual narrator, me or the voice that lived inside me, returned. *She's climbing into the backseat of her mom's car, home safe, safe and sound.*

Where's your sister? My mom was rooting around in her purse. I couldn't respond. She would know. She'd hear it in my voice.

Julie climbed into the car, wiping her cheeks, ruthless and composed. *I'm right here, Mom.*

So, what's new at the CVS? (We were notorious makeup-aisle browsers.)

Find any decent Bonne Bell lip balms, Valerie? echoed Julie, cruel.

Nope, not today. I shifted in the faux-leather seat. My back pocket crinkled. The chocolate. My chocolate. I'd sat on it.

I hid that crushed peppermint patty, my first token, in my sock drawer. On our next trip to the CVS, I took a mint-chocolate lip balm to compensate for the failure. From then on, before entering the drugstore, I applied the balm to my lips, allowing its chemicals to work their way into my bloodstream, letting them speak through me. Stealing, it became clear, was a game requiring more advanced capacities than intuition alone could supply.

Buying

By mid-July, I'd improved my technique. Julie and I wandered separately so that our surveillers (unseen, manning the video footage in a dark closet, swiveling in their swivel chairs) would have to keep track of the two of us at once. I now knew to glide straight toward Cosmetics rather than dawdling in the candy aisle. Still, Julie was much more daring. She went for the difficult items, the makeup stocked next to the 24-hour photo center where the high-school boys working in the darkroom hung out. She ripped wrapping off five-blade razors, Maybelline bronzing powder, jet-black liquid eyeliner. She stashed plastic and cardboard packaging in empty racks in the Seasonal and Bulk Goods aisles. She stuffed cosmetics down her pants and into a windbreaker worn especially for the CVS. I was conservative, dropping only products with minimal packaging, one at a time, and never more than three, into my pocket.

Julie and I didn't compare stolen goods or talk much about the game. Twenty months and two days younger, she technically wasn't allowed to wear makeup until the following year, and so stored her merchandise in a small box in her closet. I sometimes snuck into her room while she was at gymnastics practice to swipe a mascara or medicated blemish concealer. It felt like stealing from myself. *After all*, I reasoned, smuggling a waterproof Lash-O-Matic into my sweatshirt, *what's the big difference between the two of us, anyway—our hair color?*

I sat on the bathroom vanity every morning staring at my face, wondering if I could unhinge it from itself and peer beneath the veil of skin. The face didn't seem to relate to anything. If I looked long enough, I could fool myself into thinking I was looking at another girl, a double girl, and that she was looking back at me. This seemed much more likely than the idea that my features evidenced an inner design. I angled the trifold mirrors to endlessly reflect my image from all possible perspectives, receding into a glassy greenish blur. *The eyes are the window to the soul*, I whispered in a cinematic intonation to the mirror girls, applying the twice-stolen mascara. *When he looks into your eyes, he's looking straight at your soul.* Who was he? I didn't know. I stared at one eye, all mascara'd, shimmering skin and spidery black lashes, and then the other, soft and round, its lid webbed by purple veins, skin as gluey transparent as raw chicken thighs. Skin so thin that it might peel right off. Fixed on their reflection, my eyes became glassy and impenetrable, my soul inaccessible even to me.

2

Mark and Susan allotted their daughters a hundred or so dollars each for back-to-school shopping, a trip Valerie and Julie planned throughout August. During a late-July game, Julie stole a copy of *Vogue* from the drugstore, and the sisters took turns cutting out images of dreamy-eyed blondes and redheads on nondescript beaches with words like Freedom, Dream, Youth, and Beauty floating above their heads. Susan developed a roll of film from a family vacation at the drugstore and Valerie promptly took all the photographs of herself in a swimsuit for her diary, drawing thin blue lines over her hips and stomach to illustrate where her body's contours should end, were the misbehaving hunks of meat to align and conform.

I've gained 3 more pounds, she wrote below a particularly loathsome picture in a pitiful tone, *now almost ____ in total. I* must *put an end to this before school starts.* But what could she do? She stole a few Girl Scout Cookies from the kitchen and hid them beneath her pillow for evening snacking.

An unnamed hope lurked beneath her pursuit of conformity. Perhaps, if she plunged into a sea of rugby polos, tropical-island perfumes, gold-plated keychains, sea-salt hairsprays—if she dissolved like an Alka Seltzer into the realm of advertisement—she might undergo a sort of rapture, exceeding the bounds of this stinking flesh. Valerie closed her eyes and imagined a soupy, midnight-blue space, maybe a giant crystalline globe filled with sea-water, images and products bobbing about in the cool liquid. She felt her fingertips, her shins, her shoulders merging with the liquid, her particle-body dispersing to touch everything at once. She could be the toothy, athletic East Coast teenager on a sailboat; the alternative girl with dark lipstick and reflective sunglasses; the spritely supermodel skipping through a paradise of shampoo; the skateboarder with dreadlocks and spotlessly white sneakers; the serious and seductive student in tortoiseshell glasses; the young couple applying for a bank loan to finance their first house; the thin, clear-eyed old woman finally able to breathe freely again, to run through springtime meadows, to pick up her grandchild with ease, thanks to an affordable once-a-day pill. She could be all these things and more, were it not for her unfortunate, unruly, bulging body.

Her body presented a rough outline for her life, a set of rules within which Valerie was fated to move. In her diaries, effusive passages about adolescent boys in swim trunks at the popular girl's pool party commingled with lists of cosmetics and outfits she could use to create an image of herself suitable for loving. The absurd illusion of causality: *if* I'm good enough at looking like a girl, the journals read, *then* I will be loved. Never mind the baroque proliferation of identical girls across American middle schools all in search of capital-L love. A surplus of searching girls, a deficit of the emotion they sought to catch in the snares of their chandelier earrings and name-brand jellies.

A few days before the shopping trip, Valerie spent the afternoon dragging and dropping digital images of products into a blank document on Susan's desktop computer, resizing and rearranging until the screen scintillated with shirts, miniskirts, wedge heels, earrings. Satisfied with her collection, she printed the page and taped it next to the bikini photos in her journal. *Macy's, $30*, she annotated a turquoise tank top. *Gap, $55*, a pair of distressed jeans.

On a Friday afternoon in late August, she and Julie browsed the clearance racks at the outlet mall, comparing shoes and shirts to optimize swapping and borrowing potential, secretly delighted when they separately picked out the same item. By winter, though, Valerie had gained fourteen pounds and got pimply and miserable. There was no more sharing and no more pretending. For Christmas, Valerie selected her own pairs of jeans, two sizes larger than Julie's.

3

Valerie told her mom she had nothing to hide. She was stealing the bikini pictures from the vacation photo albums for her own personal use. She wasn't *behaving suspiciously*, as Susan had so rudely suggested. Her mom could read her diaries and see for herself, if she wanted. She could publish the diaries in the newspaper or on TV, for all Valerie cared. When it came time to pick a new diary for eighth grade, though, Valerie chose one with a hard cover representing smiling suns and moons, and a sturdy brass lock. She simply preferred its feel, she told Susan, hiding the key in her makeup basket.

A few weeks into the new year, tired of propping her elbow on an overturned coffee mug and leaning over her dresser to hold her face as close as possible to the mirror, hand cramping as she drew and redrew bronze sparkle lines above her lashes, Valerie moved the entire mirror-and-makeup-basket apparatus to the floor beside her bed. With the mirror balanced against the wall, she could sit on the blue shag rug and stare at her face for hours. The patch of carpet surrounding the mirror grew muddy from spilled powder and concealer and beige shimmer eye shadow. On weekend nights, Valerie painted her face with bold, experimental makeup looks. She turned the radio to the Top Forty station and danced around the room, lip-synching about wanting to be bad.

In February, Susan called her daughter downstairs, very serious. A car had pulled over in front of their house to watch Valerie dancing through the upstairs window. The person in the car was surely also being bad. Valerie could continue to dance, but only if she agreed to close the blinds. Valerie was thrilled. *It was working,* the makeup, the hours spent in the mirror practicing expressions and dramatic monologues, the studied dance moves. She didn't know much about love, but she was sure it must start with attracting an anonymous admirer's attention.

Valerie sat in front of the mirror when she wrote in the suns-and-moons diary, admiring how her hair fell over her face, her concentrated and studious expressions. It was important to will herself into different moods for the journal, making herself cry and watching her face swell and blotch to write more pathetic entries, or squinting the muscles around her eyes, seductive, to write in flowery, epistolary prose about David, her ninth-grade crush.

She wasn't writing for David, though, nor for the anonymous admirer steaming up his car outside. Writing, she discovered, had the same effect as stealing: if she fooled herself into thinking she was someone else, some bold or daring character seen by the mirror or surveillance camera, she could fool herself into narrating the most purple of prose, stealing the most unlikely of products. Sitting before the mirror, journal in lap, Valerie could feel her insides fill, momentarily, with words. The feeling didn't last, though. When she read over an entry—even one she'd written mere seconds before—phrases that had struck her as precious and clear were revealed as unfamiliar, insufficient. She was no longer one with what she'd written. To dose herself again with the feeling, she had to keep writing.

One night, in a fit of inspiration, she wrote:

February 7, 2003

For a while, I've wanted to write the story of me. Or a girl like me. And now I realize that I am doing it through this diary. (She was, at this time and for years afterward, quite taken with the idea that her life should resemble a story, a fictional work complete with: a protagonist—her, or a girl like her, the distinction quite irrelevant; secondary characters with their own resolved, but less consequential, narrative arcs; a linear progression of realistic scenes with events occurring early on predicting later ones; the crucial and long-anticipated moment of tension in Act Two or approximately ____ pages into the novel; the resolution and conclusion of major plot points, the final saying of all that needed to be said, all minor narrative arcs settled to the satisfaction of the reader before the final page, or death. Life was not to be lived, but to be neatly concluded, *the end*.)

4

Valerie lay in bed most nights with her eyes wide open to the cavernous dark, listening with a sense of dread to her own breathing. She felt the spaces between her ribs expand as she filled her lungs. Was she sensing movement or sound? She couldn't tell: even her most silent shifts in the bed seemed so loud in the dark. She imagined the night air passing through her throat, her lungs, mixing about with her insides and then, on an exhale, smuggling bits of her away with it. She didn't want it to take the secret parts, the parts that Julie, sleeping in the other bed, shouldn't know. In the daytime it seemed unlikely to Valerie that her sister could read her mind, but night heightened the ticks and moans of pipes in the house, brushed up against oil slicks left by skin on walls and bedsheets, broadcasting (Valerie worried) her uncertain fantasies against the walls.

Even with the bedroom door closed as much as her parents permitted, a thin strip of hallway light cut across the carpet and bedframe and outlined her feet like two small animals underneath the comforter. She placed a pillow over her face to insulate the secret thoughts from both darkness and sister. Sufficiently concealed, she could visualize herself naked and supine on a conveyor belt, the kind of device she'd seen in documentaries and cartoons featuring factory workers. The body on the belt, though, was not Valerie's actual body, but rather a kind of impersonal, animate mannequin. Other animate mannequins lay alongside her, a row of identical, putty-hued forms flat on the line as far as she could see. Valerie kicked her feet in her bed and the small animals flinched underneath her comforter. In the fantasy, her feet (arched and plastic) dangled midair off the assembly line. She squeezed her eyes beneath the pillow, altering the vision. A cold, metal partition appeared, about three feet high and with rectangular cutouts framing the mannequins' waists, running down the middle of the belt and cutting lower halves off from upper. Dangling feet no longer visible.

How had the mannequins gotten there? They lay down on the line, Valerie decided, and, with a pull of a lever, the machine's operator clamped the metal partition down upon them, holding them in place. Valerie turned her mannequin face to the side (replicating the imagined action by turning, too, her face below the pillow), examining the other women for particularities, distinct jawlines or veiny eyelids or silky mustache hairs. There were none. The bodies on the conveyor belt were interchangeable.

Carefully, carefully, Valerie moved her pillow from face to abdomen to replicate the feeling of the partition. Shadowy workers monitored the other side of the metal barrier, she knew, mechanical as automated factory machines and obscured from view. These men stood in position, pumping their hips into the mannequins from the other side of the partition, as the conveyor belt inched along, moving Valerie from one partner to the next. As the men worked, Valerie smiled at the mannequin next to her, who wore the same, generic face. They looked like clichés: housewives in advertisements for cleaning products and sandwich meats, with dimpled cheeks and soft eyelashes. Their mouths were the color of the lipstick Valerie had taken from her grandmother's makeup drawer the week before, Craving Coral or maybe Committed Coral.

The mannequins paid little attention to the bodies operating on the other side of the partition, whose gestures were automatic, the least personal act in the world. Unable to conjure up how *intercourse* (as her mom called it) might feel, Valerie supposed that each man felt exactly the same. She focused on the face of the woman that was also her own face, the lipstick that was also her grandmother's lipstick.

(It should be clear, but nonetheless—Valerie's bed is far from a personal space, the fantasies produced there far from original. The bed is the size and shape of beds across America, beds in college dormitories, in hospital wards, in Recovery Center rooms, though hers is a hand-me-down with elegant wood spires where wrist and ankle restraints could conceivably be installed—a compelling notion that did not escape our protagonist. The bed is positioned within Valerie's room so that a parent can peer in, observe a child sleeping sweetly, or pretending to do so. Valerie's grandfather had a home office for his dentistry practice. He built a couch and desk for the office and, afterward, used the scrap wood to build twin beds for his twin sons. What determines the proper size of a bed? The mattress that will come to rest upon it. Valerie's grandfather sent his wife to the department store with a measuring tape to determine standard mattress dimensions. What determines the dimensions of a mattress? The bureaucratic tentacle of the state. The state? Well, yes, the United States. Mattress sizes differ from country to country, and regulations determine not only standard sizes, but also materials to be used, permissible levels of toxic chemicals, measures to be taken against flammability, et cetera. Who knows what her imagination might have done had U.S. officials and bureaucrats settled on slightly different sizes for children's bedding?)

In waking life, small brown moles began cropping up on Valerie's shoulders, forearms, abdomen, thighs. *Beauty marks*, her father reassured her as she itched and picked at them, leaving constellations of scars and scabs laughing at her from her limbs. She tried to scrape them away, but the moles grew right back, making her body more individual, recognizable. Her limbs and their imperfections belonged to her.

A horrible realization: the moles would compromise her anonymity on the conveyor belt. She imagined them spreading, her
lower half infested with beauty marks of all sizes. The men on the
other side of the machine would know. They would be repulsed
by her body's stubborn outcroppings, its failure to conform. Or
maybe they'd be happy for the variety, a new thing to stick their
(she couldn't say the word, couldn't even think it) *parts* in. *I never asked for this.* She scratched at a particularly inflamed scab on
her left elbow. *I never wanted this body.* She imagined being made
only of thought, silvery tendrils of dream-stuff whirling about in
the ether, or maybe fragments of text, hanging indents, a blinking
cursor. Impossible. The thoughts had to be somewhere, and that
somewhere, whatever it was, would be a body.

Why call them beauty marks? she asked.

Her father was sitting, tired, at the head of the kitchen table in
the early evening, shirtsleeves pushed up around forearms, beer in
hand. His response came perfunctorily. *Because they make you unique.*

She slunk away, dissatisfied. Uniqueness shouldn't be a function of the body, out of her control. Unique was what she could get
at the store, the aisle of sodas at the supermarket or eye creams at
CVS: small, calculable markers that corresponded to some kind of
meaning. This one means this, that one that, and so on. Unique
shouldn't have to do with what she couldn't help, the growths and
eruptions of the body.

At CVS, Valerie stood before the CoverGirl section and surveyed concealers and powders: one designed for blemishes with
chemicals and cool green undertones; another with SPF and reti-
nol for Mature Skin; another with a smiling brunette in a sequined
dress promising eighteen-hour lasting coverage. She looked over
her shoulder a few times, studied a man in belted chinos who'd
stopped a dozen feet away in front of the laxatives, waited until
he pulled a box from the shelf to examine the instructions on
the side, and slipped the long-lasting concealer into her jacket's
sleeve, adjusting its elastic wristband so the contraband would stay
in place. The next morning, she locked herself in the bathroom,

shaved her arms and stomach, and carefully dotted Ivory–330 over the beauty marks until her skin was as uniform as she'd seen it at the factory the night before.

5

Years later, in October or maybe September, Valerie saved the letters and sales pitches she'd been drafting, shut down her computer, and took the elevator to reception, where Sylvie was watering the battery of orchids barricading the reception desk. They were the last to leave the gallery. Sylvie pressed the four-digit code to alarm the building and rushed for the door as the security system counted toward lockdown. It was long past dark.

On the subway downtown, the girls exchanged exhaustions, and by the time they arrived at the bar in Queens, Valerie was mute, skin slack and slick with city scum. She tracked bar-goers' expressions and gestures without speaking while Sylvie's eyes grew large and streams of words tumbled out of her mouth. Small islands of bodies congregated around plastic cocktail tables.

Sylvie led Valerie through the crowd on the patio to find their friend, Maria, pushing past solid forms emanating heat through cheap cotton and spandex. Red plastic straws jostled liquor and soda in Valerie's cup, condensation slurring across her palm. She put her other hand in her pocket to touch the five or six sugar cubes she'd taken from the bar's condiment tray while the bartender's back was turned. The cubes' hard edges softened under her fingers, and she brought hand to nose to smell, but her fingertips didn't smell like anything but themselves. This dampened her pleasure at getting the cubes without asking for them. She'd have to get rid of them soon, before she was tempted to pop them in her mouth during a lull in conversation. She dropped two on the ground while Sylvie wasn't looking. With a flick of her wrist, she threw another into a fake terra-cotta planter holding a fake tropical plant. The cube hit the plant's trunk and bounced across the floor.

Buying

Maria was holding a table for them, sober, hoping that an unnamed friend might stop by with coke later in the night. She wore a baseball cap and oversize glasses, and held a cup of seltzer into which she ashed her cigarette over melting ice cubes. She and Sylvie spoke, eyes locked, Maria sliding into Portuguese to complain about the latest frustration at the art magazine she edited, a new editor campaigning for *objective and impartial reviews* of gallery exhibitions. The last words Valerie caught before the conversation was entirely lost to her were *incestuous* and *roommates*. Sylvie responded in brisk Portuguese as Valerie folded her straw into four parts, and then eight, and then sixteen. She did not speak Portuguese, or any language besides English. Valerie set the straw on the patio table where it unfurled like a demented snake.

Techno coursed from the concrete and Sylvie's smoke intermingled with their visible exhalations in the cold. The scene was external and still, a movie set in service of Maria and Sylvie's rapid conversation. Valerie screened a film of herself onto the back of her eyelids, trying to concoct an important and well-formed sentence to reintroduce a language she could speak into the conversation. But, when Sylvie paused, polite, and asked, in English, what Valerie was thinking, she didn't come up with anything to say.

The door to the bar opened and two girls in fake-fur coats and long braids stumbled out, their drinks preceding them onto the patio. Nic, an art critic and part-time gallerist of indeterminate but well-groomed origin, emerged from behind the stumblers and approached Sylvie, putting his arm around her waist and gently moving her to the side by way of greeting. Nic was compact and coolly energetic, with a muscular jaw and wire-rimmed glasses. Maria barely took note of him, turning her attention from the now-occupied Sylvie toward Valerie.

Maria was a quick and brilliant monologist, and Valerie had only to nod whenever she paused, indicating agreement while, in reality, she grew lazy, slouching against the plastic lawn chair, attention occupied almost entirely by the way her jacket rose and fell over her abdomen. Neither Maria nor Sylvie wore clothes that betrayed their bodies, or else they had the kind of neat and self-contained bodies that didn't announce their digestive functions and breathing patterns. What to do with this bloated sack of organs and thoughts? Valerie fingered the remaining two sugar cubes in her pocket.

Hey, Nic said, eyes fixed upon Maria's mouth. *I know you from somewhere. I remember you. That gap between your teeth. It's one of the most subtle tooth-gaps I've ever seen.*

There was no way to respond. Maria frowned at him and turned to Sylvie. *I'm going inside for another drink. I'll catch up with you later.*

Walking home, Sylvie told Valerie about a theory she'd developed as Nic shepherded her from table to table. *Androids shaped like women are so creepy in sci-fi movies*, she said, bony shoulders jutting into Valerie's as they tripped over the crumbling sidewalk, *because they're not at all committed to their bodies. They know they've been fabricated. There's no pretense that they're natural, or that their form has any kind of meaning.*

Right, an android's body is pure utility, agreed Valerie, *so if she cares about what she looks like, it's only because she needs to be incognito enough to accomplish her goal. Not because she cares about beauty or cuteness or whatever for its own sake.*

You can't distract a murdering android by saying, "That gap between your teeth is cute"—

Yeah. If she was designed with a tooth-gap, it was probably only so she could distract CIA officers while she stabs them in the kidneys, anyway.

Seriously, what was that with the tooth-gap? The subtle tooth-gap.

I don't know. Some kind of connoisseurial approach to women, I guess.

Sylvie remembered a college boyfriend who remarked on her tiny ears or feet every time he felt nervous or insecure or bored in arguments. The compliments jolted her from language, reminding her of her hairline, her eye-shape, what her face looked like in the mirror, how her mouth moved when she spoke. The compliments did their job: they rendered her mute. But without Sylvie filling the role of respondent, without her agreements and affirmations and assurances, the boyfriend, too, became unsure of himself, faltered, fell silent. *If I were an android designer, I'd make sure to implant the most complex gear in the cutest parts. Like, my android would have super-advanced hearing and recording devices stored in tiny ears.*

That's great. Because tiny ears are both cute and a kind of impediment, right? Like, the CIA officer thinks he's talking to this regular girl at the bar, tells her he wants to get closer to make sure she can hear him, because she's got the tiniest, cutest ears.

And that's how the android gets him. Knife right into the soft part of the skull.

Jesus.

Sorry. I just meant, if anything, she's happy about her tiny ears. They're the best disguise.

6

The next morning, Valerie clawed her way out of a disturbed sleep. She was plastered to her mattress in a cocoon of dried sweat and heavy limbs, the night's dreams struggling to surface and come to a conclusion before the day's urgent tasks stole them away. In sleep, she, Sylvie, and Maria had been automatons in a New York filled with human men and replicated women. The women were happy to be homogenous. They'd proposed and voted upon the procedure themselves. Valerie and Sylvie discovered, delighted, that they often fell in step due to the identical length and composition of their legs.

The dream began: In a rigidly stratified New York, people could predict each other's occupations, where they lived, how much money they made, their favorite bars, their fetishes, how often they called their parents, et cetera, with a cursory glance at a name, a face, a hereditary chart. Valerie, for example, could be easily sorted into a genre populated by other twenty-something tote-bag carrying, art-gallery going, suburban-childhood-having humans. Despite the fact that, sociologically speaking, Sylvie, Maria, and Valerie were roughly interchangeable, they found their minor particularities (small ears framed by a tawny crew cut, a charming snaggle tooth, under-eye circles that fluctuated between *you look a little sleepy* and borderline mauve) being picked out and deployed against them. Similarly, their banal transgressions and neuroses (regular lunches of wine and oyster crackers, only getting off to muscular gay porn, compulsively ignoring accumulating mounds of student debt) were considered deep, shameful secrets, peculiar to them and only them.

Slowly, the three discovered that other genres of professional women felt the same way. Maybe Maria had been sharing stories with an apathetic luxury-car advertiser, or maybe Valerie overheard a conversation at a poetry reading. Regardless of its origin, someone began a group chat, which quickly ballooned to a conversation between hundreds, and then thousands. It was easy to pretend that the group represented the totality of women existing in the world, or maybe in all of eternity, because the message thread was so rapid and continuous. Statements appeared one after another from unrecognized numbers, and Valerie's guess was as good as anyone's as to who, precisely, her interlocutors *were*. (Such naïveté—feigned by Valerie's subconscious and excused by digital anonymity—is easy to dismiss with a cursory review of the group's formation: its network exhausted the social contacts of a select set of professional women living in New York, ages twenty-five to sixty, and better represented those who hired house cleaners than those who cleaned houses.)

Around 9 P.M. on a Friday evening, dream-Valerie picked up her phone after a shower and nap to find 637 new message alerts. The thread had recently turned to a museum curator's anger at being singled out by colleagues for a rather prominent mole under her left eye, and a 917-number proposed that all women in the city do away with their human bodies, implanting themselves instead into mechanized shells.

U know thats not a half-bad idea
They'd really have to come up with new ways to take us down a notch
You know they wld come up with ways.
But we'd at least get a few days of reprieve!
Actually, I think someone in the group works in AI at DataLab...this
could seriously be possible
    wtf
    really????
Hey, yeah, it's me that works for DataLab, I'm head of design technol-
ogy and robotics. My name's Gretchen.

Valerie opted not to voice an opinion, waiting for the phone numbers of the only two women she knew—Sylvie and Maria—to pop up in the chat. Four minutes later, Maria opined *yeah, god, this would be such a relief.* Concerns about funding were raised; one member was quite wealthy and assured the rest she'd tap into the usual philanthropic networks. An 845-number wondered *how will we get all of the other women in the city, the women who aren't in the group, on board?* A prominent intellectual promised to write an Op Ed in the *Times*; she'd argue for a *beautiful sense of equality, freedom from objectification, release from appearances.* A 718-number repeatedly asked what the automated bodies would look like, suggesting *maybe we should neutralize race, select an unnatural color, like blue or gray or purple.* Members were not sure. Objections were raised, anxieties duly noted. The group would put their collective body's physical appearance to a vote. On the day of the vote, Maria refused to participate. *They've got Gretchen from DesignLab making the thing. I know her. It doesn't matter if it's gold or magenta or teal. Any automaton made by Gretchen is going to look like Barbarella fell into a vat of Pantone.* Indeed, the final design was silver, with a poufy wig and button nose.

Once automated, it was nearly impossible to tell which body belonged to your friend, colleague, girlfriend, ex-girlfriend, and so on. The women didn't trust each other, and for good reason. After implantation in their silvery new bodies, an initial sense of peace in the city was followed by a great and sudden confusion. Thieving women snuck into homes and workplaces not their own, taking computers and appliances and the like. Identical women emptied one another's bank accounts, kidnapped those in higher positions to insert themselves by proxy into alternate lives. If you were able to remember a friend's distinctive walk (flat-footed, slow) or the sour expression she made when she was being insulted—and if you could detect a trace of this gesture on a silvery automaton—you could hazard a guess at the automaton's identity. Most women, though, were loath to reveal who they were, and even the most idiosyncratic gestures could be imitated by a skilled identity thief.

In a highly publicized case, one woman, a professor, locked up her ex's new girlfriend and took her place, thinking she'd be able to regain her former paramour's affections, if only by posing as her new love. The presumed ex, though, turned out to also be an identity thief, a woman with tens of thousands of dollars in credit card debt and medical bills who was squatting in the wealthy ex's apartment, paying off her loans using the ex's credit cards. During courtroom proceedings, the identity thief said she'd barely had to do any work to convince the professor that she was, in fact, her former love. She'd looked through bank statements and old receipts, watched a few videos. Easy.

Reporters covering the case found it difficult to transcribe court proceedings, having no way to tell which woman was speaking at any given time. They began to confuse themselves with their interviewees, and lawyers with the criminals, and soon women were speaking in tandem, completing each other's sentences, infecting each other with the desire to sabotage the entire project. It was a mess. Officials couldn't determine whether a large majority of women were suddenly participating in criminal activity, or whether a small group of deviants had taken advantage of the new system, mucked it all up. Crime rates tripled, and police were loath to arrest the hard, silvery women. The women in the group were astounded. They had not predicted this.

In the confusion, silvery Valerie wandered around Union Square where, in her previous life, pick-up artists and peddlers approached her while she was eating 50¢ hard-boiled eggs and scrolling through art-world blogs. For several days, she watched an automaton with the mannerisms of Sylvie, who leaned against the fake brick of the Whole Foods, smoking, eyeing groups of Guinean men with glinting black plastic bags, who sang, *Louis, Gucci, Hermès, Céline . . . snap 'em up before the police do!*

A select few women had escaped the automation decree by faking homelessness, dressing in shapeless men's clothes and hiding in subway stations smelling of urine, speaking senseless languages or acting otherwise deranged. Of those remaining unautomated, it was, in the end, impossible to tell who had once been a woman and who had not. The silvery Valerie didn't care. She studied the automaton she assumed was Sylvie as the Sylvie studied the peddlers.

Hey, the Valerie ventured, stepping beside the Sylvie, but not looking at her face. *Do you know of a good place to get coffee around here?*

The Sylvie looked at her sharply, squinting, not speaking.

The Valerie tried again. *I like that gap between your teeth.*

The Sylvie grabbed her forearm. *It's you.*

The two went off in search of Marias, finding several candidates: one who wore a baseball cap and eagerly engaged in exchanges with strangers, which the Sylvie thought suspiciously unlike aloof Maria; another, who sat on stoops and leaned against buildings with the exact comportment the Sylvie knew so well; and a third, combative, who snuck, stealthy, around the city with some sort of plan the two couldn't quite figure out, marking advertisements and photographing men at random. They stalked these Marias for days.

The Valerie, exhausted and despairing, begged the Sylvie for a break. Maybe a drink, she suggested, or a trip to the Russian bathhouse.

Absolutely not, the Sylvie said. She'd become obsessed with the three Marias, didn't want to abandon pursuit for even a few hours, fearing that if the two stopped following their targets, other automated women would come in and replace the Marias, kidnap or hide or kill the Marias, and the Valerie and the Sylvie would be none the wiser. After much persuasion, the Sylvie finally agreed to an hour in the steam room, advising against intoxication of any form *in the current political climate.* The two women walked to the baths on St. Marks, took towels from the hairy and potbellied attendant, and undressed.

A thick cloud of steam obscured the women's vision, and the Valerie and the Sylvie were barely able to see their own knees through the dull white vapor. The two sat side-by-side, silent, and the Valerie watched in confused amazement as shapes grew on her legs: a heat rash.

Are you embarrassed to be naked? the Sylvie asked, frowning.

No, the Valerie replied, *it's just a rash.*

I thought maybe you were blushing.

The Valerie considered this. The body wasn't really hers. It was the same as the Sylvie's, the same as all the others. Could she be ashamed of something so stupidly repetitive?

Look, it's happening to me, too. The Sylvie pressed at her thighs, marking bluish splotches in the middle of gray, her rash extending from knees to thighs.

Creepy. The Valerie poked at her thigh, and then the Sylvie's. Their rashes were different. *Let's get out of here.*

No, wait. The Sylvie paused. *We have to remember the patterns. We'll come back tomorrow and see if they're the same, and, if they are, we can recognize each other, test who we're talking to, make sure you're always you, Maria is always Maria. Once we find her. If we find her.*

But do you really want to be able to tell? the Valerie began to ask, standing up, the room spinning, light filtering in through the steam—and then the dream was distinct from Valerie, splintered off from her body and incompatible with the reality in which she found herself. She was awake.

On an evening run through a Hasidic section of East Williamsburg a few days later, she realized that the dream-automaton-Sylvie may have been trying to sabotage her, but she had no way of accessing the dream version of herself to warn her.

7

It is necessary to establish here that it is by design that the two halves of Valerie cannot communicate with each other. A pair, after all, can't coexist peaceably. Put side by side, Valerie learned in chemistry, or maybe psychology, two will tend to establish a hierarchy: sleepy-and-sneaky Valerie trying to trick waking-Valerie, waking-Valerie oppressing her psychic twin. It's necessary that they be kept at a distance, that they communicate only across the thin neural veil that distinguishes sleep from waking. In this way, they can neither cohere nor compete, although they sometimes overlap, merge and entangle, only to separate and repel each other once again. Which one can claim ownership of the name they share? Who is the rightful protagonist of this story? Both are doomed to fail at this task, this senseless contest for possession of Valerie.

8

Valerie packed her belongings into several purple plastic crates, loaded them into the back of her 1999 Ford Taurus (not even a cool old car, she thought bitterly), and drove to the campus administration building where the Hudson Valley Federal Credit Union had a small outpost in the basement. It was the last week of exams before college graduation.

Waiting in the short line of students, she picked up a brochure and scanned it, bored. *In October 1963, a group of IBM employees had a vision—to create a financial cooperative for IBM employees and their families in Poughkeepsie and Fishkill, New York. Their product line was modest, consisting of basic savings and consumer loans. At the end of their first year, the credit union had 14 member accounts and $172 in assets. Today, under the leadership of CEO Mary Madden, HVFCU boasts 121,000 members.* Her boyfriend Neel insisted that Valerie divest her money from the credit union and open a Wells Fargo account, like he had. The Wells Fargo was closer to their apartment, he argued, and besides, didn't she want to have her money in a real bank? It would be easier for their landlord, for their electric company and cable supplier. Using the campus credit union was not quite adult. They were moving in together. (Or, rather, she was moving into his apartment in Fishkill.) It was time to grow up.

Valerie directed an impatient sigh toward the boy in front of her in line who was talking loudly on the phone to his mother. She tilted her head toward the ceiling where dead flies clustered around the corners of the fluorescent lights. *I wonder if they were trying to get in, crawling toward the light bulbs, or trying to escape suffocating in that plastic hell,* she mused. *I wonder if he thinks I'm attractive.* She aimed another pointed sigh at the boy. *I wonder if he's even looked at me at all.* He hadn't. *Better that way, I don't care.*

At the counter, a woman in a plaid button-up shirt, breast pocket sagging under the weight of her plastic nametag, asked Valerie's account number, date of birth, ZIP code, and Valerie dug around in her bag for the slip of paper on which she'd noted the instructions Neel gave her on how to get all of her money out.

You're sure you want to leave the credit union? the woman (*Nina Vásquez, Senior Teller*) asked, and Valerie could tell she was a mother by her tone.

Yeah. I'm joining Wells Fargo.

Valerie smiled to convey an appropriate level of self-assuredness and maturity, hoping that the woman would recognize that she was taking a big life step, but Nina didn't seem to care. Valerie toyed with the idea of telling her about the decision to move in with her boyfriend (thus the need for a convenient and reliable off-campus bank), but Nina had finished the transaction before Valerie made up her mind. She met Neel where he was waiting for her on a bench outside, thumbing through a book, glasses slipping down his nose.

Neel had covered the entire security deposit, paternal and pleased when he told her how much money he made chopping heads off halibut, packing scallops at the fish market; she didn't have to worry, and besides, the landlord was a friend, liked his bluefin tuna. Seven hundred-ish—what remained of her savings after putting down first and last month's rent—now tucked into her canvas tote bag, Valerie trailed a few steps behind Neel across the concrete Student Union plaza and into her car, metal seatbelt fastener burning her thighs in the early summer sun. Neel preferred to drive. They would spend the afternoon purchasing necessaries to commemorate her move: a plastic shower curtain to replace his moldy one, lampshades and matching throw pillows, decorative wall hangings, kitchen tools and refrigerator magnets, plastic houseplants, and so on. Since she'd been with Neel, Valerie hadn't stolen at all, having learned from him the complex meld of guilt and joy that came with spending too much hard-earned money at the Poughkeepsie Galleria.

After a successful excursion to the Walmart, the pair stood exhausted in the early evening parking lot, heat emanating off scorched pavement. The lot had been freshly painted with neat white lines demarcating where to park, in which direction to drive, how to safely enter the store, where to return used shopping carts. Neel struggled the oversize plastic bags into the car's trunk, refusing Valerie's help. Neon lights announced a nearby gas station and Waffle House: the heterotopic suburban stretch. The sunset was most beautiful from the main shopping area in town, where the magentas and blues of the sky matched the blinking lights of the liquor store and vacancy signs at the motel.

The moon appeared, huge and ghostly, over the Wal-Mart, and Neel took the opportunity to introduce the subject of his greatest passion, space exploration, as he pulled the car onto the street. He had recently listened to a series of educational seminars on entrepreneurship and creative thinking given by a billionaire who privatized space travel. He played a lecture for them now on his Motorola. Both Neel and the billionaire considered the planets, perhaps Mars, to be the next great frontier. The billionaire spoke in a silky calm tone, but couldn't conceal his surge of excitement at the idea of seeking out a new source of danger, of mystery, and coming to destroy or dominate it. *Man looks down upon Earth from the machines he's created to encircle it and discovers it decimated, looted, neatly partitioned into grids, each module of the planet belonging to a distinct person or country or corporation. He's taken full advantage of it, conquered and possessed it,* Neel explained, *and so it no longer excites him. It's basic Freud. And now, the Earth itself, like its resources and wonders, can be sloughed off by humans like dead skin.* This all seemed quite reasonable. The next thing to possess, *of course,* would be another planetary body.

Valerie sat silent in the passenger seat, nodding, occasionally making soft noises of interest and concern. She couldn't partake in this mission of cosmic discovery and ownership and she felt vacant when listening to the billionaire's speeches on Neel's phone, but she understood the importance of supporting her boyfriend in his passions, sympathizing with his interests, reflecting agreement back to him to bolster his sense of self, make him feel heard. The moon haunted the sky above, staining it inky and deep and leaving a wake of cosmic dust in its path. She imagined the turning planets making thunderous sounds as they moved across space, sounds that were so distant and gigantic that she couldn't hear them at all. The machinations of the planets were an archaic tragedy, dramatic clashes between warring siblings, familial alliances and gods and furies who had little regard for moralistic striving or human law, who would welcome the implosion and demise of Earth and humanity as a great spectacle of punishment and suffering.

Forgetting herself, Valerie announced to the moon, *I don't think I'd go to Mars on a spaceship.* Her breath fogged the window, obscuring the sky. Neel hadn't heard her. The entrepreneur was now discussing the great financial risk of colonizing Mars, the necessity for enthusiastic high-level investors who similarly believed that humans were destined to become a spacefaring and multiplanetary species. Or, at least the five hundred or so who'd be able to afford tickets at the end of the world. Neel with his fish-market money, though a passionate believer, was of no use to the billionaire.

Buying

In the tragedy of the solar system, Mars is arid and irascible, a hostile younger brother, a planet with neither freshwater nor oceans nor dense tropical air—only the burning trial of fire and desert, loose rock and debris, cold air, thin atmosphere. The entrepreneur explained that the planet housed the highest peak in the solar system, a mountain several times taller and infinitely more treacherous than Kilimanjaro, and he imagined himself as the first to summit its monstrous heights. The planet had the most mountainous mountain and the lowest valley, he said, but no oceans, not a speck of water. It was encircled by two moons named *fear* and *defeat*, moons made from the bodies of previous explorers who'd failed where the entrepreneur was sure he'd succeed. He'd been training and testing his endurance for pain and suffering and solitude, and these trials had turned him into a real and true man, a man capable of sacrificing his humanity for the sake of cosmic dominance.

The last light of the day melted into pools of liquid gold on the horizon and then, there, gone. Sparsely placed streetlights, gaseous and flickering, illuminated white lines on the highway, instructing Neel to stay in the correct lane. Police hid in the forest beside the highway, hoping to entrap motorists, to give them fines and dishonorable marks on their records and implicate them in earthly battles between citizen and law, right and wrong, obedience and freedom. Mars was not visible. It was a cloudy night.

9

From: customerservice@WellsFargo.com
Sent: Wednesday, May 18, 2011 4:04 PM
To: valerie@SUNYschools.edu
Subject: A Warm Welcome from your Local
Wells Fargo Branch

Dear Valerie,

Welcome to Wells Fargo Online Banking. We understand that choosing a bank is a personal and important
decision, and want to extend our gratitude that you've
opted to join the millions of customers who have em-
barked on a banking relationship with us. We hope
you'll find peace of mind and convenience here—and
we're sure you'll enjoy the advantages of our exten-
sive network of over 6,200 retail locations, 24/7 phone
banking, and 12,800 ATMs.

Your monthly service fee is $10, but there are several
options to avoid this fee (and, if you're between the
ages of 17 and 24—which, Valerie, you are!—your fee
will be discounted $5. We understand and sympathize
with the tremendous financial burden you're likely
accruing right now in student loans, and want to do
our part in easing the load). To avoid the fee, you can
maintain a $1,500 minimum daily balance. Based on
the cash Neel thinks you'll be able to pick up in a few
bartending shifts—if you wear tight jeans and don't
talk back to customers who give you attitude and
manage to not burst into tears when people start waving bills in your face around 2:30 A.M.—you can probably save up enough to maintain this balance within
a month or two. (Provided, of course, that you don't
want to start paying off your student loan interest
until after graduation! Tough decisions, Valerie, but
we're sure you're up to the challenge of maintaining
healthy personal finances.) You might also consider
making ten or more debit card purchases or payments
a month, in which case, we'll waive the monthly fee
entirely. Again, Valerie, you can likely manage this—
simply stop by the Starbucks on Main Street on the

way to the Fishkill Library, do some online shopping from popular fashion retailers or cosmetics stores, and buy groceries and supplements for yourself and Neel at the organic market on your way home from the gym. Please note that the ten-purchases-a-month stipulation does not include ATM transactions.

Speaking of ATM transactions—we value loyalty at Wells Fargo. You might even say we value monogamy. For this reason, cash withdrawals made at Wells Fargo ATMs will have a $0 transaction fee. Withdrawals made at non-Wells Fargo ATMs carry a $2.50 fee on top of the ATM owner/operator's fee. Please, Valerie, understand that both Wells Fargo and other institutions need to be compensated for your ATM usage. It's simply easier for everyone if you choose to be faithful and only use Wells Fargo ATMs. We understand that cash emergencies arise—for example, needing coins to do laundry or unexpectedly finding yourself at a cash-only restaurant. In these cases, which we anticipate being rare, we don't think that the $2.50 fee is too much to ask of you. Please don't feel too guilty, Valerie. Everyone slips up sometimes. Given our relationship, we find this fee to be a minor penalty for your indiscretions. We're sure you agree.

Valerie, there are some additional fees, but don't bother yourself too much with these. Overdraft fees may be charged if you're a bit overzealous with your spending—but we prefer that you kindly allow us to kindly allow you to make a purchase for which you don't technically have funds on hand! Of course, this is precisely the type of transaction for which you'd want to use your credit card. We know that your parents got you a credit card a few years ago so that you could start to build good credit. It'll be easiest if you close that account and switch to a Wells Fargo platinum Visa—your credit score will transfer over.

Remember when you went to the used car lot with your mom? She was so excited because she'd saved for years to have enough money to buy a car outright, no payment plan necessary. She expertly negotiated with the dealer for a few minutes, the car's price dropping with each girlish gesture and laconic, knowing remark. She got them to give her the price she wanted, and then gave them her information to run a credit report. The dealer came back wearing an amazed expression—she had nearly *perfect* credit, he reported, incredulous. There she was: model citizen, lifelong teacher, a married mother of two with outstanding credit. She even still had her looks. *Here*, the dealer said loudly, *here's a life worth protecting. Here's a life worth the safest, most reliable car we've got on the lot.* She drove off in a silver Toyota Prius, adding *humanitarian* and *concerned about the environment* and *spendthrift* to her long list of accolades.

You may not know this, Valerie, but Toyota considered making a commercial about her, a thirty-second bit featuring you and your sister sitting in the backseat, singing along to the Easy Listening station on the car's state-of-the-art surround-sound system.
Valerie, your mother was a paragon of the two-earner household, an exemplary working woman. Do you think she ever struggled, ever drove that Toyota Prius to the defunct ski resort a few miles from your house and cried and hit the steering wheel in total frustration, abject despair? The lightweight frame of the car shook with her sobs. She adjusted the driver's seat

to give herself enough room to really strike the vinyl dashboard hard, turned off the headlights and hoped the cops wouldn't drive by and grow suspicious of the lone car parked in the gravel lot after dinnertime most weeknights. Remember when you told her you hated her? You threatened to open the car door and jump out while she was driving. Smart woman, excellent mother, she hit the emergency locks and reprimanded you.

Valerie, a safe car is absolutely essential, and driving is an excellent mechanism for stress release, an excuse for solitude and respite. We offer car insurance options, payment plans, even small auto loans. We understand that your Ford Taurus is working well for you right now, but imagine how you'd look in a used Jeep. Picture yourself in a black Corolla, or a beat-up Mercedes. Scan Craigslist a bit, drive past your local dealership, and then stop by the Wells Fargo to talk to one of our friendly bankers. Remember how useful and therapeutic your mother found her trustworthy car, how great she felt about herself, being able to buy it all on her own. At Wells Fargo, we want the same for you. We'll be here every step of the way. Just let us know when you're ready, Valerie.

In sickness and in health,
Your friendly local Wells Fargo family

†

10

Bond Lake Park—where Susan took her daughters to ski and skate during the day and where, when the girls were parked in front of the TV with ice cream at night, she returned alone to cry—is located on the site of a former limestone quarry that fed the nearby Lackawanna Steel Company. In the previous century, when Lackawanna was the world's second-largest steel mill and Buffalo one of America's most promising cities, high-grade limestone was quarried there and transported by rail to the firm's steel furnaces. In 1925, rising transportation costs forced the quarry to close, and the lakes and ponds within the quarry site were allowed to fill in naturally, creating a swampy nexus of shallow, interconnected waterways populated by Canadian geese and thick swathes of cattails.

The first owner of the quarry, Fredrick Bond, bought the land and divided it into twelve plots, selling most of it to local landowners for farming. The street Valerie grew up on, Meyer's Hill Road, was one of those twelve plots, a short, steep hill, now equal parts corn and dairy farmland and suburban paradise of modest, multilevel family homes. Each house on the street had at least one living room and a yard large enough that residents didn't have to see their neighbors if they didn't want to. Valerie's parents bought one of these houses after saving fastidiously during the early years of their marriage, Susan selling encyclopedias door-to-door and waitressing at a pizzeria and sub joint while her dad, Mark, finished school. Their house, a three-bedroom, two-bath, was built by a similarly entrepreneurial, ominously athletic couple in the early eighties, who put it on the market after the wife revealed over a dramatic family dinner that she'd been in love with, carrying on an affair with, the marine mechanic down the street since before they'd finished finishing the house's basement.

When Valerie and Julie's parents first brought the girls to look at the house, the two fought over the larger bedroom, not for its size or amenities, but because, over a celebratory bottle of Moscato (*Congratulations on your purchase! No, congratulations on your sale!*)

Buying

the entrepreneurial and estranged wife told Valerie's parents it had belonged to her teenage daughter, an infamous junior at the local high school. With highlighted hair and low-rise jeans, the daughter was impossibly glamorous, a little depressed. Valerie and Julie ended up sharing the bedroom. They later heard that the girl had taken up with the wrong crowd, fallen for a boy a few years too old for her, drove around in his truck getting high and wrecking neighborhood mailboxes. *She's bad*, said Susan, as if the girl had some kind of congenital defect. The girl was sent away to receive an unspecified type of treatment for an unspecified amount of time.

In the Depression years, Bond sold a few dozen acres of land too congested with hills and ponds to be properly converted to residential or agricultural use to a private investor. He had tried, unsuccessfully, to get the city of Niagara Falls to buy the land, but the city eventually got the land anyway through condemnation proceedings in the sixties. In 1976, with the nation on an upswing and recreational sports and resorts becoming popular amongst the growing middle class, a county legislator proposed turning the park into a ski slope. Fifteen acres were cleared by inmates in the sheriff's Incarcerated Workers Labor Program, and a winter sports complex and lodge were built using funds from a federal grant. Home videos neatly labeled WINTER 1996 show Valerie and Julie waddling through the lodge in fluorescent snowsuits, Julie shrieking when clumps of hard snow wedged themselves between her mittens and the elastic wristband of her jacket, Valerie sipping instant hot chocolate in a Styrofoam cup and inventing stories of artic exploration in a know-it-all tone for the camera. Valerie had sat in front of the lodge's large fire, melting, watching flames lick chemically treated logs. The chemicals produced delicate green and magenta flames. She preferred the internal absorption of the flames to the supposedly adventurous and sublime, but really just uncomfortable, activity of the slopes.

Mark and his twin brother bought their children sleds and snow tubes and their wives handheld video cameras for Christmas in 1994. Susan opened her present first and, sitting on the liv-

[55   ]

ing-room floor while the girls crawled around her lap, pulling at her
sweatpants and tube socks, assembled the device. She'd always
been handy, and as her sister-in-law laughed at herself and struggled to understand the contraption, Susan was already filming.

Is this thing on? asks the grainy image of the sister-in-law, hoisting the heavy camera onto her right shoulder, all tight, black curls
and hard vowels and corduroy pants.

*No, see, you can tell because this red light'll switch on, and when
you're filming, it'll blink, see, like this.* Susan's hand extends out from
her camera's eye, points at the power button on the twin camera,
disappears again behind her device.

Later in the afternoon, the two women crouched behind the
Christmas tree to film their husbands cleaning up wrapping paper
in new slippers, their children playing with Sky Dancer Barbies
and makeup sets, their mothers-in-law sitting on the sofa wearing
beaded reading glasses, trading back and forth the Arts & Leisure
and Local sections of the newspaper. Mostly, though, in this first
home video, they film each other's faces veiled by the bulky cameras, dueling video footage in a continuous feedback loop.

Valerie's maternal grandmother, Gloria, was the first to pro-
mote skiing. She had bought the girls ice skates for Christmas the
previous year. She bought a video camera well before her daughter
and recorded her own outdoor pursuits with the zeal and precision
of an amateur documentarian, clipped out newspaper articles on
Aspen vacation homes, and rented VHS tapes of outdoor adventure films (which she considered how-to guides) when the local
Blockbuster Video got them in stock. From these narratives of
fantastic leisure, adventure, humor, travel, and womanizing, Gloria
found she could mimic both 1) the elegance of the heroines and 2)
the reckless entitlement of the sportsmen.

When, in the new millennium, Valerie and Julie protested her
gifts of ski trips to nearby resorts—they would have preferred gift
cards to the Outlet Mall—she took this as a great personal affront.
It was an incredible privilege to be able to afford to rent skis, put
on an iridescent puffy jacket, stand heroic atop a mountain cut

through with thin lines traversing white slopes. She filled her lungs with icy breath until her sides ached, expertly planned her down-hill path, and, flipping sunglasses over hawk's eyes, submitted her body to the hard pull of gravity. She could never have afforded the sport when it was truly luxurious in the eighties, when she read about real-estate tycoons and movie stars vacationing at exclusive resorts in St. Moritz, but, by the late nineties, enough lower tier resorts had cropped up that she could spring to take her grand-daughters to experience the joy of being literally *on top of the world* once or twice a year.

Valerie was primarily interested in the ski instructors, high school and college boys who preferred snowboarding, but taught classes in both sports in exchange for free lift passes. She liked the idea of waiting by the lodge's fireplace for the instructor to finish his lessons, hot chocolate in hand, fuzzy sweater tight over large breasts (in the daydreams, she had large breasts), lacquered lips and wide, blue eyes. She imagined herself thus as she struggled to catch the lift for fear of falling for the fourth, fifth time. She imagined herself as an ice skater with powerful legs and a sequined costume and gelled hair, like the Russian Olympians she watched on TV. She had no need for this bulky snowsuit, no need for a rush of adrenaline and windburn to remind herself she was alive. No desire to tell her grandmother or sister that she was too afraid to follow them down the moderate slopes. More glamorous romances played out in her head.

11

Valerie and her high-school best friend fell in love with Valerie's first boyfriend online and simultaneously. They spent hours look-ing at his images, criticizing the chubby girl with jet-black hair and tadpole eyebrows who always seemed to be sitting on his lap at parties, gasping at his impeccable music selection and romantic poetry. The girl was *trying too hard*, Valerie said, dismissive, and Gabby agreed. Valerie and Gabby were not cool enough to be invited to the parties, but they both knew how to write, how to craft an online profile, how to be funny and smart and mimic the charming women in the romantic comedies they watched together on Friday nights. Gabby would pull the blankets and pillows off her bed and drag them downstairs to the study, creating a nest in which the two could eat ice cream and listen to Sade (Gabby's favorite singer) and watch the computer screen for signs of the boy's activity.

Ultimately, the obsession had very little to do with the boy. The goal of engaging him in conversation provided a necessary medium for the girls' bonding. They had no idea when he might sign onto his AOL account, and his unpredictable absence allowed them endless empty hours upon which to elaborate a friendship. Gabby had recently moved to Buffalo from Atlanta, and, on the first day of tenth grade in Religions of the World, both girls announced they were atheists—although maybe agnostic, maybe even a mystic, Gabby said, regarding herself as too inconsequential to know the answers to such cosmic questions. They wrote a short story about their friendship set in an alternate reality. Gabby showed Valerie pictures from Atlanta and clicked through images from her dad's recent business trip to Vietnam. In an effort to best her friend's worldliness, Valerie spoke about someday escaping her strict parents, moving to New York. She outlined for Gabby the future novels she wrote in her diaries.

When the boy's AOL screenname glowed green, the two brainstormed the best jokes, the most impressive song lyrics to quote. Gabby summoned the courage to type the message, and Valerie recklessly pressed the Send button as Gabby shrieked, covering her eyes. The two friends merged behind Gabby's screenname, *angel$tyle1988*, a single and (they thought) dangerously charming teenage girl.

In late August, just before their senior year of high school, Valerie and Gabby dressed in secondhand miniskirts and Doc Martens and went to see a band they knew the boy liked. The boy clumsily took Valerie's hand during the most romantic song, and Gabby ran to the bathroom in agony, accompanied by a secondary girl who had tagged along. In that moment, Valerie had the same sense of watching herself from above she'd felt as a child in the backyard, and ever since when she shoplifted. The movie feeling. The feeling that whatever she was doing wasn't real: plotted out in advance, it was guaranteed to end well in a rousing finale. It was as if her eyes were screening a moving image on the concert venue's ceiling, a flickering film of herself, blotchy spray-on tan and skinny legs and bottle-red hair, linked by a clammy palm to the boy from the online profile.

The boy in reality said very little and was twitchy and nervous. He explained that he didn't have a driver's license, and, before his mom picked him up, gave Valerie a chaste kiss on the cheek. She found this pitiful and so loved him immediately. Having recently secured a license and 1999 Ford Taurus (Gabby, a few months older, gave her lessons), she had no need for the boy to drive her around. She only needed him to love her—to be improved by her presence. *I am an improver of people*, she confirmed to herself in her head. She could drop him off at home next time, she promised.

12

The boy did not like to go out on dates, but Valerie did not like to stay home and make out on her couch every night. Her parents were getting angry. Her dad couldn't sleep knowing the two were fooling around downstairs. Her mom had questions: why didn't the boy want to take her out to dinner, spend money on her, like a boyfriend was supposed to? Didn't he value her? Did she really feel like this boy was a worthwhile investment? Valerie dragged the boy to a cheap Italian restaurant for their six-month anniversary to prove to her parents that the relationship was serious. They sat across from each other in the booth, stony-faced, mutually coerced. She picked at a tear in the checkered plastic tablecloth and ordered mozzarella sticks. The waitress offered them illegal cocktails, perhaps out of pity at their misery, but Valerie refused. She was virtuous and, after all, had to drive home.

Now she could tell her mom that the two were going to the movies, or bowling, or to a restaurant—appropriate, money-spending dates—and instead pick the boy up and park the car in a far corner of the Bond's Lake parking lot. On a warm and dampish spring night, a night of sweaty palms, Valerie convinced the sous chef at the restaurant where she waitressed to give her a left-over double-size sampler platter of fried foods, and she and the boy rolled up the car windows for privacy and split pizza rolls and played cassettes he had made for her of himself playing acoustic guitar really loud.

Within thirty minutes, Valerie was wedged under him in the passenger seat. She tried to arrange herself attractively and to not bang her head on the door handle, frustrated at her face muscles, seizing and twitching with pleasure despite her best efforts at maintaining an alluring expression. Gestures on both sides were easily misunderstood: an errant shin came down hard on her knee (*Is he trying to restrain me?*); a hand extracted from beneath her thigh thwacked the boy's neck. He hesitated, eyes flashing open in surprise, and shifted Valerie on top. She justified her inadvertent slap by assigning herself a new role: *I am a feisty lesbian stripper*, she thought, summoning *Showgirls*, which she had watched with Gabby. The fantasy was thrilling, though Valerie struggled to perform Gina Gershon.

She was spared an elaboration of the character: violent white light flooded the vehicle all at once, as if Valerie and the boy been transported to a brightly lit film set of a high-school make-out session. Valerie surged upright, dazed and blinded, and saw through the sticky fog of mutual teenage desire that two cop cars had pulled up, one on either side of the Taurus.

A vision of her mom transfixed in the driver's seat, waiting for an officer to approach her window, darted past her eyes. Ten-year-old Valerie, picking nervously at the rubber seal on her sneakers, watched her mom turn the rearview mirror toward her face and adjust the flyaway hairs around her ears. She applied a little lip balm, checked the mirror, asked Julie to hand her the registration documents from the glove compartment. Valerie could only see the police officer's torso through her mom's rolled-down window. Susan acted like a teenager. Sweetness and innocence, she told the girls to smile at the nice man and they did, and he didn't give them a ticket, after all. Susan continued to drive recklessly, breaking the speed limit without even trying.

Now the cops pulled the boy out of the driver's seat, asked Valerie to step out on the opposite side, to be confronted with large and aggravated uniformed bodies. The boy pulled his clothes back on, and the officers permitted him to zip his fly before questioning. Valerie began to cry on cue, theatric sobs, and the police officer on her side was at a total loss.

Why are you crying? he demanded, his tone insinuating that the only reason she might partake in sexual activity was the boy's intimidation or force, which made her cry all the more.

I'm crying because of you, Valerie sputtered, *because I'm afraid! I've never been stopped by police before!* She hiccupped a few times for effect, thought, and added, *I'm a smart girl. I get good grades. Please, whatever you do, don't tell my parents.*

How long have you two been dating? She heard the other officer ask the boy, and she listened with interest to his answer, secretly testing, hoping that he'd remember their anniversary and calculate correctly.

He said he didn't remember, *sorry, a few months, maybe a year.*

Valerie's cop asked her the same question and she wailed, *Nearly a year! I love him!* It had not been nearly a year, but she exaggerated to compensate for his lackluster response. Someone had to lend their relationship a degree of seriousness.

The police officers were not interested in staging an elaborate teenage drama with Valerie in the role of Hysterical Girl #1. They walked back toward their cars, advising her to not park at Bond

Lake again, and she called after them: *Wait! Aren't you going to write up a report? Are you going to send a ticket to our parents?*
They didn't respond. This seemed ominous. The police were a strange abstract entity with no real bearing on her life, but they could, she theorized, report back to the real authority at home.

13

This was not the first time Valerie was apprehended. A few weeks before, her mom had found a cache of cosmetics in her underwear drawer. Valerie arrived home from school to find Susan sitting at the head of the kitchen table, tinted moisturizers and split-end serums and at least twelve bottles of lavender body spray heaped between her elbows.
You don't earn enough waitressing to afford all this, Susan said. *Where did it come from?*
I have no idea. It's not mine, Valerie answered, half a lie, half an admission.
Don't lie. I found it in your underwear drawer.
Well, I have no idea what it was doing in there. Or why you were snooping around in my underwear.
It's my house, I can snoop where I'd like, Susan replied, unaffected by the insult. *You're stealing.*
Valerie was silent.
Where'd it all come from?
Why do you care?
Why do I care? Why do you need all this stuff? You think your father and I don't give you enough? Susan paused, pushing the loot away as if it were garbage. *Look around you*, she said, gesturing to indicate their general situation.
The kitchen?
Don't be smart. You think your father and I got where we are by taking things that don't belong to us? No. We made sacrifices. Listen. Your father and I work every day to provide for you and your sister.

Buying

Gabby's dad lets her shop at all the good stores. He even buys stuff for her. It's not fair.

Gabby's dad can do whatever he wants with his own money and his own child. If the other kids at school have parents who buy them useless stuff at the mall, fine. But we're not like that. I'm not going to have a daughter of mine playing rich-kid make-believe and walking around with $30 tubes of mascara because she thinks she deserves it. If you want to make enough money to buy all these luxuries someday, be my guest. But you'd better get working.

I already do, though. At the restaurant, Valerie replied, offended.

And yet you've clearly learned nothing about the value of hard work.

It's just makeup, Mom.

Susan raised an eyebrow, indicating the enormity of the stash.

It only looks like a lot because you've got it all piled up like that. In the grand scheme of the universe, though, it's negligible. Seriously. Do you have any idea how many lip glosses are currently in circulation?

It's not about how much you're taking, Susan replied. *It's about your behavior.*

It's not like I murdered someone. I'm not hurting anybody.

You don't get to make those kinds of judgments around here. I make the money and I pay the bills. That means I decide what's right and wrong.

Valerie hated her mom for so many things, but especially for the way her gaze morphed those glimmering treasures into a pile of everyday consumption. To Valerie, each item in its plastic casing, dustings of mica and bubblegum pink and mixtures of Lanolin and Red 30 Lake, was more singular and untouchable than the last. Each was a talisman, a reminder of the game and its jolts and thrills that pulled her from the onward march of her little life. The more Valerie stole, the smoother her skin, the shinier her hair, the deeper the pigments smudged on her face. The more she stole, the better she looked at the CVS, and then the Ultra Beauty Supply at the Outlet Mall, and now the Sephora on Main Street in Buffalo. The more she stole, the easier it was for her to get away with stealing.

What would Susan have to say about Valerie taking pieces of cheesecake from the restaurant on nights when her tips amounted to a few crumpled bills and some change the kids who ordered burgers-to-go left on the counter? What about the times Valerie was extra nice to the guy who operated the fryer and he gave her the mistake orders of mozzarella sticks and sweet-potato fries, which she ate in the Taurus with the boy or brought home and shared with Julie while they watched *Cops* reruns on MTV? It was so easy to steal incidentally, to just *get* things without earning them.

Later that summer, with the restaurant's kitchen empty, the dishwashers and bussers gone home, Valerie packaged a slice of cheesecake in a Styrofoam to-go container and brought it down to the dock where she ate with great deliberation and ceremony, feet dangling in the cool water. She threw a metal spoon stolen from the restaurant into the water. Why had she told the police she got good grades? Good grades meant she was a good girl, not a girl who should be talking to police. When she got particularly good grades, Susan reluctantly drove her to the outlet mall and bought her a pair of cheap sunglasses or clearance-rack jeans.

When she stole cheesecakes and spoons, she was afraid of the restaurant manager as she was afraid of the checkout girl at the drugstore as she was afraid of her mom—but not afraid enough to be *good* in any real, coherent way. *Whatever that means*, she thought. It was her last day of work at the restaurant, and the waiter she had a crush on told her she wasn't a good employee. At a graduation party in June, Gabby told her she wasn't a good friend, and they couldn't go to the mall together if Valerie kept stealing. *Or, at least, stay away from me while you're doing it. It gives me bad karmic energy. And you're more obvious than you think.*

The next morning, Valerie would pack the Taurus with clothes and books and color-coordinated dorm-room furnishings purchased at Walmart and drive across the state to college, and so tonight she planned on relishing the last bite of raspberry cheesecake and chucking the spoon as far as she could. The cheesecake tasted *good*. The arc the spoon made, the delicate splash disrupting the restaurant's reflection in inky water, that looked *good*. When she made out with the boy in the backseat of her Taurus he called her

good and when she got home with matted hair and smeared eyeliner her mom called her *bad* and since the two words could apply to
the same act, they didn't seem to have any meaning at all.

14

Valerie got up around five every morning in the apartment she
shared with Neel to study her grad school readings. She liked the
faraway opalescent glow of the early sky, and she liked to press
her nose against the window in the kitchen to create oil smudges
on the glass while she waited for the coffee machine to warm. She
usually woke to find lumpy pillows wedged between her body and
Neel's. She wasn't sure who placed them there during the night.
He watched Hollywood action movies and porn in the living room
until very late, and she often crept into the hallway, footsteps
imperceptible on the soft, standard-issue beige carpet, to stare at
his face illuminated by the blue light for a few moments, directing
all her energy at him. *You're overcome with love and desire for me, and
you want to come to bed right now. You want to touch me.*
    Neel was either serious about porn or neurotic about comput-
er security and malware, so he paid for an account on one of the
high-quality password-protected porn sites. The movies he liked
had narratives, beginnings and orgasmic conclusions; the girls he
preferred were sculpted and lacquered into thick thighs, small bellies with pierced navels, arching eyebrows, hard silicone breasts,
gaping anuses. Around 11 A.M., after Neel left for work, Valerie
snuck onto his computer and into his browsing history, clicking
on the movie he'd watched the previous night to see what got
him off. Sometimes she lay on the couch in the exact spot he'd
occupied the night before, pulling her pants around her knees and
placing his hot computer on her lap to masturbate to the same girl
he'd masturbated to, their bodies separated by only a few hours,
orgasms otherwise perfectly aligned.

15

It wasn't difficult for Neel to convince Valerie not to talk to anyone about their relationship issues. Like all dully comfortable couples, they had plenty of other kinds of problems: Neel to the tune of roughly ninety grand, and Valerie, commuting to an expensive master's program in New York City twice a week, sixty and counting.

According to the Wells Fargo pamphlet Valerie pocketed when she opened her new account, which delineated important life moments both financial and personal, Moving in Together was an essential step, one that directly preceded Saving for an Engagement Ring. Moving in Together, Wells Fargo mused, should coincide with opening a joint account. (*We'll be with you when two accounts become one*, the brochure assured Valerie. *Talk to a Wells Fargo counselor today and take your big step with confidence.*) Valerie and Neel, though, wouldn't be inhabiting that particular brand of American hetero-fiduciary conjugality. They simply had too much student loan debt to join their respective fortunes.

But they could play pretend, act as if they were mutually aiming themselves at the target of victorious, two-car-garage-owning domesticity. This required a certain degree of prevarication. To maintain their performance, both Neel and Valerie used their college degrees wisely: Neel, who had majored in political science, treated his debt as an unruly constituency to be wrangled into submission. He split the debt between different companies, compared interest rates and repayment plans, and collected books in a stack beside their frameless mattress with titles like How to Conquer Your Personal Finances and Debt-Free, Shame-Free Life. Valerie, a literature student, instead pretended her debt didn't exist. *Maybe the world will end before the debt collectors find me*, she rationalized. *Or a criminal will sneak into the database and wipe all the debts clean. Or there'll be a revolution.*

Neel wanted no such revolution. His mother, an American, and father, the child of immigrants from Surat, met in a grad program in London and moved to Queens in 1986, a year before Neel was born. Baby Neel was toted around to loft parties and art openings and evening lectures like a particularly absorbent accessory; for him, Oedipal rebellion meant leaving the city for a carpeted apartment with central air conditioning in the Hudson Valley where he could watch blockbuster movies all weekend without incurring an arty parent's forlorn sigh. The first time Neel brought Valerie home, he opened his freezer to reveal two-dozen pints of Ben & Jerry's: salted caramel, mint-chocolate chip, double fudge . . . He turned the television to a late-night infomercial and handed her a pint of marshmallow swirl, swearing that the combination would produce the best sleep of her life. *Ambrosia sleep*, he called it.

With her daughter dozing sweetly under the same roof as a man and a dishwasher and an air conditioning unit in Cherry Hill Apartments number 4B, Valerie's mother could reasonably daydream of wedding dress shopping. Valerie was on the right track. Marriage was a repetition, sure, but also a means of escape: from one treacherously comfortable life (Valerie's childhood) to another (adulthood or marriage, the two being interchangeable in Susan's mind).

A fragile aura of newfound suburban prosperity had pervaded Susan's youth. Her mother, Gloria, taped aspirational pictures of Aspen and St. Moritz next to her wedding photo on the fridge. She clipped the Buffalo Philharmonic's schedule out of the Sunday newspaper each week but, with six daughters and two sons, could not find the time to go to any of the performances.

The family had moved into the big house on Grand Island in 1970, when Susan's dad was promoted: no longer a door-to-door salesperson, he was now a proud manager at the local Nabisco plant. The family would have to move closer to the offices. *To a neighborhood with better schools*, he said. *And more privacy.*

Gloria picked the kids up after school one day in the extra-long station wagon and drove them to take a look at the place. They stampeded through the orange linoleum and fake-wood-panel kitchen and up the stairs to behold the bedrooms. Susan's older sisters pushed her aside and laid claim to the largest bedroom with the bunk beds. Her athletic brother lorded over the corner room. Susan sat cross-legged in the middle of the floor of the small room with the purple shag carpet to hold her spot. When the sister closest in age insisted that the room had been hers first, they agreed to share it, but not out of any sort of affinity. They would draw a line in masking tape down the center of the room, and Susan was ordered not to trespass under any circumstances.

There had been no such claiming of sacrosanct spaces in the family's previous home, a duplex close to the city center. Gloria and her husband rented out the upper level from an older woman who lived, alone, downstairs, their ten-person family sharing the three-bedroom, one-bathroom unit. Gloria shooed the kids outside on weekday nights claiming they needed fresh air, but really, there just wasn't enough room in the apartment for the horde to be home at once. The neighboring duplexes didn't have yards to play in— the houses were much too close to each other—so the kids staked out sidewalks and Susan practiced cartwheels in the street.

In the duplex, Gloria invited the other neighborhood wives over while her husband was at work. They smoked cigarettes and talked about their marriages, their kids. She was especially close with the Irish woman who lived next door, Kitty. When Gloria wanted to take an evening class at the community college, Kitty agreed to keep an eye on the kids, make them pancakes for dinner and pass out Band-Aids and Coca Colas as needed. Kitty's husband was the reticent type, just like Gloria's, and when Gloria picked the kids up after class, the two women stood outside together on the stoop for a few minutes, swatting mosquitoes and exchanging tips on how to best handle moody teenage daughters and passionless husbands. Gloria confided in Kitty that, when they were first talking about buying the new house on Grand Island, her husband suggested that they share the master bedroom, but sleep in twin beds. Gloria acted indifferent, maybe a little hurt, but, truth be told, she found the idea electrifying, joked to Kitty about permissible forms of birth control. Kitty revealed that her husband fell asleep in his armchair with a beer in his lap most nights. She removed the can from between his legs, turned off the light, and went to the bedroom alone, delirious at the prospect of sprawling her body diagonally over the mattress, cocooning herself, greedy and warm, in bleached sheets.

On Grand Island, Gloria dressed her six daughters in matching department-store dresses and gave the boys exacting bowl haircuts. They were now a Nabisco manager's children, and she the manager's wife. She studied magazines detailing the fashion and comportment and conversation topics preferred by the Kennedys and Shrivers and emulated the women as best she could, despite what the archbishop of the Buffalo diocese told her about Jackie, a disgrace and a sinner for remarrying after the president's death.

Gloria tried to call up Kitty when she felt lonely, but it was difficult to find the time and privacy. Sometimes Kitty's husband would get mad at his wife for tying up the phone. Kitty's husband was a psychiatrist with a home office, and she was his secretary and receptionist. They had two phone lines—one for his patients and one for the family—and Gloria was careful to always call the personal number, but Kitty's husband was wary of his wife's calls nonetheless. When Susan started misbehaving, talking back to the nuns and cutting classes at Catholic school, Gloria suggested to her husband that they might send her to Kitty's husband for analysis. Really, she wanted an excuse to sit in the waiting room and chat with her old friend. Gloria's husband didn't approve of this, though—analysis was for people with real problems, and too expensive—so the women fell out of touch.

None of the wives in the new neighborhood liked to sit on their stoops and smoke cigarettes. Gloria went out to her stoop at different times every night, no matter the weather, and peered around at the neighboring houses, but the women were never outside. At the old apartment, cigarettes had been an excuse to congregate, to sit close to the women who lived next door and gently touch knees, to laugh and blow thick clouds of smoke into the night.

Gloria gave up on making new friends and began to lock herself in the upstairs bathroom to smoke out the window instead. She lit one cigarette from the end of another as she painted her toenails pearlescent pink. She weighed herself several times and set her hair in rollers and undressed in front of the mirror, surveying the body that had once been hers. The kids never stopped banging against the wall as they played, and the older girls hit the door and screamed at her that they needed to use the bathroom to prepare for dates. She barely knew her children. There were too many of them. Strange that they'd come out of her body, one after the other. She imagined them all in her stomach at once, her bones cracking and skin stretching to accommodate hundreds and hundreds of babies. They squeezed at her organs from the inside. She stared at herself in the bathroom mirror until her own face was as alien to her as the faces of her children. If she tightened the muscles around her eyes enough, let her focus go kind of soft, she could make the mirror-face disappear entirely.

Gloria started to hate her husband. She watched his chest rise and fall at night, sometimes accompanied by soft snores, in his twin bed. She willed all her energy at him to wake up, to be filled with tenderness and to talk softly to her about whatever was on her mind. Her husband was a very sound sleeper. She considered smothering him. Instead, she began to stay downstairs until late at night, reading and chain-smoking.

One day, her oldest daughter banged repeatedly on the bathroom door, yelling about needing hairspray. Something in Gloria snapped. She opened the door and smacked the girl and screamed at all the girls to leave, to get out of the house right away, to never come back. The oldest daughter helped the younger girls put on their winter clothes and marched them, single file, down the busy road. Susan was glad to have saved her peanut butter sandwich from lunch that day, and she balled up small pieces in her pocket and fed them to herself while they trudged through the wet February snow. Valerie's grandpa, the manager, driving home from work, noticed the line of girls marching down the sidewalk three miles from home. He herded them into the backseat of the Buick, piling Nabisco sales reports and product samples in the trunk, and brought the girls home. There was no discussion of the incident.

By the time Valerie was old enough to understand her grandfather as having been her mother's version of a father, he'd parked himself semi-permanently in front of an endless stream of docudramas about World War II, the war in which he'd never fought. With the TV on, he didn't have to think about his own unheroism, the life in which he, instead of becoming a soldier, had been a product salesperson. He'd married the nicest-looking girl he could afford and they'd had as many children as she could physically tolerate and he'd tried to pay their debts and he felt the only feeling allowed to him, anger, toward his daughters intensely and evenly and toward his sons when they disappointed him. He otherwise ignored the house and family and rotation of cats and gerbils and Barbie dolls and Easy-Bake ovens and BB guns. He sat in the TV room for so long that the experience of not having spoken to anyone for decades took its toll and he retreated into images of restaged battles, emerging only to preside over the lonely empire of his own dining-room table on holidays and occasional weekends.

16

You shouldn't believe everything your friends tell you, Neel said, severing a shishito from its stem with his teeth and grimacing.

Did you get a hot one? Valerie asked. They'd been together for nearly two years and, by now, she understood the importance of affecting utmost concern for his mental and physical well-being. Neel ignored her.

Your friends don't have your best interests in mind, Valerie. You think they care about you? People only care about themselves. It's a dog-eat-dog world. They'll cut you down to better themselves.

Valerie's friends were waitresses. She doubted they were highly invested in social climbing, but Neel frequently warned her to watch her back, guard her bartending spot. He brought her to Fish-kill's two fancy restaurants—a farm-to-table trattoria and a New American spot with a $23 burger—at least once a week so she could improve both her palette and her foreign-language skills. Tonight, she was supposed to order a Beaujolais, and no, he wouldn't tell her how to pronounce it ahead of time.

Neel insisted they sit at the bar. *We're industry people. Industry people don't get tables.* The place was crowded with New Yorkers, upstate for a rustic holiday getaway. Valerie situated herself on a stool, a dripping pile of overcoats and bags to one side and jars of lemon wedges, sugar cubes, maraschino cherries—homemade—to the other. January air hit her upper arms every time a couple (smart black glasses, thick scarves, severe haircuts) entered or exited. She arranged her face into the expression of listening. She didn't have any thoughts in her head.

I'll have the Bo-jo-lee. The bartender, a soft-bellied man with a wine-glass tattoo on his forearm, gently corrected her pronunci-ation—*Ah, wonderful, the Bo-zho-lay, I'll bring it right over*—and this gave Neel an opportunity to extemporize on the town's French Huguenot history, its variously pronounced street names, the hor-rors of Americanization in general. A neighboring bar patron, alone with a crossword, disagreed. Locals should be permitted to Ameri-canize the names of the streets on which they lived. Valerie stared at her face in the back-bar mirror, trying to let all expression slip away. *Dubois* was of particular concern to Neel and the man. Val-erie relaxed the muscles around her eyes to release her skin from expression.

What do you care, anyway? the man asked Neel. *You're no French Huguenot.*

Neel was deeply offended. Valerie's face looked like a wax effigy.

I'm an American; aren't I? It's as much my history as yours. Neel had turned his back to Valerie, facing the man.

Whatever, man. I'm just saying, telling people they have to pronounce De-boyce any other way is never gonna work.

Neel asked for the check, emptied the Beaujolais, stood to leave. Valerie followed.

On the walk home, the two were silent until they turned onto Calvert Street. *You humiliated me. You didn't defend my honor.* Neel looked straight ahead, hands stuffed in pockets.

Your honor? Valerie was half-jogging to keep up.

That guy was insulting me, and you let him get away with it.

I was bored, Neel. I wanted to leave.

Bored? You think it's boring when someone threatens my reputation? He was an idiot. He was drunk and bullshitting.

I don't know about you sometimes, Valerie. My ex would've never let someone trash-talk me that way. She would've broken a beer bottle over his head.

That restaurant doesn't even have beer, Neel.

Don't be pedantic. You know what I mean.

Valerie wasn't sure what to think. Was she being pedantic? Weren't couples on dates supposed to talk to each other? Why was Neel always holding forth in the New American restaurant, lecturing the bartenders about wild fermentation and best practices for folding squid ink into pasta dough, proselytizing about the effects of mindfulness meditation and deep breathing on serotonin and neural connectivity?

You don't have anything to say for yourself, do you?

She didn't.

That's because you know you're wrong. It's indefensible, acting the way you do.

They walked the rest of the way home, Valerie trailing Neel, a scolded dog. They fought in the apartment with the beige rug for the next few hours. Neel was stern and Valerie was losing the argument, which no longer had anything to do with French Huguenots. She always lost the argument. Neel had deeper problems that he could bring out in order to win, like depression and alcohol and general feelings of malaise. But this time Valerie wanted some of the pity.

She'd learned from Neel how to deploy tragic stories. Valerie settled shrewdly on two—one in which a beloved teacher told her she *wasn't a normal kid*, and another in which she was humiliated by the popular boys in middle school—and sat on the edge of the bed, sobbing and having a *really hard time* admitting these childhood traumas. The stories were true, or as true as memories can be, but they were irrelevant to the now, and Valerie didn't feel any particular connection to either event.

Where had her childhood (in which she *wasn't a normal kid*) ended and her adolescence (when the popular boys made fun of her) began? And where did her adult self, the self that could mine her history for wounds to wield—where did that self begin? She didn't think too hard about these questions.

Neel was convinced and moved by Valerie's admissions. Neel said that Freud said that everyone had some original primal trauma. He made soft noises, pitying noises. They both knew the fight was over. Afterward, Valerie felt much more sick at herself than she'd felt when she lied about eating her roommate's leftover chocolate cake, or when she'd broken her recent no-getting edict to take a bottle of vitamin D from Stop & Shop.

Valerie had gathered all of her previous selves into the room to egg her on, give her ammunition for a performed confession. Coercing them felt no different than coercing anyone else. So, Valerie decided, even if you told someone the complete truth about yourself, it could be totally phony. She had just wanted to win the fight. She didn't care about her teacher's assessment of her relative normality, and she never really thought about the popular boys in middle school. Neel didn't seem to care either. They never touched upon her youthful tragedies again.

17

Throughout the spring, Valerie had a recurring dream that she was walking a dog through a leafless New England forest, trees various shades of decay and brown, wearing tall leather boots and

Buying

proceeding with slow, deliberate steps. She was middle-aged and quite successful, wearing a camel jacket and expensive sweater. She didn't stop to notice the forest much. She was more concerned with her own dignified image, serious patrician face, elegant hands, unhurried gait. Her phone, tucked neatly in her jacket pocket, rang in lovely, soft, jingling tones. She worried it was someone who needed her. She was an in-demand professional, frequently called upon to help people solve their problems. She sat alone in front of a massive fireplace with an unopened newspaper and glass of dark liquor. She had so few concerns of her own that other people's problems became her highest priority. She had plenty of time to think, and very few emotions. She answered the phone to hear an older and even more severe Neel on the line. He wanted to discuss a case she'd been managing. He was accusatory, the only person who could condemn this exemplary and mature Valerie. Perhaps they were both psychoanalysts. Neel, sitting in an overstuffed leather chair in front of rows of books, a lawyer in a TV commercial, scolded her because she wasn't handling the case well. It became clear to Valerie that, in this instance, she was both the patient and the doctor. She hadn't diagnosed herself properly. Neel would have to take over. He wanted her to return home promptly for treatment. She was suddenly small and squirming and, realizing that she'd forgotten to wear a shirt, entirely exposed. She asked the phone meekly what was wrong with her, but Neel refused to answer. If he told her, he said, the treatment wouldn't work. She first had to confess that she was ill, that she needed treatment, that she was incapable of handling herself. Only then would the analysis work its wizardry. She hadn't felt ill—she had thought herself genteel, alluring, complete—but she wanted to know what was wrong with her, so she admitted a string of immoralities and guilty thoughts, each more absurd than the last. She was totally, completely crazy. She stopped to await Neel's diagnosis, but none came. Looking down at the phone, Valerie, walking regally in the forest again, realized with a great and confused relief that she'd lost cell service several minutes ago, had been confessing to no one. Her sanity remained, a precious, untouchable secret.

18

Deer picked through trash by the side of the highway. Valerie sat in the back of the Trailways bus for privacy, forehead pressed to the dirty window, talking as quietly as she could to her friend Leila on the phone. Leila was racking up clinical hours with an elderly psychologist (*an old crackpot*, she complained) so that she could get her license, and, for mutual benefit, the two liked to dissect feelings in extended conversations 1) on Valerie's living-room couch while Neel was at work; 2) in the condiment cooler at the restaurant, pretending to refill mayonnaise and shivering in tacky beer-maid uniforms; 3) when Valerie took the bus from Fishkill to Manhattan twice a week to attend grad seminars at Columbia with a very important professor who'd been big in France in the sixties.

Leila was training in self-development and life stages. She advised taking control of your situation, making the best of it, setting boundaries with unhealthy friends, confronting and cutting out toxic ex-boyfriends and cousins and catty waitresses who gossiped about your having seduced the Thursday afternoon bartender, who was married. *I didn't even have sex with him*, Leila complained, *just a hand job out by the beer bottles. And then we sorted them for recycling.* Leila was a confident girl, short and big-haired, with pockmarked cheeks. She wore oversize sweaters and tight jeans and was an excellent flirt. She revealed intimate details about her romances in their conversations, to which Valerie replied in oblique and allegorical terms.

Valerie occupied her seat next to the bus's bathroom, tolerating the periodic flush and ventral smell of the roving Port-a-Potty. She had debated for several weeks whether to come clean to Leila about her and Neel's problems. Neel had cautioned her that discussion of any aspect of the relationship with friends or therapists or coworkers (even strangers, he said) was a mortal sin against the sanctity of their romantic bond. But, Valerie rationalized, she and Neel didn't have much of a romantic bond, or at least one that she'd consider sacred and managed by a higher power. Confession to her friend/therapist/coworker would only be a minor transgression against nothing.

As the bus slunk away from the city and back toward Fishkill and Leila and Neel, Valerie felt herself slipping from attentive-silent student to attentive-silent girlfriend. The bus was a weird in-between space holding the commuters, who didn't converse or look at each other during their two-and-a-half hour, seventy-five-mile process of shedding one face, rearranging and making believable another. Valerie worked up the nerve to tell Leila the secret exactly sixty-two and a half miles into the drive. Blanchot, who she'd read that week, could turn language into an opaque surface, speaking beside the point, around the point, evading the point, and so Valerie would try this, too:

> Valerie: _____ [an evasive monologue meant to communicate something without having to say what] ... *and we don't talk about it. We don't communicate at all, really. He doesn't like when I bring it up.*

> Leila: *Wait, when you bring what up? I'm not following.*

> Valerie: *When I bring up the problem. I just told you.*

> Leila: *Come on, Valerie. You didn't tell me anything. You just rambled on for five minutes about contemporary conditions of alienation and the impossibility of actualizing heterosexual desire.*

> Valerie: *Yeah, well, that's the problem. A standard, run-of-the-mill straight-people problem. Plus, my brain doesn't work when I'm around him. I can't read, can't write, can barely speak, can't focus at all. We don't touch, just move around each other: 1) He, on the left side of the living room with a book open beside him. Me, in front of the kitchen*

sink, glowering in his direction; 2) He, fallen asleep with
his computer still open on the couch. Me, huddled in bed
upstairs and listening like a scared animal for signs of life
below; 3) He, taking a business call from the fish market on
the porch so I can't hear. Me, sitting in the bathroom and
staring at my reflection. It's paralysis. I'm mute, but it's
not only that—if I could speak, there'd be nothing to say.
I'm stuck in this abyss, like the longing gnawed away at all
the other parts of me until it was the only thing left. And
now I spend all day puttering around our apartment like
a weirdly desirous ghost. It's intolerable, my cells on fire,
waiting, trying to make myself as invisible and available
as possible. Like, if I could just disintegrate, become not a
person but a palliative, if I could make it [Valerie meant,
but couldn't say: *my body, desiring and revoltingly phys-*
ical] *go away, love might emerge. He might be born from*
my nothingness whole and ready, and I might rejoin flesh
with presence with thought, suture throat and language and
speak freely, an outpouring of silent words that bind us
together. But just look at me, I'm real and I can't disap-
pear and despite all my trying, I'm still so horribly this
[she gestured at herself, invisible to Leila].

Leila: *Valerie, what the fuck. I have no idea what you're*
saying. Spell it out for me like I'm a moron.

Valerie: *He won't have sex with me. Ever. He refuses to*
touch me at all.

Neel stepped carefully over and around Valerie, smiling politely
while maneuvering. Valerie often thought about the few times in
her life she'd visited friends or grandparents in a hospital, how
twitchily she'd sat at their bedside, how she'd avoided leaning in
close enough to smell their breath. She must smell rotten to Neel.
She must look sick.

Buying

As soon as Neel left the apartment, Valerie came rushing to the surface, violently contorted like the Francis Bacon paintings she was supposed to be studying in Postwar Critical Theory, writhing and sobbing silently. Neel didn't like the neighbors to know his business. When it was time to stop crying, she stood before the bathroom mirror and told her image to snap out of it; that's enough, now, dummy; it's time to snap out of it, and once the image had complied, she gathered herself and sat on the couch with a pencil and paper.

It's been nine months without this or that variation of _____ [sexual behavior or act] *because of* _____ [offense conceivably caused by her body]. *It's been five weeks without talking about it. It's been thirteen days since I've registered any sort of complaint re: the situation, the suffering.*

> Leila: *Have you tried speaking with him more clearly about it, maybe?*

Valerie made a face at the phone. Leila didn't understand. As if an argument for the Human Rights of Girlfriends might be drawn out of her pleas. She, a serf in rags scuttling across the polished floor of the feudal court to prostrate herself before her lord. He, sitting in front of his computer, productive, Long Island fishmongers on his phone.

Over their two-year relationship, Valerie had expected a trajectory of gradual improvement to mark itself on the calendar hanging in the kitchen, a future of reasonable expectations. The relationship had become an endurance test that she agreed to withstand, twisting and transforming its flaws into complicated disquisitions and justifications until she was, at last, satisfied at her decision to stay.

Photocopied essays by postwar critical theorists piled up beside their bed. When Valerie tried to read, the words of these mostly dead, mostly French men flowed to the surface of the Xeroxed pages and conjoined and multiplied and began shimmering, taunting her. Determined, she read sentences again and again, out loud, in her head, copied into her notebook. She tried to find counsel in Derrida and Barthes on _____ [*subjects related to the problem*] but after months of this, it became clear to Valerie that the problem was inexpressible in this language, which was the only one she had; _____ couldn't be dealt with in terms that these words could even approximate, let alone begin to fix.

Leila: *So, if you don't mind me asking, why are you still with him? Why don't you just leave?*

Valerie: *I thought I could make it better. I thought that was my role. And, you know, once something's set in motion, it's difficult to make it stop. What's that called?*

Leila: *I don't know, Valerie. Why don't you tell me.*

Valerie: *The law of inertia, I think. The tendency to stick on the same track unless met by an equal and opposite force.*

Around Newburgh, the day burst forth into a gray and punishing rain. The bus inched past a construction site, workers in bright orange rain jackets and galoshes. A siren lazily announced its presence in the distance.

Leila: *You know, the way you're justifying the whole situation, I'd say you get a kind of kick out of it. Right? Hear me out. I'm not being a jerk; I swear. But sexlessness is kind of an interesting problem. Why be with a man at all unless he's fucking you? You probably have some deep-seated attachments to the performance of heterosexuality, is all I'm saying. Rooted-in-childhood-style attachments. Like, what's so great about men without sex? What's so great about living with Neel? Talk your way around it all you*

*want, but my professional opinion is that there's some part
of you that enjoys suffering silently and doing the dishes.*

Valerie: *You're seriously going to tell me I want my own
oppression? That's messed up, Leila.*

Leila: *Do you even want to have sex with Neel?*

Valerie: *I want him to want to have sex with me!*

Leila: *That's not what I asked.*

Valerie: *Do I want to have sex with him; do I want him to
want to have sex with me—what's the difference?*

Leila: *What's the difference? You're hopeless. Totally
hopeless.*

Valerie made another face at the phone, promising to *think about
it*, and invented an excuse to end the conversation. She should've
known better than to tell Leila. Now there'd be someone nagging
her, keeping tabs on her progress toward leaving.

When Valerie's semester ended, Neel suggested going to the
trattoria to celebrate. He wouldn't even test her wine skills. She
could order a plain old Cabernet, if she liked. After two drinks
(her) and five (him), Neel began telling her about a dishwasher
at the restaurant adjoining the fish market. He'd fallen in love
with one of the waitresses and, improbably, they had a romance.
Angry and sullen and poor, the dishwasher made dirty comments
about all the waitresses and picked fights with the manager. The
waitress was a practical single mom without a green card who'd
taken the job to save for her son's education. She dumped him,
of course. The next evening, he came into the fish market after it
closed, drunk and sweating, waving a gun around and demanding
to know where she was, threatening to kill her and himself, too.

Neel calmed him down, got the gun away from him, gave him a Budweiser and a glass of water and listened to sorrows voiced in anguished, intoxicated tones.

He's just like any other man, Neel sighed into his drink, sympathetic. *All he wants is a woman to love him.*

19

The problem with [*sexlessness*] being unutterable is that it takes on the status of the eternal and primordial and natural. All Neel could do was shrug his shoulders. It was a fact beyond language. It would not change. Who was he in the face of earthquakes, monsoons, the irrefutable truths and mechanics of human nature? No one person, and certainly not Neel, could be held accountable for [*her body, her longing*].

Valerie's internal monologue grew increasingly dramatic. When she stood in the grocery-store checkout line surveying magazine covers, she felt a sense of solidarity with trapped miners and earthquake victims and women chained up in basements. *Unspeakable suffering, violence beyond words*, images of unidentified corpses already merging with landscape, and Valerie nodded, comradely. Outside language, on the other side of discourse: what could be done with something that [*unfortunately but undeniably*] exceeds available tools? Valerie imagined herself filing complaints, writing letters to the editor on behalf of all the world's sufferers, each returned with a note in Neel's handwriting. *There's no accounting for tragedy.*

No forcing it, either: Neel wasn't to blame, he said. [*Sexlessness*] was simply a regrettable result of one of the world's most mysterious forces, carved in stone and writ since time immemorial. Just as Brad couldn't help but want Angie and Romeo couldn't help but want Juliet, Neel couldn't help but not want Valerie. If she'd just leave it alone for a while, maybe things would change.

1) *You're emotional,* he sighed, looking up from his computer as she sat on the floor before him, asking him to discuss [*sexlessness*]. *Try to get a grip on yourself. We can talk once you've calmed down.*

2) *This is insane,* in the morning, when she snuck her hand across the bed to touch his shoulder, voice breaking. *If you'd just leave me alone, let me deal with it my own way, it might get better. You just won't let up.*

3) *You're making that up; you don't remember correctly,* when faced with her timelines and lists. *I thought we were past this.*

4) *That's not a sound argument,* at the bar, after she outlined research and readings and reasons in an uncertain, shaking voice. *It's more like . . .*

5) Or, most simple and frequent: *yes, but . . .*

In September, Valerie returned to the apartment after bartending to find a decadent spread covering their dining table. Two plates of lobster, lemon wedges, tiny red potatoes flecked with whitish globs and spots. (*Hardened butter,* she thought. *They've gotten cold.*) A shiny, lumpy cake buried under dense whipped cream. Neel had made a feast. He wanted to have a romantic evening, to spill his guts and feed her shellfish and fill the space between them with Hallmark gestures. Lobster and whipped cream. Valerie didn't mind the cliché. She would heat the potatoes while she waited for his return. She would allow no lukewarm spuds to dampen their passion. She set the oven to 300°, grabbed a pan from the cupboard, stabbed at a potato with a fork. It resisted. She poked at the potato again, and still it defied her. It was then that she realized the meal had no smell. Of course it didn't. The food was made of plastic. Crude and horrible, cold and with an uncanny gleam.

She waited for the astonishment to pass, for reality to recompose around the inanimate crustaceans.

Neel emerged from the bathroom, wiping his hands on a sweat-yellowed T-shirt. *Hey. Aren't those funny?* He nodded at the plates. *The manager at Cardullo's gave them to me when I dropped off this week's shrimp order. They were on display behind the counter for decades. Pretty kitschy, huh? Very seventies.*

A plane crashed, an insult hurled, a bone broken. The cause is clear. Harm hits the body all at once. This was another kind of problem, though. It had accumulated so slowly, an event lived daily. It was difficult to imagine life otherwise, so structuring of reality had the problem become. Valerie couldn't leave Neel over a plastic meal, couldn't leave him because of strained silences and absent desire and nighttime pornos. It simply did not add up.

She began hoping for a terrible crisis like betrayal or illness or death. *That's not atypical*, Leila reported when Valerie confessed she lay awake at night, fervently wishing not to hear the metallic click of the door or smell the sudden waft of fish guts. Hoping she'd find his body in a ditch or get a call from the hospital. *Most of the patients in my women's group have recurring fantasies that their boyfriends will die in a tragic accident.* Leaving, unlike Neel's untimely death, would require that Valerie make a decision. It would demand definitive events and suitcases packed and futures abandoned. It seemed tiring. *And, after all, our problem is common enough*, Neel told her. *Probably your parents are this way, and my parents, too. It's just that no one talks about it. So, you can't go around getting all upset with me just because of* [sexlessness].

20

The waitresses struggled with inertia. *Restaurant work*, it seemed, as they rotated between tables of frat boys and married couples, noting hamburger temperatures and beer orders and allergies, *is for people who've been diverted from their desired life-trajectory, who haven't been able to accomplish the next step in time.*

In time for what? Leila couldn't say. She imagined her future unfurling before her like a Google doc. Under the doc's current heading, *Leila: aged twenty-four to twenty-seven*, was a checklist: she would date several men, some seriously, and toward the end, fall madly in love with one and get engaged. This, she calculated as she stood before a family of five, nodding and writing BLUE HAT—WELL DONE in her notepad, would allow a one-year engagement, a wedding before she turned thirty, several years to enjoy marriage before giving birth. The pregnant woman at table seven couldn't have raw onions in her side salad. Sautéed onions on the burger were fine. Could that be real—a raw-onion allergy? Leila pressed the appropriate button on the wait-station computer terminal. The mother was committed to her husband and her haircut and the lump of flesh in her flesh and to not eating raw onions. Leila was committed to getting away from the restaurant, achieving professional success and personal fulfillment, *making it happen*, whatever the cost. What was *it*? Leila sent the order to the kitchen. *It* involved becoming a woman who could be picky about her onions.

After their Sunday-afternoon shift, Valerie walked over to Leila's, two blocks from where she lived with Neel, and parked herself on the kitchen floor smelling of Worcestershire sauce and beer. Julie had recently arrived in town after an unsuccessful backpacking trip in Europe and was crashing with Leila; she texted Valerie that she would be there soon, would contribute boxed wine and a bag of pork dumplings. Leila would contribute *sparkling conversation*, she said, and a floor to sit on. Valerie didn't have to contribute because it was her turn to be pitied. This was an unspoken rule: if your boyfriend is giving you a hard time, other girls will take care of you.

So I sat there, pretending to cry. I knew it'd be good for his ego if he thought he made me really upset, but I'm not upset anymore. Just bored. Bored with how stupid and hollow it is having to create this thing with him, this cardboard cutout of a reputation that I sit next to at the bar on Saturday nights. Valerie prodded a half-eaten dumpling with her toe. Would the girls notice if she ate it off the floor? She nudged it closer.

Leila suggested that Valerie reclaim her agency. She sketched a plan by which Valerie could slowly move away from Neel, promising her she'd feel much better once she began to take steps. Soon, said Leila, practical and planning, Valerie would quit bartending and have satisfying work, even a job in New York, would be dating again, back on track. Leila understood, of course, that it was a crushing blow, losing one of those major success markers, an indicator of a life stage she'd seen in the Wells Fargo pamphlet.

Julie thought that the prospect of Valerie reorienting herself toward a different man-shaped target, Leila planning a wedding without having met a husband, the waitresses and Wells Fargo's life stages, were ridiculous, self-destructive. Why, Julie wanted to know, should Valerie be invested in the future payoff of a nonexistent relationship that, evidence showed, would likely make her desperately unhappy? Valerie pressed Julie to tell them if it was the same in queer relationships. It was not, Julie reported. No one knew whether to believe her.

Valerie remembered what their mom said when Julie announced she was gay: that she would mourn the loss of her own future, the one she'd always imagined, with one white wedding per daughter, two sons-in-law, four or five grandkids, two reassuringly balanced families visiting her and Mark on the holidays. *Lots of gay people get married*, Valerie had retorted. *And what about adoption?* She didn't want to say the words *artificial insemination* to Susan, and strategically decided to omit the fact that Julie had recently been quoting Lee Edelman and dotting casual conversation with derisive mentions of *homonormativity*—not that Susan would know what that meant.

Forget Neel. We should all move to New York. You can finish up grad school and Leila can put in her clinical hours at one of the psych centers down there. I could use a new scene; I've nearly dated through the dykes in this town, Julie suggested.

[86   ]

Buying

You've been here for two weeks, Leila said.

Exactly. There's approximately one fuckable queer here besides me.

At the restaurant, the manager scolded Leila and Valerie for gossiping [*talking to each other*] when they were supposed to be working [*talking to customers*]. Outside the reach of his surveilling ear, though, conversation proceeded circuitous, speculative, simultaneous: *yes!...and...I've also...* Talking together and all at once, the friends exceeded themselves.

Gossip, an amalgam of *god + sibling.* A relative, a close friend, she with whom one shares idle speech. Idle speech, the essential act of exchanging information: which waitress was unhappy in her relationship, which bartender shared tips most equitably with the wait-staff, which chef to avoid drinking with after the dinner rush on account of rumors he had been *not so nice* to the new girl, who'd quit after a few weeks. Hearsay, unreliable as evidence, not worth bringing to the police and useless before judge and jury. The list of men to avoid going home with on the stall door in the women's restroom, the phone call from an unknown number and a soft voice on the other line saying, *is he your boyfriend? Because,...* the sharing of information and encouragement and the offering up that *if you need to leave tonight, you can stay at my place for as long as you'd like, and I hope you do leave tonight, and I hope you can slip away quietly.*

21

At the beginning of their relationship, [*sexlessness*] still only a faint worry rattling around her skull, Valerie walked around Neel's beige living room in her floral-print underwear, a pair that was available that season at every mid-size mall in America alongside magenta briefs and multi-stripe boy-shorts and sheer mesh stockings and fluorescent thongs. Neel sat at the kitchen table, studying the week's inventory for the fish market. Red Snapper, Yellowtail Tuna, Grouper: Neel's fixations. He squinted at Valerie from under his glasses.

Are those underwear from the Gap?

Neel's tone was measured, curious, but a susurrus of secret meaning leaked out from beneath the question, behind the veil of glasses and skin and bone.

Yes, Valerie responded, The underwear were from the Gap.

No more needed to be said: Valerie could clearly imagine a scene in which Neel and a previous girlfriend had gone to the mall, walked together into the store, laughing and poking each other's sides, she a bit nervous and proud to bring a boyfriend in to pick out panties. Neel stood to the side as the ex browsed, bored and indifferent to the shades, styles, fabrics. They'd shared an Orange Julius and two oil-slicked slices of pizza at the food court. They'd compared purchases on the drive home. For months afterward, the Julius-drinking ex had flounced around Neel's apartment in the floral-print underwear before Valerie had even existed. (Or, she corrected herself, before she'd existed to Neel.) The Julius-drinking ex had stood, languid, in the kitchen before an open dishwasher, complimenting the floral-print underwear with one of Neel's shirts and a sexy-homemaker stance, just as Valerie was attempting now.

The underwear had been a deliberate choice, an item Valerie thought sure to lure Neel into unbridled lust, communicating as they did a kind of unthreatening vitality and youthful naiveté. At his question, though, thousands of possible wide-eyed and half-dressed ex-girlfriends extended before Valerie. The underwear could plausibly fit any female body. Her own pale legs, bruised knees, wide hips were thrown into relief with the infinite variations of *girl* cheap cotton could define.

Two years later, near the end of their relationship, Valerie skipped class to see an exhibition of Agnes Martin's paintings in Chelsea before taking the bus home to Fishkill to bartend that evening. Innocent Love, the series was called, but Valerie didn't read the wall text. She stood in the sterile white gallery for a long time studying the imperfection of Martin's pencil lines. The graphite marks were barely perceptible, tentative and exploratory—apologetic, even—attempting unsuccessfully to follow solid painted swaths of pale pink, blue, glowing yellow. Martin didn't draw the lines and then fill them in with paint: the broad blocks of color came first, then individual lines trying to track the borders, form the prescribed outline, exposing their particularities even as they tried to conform.

Valerie wanted to tell Neel something about the paintings, about trying to trace lines around her own existence, about why she was fantasizing her escape to New York with Julie and Leila, but she couldn't articulate it.

The paintings were the same colors as her old floral underwear, but the cheap chemical dye of the briefs was ugly and common in comparison. At the Fishkill Wash & Dry later that week, trying to sequester her dirty clothes from the eyes of the middle-aged woman on the phone and the alcoholic wandering around watching spin cycles, Valerie noticed the threads holding the underwear together had become more pronounced as the flower print had faded. It must've been the harsh detergent the laundromat gave out for free. The threads were beginning to unravel, the edges of the lace pilling and ripping, and she noticed that the seams weren't quite right. She could see where the hands operating the sewing machine had faltered, deviated from the pattern, a line flying off in the wrong direction for a millisecond. The underwear were, against themselves, extraordinarily particular. How many pairs were currently in circulation, she wondered, and how many girls pulled them on unthinkingly, daily? How many particularities masked by the ugly imperialism of identical floral-print briefs? The look of the underwear seemed linked to the shiny brutality of the system that produced and circulated them, but she wasn't sure how. It wasn't a topic she could pursue for a grad school essay, anyway. She watched the rotation of the drum as it tossed her clothes and forgot the metaphor.

22

I think I'd like to get out of Fishkill, Valerie proposed abstractly one morning, making coffee as Neel transposed his sleep-gorged body from bed to couch. This was her first step.
But all of your friends are here. He was disturbed by this idea, voiced so casually. *And I can't afford rent on this place alone.*
I think Leila's going to move down to the city soon. And Professor _____ asked me to help him get his archives in order, plan some department events . . .
This was a lie. She'd conjured it on the spot, culled from a dream or delusion she'd had the night before. (*Dreams don't have any meaning,* Neel told her when she'd relayed one previously. *They're basically like any other bodily excretion.*)
The dream, folded into language and ironed flat:

> Valerie and the waitresses worked on a tropical farm, planting and tending to row upon row of bright, fragrant flowers. A strange alchemy begun by the waitress's work transformed the plants into a noxious chemical river nourishing an enormous figure sitting in the middle of the farm, who the women referred to as _____. Wasps who were waitresses worked alongside the human waitresses, also tending to the flowers. Everyone knew the flowers to be female. The gender of the plants seemed clinical, factual, nothing to fuss about. The wasps went about impregnating plants; Valerie herself was assigned the task of impregnating those flowers that the wasps missed and killing the flowers that struggled with infertility. *But how can I impregnate a plant?* she asked the enormous _____. He didn't respond. Instead, he morphed into a serious and small old man, her professor, an esteemed philosopher-slash-theorist sitting at the head of a dinner table. It seemed quite natural that

the tropical island was now the interior of a New York apartment. The guests drank the fragrant fluid she'd moments ago been extracting from the plants. It continuously regenerated in delicate crystal glasses. The serious philosopher who was at the same time the enormous _____ charmed the dinner guests, and Valerie found herself conversing with important and wealthy New Yorkers with ease. Words fell from her mouth, but they were not her own. The words knew their place better than she did, and so she allowed them to flow forth. She complimented the other guests and gazed at herself from above, enchanting and elegant and dressed in sumptuous white fabric. The enormous philosopher _____ at the head of the table smiled at her, approving, his hair as white as her clothing. She realized that she had one of his books in her bag and excused herself to find it. Maybe he would sign it for her. Her bag was in a large pile of laundry shoved into the corner. She spilled the contents of the bag everywhere in an attempt to find the book, which, she remembered as she rifled through the pile, she'd ghostwritten for her professor. Make-up bottles and powders hid the book from her sight, jostling and spilling their contents onto the carpet, staining her fingers and clothes. Hands groped at her limbs, her hair. She allowed this. It was, after all, her fate. She looked up to see the dinner guests standing from their chairs, scowling at her, arms crossed. Stumbling, excusing herself, Valerie fumbled her way along rigidly gridded streets to an austere modernist hotel with soft purple lights. A valet offered her a bedroom with a sweeping view of the city, far above the dirt and turmoil of the street. The valet was very polite. Valerie wanted to gain access to the room, but knew that she'd have to marry the philosopher _____ in

exchange for the key. A repulsive thought. Standing
before the now-judgelike valet, she realized in a calm
horror that she already *was* married to the philosopher
_____. He was waiting for her in the room.
She walked forward, resigned, to the elevator, which
opened on cue, as if the scene had been scripted.

This was the end of the dream that had no meaning.

So, Valerie continued to Neel, *I thought I might move to New York
with Leila and Julie and get a job somewhere. I mean, it's getting difficult
to travel back and forth.*

And what'll I do?

Stupidly, she hadn't prepared for this question. *You can come,
too, if you'd like.*

Neel gave an exaggerated sigh, pulling a pillow onto his lap
and situating a business-management book atop. The discussion
was over.

Valerie no longer hacked her way into Neel's computer while
he was at the fish market to monitor his Internet activity and chart
his sexual proclivities. Instead, she browsed listings for jobs and
apartments with the intense pleasure of one who has an open
secret. *Assistant needed—excellent language skills necessary,* read a post
on an Upper East Side gallery's website. *Young and ambitious person with outstanding written and oral communication skills. Advanced
degree and stylish preferred. Tasks include embodying and ventriloquizing
brand identity; drafting all communications for gallery director; writing
press releases and exhibition texts in brand voice; conceptualizing essays
for gallery publications; answering the telephone in soothing tones; giving
tours and extemporizing on the historical importance and aesthetic value
of all paintings, sculptures, and mixed-media works under gallery pur-
view; being presentable and professional and appealing to collectors who
will buy artworks, wishing they could buy you instead.*

Valerie submitted a lengthy and imaginative résumé. She
appropriated a smart cover letter from a Job Applications and
Career Search Advice chatboard, making minor alterations and

adding relevant personal information. *I am* _____ *and can provide skills bolstering company* _____, the form letter suggested. She considered, amended: *I am malleable, a quick learner, and can provide skills bolstering company image and reputation.* The gallery directors were impressed. They didn't recognize the name of the school from which she'd received her undergraduate degree, but they were happy to employ her while she completed her prestigious master's program. When they called to set up an interview, Valerie answered the phone in a professional voice and promptly drove to the Poughkeepsie Galleria to purchase a professional outfit.

At the very least, Susan advised when her daughter called, *it'll be a good line on your résumé. This job will increase your marketability for the next job, the good job, the one you really want. Think of it as self-improvement. It's an investment in your future.*

At her mother's urging, Valerie had been adding lines to her résumé for as long as she could remember: piano lessons and travel and volunteer work and sports at which she'd been awful made her an attractive college prospect; alliances with high-profile professors, internships, and summer courses (and, of course, the boatload of loans that made this all possible) made her an employable worker. Susan thought these activities and lessons were excellent for her daughter's self-esteem. Valerie considered adding further line items to the résumé, expanding it to include her uncertainties and worries, her defining neuroses, the instance of her birth and her ultimate trajectory toward death, the quick burn or slow decay of her body, the moment in which any matter that once comprised her ceased entirely to exist, eaten by bacteria and cockroaches and mushrooms.

Despite the commonsensical grid and rigid social structure of the city, Valerie didn't know New York outside of the three-block vicinities of Times Square and the university. Lost on her way to the gallery in a fitted skirt and heels and a silk blouse, she ran, sweating, past the United Nations, its flags and stately cul-de-sacs, past Trump Tower, the tycoon's name in outsize gold letters high over the doorway. Words and images and reputations stood in for human bodies, she understood. This would be her job.

Practicing for her interview as she hurried up Park Avenue, Valerie silently babbled about artworks in the tycoon's copywriter's voice. *A very fine painting, the best painting, a most outstanding painting.* She limped swiftly past an organic dry cleaner, a bookstore named after Shakespeare, a Pakistani deli. How could her jabber harden into actual authority? *At some point in the farce,* her internal narrator concluded, *all you have to do is hire people. You have become money, the image of money, which is money.*

Despite Neel's primers on Beaujolais and her teenage evenings with *Vogue,* Valerie knew little about the priorities of the rich. They, an anonymous and shadowy coterie, had public relations departments and wellness teams and speechwriters and troupes of domestic servants. When exposed in less-than-legal dealings, they were loud and offended. Valerie continued to practice: *These slanderous allegations have damaged the thing I hold most dear: my image.*

She was interviewed in a room with mirrors on all four walls. Valerie sat with her own reflection in endless proliferations, her face morphing into liquid green abstraction. She received an employment offer from the gallery in the form of a love letter. On her first day of work, the director of sales walked her through the Madison Avenue offices, explaining her new role:

> *You'll be the voice of the gallery and speak on its behalf at all occasions, creating speeches and correspondence and conversation topics for the top-tier directorial staff, drafting emails and messages to clients and adopting a pleasing, welcoming manner to tour clients around exhibitions and viewing rooms. You'll have an innate understanding of all matters interpersonal and cerebral, and you'll realize that language can be used to disguise, to dissimulate, to manipulate, to smooth over, to reframe, to create the image of IWC gallery as an exclusive, trustworthy, high-end experience in the consumer's mind. Our clients want to feel*

*smart, savvy, and special, as if they've earned their money
through their own expertise and cunning and intelligence.
Certain that they now have the opportunity—no, the privilege—to spend it at a gallery operating at an equivalent
level of success. These people, they believe that once their
money reaches a certain level of, hmm, I guess once it's in
the hands of someone—namely, themselves—living and
working at the highest echelons of circulation, they would
hate to see it fall to a lower tier. Degrade in stock, so to
speak. And so they like to give their money to IWC, because
it ensures that the new owner of the money will value it as
much as they did. It's a special feeling, the attachment our
collectors have to their money.*

Valerie imagined the collectors as fat and fussy infants being
spoon-fed artworks in various formats—as objects, as descriptions,
as monetary values—until they found a mode so palatable that
they were overcome with an urge to spend. And, with every purchase, they increased their value, added to the portfolio of objects
and events and images and rumors that was them. Valerie realized
that she was like this, too. She could be like them while also being
bought by them daily. It was all very confusing.

*I'm sorry, we were talking about the role you'll have here.
Ah, yes! Here we are at the desk of our wonderful Sylvie.
She's just absolutely spectacular at recognizing our clients'
faces, answering our phones, entering data. She will do
all your data entry for you, order books you'll need for
research, place your dinner orders on nights you'll work
late. She can even help copyedit. Sylvie, smile and say
hello.*

Sylvie reached out from her seat behind a phalanx of orchids
and handed Valerie a stack of papers to sign, contracts indicating
that Valerie relinquished all ownership of intellectual property,
abdicated the rights to her writing, her language, her voice.

The contracts cast a spell and, within a few days of beginning her job at the gallery, Valerie felt herself in a strange new relationship to words. They were light and bouncy. They shimmered and flitted about, exquisite phrases loosened from referent. *In a gestural burst of vermillion at the canvas's center, the painter unfolds a drama of ravishment across the surface, crimson and ruby circling back in centripetal folds to a dynamic core.*

Soon, Valerie could sculpt strings of words so stunning, so free, so utterly ahistorical, that she sat enchanted, transfixed for hours by their effect. Text was now a substance with which she could work, a lovely raw material, rare and precious like dark obsidian, malleable like bubblegum.

She was so preoccupied with language, so busy with work, that she barely had time to mourn her bartending job and Neel, or celebrate her move into an unevenly floored duplex in Queens with Julie and Leila. Her old life simply faded away. Her new life was now as the gallery directors promised it would be: work was her only desire, her true love, her greatest passion. She forgot about problems and forgot about sex. All the pleasure to be had was right there, in the art world.

23

Tired, I'm so tired, Xiao typed into an empty text box on Taobao. *Sometimes, I just want to give up my life. I don't want to belong to myself. I want to live online and let the netizens arrange the rest of my time for me.* She moved her cursor to an empty square prompting her to enter a HEADLINE and paused, considering. *Xiao's Store of Remaining Life Time*, she wrote, rereading the title three or four times. It wasn't catchy enough. She deleted a few characters, tried again. *Xiao's Remaining Life-Time Store: Extend Your Own Life by Taking Time from Me!* Much better.

Special skills and expertise, the next box requested. She skipped over it. She had a degree, sure, but so did hundreds of thousands of other young people, cramped in shared apartments outside Beijing. None of her skills were particularly *special*, and she definitely wasn't any kind of expert. She lived with three other girls much more specialized than she: an accounting student who interned three days a week at the Huaxia Bank, a nightclub hostess who'd just completed her hospitality degree, and a biomed major who stayed home with Xiao most days, painting her toenails and complaining about her professor. She'd been trying to sleep with him for the past two months. Her classes were online, so this endeavor was significantly more challenging than she'd anticipated.

Xiao already had a Taobao profile, a clothing store selling faulty designer knockoffs: poorly stitched or mismatched at the seams, uneven collars, shoddy dye jobs. Her friend worked at the company's factory outside the city doing quality control and smuggled the passable offenders to Xiao, who gave him a small cut of her profit. He had recently started conducting evaluations for a makeup company, too, so Xiao expanded her business to include nail polishes and cuticle serums. Even so, selling things online was boring and barely profitable. She had to find another way to make rent this month. But what could she do?

Xiao pulled her legs against her stomach, watching it crease into four fatty folds, and curled her toes under the overheating laptop. It needed a break, and so did she. According to her father, who refused to visit Beijing, she was *definitely happy, or at least going to be happy very soon. I'm at the beginning of my own personal life story*, she thought, parodying him. Yeah, right. The laptop had not yet cooled down, but she opened it back up.

When are you all going to be home? she wrote in a chat to her roommates. *Not till super-late! Working*, the hostess typed immediately. *2–3 hrs*, replied the accounting student, *haven't left the city yet*. The biomed student didn't respond. Her school had a mixer that night, one of the few in-person events of the semester. Right now, she was probably trying to get drunk enough to walk up to the professor and say something like, *Oh, wow, I hadn't realized from the video feed how tall you are!* She'd practiced the line on Xiao a few times before she left. Maybe he'd turn her down. Maybe she'd respond that she was coming home soon. Xiao stood up, opened and shut her minifridge a few times, considering a container of leftover pork ribs and daikon soup. She cracked an egg over some instant noodles instead, pressing a familiar set of buttons on the microwave.

The night before, she'd ordered takeout with the med student and hostess. The three had sat side-by-side in the bathtub trading dishes across laps, knees draped over the tub's edge, feet knocking into feet. Xiao took her Styrofoam pot of noodles into the bathroom, situating herself in the position she'd occupied the previous night, remembering the med student's thigh against hers, sweaty skin and fine, black hairs. She liked the way the med student smelled, musty and comforting. Rodent-like. Xiao imagined she'd be great working in a lab with thousands of mice, wearing a white coat and glasses, brushing against her professor on her way to deposit a dead mouse into the biohazardous waste container. Xiao had no idea what a bona fide biomed student, one who took classes in a classroom and not on a computer screen, actually did. Whatever it was, it was a shame that her friend would never get to experience it.

Adjacent buildings cast long shadows against the bathroom wall, and Xiao watched them fade and crisscross in the orangey light. When the boys upstairs got home, she planned, she'd listen until she heard one of them peeing in the toilet, and then she'd stand on the sink and tap messages in code on the ceiling. The code would mean, for example, *you're smelly assholes and you use all the building's hot water and I hope you die*, but they wouldn't know that. They'd probably think she was flirting. Xiao thought again about the med student. She considered getting up to turn on the wireless speakers so she could play Brahms's Symphony No. 1 in C minor and paint her toenails. The speakers were new— the hostess bought them a few weeks before and installed them in the bathroom, the apartment's only common space—and the roommates used them to dance to pop music on Friday nights, four jubilant bodies grinding and bouncing to sticky synth beats, bare feet on faux-tile floor. In undergrad, Xiao's music professor said Brahms had copied Beethoven, but Xiao didn't care. Unlike herself, Brahms had ambition. He wanted to be the best, even if that meant plagiarizing. Xiao decided to preserve the sanctity of Brahms and spare him the bathroom. The shadows on the wall faded to reddish black.

The med student, too, had ambition, thought Xiao. She'd been the one to scout out the apartment, to find the other roommates online, introduce them to each other, collect their security deposits. *An hour and forty-five minutes into the city*, the listing boasted. This turned out to be a sham. The commute was two hours. *It was the only choice*, thought Xiao. *I couldn't go back home. It'd be awful and everyone would know I didn't get a job.* Some of her college friends were married by now, and her best friend Ling was considering divorce. She and her husband hadn't been able to afford to move out of the apartment they shared with his finance coworkers. Understandably, this put a strain on the relationship.

When Xiao met Ling at the McDonald's earlier that week, her friend ate crispy chicken and iced tea and blamed her husband for the collapse of the marriage. He was supposed to have achieved some level of success by now, supposed to have made enough money to at least get them their own home. She wanted kids, and you couldn't raise kids in the *slum*. Xiao shot her a look. *Stop saying that. We don't live in a slum. Your apartment is fine, better than mine, and if you want a new one so bad, you should get a job, too. Or at least sell some stuff online.* They'd had this conversation so many times that they barely had to use words. *At least you're not living underground,* Xiao said, stirring her sundae.

Ling's husband had suggested moving to a smaller city, but Ling couldn't bear the thought of leaving Beijing, all her friends, *the dream*, she said, gesturing around. Xiao looked around the McDonald's, half expecting the dream to materialize on its walls. Nothing. Just shiny white tiles and screens flashing deep-fried shrimp and yogurt parfaits. Ling was going on about how her husband should try to move to the U.S. for a year. *Yeah, but in the U.S., all of the kids with college degrees are unemployed, too*, Xiao replied. How could her friend have become such a cliché? The screen broadcast a ketchup packet and a pepper performing some sort of mating dance, getting closer and closer until they merged in a burst of smoke, producing a new, spicy Sichuan ketchup. Xiao rooted through their crumpled to-go bag. Had they received the new ketchup? She found only two packets of honey mustard and a few stray fries.

The previous night, after the hostess went to bed, Xiao and the med student lined up a few nail polishes at the edge of the bathtub, wine coolers between their thighs. It was nearly 2 A.M. Xiao selected a color to keep for their pedicures and photographed the rest against a flower-print blouse that served as a backdrop for most of her online store's photos. She toyed with a nail polish cap for a few moments, picked at her cuticles.

I don't think I can keep doing the makeup store much longer, she said, looking at the dirty underbelly of the sink. *I don't know. It's just that it doesn't really seem to be going anywhere.* She caught the med student's eyes, sympathetic, questioning. Xiao's intestines flipped around inside her. She blamed it on the pork ribs. *I have so much time on my hands . . .* she let out a faint sigh, pulled at a hangnail on her pinky. *Every time I make a plan for what I want to do with my life, it collapses. I wish there was a way to stumble upon a task, some vapid job to occupy all this time and help me make money. If I could get someone else to make a plan for me . . .*

I mean, you're doing everything right. Online business is the best option right now, the med student said, encouraging. *You should concentrate on that.* She and Xiao studied the polishes, a neat row of pastels and shimmering metallics situated precariously on the polyester shirt. *But you don't have to sell nail polish. Fuck it! Let's keep this one for ourselves.* The med student grabbed a turquoise polish and set it by her foot, taking a long drink from her cooler.

Yeah, I kind of wanted to keep this one! Xiao took a silver confetti polish from the lineup.

But, you know, that's not a half-bad idea, asking other people to give you tasks, the med student continued. *People need babysitters and errand girls all the time. Imagine how much time the average person wastes, online shopping, buying groceries, waiting in line for a metro pass. You could be, like, an all-purpose helper. You could make the profile really generic and friendly looking.*

    I don't want to make plans, though, Xiao said. *I don't want to advertise specific skills or have to get good at anything. I just want to let go of control. If I plan it too much, I know it'll go wrong. Like, if it's some kind of start-up—it'll just fail. This feeling, you know, it's not just about a job, or money. It's bigger than that. It has to do with the whole arrangement of the world. I don't fit in. I don't care about ambition.*

    The med student plugged her phone into the speakers and put on melancholic pop music, a vocoderized voice urging the girls to stay in the moment, live for tonight. They gave each other sloppy pedicures, dangled their feet in the air for a few minutes, finished the six-pack, and opened the window to let fumes out and smog in. The med student said goodnight, picked up the Q-tips and empty bottles, and departed to the bedroom she shared with the hostess. Xiao turned the bathroom lights off and sat turning the silver confetti polish bottle, wishing it might cast disco-ball reflections on her legs. *Follow the dream and keep your feet on the ground,* she sang under her breath, rotating the bottle to the beat and visualizing dancing ketchup packets until she was exhausted.

    Now, here she was again in the shadowless bathroom, alone with her noodles, without the med student and without Brahms. No wonder Ling wanted a divorce. Work was miserable. Not a single one of her friends had a job they liked, but still they crowded onto buses headed into the city every day, traveled for hours to sit at call centers and banks and dumpling shops, returned home to heat up takeout in their apartments' shared kitchens.

    Occasionally, a story came out in the press about a young entrepreneur who made millions, whose webstore or tech start-up took off unexpectedly, who got married and bought a home and clothes and furniture for the photo-shoot. The *Unlimited Creativity Generation*, the article would proclaim, encouragingly noting young people's solutions to *changing employment channels*, their *capacity for hard work, willingness to endure hardship,* and *innovative communica-tion skills.* In other words, if your online makeup store failed, or if you thought it was a bore, the problem was you.

Xiao dug a cigarette out of the junk drawer where the girls kept a pack, *for emergencies,* the hostess said when she first stocked the menthols. She yanked the narrow, heavy window open and inhaled heavy summer heat, flicking the shared lighter and puff-ing. She took a long suck and held the smoke in, squinting down at rows of concrete apartment buildings on the industrial street, yellow light bulbs and neon signs blinking as far as she could see.

I'm wasting my time. She focused on a bluish glow emanating from a neighboring building's sixth-floor window. *But I kind of don't mind.* She liked to pick a particular light and imagine the person who'd turned it on—a young mother stir-frying vegetables for her-self, hair in a ragged ponytail, listening to the radio and singing along softly after putting her child to bed, or maybe a student tak-ing notes quietly so as not to disturb her girlfriend sleeping by her side, or a teenage kid staying up on the Internet, browsing forums and making obscene posts under a pseudonym. Xiao took another drag, coughing, wishing she could be more like the med student, who claimed to enjoy the burning sensation in her lungs. *I'd feel better if I could get to know all these people, talk to them, get them to tell me how they went about finding purpose in life. Of all the people behind all the lights in the city, someone should be able to find a use for me.*

24

Postwar Critical Theory final draft THISONE.docx

This year's Triennial curators justify the exhibition's so-called *dual globalities framework* by turning to his-torian and scholar Fernand Braudel, who charts the emergence of two types of cities, coexistent and com-plementary, though often engaged in fierce ideological battle: the capital city and the maritime city. The capital city, sheltered by expansive landmass, inhospitable mountain range, river, manmade wall, is the central and dominant point, the node from which civilization is defined and defended. In 20 BC, Emperor Augustus erected the Milliarium Aureum, a gilded milestone in the Central Forum of Rome. Before the empire's collapse, all distances were measured from that singular point; all mile markers bore its insignia. From the stone proliferated an outward sprawl of increasingly peripheral municipalities and towns, all looking toward the Forum.

A citizen desiring more from life than is offered in their birthplace—an artist, the curators suggest—moves progressively through the hierarchy of municipalities until they find themselves in the glimmering capital. There, this artist encounters other artists, designers, writers, thinkers, chefs, musicians, architects, and so on—all of whom meld to form a relatively homogenous style, which the citizen's birthplace in turn reclaims as its own, its greedy and selfsame identity. The capital thus assembles the frenzied creations, blunt impulses, and shadowy languages that foment in peripheral areas into a systematic, bona fide, nation-born culture.

Representation of the great historic capital city in the Biennial falls along predictable lines: Paris and Beijing, as well as Madrid, are counted among the cities whose intense periods of creativity have been recast as national traits. The particular and individual works of artists and performers and filmmakers are joined together in the great collective body of the arts. Viewers and admirers of these arts stand under their umbrella of brilliance; these brilliant, art-canopied culturati move through the city together and speak at the level of discourse. In due time, their discourse becomes a law that rules over them, external to the very forms and peoples who first produced it.

The exhibition's imaginary of the maritime city, by contrast, figures it as devoid of historical or regional identity. Marine vestibule to the country's interior, the maritime city mediates between ocean and land, playing boarding house to ships and sailors of diverse ports. In the antechambers of the maritime city intermingles a heterogeneous miscellany drawn from each element—person or commodity, microbe or pest or foodstuff or idea—that passes through its gates. Maritime cities, unfixed from any national affiliation, form networks with other maritime cities. Trade routes emerge; commerce becomes global; trends accelerate, cultures intermix.

This is not a new phenomenon, of course: young women—for example, the author of this essay—have been living alone or in small groups in port cities since at least the twelfth century, working as butchers or candlestick makers, joining guilds and being tracked in the social registers. Anxieties about cosmopolitanism and globalization come into and out of vogue every few generations, residents of *nowhere in particular and everywhere at once* pen theories of exile, transients wander the streets of maritime cities having been dispossessed, long ago, of the meaning of the word *here*. Amsterdam, selling weapons to any country regardless of national allegiance during the Thirty Years War, exemplifies the promiscuous priorities of the maritime city. New York—the city to which this author recently moved, and in which she now writes—is a maritime city par excellence.

Life in the capital city is characterized in the gesture of looking over one's shoulder while walking down a narrow cobblestone street. Marble buildings, enveloping the pedestrian, take on the character of strict authority: the capital's institutions determine standards and standardize culture; its lawmakers hold ultimate decision-making capacity. Monuments and government buildings and long histories loom at every corner, and the movement of bodies about these structures is rigid and frightened.

The port city, on the other hand, holds the gesture of the drunken and rancorous stumble, usually ending in whatever alleyway or stairwell suits the revelers best for sleep or sex on that particular night. Life in the port city is erratic, identities pass with passing styles. New Yorkers find common cause with polluted droplets emerging off the East River on cold mornings in a nebulous haze or pouring, hot and oppressive, from manholes in Times Square on summer nights.

Sitting in the basement reading room of Columbia's art history library, Valerie paused to consult a glossy exhibition catalog, taking vague notes for the next bout of final-paper writing. Scholars lined the cubbies, faces bloodless in the harsh fluorescence and skulls propped with clenched fists as they flipped page after page. Valerie's was one of the few desks available to master's students; most were assigned to doctoral candidates. Jeremy, his desk stacked with slim, metallic volumes on Japanese database culture, who bragged about having *spent a lot of time in Tokyo*; Demetri, his father a famous collector and who used his mother's last name and who wanted to *disrupt the thematic and temporal modularity of art history by tracking ideas across space and time* (such *subterranean resonances* would increase the value of a collection he'd soon inherit to the tune of millions); Anya, her readings on the perestroika and Soviet architecture alongside biographies of Lenin and Alexandra Kollontai, who Valerie had only ever heard say *mmmmm*, gazing glossy-eyed over her interlocutor's shoulder. Valerie's master's program was understood by the doctoral students to be a cash cow, luring in curatorial hopefuls and funding PhD stipends with their tuition. Valerie hadn't known that doctoral students received stipends. She'd been operating under the assumption that doctoral students were bankrolled by family wealth and that she and her fellow master's students, spending only eighty or ninety grand on a degree, were the frugal ones. *We're basically here just to keep them afloat*, another curatorial student confirmed before class one day. Skimming the catalog and staring at the back of Anya's head, Valerie tilted her chair. It hit the desk behind hers, making a deafening *thwack*. Anya turned to glare at Valerie; Valerie turned back to her book.

In an interview at the back of the catalogue, a video artist explained to a curator that China had been technologically dominant for much of written history. The country was once led by Nanjing, a port to Japan and Southeast Asia and inlet to nearby Shanghai. In the early fifteenth century, the Portuguese planned their route around Africa to India, conquering markets and people along the way, establishing dominance of the unknowable hydrosphere, the trade routes therein. At the same time, China's imperial rulers sent massively armed ships to explore and trade in the Indian Ocean, reaching the eastern coast of Africa. Whether by chance or deliberate decision—the artist didn't presume to know the intentions of fifteenth century sovereigns—the monarchs did not bid their ships circumnavigate Africa, though their military certainly had the navigational and economic capacity to do so. Instead, their fleet remained squarely on the eastern side of Africa, and Europe untouched by the Eastern military. In an alternate history, the Chinese certainly would have conquered Europe, discovered America. *Viewers of this New York exhibition*, the artist claimed, *likely would have been born speaking Mandarin, had they been born at all*.

It was difficult for Valerie to tell if the artist's alternative history was trustworthy. His claims were so sweeping, so general, like regular people didn't exist, only kings and countries. Contemporary artists were wonderful at speaking. They made the most daringly speculative claims to justify their work, which, more often than not, stood rather dully alongside the words that issued forth from all corners of the art world to explain it.

Of course, Valerie wrote, allowing herself her own speculative leap, *the curators' imaginary of the maritime city forgets its ghostly doubles lurking beneath the hydrosphere's well-charted surface, infinite histories that can't be unhidden.*

The unwritten lives of those transported in the bellies of ships, born of oceanic displacement, torn from inheritance of any solid ground—Romans traded back and forth over the Mediterranean, Africans across the Atlantic, indentured laborers from India and China through the Indian Ocean. Round after round of violence and departure. It's no wonder that Moses's emancipatory power lay in his ability to part the sea, Noah's in his ability to rescue animalkind in an all-encompassing ship. Another haunting absence: the ocean's ecology, infinitesimal glowing plankton and morphing single-cell organisms too prehistoric to perceive, chemical-tainted coral and ever-heating currents carrying marine life in decades-long journeys that flash by in the blink of a human eye. And yet another: the hallucinations of sailors adrift too long, visions that overtake the senses and entice the mariners to drink saltwater and make love to manatees and throw themselves overboard and generally behave with no regard for mission, state, or fellow countrymen (save for when they're jerking off said countrymen in the ship's hold, drunk on dehydration and desire); and then another, Internet cables that run parallel to geological fault lines on the ocean's floor, gnawed on by sharks and crustaceans, overgrown with slime and ooze and encrypted with codes detailing the darkest secrets of warring countries above; and then another, a dumping ground owned by no country, to which no one person can be held accountable; and then another, a liquidy imaginary in the mind of neoliberal financiers whose offshore accounts grant them dominion of no-land and every-land at once; and then another, a dark and roiling grave into which women, naked and pregnant, were flung from American-made airplanes by the Chilean junta. *If you kill the bitch, you kill off the offspring,* said Augusto Pinochet. Below the sea's surface, starfish—exquisite, primordial creatures visited by American children and their nannies at the Los Angeles aquarium, an ocean served up for consumption—feast on decaying their flesh.

Valerie considered the paragraph, deleted. She was no contemporary artist. Her professor would expect a more formulaic conclusion. She toggled her internal narrator from *emerging artist proselytizing onstage at a swanky symposium* to *academic critically criticizing all that exists*:

It's not that the histories the curators present to justify their choices are untrue, the critic wrote. *Rather, it's the way the historical facts are selected and arranged. A novelesque structure is a good tool for producing history: two incompatible siblings, the capital city and the maritime, churning out two distinct streams of artists who meet, in the present, in this exhibition. But, does not Braudel's capital|maritime distinction merely replicate, if through a different lens, an outdated two-worlds framework? And, if curators residing, still, within such a historical structure's clutches can so easily identify its scaffolding, could it still be said to retain any explanatory power over them and their preferred artists?* The curatorial team, arms crossed and haircuts severe, glared at Valerie from the catalog's jacket. She reread her closing paragraph, adding a comma, removing a word. She couldn't work up much enthusiasm for such Hegelian questions.

25

Who *could* work up the enthusiasm for such Hegelian questions? Valerie's professor, that's who. Her mother had advised her to *make connections in case you need recommendation letters in the future*, and, after a scraggly haired lecturer in the department listened to Valerie ramble about contemporary art and embodiment, the circulation of capital, the impossibility of just representation, he suggested she speak with Professor _____. *He knows the artists you're talking about personally. He's very tapped into that whole network. And I heard he's looking for a new research assistant to do some indexing and fact-checking.*

So it came to be that, having spent the morning in the library with exceptionally cosmopolitan curators, Valerie sat outside Professor _____'s office with no real objective other than to, as Susan had put it, *make herself known.* With its marble benches, polished wood, and stone-floored chill, the art-history wing more than vaguely resembled a cathedral, one punctuated by Scotch-taped posters announcing department opportunities and events. *Gain a deeper understanding of the foundations of Western art history and culture with a weeklong intensive in Florence. Pace Gallery seeks experienced provenance researcher for part-time work.*

Professor _____'s office door (heavy, carved mahogany, a sizable brass plaque accommodating his title) was propped open with a book, and Valerie could see another student's nodding cowlick, Professor _____'s fleshy and folded hands, a brass lamp, a pile of papers. Two authoritative tenors emanated from the office, words inaudible but meaning clear. *An academic peepshow,* she amused herself, studying the visible sliver. Having attended a year-and-a-half of seminars and lectures, Valerie had seen enough of the aura of expertise. It wasn't located in the speaker alone. The men who raked their fingers through their hair and swept their hands across podiums had the capacity to magnetize and mute their audiences. (She was easy prey.) They treated their brilliance like a prized possession, groomed and guarded. Valerie saw Profes-

sor _____ nod, serious, at the cowlicked student's statements. Cowlick turned simpering and wag-tailed, a poodle praised
for tricks.

After three or four more minutes, Cowlick packed his bag and
struggled with the door, staring blank-eyed at Valerie before piv-
oting away.

I see you sitting out there, Professor _____ called from the
office. *Come in; come on now; don't be shy.*

Valerie arranged her wool coat over her arm in what she thought
might be an elegant drape, wedging notebook and pen against her
chest. This studious configuration, though, proved a hindrance at
the office's massive door, which barely budged. Abandoning her
pose, she struggled the door open with her whole weight, already
dreading doing battle with it on the way out.

Ah, good. Hello. Professor _____ sat calm at his desk.
You're in my Postwar Critical Theory seminar, yes? he said, examining
the notes he'd taken while Cowlick was speaking. *Remind me of
your name.*

Valerie responded, situating notebook in lap and assuming a
suitable posture in the folding chair at the office's center, far away
from Professor _____'s large desk.

*That's right. I knew it started with a v. Vanessa, Victoria, Valentine,
Valerie. You work for IWC, yes? Quite a tough gallery. That era of powerful women. Sharks, all of them. You must be very bright to pass muster in
that environment. Anyhow. What brings you here today?*

It seemed uncouth to ask outright about _____'s
more-famous friend, the theorist whose work Valerie wanted to
theorize, so she enthused, instead, about the gallery's current
exhibition, focusing more on the cross of her legs than the words
issuing, automatic, from her mouth. As she spoke, her mind fed
her progressively repulsive ideas: *ask about his wife. Make up a
rumor about Cowlick wanting to blow him.* Was it the fact that she sat
exposed, the chair's cold metal against her thin polyester pants?
Was it that his reputation hung heavy in the room, making the air
dense and thick? *Crawl across the room on all fours. Offer to blow him*

yourself. Slap his face. Get him before he gets you. The thoughts felt protective, even dignifying.

Professor _____ cleared his throat, indicating that he'd had enough of her speech. *Well. That's all very good. Tell me, Valerie, did you come here to discuss anything specific? Your research, perhaps?*

Oh, no. I'm sorry. Jones told me that you might be in need of an assistant, and I've been doing some archival work, indexing, proofreading, for the gallery. I thought I could lend a hand.

Professor _____ leaned back in his chair and Valerie made an attempt to scrub herself of all improprieties. The brass lamp's yellow light shone on the bald spot on his otherwise white-haired head.

Well. That's an interesting thought. As a matter of fact, I'll be out of the country next semester, so we wouldn't be able to work together in person. It's your last semester, no? I hope you don't mind. I'm traveling to Hong Kong and Beijing for research. A kind of ethnographic exploration of what contemporaneity means in the Chinese context. But I've been meaning to finish this side project for ages now, and perhaps you could help while I'm away. I wouldn't be able to pay, of course.

That's fine, Valerie said. *I have the job at the gallery. I don't need to be paid.*

It'll be only a few hours a week, I suspect. And the department can sort out a nice title for the position.

He looked at her, expectant. She fished around for something appropriate. *What's the project about?*

Ah, yes. I think you'll like it. It's a little collection of interviews I did in the sixties and seventies. French Philosophy in New York, *I'm calling it.*

That sounds fascinating. Another ethnographic exploration, no?

He looked at her sharply. *No. This is a book of philosophy.*

Oh. I'm sorry. I just thought, you know, interviews, a specific milieu ...

No. Well. I'm sure you'll better understand when the texts are in front of you. The manuscript only needs some minor copy editing and fact-check-

ing, anyway. Here, I'll give you some background readings so that you might acquaint yourself with the scene.

Clutching four books written by three serious-faced men, Valerie found the cowlicked student outside, waiting for the elevator. He appraised the books in her arms. *That one's brilliant,* he said, nodding at Serious Man #2. *Have you read his work before? Professor _____ lent it to you?*

Yeah, I'm going to help him with a project.

Great, good stuff. That book is really genius, you know. He studied her. *You're in Postwar Critical Theory, right? You sit in the back. I've never heard you talk. How come? If you're researching for _____, you must be pretty bright.*

Walking to the 116th Street station, Valerie rehearsed the two conversations in her head. Had Cowlick eavesdropped on her conversation with Professor _____? Had the two men made a secret pact to use that word, *bright? Very good, very bright,* she repeated to the rhythm of her steps. *Bright* was Valerie, that parrot of intelligence, an outstanding specimen. *Brilliant* were the philosophers in her arms, their words transcendent. She imagined herself, old, in a room stuffed with reams of paper, diplomas, trophies. The record of her life. *You're very bright,* the standardized test results and titles and reviews reported, *even exceptional, but brilliance can't be measured. None of us can be certain whether or not you've got it. The cream simply rises to the historical top.*

How could a judgment of exceptionality be bestowed upon her? How would the worth of her words be assessed? By the laws she obeyed, the ways in which she governed herself? Her life had so far been utterly unexceptional, an impersonal scurry along typical routes in a vessel not of her choosing. Should future archivists and researchers look back through Valerie's papers as she'd been assigned to look through the philosophers', she thought, they'd find no early indicators, quantitative or qualitative, of transcendence, no signs of brilliance. She'd cared only about mundane social interactions and visions of glamour and her own roving thoughts. She hadn't been exceptional. She'd just wanted people to like her.

Alone in a car on the downtown train, Valerie stared at the gray-faced philosopher gracing the book on the top of the stack. *You're very bright*, he complimented her, winking.

Thank you, she responded. *And you're an exceptional specimen for my ethnographic research.*

The philosopher's photograph was offended. *I'm no ethnographic specimen. I'm a philosopher.*

Valerie had suspected the image would respond in this way. *Ah, but you're wrong. You see, some compatriots of your compatriot, Braudel, told me something very interesting this morning. Had China decided to send ships a few miles farther several hundreds of years ago, you'd have been a big nobody, and this book you're sitting atop would have been written in Mandarin.*

No, the philosopher responded, dejected. *I wouldn't have been born. And this book wouldn't have been written at all.*

26

People's time can be a commodity. It's your right to arrange Xiao's life, and it's her obligation to serve you, Xiao typed into the website headline, selecting purple bubble font in a subtle, glimmering gradient. She leaned her full weight into a worn office chair the med student had picked up for her on the side of the road. The knobs that were supposed to customize the height of the seat and the relative uprightness of the chair were nonfunctional; tilting backward in a gesture of completion, self-satisfaction, was a dangerous move.

It was now nearly 2 A.M., her second night in a row up so late. Did the hours always have to repeat themselves? The med student still wasn't home. Xiao cursed the day, with its melancholy morning that had turned into a gray-blue afternoon, the kind of afternoon that made her suspect time was inconsequential or maybe an illusion. Dark came early, before evening and before the two girls had decided upon the med student's seduction strategy. By now,

Xiao's lonely night thoughts had had hours to assume their form, become real. As real as thoughts can become on the Internet.

Xiao set three price levels for customers to purchase her lifetime, allowing users maximum choice and flexibility: 7¥ for eight minutes, 33¥ for an hour, or 175¥ for a day. The levels could be mixed and/or matched, of course, depending on the request. But no matter the difficulty, the intensity of engagement, or the travel or effort or thought dedicated to the task, it would be priced the same. This was only fair. It would be impossible to figure out how to assign specific values to all of the hopes, services, demands, missions. The only certainty she possessed, could put a number on, was the standardized and measurable units of time that would structure her life from there on out.

I'm telling you, this website has potential, she said to the hostess when she came home from work. Xiao followed the hostess into her bedroom, yammering excitedly in the early morning light as the hostess took off her polyester dress and hair extensions, scrubbed her face, picked at the skin between her eyebrows. The med student's bed was empty. Xiao sat on the floor. *Every day is going to be different, a guided venture into the unknown, organized by the wishes and whims of the Internet. I won't have to make any decisions for myself, except for which requests I'll select. Like a multiple-choice test where the options are all acceptable. I bet people will never stop needing me.*

Xiao was right: people never stopped needing her. Her life continued in this way forever. She became so useful and accommodating that she did not die. She did not quite live either. Her flesh grew doughy and malleable, her clothing and hair soluble, her tone semifluid and monotonous. Her voice spoke only words that her clients asked her to say. It sometimes created stumbling arrangements out of the predetermined words, garbled last retches of their own grasping vision. The purchasers of her time took her plastic and melting flesh, carefully remolded it, reshaped her into new forms daily. She was eternal and pulsating wax, without life or death, strangled and then resuscitated by the hands that shaped, the words that spoke, the calculations that made and remade her again and again in slightly different iterations, a girl-form as mute and warm as the sticky balls waiting to be tenderly folded and baked into sweet, decorative pastries in Beijing cake shops in the purple morning light.

27

A few nights into her first high-school waitressing job, while carrying a tray of half-empty glasses dirty with lipstick stains and cigarette butts, beer foam stuck to the sides, Valerie tripped over a thick rubber mat in the restaurant kitchen. Glasses tipped precariously, fell, shattered, as she grabbed at broken water goblets and tumblers. Shards shaved thin layers of skin from her forearms, the only part of her body free of raised moles and freckles. Valerie watched, transfixed with horror, as thick blood oozed forth from the wounds. *It shouldn't be possible*, she thought, *for something to so easily slice open my skin.*

The older waitresses gathered around, cooing, escorting Valerie out of the kitchen and onto the cement patio. Someone procured a first-aid kit as she sat on the concrete, mute, staring at viscous beads of internal matter coating her arms. *I didn't know this stuff was inside me*, but there it was, seeping out from just beneath her skin. Looking at the globbing matter felt nothing like looking at her face in the bathroom mirror, *but it's still looking at myself, I guess.*

Valerie fainted and the waitresses gasped, frantic, and searched through the restaurant's marinara-stained employment forms for emergency contacts and medical information. The chef excused himself to the patio to see what all the fuss was about, where his waitstaff had gone, and when Valerie woke she was reprimanded for causing a commotion in the middle of dinner service.

Go home, the chef said. Valerie protested that she could get back to work, could polish silverware and take orders and refill water goblets and run salads from kitchen to dining room all night.

No, the chef said, scowling at her arms. Valerie walked home, dreading her parents, who already thought she didn't have sufficient entrepreneurial spirit.

Several weeks later, Valerie's father announced that they would go see a traveling exhibition of plastinated bodies. *To toughen you up*, Mark said, and Valerie stared into her oatmeal, remembering just how tender she had proved to be, so easily cut open. Twenty or so corpses on a grueling international tour, Mark reported. They'd be in town for just a few weeks before shipping off to Miami, their fourteenth stop on a long list of cities large and small. Valerie imagined the corpses on the go, stacked in oversize trucks, fascia and bones and nerves jostling as wheels hit potholes on the interstate, chatting with one another about the demands and discomforts of business travel.

The bodies, donated for research to the Chinese government, had been preserved and hardened and turned to rubber and plastic or silicone, a complex chemical process. Valerie's father pushed a colorful pamphlet across the table. Small text below a flexing corpse thanked the living families of the dead bodies for *gifting their loved ones to science, for furthering human progress*, but the newspapers reported several days later that the bodies hadn't been gifted at all. They were political prisoners, executed and deposed to the lab. At school, Gabby said her dad said you couldn't trust the papers, especially when it came to China. The exhibition continued despite the controversy. Ticket sales increased.

Valerie and Mark waited in line outside the convention center for an hour before the doors opened. He paid the entrance fee for two ($50) and Valerie extended her hand to receive a smudged human skull in red ink. The exhibition, its theatrical lighting and swelling music, began with the skeletal system. Viewers progressed through dark and dramatic rooms, each adding a layer (muscular, digestive, respiratory, urinary, reproductive) atop the skeletal base. The human body is mysterious, the lights and music and cavernous rooms said, but not so mysterious that it can't be laid bare for you.

Buying

Valerie stared into the bulging eyes of a skinned Olympian (or a political prisoner or donated dead guy posing as an Olympian) holding a discus and crouching, tense and ready. There was a lump of some sort embalmed in his throat. He had died and been preserved and sold to a multinational corporation and packed and installed and shuffled about, lit just so, with something still *there*. A piece of food, something to say, Who knew?

Do you see that? Valerie asked Mark, but he didn't.

Valerie imagined being a body that didn't decay, wasn't buried or burned or drowned in the sea, but was preserved, a rigid relic set atop a pedestal to be gawked at by a global clientele in plastic sandals and cotton T-shirts. Technically, *no photography* was allowed in the exhibition, *but the gawkers would take pictures of me anyway*, Valerie thought, bitter. Selfies beside her paralyzed corpse, posing and sticking out tongues and crossing eyes and smiling, hands outstretched and fingers forming all sorts of signs.

Valerie's fingertips began to tingle with television static at the thought. The static slowly crept through her synapses and nerves and then started again in her feet, seizing her tendons, wrapping around kneecaps and thighs. *I feel weak*, she thought, but she didn't want to say anything. After all, she was there to be toughened up. Exhalations, maybe her own, echoed oceanic in her skull. It was difficult to tell if she was hearing or feeling or imagining. Blurred white patterns danced in the corners of her field of vision, undulating, taking over, and she reached for the Olympian's glass case, *I don't feel so good; I think I'm going to be sick—*

And then Valerie was sitting on a hard metal bench outside the exhibition, a woman with tropical-breeze-scented hair and a red polo shirt emblazoned BODIES stroking her forearm and her dad kneeling before her with an orange juice in his hand. She was okay, was alive, and he was sorry but unsurprised she'd been upset by the corpses. Valerie assured him that no, she was just a little bit hungry, and they picked up Chinese takeout on the way home and ate egg rolls and fried rice out of cardboard boxes together in front of the television. Politicians argued with CEOs on the nightly news. Valerie and Mark forgot all about the bodies.

28

I literally went insane, Julie announced to her audience of two, staring at folds of thin fabric in her hands. She picked a sheer green shirt from the pile, pressed it against her cheek. *I don't even remember getting this one. It's like, when I'm at the store, I'm in a trance. It's hypnotic.*

She'd bought eleven oversize shirts, a blazer, two silk scarves, a pair of faux-gold clip-on earrings, platform leather boots, a leopard-print overcoat, spandex athletic pants, and a pillbox hat from the used clothing store on 125th Street. Home in Ridgewood and rejoined with her sanity, Julie coated her mouth in blue lipstick and swaddled herself in the velvet blazer. Valerie and Leila sat side by side on her bed before a bay window that looked out on Wilson Avenue. The September sun cast the Iglesia Presbiteriana across the street in harsh, white light. Valerie directed sly glances at Leila, who pretended to care deeply about Julie's fashion choices, nodding in agreement while Julie mused on the *theater of the self*, the *drag of identity*. Mimicking Leila, Valerie marveled at her sister's reflection in the full-length mirror, shoulder-pads and heavy eyeliner and secret lingerie visible when she twisted her torso into an elegant contrapposto. Julie still had the same thin hips and high, narrow forehead of middle school, now with a cropped-close haircut. She could call wearing clothes *drag* because she passed, easily, as *girl* or *boy*.

When Valerie got dressed it didn't feel like the fun kind of drag, glitter and men's suits and decades-old dresses. Standing before her closet in the morning, she thought about the paper dolls her mom had given her long ago, old-fashioned toys, and she imagined her arms flattening, fat and blood and fluids seeping out through her pores, flesh desensitized and rigid, nerves dissolving. The paper dolls were genderless clones until you put on their bright cutout clothes, careful not to tear the flimsy fiber and amputate an arm or lacerate a thigh. When they were dressed, they were complete. Why didn't it work this way for Valerie? She tried to dress herself up to be herself. But her clothes, selected to represent an aloof, self-possessed graduate student-slash-art-world girl, made her feel like an overstuffed sausage, insides turned out, mucus-dripping entrails sewed onto a black cashmere turtleneck, shit smeared on wool pants.

Julie styled Valerie for their nights out as an ironic, frumpy nineties student in turtlenecks and thick, inflexible jeans, hair braided, belt buckled tight. This particular look, Julie thought, convincingly restrained Valerie's anxious body. Valerie couldn't stop nibbling on healthy foods because she was so afraid of gaining weight. She perched on the bed with a handful of almonds and a Polar Seltzer, awaiting approval or direction. *Wear your fuzzy black turtleneck, I guess,* Julie said to Valerie, pulling on wine-colored Doc Martens and sucking in her cheeks to examine herself in the mirror.

In moments of extreme sartorial distress Valerie called on Leila, readying herself across the hallway in her own room, the apartment's largest. She'd arranged three Mexican prayer candles and four succulents on her dresser, and ashed cigarettes into the plants' dry soil while spraying her hair into thick, matted clumps. Her laptop, perched on a nearby stool, cycled between recommended YouTube lectures on depth psychology and a podcast on Lacan. Leila had abandoned her conventional therapeutic education upon moving to New York with Valerie and Julie. Now a year into what she called the *new approach,* she talked about *drives* and *phantasmagoria* a lot.

Will you wear a dress with me to the bar? Valerie asked, hoping the question wouldn't prompt intensive analysis. Yeah, she'd wear a dress, Leila responded, but they'd have to be sure to not both wear the black one from H&M.

Leila, confident and directorial, smoothed the dress over her underwear, ran her hands over her ribs, long neck craned, appraising, hoped that whatever the dress was doing aligned well enough with the Platonic imaginary of *girl* that a guy would notice her, choose her out of the available varieties of *girl* on display at the bar that night. She'd try to feel special to have been selected, and they'd fuck and mime a perfunctory amount of affection and she'd sit on the edge of his bed in the early morning wondering, vaguely, if she was supposed to want him to ask for her number, hinting that she'd be free for breakfast. Breakfast, conversation: pleasures she was supposed to crave, to ask for. She didn't care anymore. It was hard to remember why she'd ever felt so attached to the idea of a future. Life was much better, she decided, when she situated herself in the little gap between the present and the past.

For example: last weekend, she'd slept over at someone's apartment. His phone started ringing around 7 A.M., long before she had to perform the *how do you take your coffee* number. Freed from bagel and/or omelet obligations, Leila rooted around for the lacy underwear she'd picked up at a 7-for-$25 sale at Victoria's Secret near Bryant Park. She'd browsed piles of lace and mesh and cotton blend, knowing the slivers of fabric were supposed to make her feel anticipatory, ready for sex and excitement.

Choosing underwear was like choosing who she wanted to fuck: it was supposed to make her feel free. Leila wasn't sure what she was supposed to be *free* from. Freedom from morals, from obligations? Freedom from rules? Her phone pinged, reminding her to take her birth control pill. She felt nauseous. She dug around for her wallet, finding a switchblade in the mess. She placed the knife on the boy's dresser, remembering that he'd pulled it on her as they were fucking, held it against her neck, threatening to kill her if she didn't do exactly what he said. But it was a game, not serious. *Still*, Leila considered, *there's something off about this one.*

Satisfyingly scorned on the walk to the subway, Leila slipped a Valium from jacket pocket into mouth to console herself and bought a bran muffin and burned coffee from the bodega. Four sugars in the coffee, sticky white paper packets crumpled and tossed onto the sidewalk. It felt good to litter. The garbage can on the corner of Elizabeth and Houston warned her of a small municipal fine for her transgression. *Good, I hope they fine me.* It was her small but significant *fuck you* to the dress and the boy and the underwear and the knife and the ringing phone.

Soon, though, littering didn't feel like enough. The autumn day flattened, and Leila was tranquilized, gliding on the sidewalk without effort, without obstacle, noticing her breathing heavy and constant and slow, her body operating at a remove from her mind. She considered an afternoon in bed watching reruns and masturbating and online shopping, and imagined that she'd run into Julie, who'd be at the kitchen table where she sat most weekdays, half-dressed and earbuds in, editing online articles and updating *Teen Vogue*'s social media accounts from her phone. They'd discuss the boy, how fucked up it was that he didn't ask for Leila's number, how Leila shouldn't expect anything from men and should use them for sex until she finally just admits she's bi. (Julie would only hint at this, though.) *After all, it's what they've done to you for years*, Julie would say, and Leila imagined feeling momentarily galvanized by the idea of female sexual revenge. *Desire can be channeled through political routes*, she told herself, unconvinced. Maybe it could, maybe it couldn't.

It wasn't until she turned the corner onto Broadway for the Queens-bound M train that she noticed blood trickling down her leg. Her underwear was soaked through. It wasn't time for her period. She'd forgotten to take her pill, for how many days she didn't know. Leila stripped the underwear from beneath the dress, balled them up, and buried them behind a dying honeysuckle bush across from the CVS. They'd never fall in love, never be removed lovingly, tenderly, never be appreciated for their delicacy, for what they communicated about their wearer. *A waste of money*. She would pop into the drugstore to buy tampons, a three-pack of Hanes.

Leila scolded herself mildly through her protected narcosis while deciding between Tampax and OB. She'd fallen for the narrative the underwear communicated. Love, she reminded herself, was a series of biochemical reactions sublimated within a framework of oppressive cultural mores. She'd shoot over to Ridgewood, stop by the apartment and grab her journal, change into jeans, sit on a sunny bench near the park and the fish-fry joint. There, she could observe the intersection with an anthropological eye and write as if she was Claude Lévi-Strauss or whoever, one of her favorite weekend Valium pastimes. She'd forget about the boy and the underwear.

29

Point out that what appears, in history, as being <u>eternal</u> *is merely the product of a* <u>labor of externalization</u> *performed by interconnected institutions such as the family, the church, the state, the educational system,* Pierre Bourdieu wrote, and Leila, sitting on a bench at the intersection of Halsey and Howard, copied into her notebook, drawing several arrows and stars alongside. ***N.B. ETERNAL***

She liked to keep books by several men in her bag, sampling back and forth, as promiscuous in her reading habits as she was in her sexual excursions. Julie made fun of her for stashing perfume samples and cash and two forms of ID alongside her weekend reading. But Leila liked to read on Valium and a hangover. It helped ideas permeate her consciousness, find the rhythm of her own mind.

<u>Naturalistic</u> *(but not natural,* → *what is natural? If something is* <u>natural</u> *it can't be* <u>political</u>*)*, she wrote, *and* <u>essentialist</u> *visions of difference*, like the one Leila had read in a psychology book that morning, about men being creators, individuals, expanding civilization and dragging society into the future and building and acting, always moving, and women being *intrinsically not individual,* inherently collective because they always contained the possibility of *child* within them ... she lost her train of thought. The texts were utterly contradictory.

Leila was certain she was more intelligent than the men who wrote the readings. She didn't take them too seriously. It was much more interesting to read a bit and let the words drift away, think on vaguely related themes, allow herself to halfway forget. So many psychology students were supremely invested in the texts, proselytizing about Freud and failure and interrupting each other *yes, but*— with imperious expressions and persuasive rhetorical flourishes. At first, Leila was stumped by the classroom discussion. It was as if the students spoke a different language. They all seemed to really get it. After a few weeks, though, she realized that she understood as well as anyone. The other students didn't care about communicating. They were speaking in order to be right. Obviously, from the way they acted, only one of them could achieve this distinction. They began to imitate each other, getting much better at arguing because of the relentlessness with which they pursued it, each trying to put the others in the wrong.

She practiced their styles of speaking and reasoning when she was with her friends at their apartment, starting conversations about the politics of desire or the myth of sociopathy or incorrect interpretations of the death drive. She eventually got good at it. Her friends sat silently listening to her, impressed and annoyed. They didn't respond after she extemporized. When, finally, Leila had an entire conversation with herself before a room of mute girlfriends, rehearsing arguments as if they were biblical truth, she knew she'd succeeded.

A pick-up truck honked angrily at a slow-moving sedan that couldn't decide whether it needed to turn left, toward Bushwick, or proceed into Queens. Leila willed herself back to the text. Deterministic roles are forms of *symbolic domination*, and she drew big stars next to this phrase. *I have always been astonished by . . . the fact that the order of the world as we find it, with its one-way streets and no-entry signs, whether literal or figurative, its obligations and its penalties, is broadly respected; that there are not more transgressions and subversions, contraventions and "follies."*

Leila sighed, closed the thin book, watched traffic. It seemed like a lot of work to start some contraventions and follies at this point in the afternoon, and she was tired from the hangover and pharmaceuticals and laborious reading. Hours could pass on a single, mesmerizing stream of thoughts. It was important to take notes or else she wouldn't remember anything.

Leila's chosen bench was in the middle of a complicated intersection adjoining Brooklyn and Queens, four sets of red and green lights blinking, drivers (for the most part) respecting the signals, and bicyclists, not. She liked the intersection because of its chaos, the incessant pressure that the external scene exerted upon her and Bourdieu, the danger of being hailed by the huge man in an oversize polo selling sunglasses, or the two women offering dollar-a-bunch carnations, should she look up from her book.

About six months ago, she'd been walking toward the intersection when a cop standing outside the NYCHA housing projects nodded at her. She nodded back, obligatory, only so that he might release her from his gaze and allow her on her way.

Hey, I've never seen you on this block before. Do you know where you're going?

Leila paused, annoyed, fixing her face into a protectively vapid expression. *I'm fine, thanks. I live just a few blocks away.*

What's a girl like you doing living in this neighborhood?

The question was absurd. Leila was one of hundreds, maybe thousands of passably white-looking, decent-haircut having, canvas tote-bag carrying young people who had moved into the neighborhood in the past year alone.

I like this neighborhood. I live with my friends. She paused, invented. *I'm meeting them for dinner soon, actually.*

You live on this block?

She didn't. *Yeah, closer to the park.*

You should be careful around here. This neighborhood is crazy. Three shootings last night alone. I have to stand outside all day. We got the big lights coming in tomorrow. Should make it a little safer.

Leila made a tentative move forward.

Hey, wait, before you go—I know I'm not supposed to do this, I swear, but would you like to get a drink with me sometime? Give me your number.

She'd known it was coming as soon as he'd started rambling on about her needing to be careful. *Oh, sorry. Thanks. But I have a boyfriend.*

The cop held up his hands, made a backward motion. The

skin of his palms, she noticed, was surprisingly smooth and pink, a little bit oily. He was as young as she. *Okay, okay, my bad. Hey, you look a little bit Greek. Are you Greek? Part Italian?*

No idea. I'm a mutt, she lied.

What, you're adopted or something?

Leila didn't respond. Maybe he'd interpret her silence as sorrow, be ashamed for asking so invasive a question.

What about your boyfriend? He live around here?

She knew what that question meant. *My boyfriend lives downtown. Works in finance.*

He's Italian, too?

He's white.

The cop nodded. *Got it, got it.* Well. Stay safe.

Leila had abandoned her plans to sit at the intersection, making three additional turns before proceeding home. Left and right, left and right, checking over her shoulder each time.

Months later, the interaction still troubled her. She tried to focus again on the park, her book. Bourdieu consoled her, explaining (and she underlined), *the most intolerable conditions of existence can so often be perceived as acceptable and even natural*. Leila drew proliferating circles in the margin. It wasn't her automatic answers that bothered her (*I'm a mutt. The park. My boyfriend, finance, white*). It was the fact that precisely *those* answers had been the ones implanted deep inside, held in reserve, waiting to surface in a moment of danger. She hadn't come up with the answers on her own. But she'd used them when needed. And maybe, in speaking them aloud, she'd etched their usefulness deeper into her own brain, and the cop's.

Leila copied a few sentences at random and again watched the traffic lights. She thought she'd read a passage about traffic lights on a previous Valium afternoon, but she couldn't remember it now. *Green, go. Red, stop.* It was satisfying to watch the cars obey.

When she began experimenting with sadomasochism, her twin sister, who was surprisingly aware of the basics of the system (*on a purely theoretical level*, she assured Leila), suggested that Leila use the traffic light code. *I already do*, Leila told her, but she proceeded to explain nonetheless. *Yellow* would mean *slow down, be careful*, and *red* would mean *stop; please stop; let's get out of this game right now*. You could exit the symbolic structure of S/M by simply invoking your own personal deus ex machina and, with a single word, the whole order of signs and connections and oppositions came tumbling down. You couldn't exit the symbolic order of real life.

How do you know all this? Leila had asked her twin, a bank teller living with her fiancé in Rochester. A comfortable life.

Her sister sneezed. *I found it online.* She was unshockable.

The reason the traffic light system worked so well in S/M, Leila thought, is that everyone already knew what it meant. It was so deeply ingrained that you barely had to think about it. You saw green and went ahead. You saw red and slammed on the brakes. All the world's brains had learned the system so well that, at this point, it would be nearly impossible to reroute the corresponding actions—and the universality of traffic lights meant that Leila wasn't sitting at the intersection watching a string of car crashes.

Two bicyclists slowed, circled, pedaled through a red. Leila imagined a symbol-free intersection, drivers pulling over and rolling down windows and discussing how they should proceed and agreeing based on a particular circumstance. A whole new language of how to drive would have to be invented, would eventually be systematized. She remembered the previous evening's encounter, the boy with the switchblade. What if he'd had to negotiate with her exactly when to pull the knife out, explain what his actions would mean? The thought made her laugh. Of course he didn't need to do that. He could assume what her role would be, and he'd assumed correctly. Red and green lights made it all go so smoothly.

When Leila's father first taught her to drive, he instructed her to use turn signals all the time, even when she was turning out of their driveway. Her high-school boyfriend teased her for this. *You're thoroughly programmed*, he told her, miming a robot and lording over the car from the passenger seat. *It's like you've got this innate obedience.* Boyfriends liked to talk like that to Leila because her parents were from Morocco. She was *a little exotic* which, in the mouths of American teenage boys, meant *hopefully kinky and submissive.*

Her use of the turn signal, though, had nothing to do with obedience. Her muscles had simply habituated the gesture so completely (light press of right foot on left pedal, flick of left wrist upward or down, eyes to each side—once, and again—before easing of foot and its shift to the right, turn of the wheel, turn of the car) that the signal exceeded communication, became another step in the process of making a turn. After her boyfriend's observation, Leila started running red lights when the roads were clear, like she was transgressing some higher authority, being bad. But maybe there was no higher authority. Leila never once got in trouble for running red lights on lonely nighttime roads.

She picked at a thread unraveling at her shirt's hem. Her arms were still dark from the summer sun, stubbly from shaving and goose-pimpled, and she ran her hands along her wrists without desire, scientifically observing herself. What kind of body was this, *exotic* in its suburban high-school desirability, a law-and-order worthy specimen when making its way from Queens to Brooklyn? The question felt like too much. It would've made Leila want to cry, but Valium ensconced her in a sense of profound calm.

Leila tucked Bourdieu back into her bag, thinking instead about an article she'd read a few years back about medieval Spain, about sex workers, about how men in particular tribes would all use the same prostitute to define their relationships to one another. They'd all come inside her or on her and their liquids would mix and congeal and inscribe invisible masculine bonds within her body. The prostitute wasn't real; she was a symbol of their community, a collectively owned natural resource, a way to define the group without land borders. *Except she* was *real*, Leila thought, angry on behalf of all medieval prostitutes. She considered calling her twin to tell her about the prostitutes, but she probably already knew about them, too. When Leila had told the story about the cop to her sister, she'd simply yawned and reported that Leila had deployed *protective self-fabulation*, a common tactic used by women-on-the-ground.

Protective self-fabulation?
Yeah. You invent other selves and play-pretend that you're them, only for a minute, to get yourself out of a bind.
How did you come up with that term?
I didn't. I learned it from an NPR podcast.
Leila's sister listened to podcasts and browsed the Internet on slow workdays at the bank. (*Something I absolutely wouldn't do if it weren't explicitly allowed,* she assured Leila.) For her, worlds of information were always within reach: diagnoses and solutions for every problem, *interesting* historical tidbits, instructions on the gamut of behaviors and mores: sexual, medical, educational. She had an endless repository of knowledge to be called upon in times of crisis or boredom. Because of this, she exuded perpetual calm.

Leila flipped through her notebook. *Indeed, our body is but a social structure composed of many souls,* she'd written in an undated entry. An entire social structure of souls, of selves, each with a range of expression (*authentic* or *fabulated,* she intoned in her sister's voice), impulses and yearnings, a sensorium, each struggling to seize the muscles and limbs of a single physical body. Leila attempted to locate her souls, name them, but found that she was able only to come up with a list of their preferred products and brands. One soul, serious and sensual, liked expensive lattes and reading books shipped to her by two-day Express Mail at the intersection. Another soul, a bit more punishing, used Valium like she meant it.

I contain multitudes; I contradict myself, she wrote ironically in her journal, *and so I spend more $$$.* No wonder early advertisers targeted women primarily, as she'd learned last year in the Psychology of Economics. Historically, her professor reported, women had huge amounts of influence and control as consumers, spending money they couldn't earn—and not much power anywhere else. Convince someone their only shot at freedom is tied to the act of purchasing, and they'll feel expansive and empowered the more selves they have to buy stuff for. It was all so dreadfully predictable. It was despair epitomized.

An older man, also North African, she guessed, sat on a bench across from hers. The street was momentarily quiet and sunlight cut diagonal lines across Leila's legs, which she stretched, treating her bony ankles to its warmth. Certainly the man was not ugly, but he was decades older, dumpy, mustached and balding. He took an old radio out of a reusable grocery bag, settled its dial on Whitney Houston, the song almost over. Whitney mourned in A minor and Leila felt something in her chest unclench. She supposed she could add the *protective self-fabulator* to her inventory of souls, one to be worn like a mask to safeguard its more fragile companions. To some degree, she reasoned, each soul rose to the surface in a moment of self-preservation. An army of mask-wearing souls to keep her body alive. Her body, this body, stubbled arms and bluish veins and thin membrane encasing organs and plasma, masks and markets tangled inside.

30

The painting, Valerie and Sylvie decided, looked nothing like its photograph. Rather, the painting looked nothing like the photograph its previous owner had sent last week, the photograph Valerie used to write the sales note. Maybe the pictures Tom and his assistant would take that morning would look better, Sylvie suggested, hopeful. Why did Tom have to take photographs of the painting, Valerie wondered, if the collector was coming to look at it in the afternoon? *The collector probably wants something to take home, show his wife*, said Sylvie. *A souvenir.* They both knew the conversation was beside the point. The painting needed to be photographed because it was expected to be photographed.

At first, the painting looked even less like its photograph: three Matisses arrived from the Geneva freeport in the same shipment, and the art handler called Valerie and Sylvie over to watch the big reveal of the most highly valued, a loosely rendered depiction of a woman with short black hair painting, alone, in front of a window. *I think Helene's going for around thirty mil with this one*, the art handler reported, tossing the box gently from hand to hand to impress Valerie and Sylvie. When he cut the tape, removed the packing foam, and lifted the tissue paper with gloved fingers, the girls saw only a blotchy, wild vase of flowers. No one knew if they should be concerned. Had the freeport sent the wrong painting?

The art handler checked the box's label. It was correct, or rather, it was incorrect: *La Séance du Matin*, the sticker declared, the title of the expensive painting, decidedly not in the box. He cut a second box open, significantly less careful with the tape and staples and paper and foam. A sensually seated black-haired woman in a Mediterranean studio peered out. The art handler was both relieved (at finding the painting) and disappointed (that the spectacle had fallen flat on Valerie and Sylvie), and told the girls that they better get back to work. The collector and his advisor would be there at 3 P.M. Didn't Sylvie have to be at the reception desk to intercept the Fresh Direct delivery? Didn't Valerie have to finish preparing the files?

Valerie sat at her desk, drinking an espresso from the previous week's Fresh Direct order and scooping out the bowels of an avocado. The sales note was nearly finished; she'd begun it the previous night, plagiarizing copy from a 1950s catalog on Matisse's Riviera period that said the painting was *resplendent with brilliant morning light, both an encapsulation of the artist's simple seaside lifestyle and a complex meditation on creative identity, the role of the model, the impossibility of representation.* She consulted the old .jpeg, trying to find something in the image to substantiate this claim. It was off-tone and pixelated. The work had been in the same collection for the past fifteen years, Helene said (fourteen, actually, the provenance reported), and so the most recent photograph was from around the turn of the century, hadn't been properly digitized, was not, so to speak, *representative*.

Helene's assistant, Françoise, provided a PDF of comparable works sold at auction, each priced between eight and twelve million, each from the Riviera period. *This should give you a sense of what we're going for,* Françoise wrote in the email. *Helene would like you to emphasize the impeccable provenance, never auctioned, one of the last Nice paintings to remain in private hands. Exemplary of the period. Matisses with such complex patterning are rare to come to market.*

Catalog essays on Google Books, images removed for copyright purposes, told Valerie that *windows are a key motif in Matisse's Riviera paintings.* From this, she extemporized, *the artist became enamored of the brilliant sunlight in the south of France after a 1904 trip to Nice; indeed, his Riviera paintings as a whole can be seen as an extended ode to the interplay of dazzling light and shadow he found in the region.* She paused, considering the painting's pixelated counterpart. *Here, notably, the artist's female sitter is at ease before an expansive horizon.* While open windows in Renaissance portraits of women *provide moments of tension,* Valerie typed, *given the Renaissance-era matriarch's role in the home, and her inability to travel the roads depicted sprawling out behind her, Matisse's sitter is blithely untroubled by the sea beyond the studio's closed window.* Valerie added a few adjectives: *meditative, expansive, unexpected,* feeling less blithe and untroubled than the sitter. She consulted Wikipedia and matissefacts.org; the sitter became Matisse's *beloved studio assistant,* the painting a *commemoration of her attentive, joyful spirit.* Valerie concluded with a few sentences about the work's provenance, using the words *inherited, newspaper, avant-garde, Yale*—a pompous vocabulary. The text could only be written because it had no author.

Now, having seen the painting in person, Valerie could revise a bit. The second paragraph needed a transition sentence. *The present painting is remarkable for its consummate synthesis of the essential pictorial qualities that Matisse explored at the height of his career,* Valerie wrote. Not even esteemed university professors sitting at walnut desks with quill pens in the middle of the nineteenth century could get away with such prose, she decided. Only unnamed artworkers. To the third paragraph, she added, *handled by a lesser painter, the sitter's pose, as if straddling her canvas, might be construed as explicit eroticism; in Matisse's masterful hand, though, she is imbued with creative force, her energy diffused throughout the canvas in an atmosphere of luxurious, generalized sensuality.*

Matisse had little regard for the realities of dimensional space. A diaphanous curtain overlapped and then, improbably, snuck underneath the windowpane; faraway palm fronds were foreground patterning; stark black shadows pushed forward into Valerie's computer screen, outpacing the objects that should have created them. Matisse *complicates and subverts perspectival conventions,* Valerie copy/pasted from a 2011 press release for an exhibition by a contemporary painter.

She consulted the image again. You couldn't see what the woman was painting. *With its back to us, the sitter's canvas presents an enigmatic void in the middle of the work.* In fact, Matisse's assistant had positioned two chairs to face each other, as if she were expecting an intimate, maybe confrontational, conversation, but no interlocutor appeared. Instead, she straddled the second chair, placed her palette on its seat and her canvas upright against its back. Maybe she was painting her conversant into being. Maybe she was ripping off Matisse. There was no way to tell if she was any good at painting, since Matisse didn't let you see her work. Strangely, the painter's palette was paintless.

A vase of flowers by her side: Valerie should probably insert somewhere in the note that the assistant was painting a vanitas, a still life, should probably riff on the still-life-as-object versus the woman-as-object, throw in some text on the gaze. *Feminist criticism still life vanitas gaze,* Valerie typed into her Google search bar. Email alert: a downtown gallery announced an opening that evening. An artist in conversation with an academic, followed by a Q&A, drinks. Another alert: *Valerie we urgently need to send the sales note please send me a full PDF with new images provenance note certificate of authenticity,* the subject line read. The body of the email was empty, save for Helene's signature, a little gray skyline of text, prone, as Matisse's painter surely wished she could be after such an exhausting modeling session. Valerie's phone rang: FRANÇOISE, the screen announced. *Valerie Helene wants to know if you could print the* materials for the Matisse and bring the file over to the viewing room before the viewing after the photographs are edited,* Françoise said, breathless. *Thank you!* She hung up without waiting for a reply.

The painting's file included: 1) Valerie's sales note; 2) a thoroughly fact-checked and then selectively edited provenance; 3) a condition report and certificate of authenticity; 4) Françoise's list of comparable works to have sold at auction (works that failed to sell cropped out); and 5) five freshly edited and printed photographs. Each photograph served a purpose: the first was *representative* of the painting like a mugshot in a lineup, hanging on the wall head-on and approximately six feet tall; the next two *connoisseurial*, detail shots of *painterly incident*; and the final two *experiential*, images of Sylvie standing before the painting, back to the camera, transfixed.

Tom always makes me stand in front of the paintings, pretending to look at them, Sylvie told Valerie during her first week at the gallery. *For scale.* Sylvie was small. The paintings looked large in comparison.

In one image, Sylvie wore a loose black dress, her hair swept over her shoulder, her cheekbone just visible against Matisse's violet stripes. What, precisely, would the collector think Sylvie-in-the-photograph could see that he couldn't? In a second photo, Sylvie sat in front of the canvas, arms winging, fingers pressed into the wood bench. She looked like she was about to fling herself into the painting. Like she'd forgotten the surface of the canvas would present an obstacle, was preparing herself to leap into the scene. It was believable enough as an image. Maybe the collector would want to come back to the gallery and buy more paintings, if only to find the girl in the photograph, see her face, ask her out for oysters and white wine and then belittle her for being a receptionist.

When the collector and his advisor arrived, after she'd taken their coats and offered them espressos and called Françoise to announce their entrance to Helene, Sylvie pulled up the surveillance footage. The security guard was on the second floor, walking infinity loops around a statue, or rather, a statue that was two statues, two busts on two pedestals situated to stare at each other. He was staring at his phone. Françoise shot across the frame at a near-gallop, ignoring him, up the stairs to the third floor, out of frame through the vestibule, back in frame before entering Helene's office. Valerie, hailed by email, arrived at Sylvie's desk and crowded next to her to watch. Sylvie clicked on the footage of the private viewing room to find Helene standing, spotlit with her back to the Matisse, the collector near-reclining on the velvet couch, his tense-looking advisor squished into couch-space beside him. Helene was gesturing like a circus conductor. They couldn't hear a word she said. (The gallery's surveillance cameras recorded only visuals.) Sylvie's phone rang, flashing FRANÇOISE.

Valerie, Helene would like you to bring the Matisse catalog to the viewing room immediately, the phone's speaker reported. Françoise didn't ask Sylvie if Valerie was at the reception desk, didn't address Sylvie at all—apparently, she, too, was watching surveillance footage.

Walking to the viewing room, heavy book under her arm, Valerie strategized a plan to prove her savvy, her wiles, to Helene and the collector. She'd offer a useful remark, but would remain appropriately deferential. She'd help close the deal.

The viewing room was as silent as an airport chapel and twice as still. Valerie heard her heels cross the floor at a precise clip, saw herself deliver the book to Helene's outstretched hand.

This piece would be a wonderful complement to your Brancusi. The gold tones, the theme of the enigmatic face …

Helene and the advisor turned and stared. There: Valerie had spoken. Her comment proved she followed the art press, where the collector had bragged about his Brancusi purchase in the *How to Spend It* profile the previous week. Valerie stood waiting for a response, as blank as the canvas in the middle of the Matisse painting, the mute object, the decorative thing.

This painting will not hang near the Brancusi, Helene articulated. The advisor busied herself with the crease in her pants, leaned over and whispered in the collector's ear.

Buying

Oh, it's fine; don't ruin the fun, said the collector, cracking his knuckles, jostling the advisor with his elbow. *This piece is going straight to the Beijing freeport,* he told Valerie. *It's not going to complement anything except Styrofoam and packing tape, at least not till the end of tax season next year.*

31

Valerie didn't know whether her parents were rich or poor or Democrats or Republicans or anything at all, really. She'd asked her mother once when she was younger. *Your father and I don't believe in defining ourselves by our income or political beliefs,* Susan replied. *We're normal. Just normal, average people.*

They believed in something, though, because they made jokes when she arrived home for Christmas with books by Gramsci and Marx, and worried aloud about her studying at a school that had played such a big part in *that '68 stuff.* They were Americans. The point of college was to train to be industrious and get a good job, they told her, not to be locking professors and deans in administrative buildings and chanting communist slogans. Valerie told them that no one in her class was worried about imprisoning professors. They were too busy theorizing the slippery relationship between art and commodity, trying to ethically justify a degree designed to turn them into gallerists or dealers.

Valerie's uncle was a communist and a Buddhist, but he was ten years older than Valerie's father, so that made sense. By the time Mark was old enough to vote, Jane Fonda had switched from protesting the war and befriending Black Panthers to making aerobics videos, and most of the generation made the shift along with her. Valerie's mom stocked their refrigerator with yogurt and wheat germ and refused to pack soda or Oreos in the girls' lunches. With Valerie and Julie sitting on her bed watching approved MTV afterschool programs and eating low-fat cheese snacks, Susan performed leg lifts while ironing her work clothes. She never lost her balance. It was important to have a healthy body.

Valerie was expert in health and wellness and the general improvability of the self by the time she began working at the gallery, so her manager frequently sent her out to pick up vitamins and green juices and ginger immunity elixirs for the staff when the weather was bad. HR was concerned that everyone would get simultaneous chest colds. Calling in sick was frowned upon as a moral weakness. A high-end pharmacist on retainer administered compulsory annual flu shots and brought supplies of exquisite probiotic formulas. Salespeople compared stories of flying to Miami and London for the art fairs with splitting migraines, bouts of bronchitis, herniated disks. The senior director boasted that he made his biggest sale ever in a fog of illness so intense that he later couldn't remember the particulars of the deal. His assistant had to play dumb to get the client to tell them the terms of the agreement.

It was February, prime cold and flu season, and staff morale was dropping. Valerie emerged from the subway station to a flurry of text messages from Helene and Françoise and HR asking her to please arrive with a first-rate selection of energizing green juices and restorative teas for the entire staff. While she was at it, HR added, if she'd be so kind, could she also purchase backups of Helene's supplements? She was running low, and relied on her regimen to maintain not only her physical health, but her emotional stability, productivity, and feelings of joyous connection to her work and family.

When Helene early on discovered Valerie's obsession with calorie counting and organic vegetable consumption and rigorous aerobic workouts, she shared a bottle of her most potent multivitamin with her. *BrainBoost Extreme*: Relaxes your mind and body so that you can work at absurdly efficient rates, all the while projecting an aura of radiant health and happiness. Cultivates a sense of love and connection to your work, allowing you to feel enjoyment in rigorous task completion for up to eighteen hours a day. Accelerates restorative response to decrease necessary sleep duration. Cleanses all toxins accumulated since birth from the body within five days of recommended usage. Multiplies effects of exercise threefold so as to spend less time at the gym. Mental synapses proven to work at nearly twice the normal capacity, activating previously unknown areas of the brain. No side effects whatsoever. A state of physical and mental superiority guaranteed or your money back.

In addition to the BrainBoost, Helene would text Valerie some other vitamins she'd like her to purchase, HR added. *Please keep your phone handy so as to not miss her messages, and please check online reviews and ratings and prices of requested supplements so as to ensure you are purchasing the best brands.*

Fuck, Valerie's phone was dying. It buzzed with a message from Helene. *Resveratrol collagen blend, high polyphenol count. Nootropics for brainwave optimization, not the ones that make me nauseous, though.* Then, another message, nearly immediate. *Please ensure all are gluten-free capsules.* Would Helene also prefer vegan capsules? *No corn no soy more important*, Helene responded. *Chaga Reishi mushroom blend for immune support, at least 110mg Reishi.*

Julie texted in the middle of Helene's onslaught. *Hey, hows work, u wanna go to the movies tonight?* Stupid Julie, needy Julie, Julie whose communications were using up immense amounts of Valerie's battery life. The iPhone's percentage dipped precipitously: six minutes of remaining battery life dropped to two minutes in less than ten seconds. The PR girl had told Valerie she should get a portable charger. She was always so relaxed, her phone's battery supply continually nourished, never concerned that she was running out of time. Valerie's phone must be one of those malfunctioning ones. It was always dying. Each day was a race against the battery's clock.

An automated reminder to update her software popped up. She never remembered to update her software, so the phone regularly complained. Updating took precious minutes of screen time—time when Helene might call or an urgent email might come through. She selected that her phone *remind me later* to make the update, although she had no intention of responding to its later reminder. *When?* It wanted to know. *Remind me again in an hour*, she selected.

Helene continued to add to the list: turmeric pills, for inflammation and blood flow support; cordyceps mushrooms, for enhanced white-blood-cell response and cancer prevention; L. Reuteri probiotic strains, because she hadn't been breastfed and now needed to replenish that particular gut bacteria daily. Did the organic grocer have L. Reuteri? No, but they had Lactobacillus, a close cousin, which the organics reviews website recommended under the headline, *Customers bought these products together*, suggesting that she might want to purchase a bundle of probiotic strains. It wouldn't do. It wasn't right. Another email from PR. When would the press release be ready? *xoxo take your time, of course! but within the hour would be best*. Valerie dashed off a quick response. PR's email signature included a typo disclaimer, explaining that she emailed so rapidly that it was impossible to monitor language usage. Another text from Helene. Please get the brown seaweed gel by BioLineRX, $85 per ounce, *not* the green seaweed from China, $52 per ounce. *Yes, of course, I agree; the brown seaweed is best*, Valerie responded, careful to be polite and articulate. Her phone buzzed, a text from Françoise. *Where are you? Please urgently return to the gallery*. Valerie furiously typed a response. The phone blinked, its artificial bluish glow flickered, died. She looked up, desperate, drunk on adrenaline. She hadn't read Helene's last text. She was no longer connected to her work. She had no idea what to do.

32

Valerie staggered toward the prepared foods buffet, a cornucopia of hot vegetables and pilafs and lasagnas and soups made daily by the Korean couple who ran the store. The tile floor, recently swept, quivered as a train pulled into the subway station below. Reality came into view slowly and as something precarious, shimmering and stone-still compared to the hypnotic velocity of the screen. Valerie was aware of being watched. She glanced over her shoulder to check for cameras and performed a quick inventory of the store's occupants, a tic from her CVS thieving days: a woman, pale and pregnant, browsing blueberries and cradling her plastic basket as if she were practicing holding her child; a Latino kid in a faded sweatshirt stocking bags of coffee beans, separating ground from whole, dark from light; a gray-haired woman, thin and skittish, dancing careful paths around cardboard boxes piled with produce, fondling tufted carrot greens with a dry, vein-crossed hand; a man wearing jeans cuffed around tall cowboy boots, a snow-stiff scarf and ribbed hat obscuring his face.

This man, he'd seen her, too, caught her surveying the store. Valerie emptied her eyes of feeling and averted her gaze, focusing hard on a stack of plastic-wrapped vegetarian sandwiches in the buffet case. *If you can't see him, he can't see you.* Child's logic, sure, but Valerie had lived in New York just long enough to know that a woman who maintains a crossed sightline with a stranger opens herself to interception. Some women are opposed on principle, but Valerie was not one of these. For the past few weeks, she'd been daring men on the subway and the sidewalks to meet her gaze, wanting to test advice picked up from an email newsletter called *Power Tactics for Professional Women*, which she'd signed up for after a particularly abysmal performance in a gallery staff meeting. Turn the tables on your interlocutor, the newsletter advised. Don't let him question you. Question him, instead! Today, though, Valerie had no time to rehearse power tactics. She had to figure out a way to charge her phone. She had to get back to work.

I'm blocking the camera; go ahead; put it in your bag.

The man in the cowboy boots had crossed to stand beside her. *I have to say*, the man said, unwrapping his scarf and removing his hat to reveal a mass of dark hair knotted at the nape of his neck. *I'd have chosen something a little tastier, and a lot more expensive, but go on; go for it.* One eyebrow, she noticed, was split by a shock of gray.

The eyebrow unsettled her, though she couldn't say why.

Go for what?

Put that sandwich in your bag. He indicated a security camera watching from the tiled ceiling with a discreet nod. *Better do it now.*

I wasn't going to put a sandwich in my bag.

Oh, right, got it, and he nodded at the supplements in her basket. *Smart choice. Hey, what's that? BrainBoost?* The man surveyed the bottle, surveyed Valerie. *You don't need a brain boost. You're picking it up for someone else. So, that would make you a personal assistant to a . . . film producer. Or an Upper East Side nanny, who speaks five languages and takes the kids to the museum. Except, if you were a nanny, you'd have brought the kids with you. Kids are the best alibi. "Oh, I'm so sorry, it completely slipped my mind to pay, these little monsters have been keeping me up all night."*

He bounced forward and back, at once restless and at ease. *Come on now. Put the vitamins in your bag. The cashiers are on your side. They all think you're busy tolerating some jerk trying to pick you up.*

You're not trying to pick me up?

No way. I'm here for moral support.

Valerie examined the stranger's face for condescension: he had a pretty mouth and clever eyes that, on a different man (or, she supposed, on the same man but a different day), could have easily spelled *asshole.* Now, though, his face was open and earnest. She rolled her eyes, mostly to give herself something to do. *Power Tactics for Professional Woman* hadn't prepared her to be morally supported by an attractive stranger in the organic market.

I'm not going to steal just because you tell me to, she said. *I have no idea who you are. Maybe you're an undercover cop.* He tilted his head back with real delight and gave a quick, hard laugh.

Besides, Valerie continued, *I've got to get going.* She hallucinated the metallic ping of her iPhone's alert, pulled the lifeless metal biscuit from her pocket and lamely pressed its flat, round button. Odd to not feel it yield to her touch. Odd to have to speak aloud, unscripted, to this bouncing man.

Going where?

To work.
Where's work?
A gallery on Seventy-second.
What gallery?
Just a gallery.
Any old gallery?
Yeah.
So, not a nanny. Any old gallery? I bet contemporary. You've lived in
New York less than a year. Came to get to the heart of the culture industry.
And here you are, stealing health food on Jeff Koons's dealer's time.
I'm not stealing anything.
Those bottles must add up to at least $300. You could buy vegan
sandwiches for months. Hey, I'm serious. Don't look at me like that.

When he used that word, *serious*, Valerie had the distinct sense
that they were in a movie. She sighed an exaggerated, scripted sigh
and, in a single gesture, opened her canvas tote and dropped a
bottle of BrainBoost inside. The handsome man broke into a handsome grin.

Now, why would you go and do a thing like that? Do you always do
what people tell you to do? Don't you know stealing's a crime?
You've got to be kidding me. Valerie went to fish the supplements
out of her bag; he reached over and, gently, closed his palm around
her wrist.

Don't do that. Careful. He dropped her wrist as quickly as he'd
grabbed it, but not before she'd had a moment to conjecture wildly
about the gesture's meaning. Alertness and care, she thought. The
capacity for an addict's or pet's level of devotion. Maybe she was
exuding Power Tactics, after all.

What would happen if you got caught stealing in the middle of the
workday? The man settled again into cheerful banter. *I bet the police*
would hold you at the station for a few hours. Take your picture and ask
some questions. Would you get fired straight away if you didn't return to
the gallery after your lunch break?

Valerie had no idea. There was no world in which she wouldn't
return to the gallery after her lunch break. *If I didn't go back after*

lunch, she said, slow, *they'd give all my tasks to the receptionist. She'd have to stay late. And they'd never leave me alone. On my phone, I mean.* She groped again for the dead thing in her bag.

Ah, but you'd be behind bars. No phones in the holding cell—I know that for sure. So, what would you do after the police released you and the art dealer fired you?

She looked over the man's shoulder, scouting an exit route. Through dried goods, chocolates and specialty coffees, past checkout, free.

You'd turn to a life of crime.

Crime was one word for it. She'd been caught trying to catch some eyes.

No, I wouldn't.

Listen. I've got a feeling about you. You'd absolutely lead a life of crime. I'm serious, I can see it in you. I'm never wrong about things like this.

A stooping and sunspotted woman in a hairnet appeared beside the buffet, smiling at the man and shuffling him to the side to scoop steaming globs of food. Valerie calculated the nutritional contents of a mass of yams and lentils, which looked to have some kind of walnut crust, a layer of spinach, probably a bit of olive oil. *Coconut oil*, read the label pasted to the inside of the glass. Who could trust a label?

Do you want to be friends? The man had stopped bouncing.

Look. I've got to get going.

Ah, a serious woman. No time for friendship. He stepped to the side and extended a palm to clear her way.

No matter—she was off-balance and staggering, *late for work*, she reminded herself, *late.* She squeezed past the prepared foods and out the door, rejoining businesslike New Yorkers in tall boots and wool jackets on cell phones with beautifully dressed children in tow. It was somehow afternoon. She'd missed half the workday, and realized only a few blocks later that she'd forgotten about the BrainBoost in her bag. *Idiotic*, she'd vowed to be done with shoplifting years ago when a security guard followed Julie outside the

Poughkeepsie Galleria to the parking lot, forced her to take off her coat and empty her bags. Neel fumed about her sister's *reckless behavior* and Valerie picked Julie up from the police station in the Taurus, promising not to tell their mom, not to tell anyone. Now Valerie would have to go back to the grocery to pay. She'd explain to the cashier, get a proper receipt, go straight back to the gallery.

Outside the store, she rooted around in her bag for the supplements, finding a rough piece of paper. A coupon booklet advertising strawberries, ten digits scrawled in blue pen, *your friend, Ted*. A phone number. Valerie snorted. *Corny*. Moral support, indeed.

The store's aisles glimmered fluorescent. The hairnetted employee continued to scoop prepared foods and the pregnant woman continued to shop, but the man—Ted—was gone. Valerie walked alongside crates filled with onions and bananas and greens flown in from Mexico. How could he have disappeared so quickly?

Good intentions forgotten, Valerie left the grocery and turned down a side street. A film crew had lit up leafy trees and cobblestone sidewalks and elegant wrought-iron stairwells with hard, bright floodlights. Figures in black sweatshirts sporting wires and headphones and clipboards directed her to pause as they finished a scene, escorted her to the other side of the street, led her through a sea of actors and extras and stylists eating prepared sandwiches and rehearsing lines. She ducked underground at Lexington Avenue, felt in her pocket for her MetroCard. Not there. The station was empty but for discarded one-trip cards, crumpled Taco Bell wrappers, rats scurrying along the tracks. She looked from side to side and, seeing no one, tucked under the turnstile, hair blowing in the rotten underground wind as the express pulled in. She pushed her body into the mass of bodies, backpacks, strollers, teenagers, everyone on cell phones, sweat and flesh and decaying matter shuddering forward as the dark water of the East River rested still and heavy above.

33

Julie was scavenging in the refrigerator for a half-eaten bagel or leftover salad when Valerie came home, deposited winter jacket and bag in a pile on the floor, and produced a scrap of paper torn from a coupon booklet, farm-fresh strawberries, $3.99. Valerie recounted the conversation to Julie. *He looked a little wild, like that painting by Courbet.* Julie rolled her eyes. *I have no idea what that means*, and Valerie plugged in her phone, waited for the device to siphon some life from the circuitry in the walls, and Googled the portrait to show her. Should she call him? *Not until we figure out who he is*, Julie decided, leaning against expired mustards and half-full wine bottles in the refrigerator door before finally shutting it.

Pulling out her own phone, Julie searched valiantly for records of this *Ted*'s existence on social media sites, networking profiles, domain listings, shady for-profit pages promising police records and full addresses and credit scores associated with any phone number for a small price. No social security number concealed by X's, no address history, no property records, no voting history, no records in criminal or civil court, no old social media profiles he'd forgotten to delete. *No luck*, Julie concluded after several glasses of wine and a dozen failed search attempts, the sisters cross-legged on the kitchen floor.

Maybe he's not real, Valerie suggested. Julie gave her a look.

Don't be ridiculous. You met him, didn't you?

Yeah, I guess.

And he somehow wrote his phone number down and dropped it into your bag without you noticing, Julie said.

Yeah.

So, he's sneaky in real life, and invisible online.

Invisible online; the suggestion as outrageous as the idea that he was a phantom or figment. What person living in New York couldn't be found online and rightfully scrutinized? Homeless people, the criminally poor, illegal immigrants, old women who'd never made a name for themselves, never owned property or voted or divorced—that's about it. Valerie and Julie and all their friends and everyone in the world by extrapolation had multiple online personas at their disposal: dating personas, professional personas, personas constructed of carefully photographed and rephotographed staged moments, impersonal email accounts to tie all the distinct selves together.

Like how the body ties together all the consumer selves, Julie said, remembering something Leila had said, cornering Julie as she came out of the bathroom and extemporizing on psychoanalytic theory the previous morning.

Valerie looked down at her lap and noted her body's miserable banality, aligning just well enough to pass as *woman*. Would *Ted* on the scrap of paper even recognize her should she pass him on the street or step into the same subway car?

Grown bored with their investigation, Julie was now tearing bits from a bagel, chewing and complaining about Leila's incapacity to follow their newly implemented cleaning schedule. *I bet she's using psychological tricks on us to make us believe she's cleaning the bathtub when she isn't.*

You think so? Valerie said, stifling a yawn. A worthy hypothesis, but she was too distracted to care much about soap scum or hair in the drain. She retired to her bedroom and sat on her bare mattress, folding laundry, willing her body toward numbness, into sleep. Surely, despite the washing, there must be traces of her skin on the clothes and sheets, and traces, too, of bodies encountered years ago, of past selves, of her mother's hands who'd folded the clothes when Valerie returned home for the holidays, of the retail workers who stocked them in now-closed department stores, of the garment workers who sewed thousands of versions of the same shirt, tired and calloused hands finishing each shirt with *Instructions for Care* affixed to the back collar. *Instructions for Care*, how to care for the thing, how to care. Valerie fingered the strawberries coupon, now smudged and creased. She had to wake up and get ready for work in approximately six hours, her phone reminded her. *Where did you go with supplements? Are catalogs for exhibition on the way to the printer?* demanded an 11 P.M. email from Helene. Valerie placed the coupon beside her bed. She'd decide what to say to everyone tomorrow.

34

February in New York was pitiless and long. Valerie carried Ted's number around in the pocket of her coat like a talisman. Was this how real lovers met? Saying things like *I've got a feeling about you* to strangers in the grocery? Valerie's coupled friends and acquaintances usually claimed to have met their partners *at the bar* or *through friends*. This was a lie: they'd all met on dating apps.

In the first month after she moved to the city, Valerie had taken herself to after-hours lectures at the Whitney and Thursday-night openings in Chelsea, hoping to be swept into the discursive flow of the art world. Soon, though, her tasks at IWC swallowed up the hours allotted to other galleries' openings, and then the hours allotted to after-opening dinners and cocktails, until the exhausting work of selling art made it impossible for Valerie to keep up with contemporary art's social marching orders. The only openings and parties she was permitted to attend were IWC's, and those only when Helene needed a young woman at her deploy to lure in gnarled collectors and open-shirted, hairy-chested artists, give them a pretty face to whom to condescend over tartare and champagne. Chelsea and SoHo gallery assistants seemed to have already laid claim to the friendship of all the city's film programmers and magazine editors and museum educators anyway, and so, when Valerie managed to leave work in time to attend another gallery's opening, she found herself alone in white-walled rooms that crackled around her with conversational intensity. She learned to make her exit before enclaves of after-partiers formed, their income levels and professions distinguishable by the restaurants to which they flocked: downtown dealers to an old-school Italian place with high ceilings and steak tartar, academics to a middling

Moroccan joint near NYU, and critics with massive online followings to a glorified dumpling stand in Chinatown. There was a particular kind of loneliness, Valerie found, in walking herself to the Brooklyn-bound M train after attending an opening alone: the solitude wasn't necessarily unpleasant, but it left her brimming with language, wondering what language brimmed in strangers across the subway platform, too.

Now, though, the city had offered her an interlocutor.

Why do you think he came over to talk to me? she asked Julie. Nearly two weeks had gone by and she hadn't called the number in her pocket.

He's probably a pickup artist. Or trying to steal your liver to sell on the black market, Julie responded, and Valerie dialed the number that afternoon to prove her sister wrong. Ted picked up after the second ring.

The sandwich thief! he exclaimed, as if no time had passed since they'd met in the store. *I was just thinking of you this morning. Do you want to get a coffee? Meet me at the corner of Mott and Prince in an hour?*

She arrived to find him sitting on a stoop in the same cuffed jeans and elaborate boots, his hands gloveless and palms turned up, a mash-up of devotional penitence and showy seventies masculinity. *It's too late for coffee,* he said, apologetic. *But I discovered something.* He tapped his foot, the stoop a patchwork of thick glass and slender iron lines. *See the glass bricks? I bet they were used to let daylight into the basement from the street before electric lighting. Probably a department store.*

A department store?

Sure. And see these little bolts on the building's facade? It's made of cast iron. Makes for large, open interiors. For shopping. Or not shopping, he said, checking her face to see if his joke had landed.

They walked through SoHo. Before an elegant, slender building joining Mercer with Spring Street, he paused to point out a triptych of second-floor windows. *Donald Judd's studio,* he said. *He was your kind of guy. Serious.* Glass panes reflected the flat December sky back to itself.

Ted stopped her in front of a glowing CVS, models dancing and laughing on loop in video screens abutting the store's revolving doors. *This is the place,* Ted said. He jiggled his pockets, rocked back and forth on his heels, looked at Valerie with a cocked brow. *Ready?* Before she had time to ask *for what?* he'd slipped inside. The models onscreen gave Valerie a series of encouraging winks and nods: *you're along for the ride,* they said. *Be along for the ride.*

Ted was puzzling over a vending machine in the drugstore's entrance. *I usually go for the most expensive thing,* he said, scanning its wares, *but Pop-Tarts? Really?* He clucked and fiddled with the machine's buttons like a parent making their child aware of being seriously disappointing. *How about salt and vinegar chips? Peanut M&M's?* Ted pulled a handful of quarters from his pocket, feeding them to the obliging machine one by one. Opting for two of every flavor of pretzels, he held a coin close to Valerie's face before flipping and catching it, tucking it away. The quarter had no face. *Can't give away all my secrets yet,* Ted said, and strode into the store to grab a plastic bag for their snacks.

The sky darkened to a vivid indigo and streetlights cut hazy globes of yellow into the night. What little conversation remained between them relaxed into a comfortable drone, background for Valerie's looking. She had never walked anywhere in New York without purpose. At a tiny Greek bakery off Canal Street, they stopped for $1 pastries that collapsed at her touch, golden, glazed shards flaking into the folds of her scarf. The pastry had a rich sweetness she couldn't place. Something brought to the precipice of burning, but rescued just in time.

When the cold won out and snow, fluorescent in the streetlights, slicked the sidewalks, Ted led her to a construction site on King Street. She stood, staring at his hands, as he picked the makeshift plywood door's lock. Its latch gave a metallic exhale and released, and he grinned at her, eyes filled with cold, gray light. *I can break into or out of anywhere,* he said, pulling back the giant tarp covering a bulldozer's cab and hoisting himself inside. *I slept here earlier this week. I hid some booze.*

Ted's beauty made Valerie suspicious: the precision of his nose, the strange eyebrow, the way he moved with ruthless grace. Now, with the liquor's first pricks, she allowed herself to really look. A generically good face: clear skin; broad, white smile; decisive jawline; pretty lips. So good as to be forgettable, save for that jolt of gray above his left eye. She decided that it would be wrong to ask him what he did for a living. All New Yorkers had a well-worn speech queued up to explain how they spent their time and got paid for it. She didn't necessarily care to hear his.

Ted had nestled their bag of snacks, untouched, next to a jar of quarters on the cab's floor. After a few minutes, he selected a coin from the bunch and handed it to her. Like the coin he'd flipped in the store, it had no face, no markings whatsoever. A blank slate awaiting an identity. *Knockouts from junction boxes*, Ted said, indicating a dark corner of the construction site. *Got 'em right over there.* Wind flapped at tarps, sending the occasional stray bottle rattling across the pavement. *You can find these anywhere there's electrical work being done. New machines won't take them, but older machines will. MTA ticket machines, parking meters, vending machines, highway tolls. Arcade games where you can win stuffed animals and shit. They work about sixty percent of the time.*

Valerie studied a faceless quarter, willing it to speak, but it had a quiet resolve and so did she. The interior of the cab was warmer than she'd expected. They could stay here all night. Ted punctuated their silence with occasional remarks, and Valerie allowed his speech to wash over her. Neel had spoken a lot, always mistaking Valerie's silence for studiousness. Ted didn't need her encouraging nods or questions: he started and stopped as he found and lost things to say, allowing stillness to settle. Valerie took this as a sign of maturity. *Here is a person comfortable with the void*, she thought. Occasionally, he gave a strange, hard laugh, a laugh like an exclamation point, at remarks she hadn't thought were funny. *Here is a person at ease with his peculiarities*, she decided. He leaned toward her with the flask, and she felt his warmth as he leaned. She wanted to be able to laugh the way he laughed, to fall silent the way he fell silent. She wanted to feel that kind of ease in her own body.

Julie rolled her eyes when Valerie came home in the morning to change for work, eyelids purple and puffed. *So, your mansplaining boyfriend knows where a famous Minimalist artist lived, and he snuck you into a bulldozer,* she said, humming a few bars of Shania Twain to make her point. *He probably uses that Donald Judd line on every halfway artsy twentysomething he meets. But most of them aren't suckers like you.* She followed Valerie into the bathroom and stood in men's Calvin Kleins, coffee in hand, while Valerie gargled mouthwash and smudged color onto her eyes.

He's not my boyfriend, Valerie said, pulling on sheer stockings. She wasn't sure what Ted wanted from her. He hadn't hinted at some nebulous *practice* or *project* in the way that networking artists did, and he hadn't attempted a cinematic make-out or asked her back to his place in the way that men selected and soon discarded from dating apps did.

He's not your boyfriend yet, you mean, Julie replied. You get attached quick.

35

That night, Valerie dreamed of herself and Julie, small, playing tag on a steep hill in warm summer dusk. At the hill's base was a marsh filled with marine life, seaweeds and fish and snakes and alligators, water dark in the twilight. (*Alligators?* asked Julie, eyes wide. *Alligators,* Valerie confirmed.) The girls could not see the danger, but felt it in their bodies. They played nonetheless. Julie ran close, closer to Valerie, and Valerie made a daring leap down the hill. She lost her balance and fell toward the water, grasping silently with animal claws at the soft dirt, neatly mowed lawn, pebbles and mud coming down with her toward the river. She was much stronger than she'd thought herself. Her arms, grabbing, didn't belong to the girl Valerie, who wore soft fabrics and played with Barbies and drank orange soda. They belonged to a creature that wanted to wildly thrash and claw at the Earth's surface. A creature that knew what death was and didn't want to die. Valerie didn't want to save herself, no—she wanted only to expend every last bit of energy, lay every muscle to waste. She kicked with small crab legs, clawed with talons, reined herself in and returned to herself in a breathless stupor just short of the water. Standing at the foot of the hill, she dipped human hands into the swamp, knowing—but how?—that she would no longer fear it. She was a part of it now. The water's surface responded to her hands with an oily glow, marvelous creatures rising to meet her, emerald seaweeds and nightmarish fish greeting her and beckoning her to join them. Julie called her name, though, and, at once, Valerie was back in their game. She forgot the wondrous signs of the swamp.

36

Four days passed: the hum and rattle of the subway, spasmic ping of email alerts, Valerie's legs heavy and twitchy under her desk. Ted called on the afternoon of the fifth day, and she hid behind a projection screen suspended from the gallery's ceiling to make plans for the evening. They'd meet at a bar near St. Marks. She'd tell him about the catalog essay she'd been writing for the gallery on the *aesthetics of acceleration*. The phrase wasn't hers: she was writing, as always, under a trendy intellectual's multihyphenate name.

Valerie arrived first and situated herself in the row of crepuscular figures silhouetted in red and orange light. She studied the hunched forms around her. An old man with a hard face sat at the end of the row, his outline distinct even in the dull light. Alone and proud to be alone, a hardcover book before him, his thick wallet on the bar top. It was Professor _____, whose interviews she'd edited while he was in China, and then, when he returned, whose recorded observations she'd transcribed, papers she'd organized, scribbled notes she'd quilted into arguments.

When he was traveling, he rang her at odd hours to hold forth about *unique forms of creative production emerging in the Chinese context* in a jovial tone. *Take notes*, he instructed when he felt a particularly sharp insight coming on. *It's important that we get the minor '68 texts properly translated*, he told her. *So that the Chinese can better understand their political situation.* Professor _____ didn't seem interested in texts written by Chinese theorists and activists, which Valerie assumed were more relevant to their *situation* than French-language pamphlets circulated fifty years prior by her professor's more-famous friends.

More often than not, Professor _____ addressed her by the wrong name: *This is great work, Victoria*, after a two-hour turnaround on a preface for the sixties interviews. *Could you tighten up the conclusion to the third section, Vanessa?* after receiving manuscript notes from his publisher. She'd seen him for the last time six months before. *I'm sorry to call you on your gallery phone, but I couldn't get through to your cell. I've just received the final layout for the China book. Could you come to my office after work and give it your eye?* She'd hailed a taxi to Morningside Heights at 7 P.M., marking the manuscript while he took an endless telephone call. When she was done, he offered whiskey, standing much too close, holding her hand much too long, squeezing her knuckles tight. While she calculated the distance to the door, made an estimate of her weight against his, she breathed the most awful wind from his half-parted lips—an animal had died inside him and was rotting. She refused the whiskey, took a step back. Professor _____ dropped her palm with a sigh. The next day, Helene announced to Valerie that she wanted him to write an essay for the gallery's upcoming catalog. *You'll sort the particulars*—and sort Valerie did. Professor _____ was busy, much too busy, to draft the text on his own, *but of course, my dear, you're welcome to write something up on my behalf. By now, your words are as good as mine.*

Buying

He now sat hunched on a barstool, fingering a tumbler of whiskey, regarding the bartender with a nod, cracking his neck side to side. Panic seized her jaw and slid down her spine. *Unlikely that he'll notice me*, silent and scarf-swaddled as she was. *Unlikely he'll care to talk, even if he does.*

The unlikely always lurks too close: _____ saw her immediately, beckoned her to him, asking how she was, if she was cold, tired, needed a drink, steering her onto a stool and signaling the bartender. Valerie found she couldn't speak quickly enough to refuse, undid her scarf from her throat to itch at her neck. Though growing old and white-haired, _____ was the kind of man whose many accolades have only ever oiled his own skin and hair, smoothed his tan and unworried face. His substantial jowls had sagged farther, though this gave his lips the appearance of being always slightly parted, on the verge of speech. His hair, thinning only mildly, was white and tufted. Each uneasy response that trembled from Valerie's throat (*I'm fine, thank you. A red wine, please. Oh, sure, what you're having. A Manhattan is fine.*) landed in a watery arrangement on the bar-top, an easy mirror into which he peered and saw himself, pleased:

> 1) When he quizzed her on what she'd been reading lately (a book by a lesser-known philosopher in his circle): *Yes, in fact, I know him well. One time, we rode together in a cab from the airport, and he told me . . .*

> 2) When she mentioned the gallery: *Ah, Helene. We once sat next to each other at a dinner party, and she had the most intelligent interpretation of my second book. Would you imagine, she actually understood the whole second section as a metaphor for . . .*

A strange sensation: Valerie felt something small and weak rustle in her lungs. A word? With an exhale, mothlike, it escaped her body to flutter toward the sound of his voice, crystallizing into a small insect on his face. (*I haven't eaten enough today*, she thought, noticing the insect now winged and emerald green. *The booze is getting the best of me. The professor got the best of me.*) The insect, much like Valerie, found it difficult to speak an original thought. As the professor held forth, it repeated back to him his own words, reformulating his sentences in reverberations, insect carapace a supple and reflective screen casting back condensed and arranged transcriptions. Professor _____ was penetrating and sly, carrying on now about a reviewer who had simply missed the crux of his argument, now about the keynote he'd been outlining before she and her insect arrived.

Valerie-insect crawled in rapid circular routes across his ear canal, into the recesses of his skull, out his muscular throat, dancing along his lips to bring his words quickly back to the eager receptors of his own ears. In human form, Valerie grew tipsy, skin warm and throat loosening. Where was Ted? If the cute, sly insect could keep Professor _____ going for thirty more seconds, she could check her phone while, close-eyed, he sermonized—

Ah, it appears we'll need another round. Still Ted did not arrive, but the cocktails did, and the professor charmed and cheers'd, clinking his glass against hers so that its liquid sloshed and its maraschino cherry unmoored, bobbed, disemboweling syrup into her drink. *That's quite enough about me. Now it's your turn. Tell me, what did you think of the essay I wrote for your little catalog?* The bartender, thin and bearded, refilled Valerie's water glass with a wink.

So they would play this game, the game in which they both pretended Valerie hadn't written the essay. She gathered her face into a vapid expression, praised the general thrust of the essay, highlighted a few key phrases she'd memorized: *the way you described the canvas's subversive potential, its playful inversion of the rigid codes of identity, of representation.*

Ah, yes, _____ mourned into his drink. *It's a shame, the chicanery we find ourselves obliged to produce.*

Show tolerance, the winged insect, now a cartoon, a decal superimposed on the screen of this encounter, whispered to Valerie.

Buying

So, Valerie said, *you don't agree with what you wrote?*
The insect, relieved, continued to fly.
*What I wrote may have been true when the work was first painted.
But today . . . I'll say only that I don't trust any woman who can sell the
sublime in the way Helene can. You and I, though, we're but cogs in this
beastly machine.*

Valerie-insect paused, scuttling from mouth to ear in glossy,
circular route. Who was this *we?* An absentminded colloquial-
ism? Or a slow-motion fusion, a now-durable bind of "Valerie" to
"_____"?

Valerie offered, cautious, *it's different for you and me—isn't it?
Helene is my boss. If she's not happy with my writing, I can't pay off my
student loans. I can't afford my rent.*

Ah, but there are many ways to pay rent, _____ said. *You've
always positioned yourself adjacent to the subversive. The iconoclastic.
While you complete your assignments, get your As. Don't think you're
beneath notice.*

The assessment stung. Valerie wanted to sting. She wanted to
hurl herself at him, but, composed, she heard herself intone, *I'm
not sure I understand what you mean.*

*In class, you were so interested in the German terrorists, the student
protests, the radicals in Italy. It was obvious. You see?*

You barely knew my name when I was your student.

_____ laughed, looked at her sideways, hands cupping
an empty tumbler. *I always knew your name, even before you came to my
office. Calling you Victoria, Vanessa—that was a little game.*

Had they been playing a game? Games demand that partici-
pants submit to a particular set of rules. Governing principles, codes
of conduct, conditions that must be accepted before players begin.
Even tacit agreement, agreeing without actively admitting you're
opting in, can be a position. She thought of herself as an insect. She
thought of signing _____'s name over her words, of trailing
after Neel, responding to *Victoria,* crying to police. She hadn't chosen the role he'd assigned her. Nonetheless, she'd played.

_____ filled her silence with elaboration. *You realize, of course, that the first email addressed to "Vanessa" contained my notes for the chapter on split subjectivity and identity formation. The salutation was my little joke, my variation on the theme.*

I had no idea.

Of course you knew, said the prickling _____, turning to his glass and signaling the bartender. *It was our game.*

I didn't know it was a game.

Don't be foolish. We both knew. Don't tell me you didn't. You'll make me sound like a monster. You'll ruin the fun.

Fun. It would be fun to destroy him, to consume him. The desire rose, ancient and anarchic, dancing in her kidneys, drumming at her lungs. She thought of her urge to slap _____ in his office. Playing with Julie in the swamp as a kid. Ted's face in the fluorescent grocery light. She thought of nothing while her fingers itched to grab those little tufts of white hair lining _____'s ears, spill his blood and bones and brains across the oak bar.

I've offended you, said _____. The bartender turned on a mechanical sort of jazz, and Valerie saw that she'd eviscerated her wayward cocktail cherry. Her fingernails were gunked with its guts.

I wonder if you'd like to try a different sort of game, she said, and she watched as his eyes glinted beneath his eyebrows, quirked at her unexpected engagement. It was kinky. She outlined the rules: she and _____ would each select, at random, a sentence from the book he'd brought to the bar. One would explicate the given sentence in prose; the other would make a poem out of it. Whoever served the sentence better won. She made a bet with herself: should she lose, she'd turn herself permanently into an insect. Should she win, she'd never speak to him again.

All right, _____ agreed, *but let's establish our stakes.* Valerie didn't have any cash. *If I win*, he said, *my reward will be the winning. If you win, I'll give you a bill from my wallet.* He pulled apart its leather lips to show her, as if money were candy and she a wide-eyed child.

Ted found her on the street and held back her hair as she vomited. Sea creatures swam in her puke, undulating and curling in pools of foul liquid. Between heaves, she tried to tell him about her suburban home, the skiing trips and makeup and diaries, the stories she read online about girls in Beijing who sold their time, her ex who preferred porn to her body, the time she'd been staring at her disembodied head in an art museum mirror and a wrinkled woman with frosty lips and a blonde bouffant emerged from the stall, held her veiny hands in front of the faucet to admire her nails and glittering rings, raised her eyes to appraise Valerie's reflection. *Very nice*, she reported. *Very neat.* Valerie had never been afraid of the police, the police who loved all things neat and compliant, and when she was sixteen they'd surrounded her car and she'd worried only that the boy she was dating wouldn't offer a validation of their relationship. *I've always been good*, she sobbed, *gotten good grades, eaten healthy foods, been a hard worker. I've always been normal. I've always been told I should survive.*

III.

STEALING

1

Ted rode you home on the back of his bike, your arms tight around his waist, laboring steadily over the Williamsburg Bridge and not saying a word about the stink of vomit. You shifted your weight against his and adjusted your legs so he could pedal, and the animal you became together was alive, snorting and solid. He leaned over the handlebars and you did, too, and you sailed past a spotlit bank and a waterfront construction site. The bike was so fast that the singular precision of things blurred away. Past a statue of a man on a horse, bronze and tall and dead; through an intersection, red light, patient cars. Ted sang loudly, creating nonsense melodies and strings of half-words.

Your soundtrack, he shouted, voice lost in the oncoming traffic.

What?

I'm singing you a soundtrack. You know, for the film you're screening in your head.

You could barely hear, couldn't see beyond what traveled with you on the bike: your legs wrapped around his, arms disappearing in front of you, embracing him. It was the closest your bodies had been. When you breathed in, the winter air was cut by his smell of alcohol and sweat. You pressed the side of your face to his jacket, noticing fine, dewy hairs clinging to his neck.

Hey, he yelled, tossing his voice over his shoulder for you, *that was pretty impressive, what you did back there in the bar. I came in about halfway through, but I hung back. It was incredible to watch. I'll bet you took $300 off of him. See, I told you you'd live a life of crime.*

That wasn't a crime, but the wind caught the words in your throat. The night was cold and its edges vivid and, when Ted turned onto a busy avenue, colors exploded into you through a thin veil of mist: the yellows and blues of a neon sign, a wall of ribboned and artificially colored bouquets, a traffic light's sea of bobbing, flickering reds.

Are you hungry? Ted asked and, before you could answer, he had eased the bike over the curb in front of a grocery. *Let me cook you a steak. We'll pop in here quick.*

In the pet-food aisle, he plucked two filets mignon from your basket and tucked them, along with a stick of butter (*Vermont Creamery*), under his jacket and into his armpit. He loosened his belt a notch and snaked a bottle of wine down his jeans. *Voila*, he grinned. *Can you buy the greens?* You stood next to cans of cat food and kibble, feet heavy and cold. *Hey, you started it*, he said. *I'll meet you outside.* He turned, paused. *Oh, and could you make sure to grab a bag on the way out?*

A bag?

You know, a plastic bag. From the cashier.

But if I'm just getting greens—

Trust me, he said and, in spite of yourself, you did. *We'll want a bag.*

You waited in line with a box of spring mix. *Don't look at the cameras*, you recited to yourself in a child's nervous singsong. Ted walked out the door, too calm to be real, as you handed the cashier your credit card, $4.99. A bag, yes, thank you. Ted walked you and his bike around the corner, filling the bag with wine and steaks, a jar of honey, a sleeve of goat cheese, some truffles, the butter. He shepherded you into a brick building and up two flights of stairs. The apartment was spacious and sprawling, with low ceilings and dark walls.

This is your place?

Not mine. It's a friend's, he said, putting a heavy pan on the stove and turning the knob till it made flame. *Do you ever get asked to house-sit? It's the strangest thing. These people don't have pets or plants, and they already have a maid who comes on Mondays. And yet they ask me to stay for weeks at a time.* He turned from the steaks to gesture at the apartment: an austere couch, upholstered in suede the color of mink; floors black and marbled, corners sleek, wires hidden. A cold war bachelor's technological lair. *I feel like a night guard at a museum, puttering around, making sure someone else's loot is secure.*

I've never been asked to housesit, you said. *I've never been in an apartment like this.*

Never? he asked, genuinely surprised. *Not even for one of those fancy gallery after-parties?*

I don't go to the after-parties, you explained. *I don't even go to the regular parties unless my boss asks me to, which means I'm aging-and-married millionaire bait for the night. Usually, though, I just go home.*

And there's your mistake. You'll never get a house-sitting gig by just going home. It was part of his general strategy, he explained. *Living off the land,* he said, and waited for your reaction as if he were sure it would please him. *And by that, I mean, taking advantage of the fact that thirty percent of this city's apartments are empty seventy percent of the time.*

And stealing filets mignon, you said.

Yes. He stole nearly everything, he explained, paused, amended. He stole everything. *But I try to not take things from small places. Or, when I do, I take only what I need to survive.* He regarded the wine, its purple-soaked orange sticker, *$58.* Well, *survive* was one word for it. It wasn't hard once you learned how, he explained. He saw it in you when he first met you, and he'd seen it again just now at the bar.

You saw what in me?

You know.

You sat at the counter while he flipped the steaks to reveal their perfectly charred undersides. The barstool was tall and your feet dangled. *You make it sound like part of a grand strategy. But I wasn't stealing. We played a game and I won.*

Ted laughed and turned from you to search the cupboards. *A game, huh?* When he turned back, two heavy plates in hand, his face was apologetic. *That sounded sarcastic, didn't it? I didn't mean it that way. But, in my opinion, stealing's a game, too. I play to win.*

Doesn't hurt to look like you, you said.

Or you, he responded with a wry smile. *Like I said. I have a feeling about you.*

You sat chewing at a fatty bit of steak, wanting to ask how his game might work for those who couldn't disguise their desperation behind a facade of tall and amiable and white masculinity, but you were too afraid to spit a mauled hunk of gristle onto your plate so that you might speak. Ted surveyed your face and held his hands up in a gesture of mock innocence. *Maybe other people have different tricks; I don't know. I only know what works for me. I don't have money and there's all this wealth around me, so I take what I can.* He came to sit beside you, feet knocking gently against yours, and then his gaze was on you like a bedside lamp at night. You swallowed the mass of meat in your mouth, fat and oils dissolved in your saliva. How to respond to this stranger, his knee snaking between yours, intruder, sending a shudder up your guts and through your center. No one to tell you what thought to think; that, and more: his effortless lean against the dark of the room, keeping it from you, his eyes hard and bright and saying, not precisely but somehow, that you might move toward him, might lay your palm to his thigh. You sat still, toying with your wine glass.

What was that ridiculous phrase your professor used to describe you? "You've always liked to position yourself just next to the subversive."

That's you?

He laughed. *You sure seem to think so,* and it was true, you did. You felt a sort of nervous, unstable energy in your calves, and put a hand on his leg to steady yourself. His body was much more solid than you'd known one could be. Your mind fed you pornographic images: you dropping to your knees and unzipping his jeans and sticking out your tongue. You taking off your clothes and doing a little dance. He reached for your hand and held your wrist, and then his mouth came down on yours and vertigo sank and swelled your insides.

You knew of only two ways to communicate, and regularly fumbled both: there were words and ideas, transmitted in language, which seemed to function well enough with professors and friends but worked much better in your head, and then there was the jointed skinsuit you wore as a body, to be arranged into positions spelling *girl* in situations defined as *sex*. Most men required only that you perform *girl* well enough that they could articulate themselves against you as *man*. This meant holding still and whimpering little animal noises at the right moments, pretending to be overwhelmed by a power that felt like nothing much. Performing passivity was a lot of work. You dreamed of no work at all. Your fantasies were the usual—*hold me down until I can't even wriggle a toe, slap me till I'm scared and put your hands around my neck. Inflict some pain and tell me I like it. Say I'm the same as all the others but you love me the best*—but you'd thought them impossible to realize, an armature of language applied to two groping masses of flesh. When Ted held your wrists behind your back, though, your shoulder burned wordless with pain, real pain. When you fucked on the floor, language extinguished. *Who is this person*, you wondered, this person pinning your knees to your shoulders, hands holding firm your chin to feed fingers into your mouth. Who knew there was so much to take, you thought, and that word, *take*, careened pornographic into your present, splintering you and then disappearing again until your watching mind saw only flickering projections of white light.

You slept a heavy and dreamless sleep that night, shifting into gray wakefulness only twice. The first time, you felt your body held and protected in Ted's grasp. The second, you sensed yourself immobilized, caught.

2

In the morning, Ted led you to the fancy coffee maker. It ground beans with the press of one button, and then produced either a single- or double-shot espresso with the press of another. By the third espresso, armpits soaked with caffeinated sweat, you realized that Ted's eagerness was not about showing off an expensive machine or discussing the aromas of varietals. He was just excited to give you something. *Ted the provider.* You sat by his side on the stoop, cup in hand, feeling positively rich. You would take the day off. You would email HR that you were terribly sick.

Around 9 A.M., though, the anxiety of a day without work set in. You told Ted you should go home, and he offered to ride you on his bike. *I've got to meet up with Virginia, anyway*, he said, and you deliberated whether or not to ask. *My former partner in crime*, he offered, reading your silence. *My ex. We're doing a work thing today.* Ted was not the sort of man who emanated entrepreneurial spirit, and the fact of the word *work* in his mouth startled you out of suspicion at a hovering ex. You tried to imagine Ted as a man at work. Your mind summoned a montage of hard hats and cowboys and bikers, which you indulged until you realized you'd replaced Ted's face with Freddie Mercury's.

At your apartment building, an unbeautiful brownstone, Ted checked to make sure you had your wallet, your ID, and stood back as you groped for your keys, taking inventory of the apartment's facade and then you, giving both an approving nod before he waved and rode away. You staggered inside, dizzy and slow. Pausing at the kitchen table, you ripped and emptied the envelope that bore the April electric bill (*Do Not Discard: Important Information about Your Account Inside!*) and stuffed in the cash you had won from Professor _____, crossed out the Con Ed address and tucked it in your bag.

Upstairs, you sat at your desk and stared at your bookshelf. Yellow and pink and blue and green covers, neat white titles. Some with dust covers, large and heavy, others pocketsize, or, rather, suit-jacket-pocket size. All stamped, neat and official, with famous names. When you cleaned your bedroom on Saturday, you lined a row of nail polishes in front of the books. Proud soldiers in formation, deep violet to shimmering pearl. The bottles were profoundly ugly, each bearing the name of its maker and capped with shiny white plastic around which sloppy polish congealed. Each destined to be shrouded with AstroTurf in a landfill because living grass refuses to grow atop sloping hills of waste. Why had you sorted them? No big secret: you took great pleasure in organizing your things. You opened your computer, clicked on the Microsoft Word icon, made it bounce.

Stealing

Document1.docx

Valerie, I was you once.

When you were born, a sheet of paper gave you a name, made you real, made you whole. You found yourself well suited to the form that preceded you. When you watch videos of yourself as a child, pretend-cleaning the floor with rags, pretend-dancing with your father, pretend-domesticated with your plastic oven, you smile an empty smile at the images. You were a pretty child.

Who first taught you to perform these tasks? What cruelty did you feel toward the linoleum when you first took a wet rag to it? They want you to feel shame, to sweep these questions from the corners of your small cage, to decorate the bars instead with shining ribbons of every color. Valerie, did you ever want to shut your captor's hand into the oven along with your plastic pie?

Your captor? Who's that? your professor will demand when you submit this text. *Be specific in your use of language. Revise and resubmit.* Have you ever refused to revise to his specifications? Have you ever wanted to lodge yourself like a thorn in his side, bleed him dry? Killing him would be a suicide, to be sure, but not the one they (yes, *they*) expect you to commit.

You have several times, I know, stared at your face in the mirror and felt a flash of hatred for the products you were about to apply. You have found yourself performing affectations, smiling innocuously into the face of authority. Valerie, *try this one simple trick to erase years from your age*: when you're next at the store, tuck a bottle of supplements into your bag—first the one with the blue text promising shiny hair and lubricated joints, and then the green bottle stamped with flowers, *grass-fed and pasture-raised*. Smile your natural-toothpaste smile at the checkout girl as you walk past. She isn't your enemy. She takes things, too, when she stocks shelves at night. Look up, to the left: your enemy is the surveillance camera, hovering watchful above you and implanted deep inside, broadcasting your image back to you from the corner of your mind's eye.

The camera loves you, the yearbook photographers said. Your bouncy ponytail, your quick step. You radiate health, pleasure, restraint. You are the picture of morality.

How to take revenge on this image, yourself?

Valerie, after you exit the store with the products in your bag, begin ingesting immediately. Hate the products as you consume them, hate them for their metallic labels and slick brand names and cellulose encapsulation, and allow the hatred to commingle with probiotic and herbal tincture and vitamin and allow it to make you stronger, enliven you. Thieve these supplements by the dozen. Cease to purchase your detoxification teas, your vegetable juices, your spandex leggings—steal them instead, steal everything you need. Begin to disappear from the register.

Forget to post that image to your digital profile; neglect your exercise class. *Where did she go?* the cameras ask. *I'm not sure*, your manager replies. Valerie, cease to be productive. Work on useless projects, poems and lists not intended to sell a single thing. Type nonsense into blank emails, *hard at work* when HR walks by. Form alliances with they who work beside you; plot in private languages while sitting at your desk. Gather the personal information of the executives; print out files with classified information and stash these beneath your mattress as collateral. Smile at your colleagues. You love your work. In morning meetings, take diligent notes in the form of a tell-all exposé.

In your last month of employment, purchase things on the company credit card. *What should I buy?* Anything at all. Change your last name and address in the directory: they barely remember you, anyway, can't find you when you're gone. On the day before the Amex statement comes, tell HR you're going away for some time.

How long?

Just some time. A sabbatical, a residency. Something restorative, that's all. Of course you'll still be available on email. Of course you'll come back.

Will you, though? Will you come back? Valerie, take your company phone and disconnect it from its provider, wipe its data and replace its SIM card. Ride your bike around the city and eat the stolen office snacks stockpiled in your closet and when you run out of food, steal from the top salespeople whose information you've gathered, the ones who ignored your proposals in meetings, who told you that you were *just wonderful* at data entry, that you should dedicate your

life to data entry—siphon their accounts dry, one by
one.

Valerie, steal into the university library at night like a
stowaway awaiting passage to a new life. Take Wite-
Out and fine red pens with you into the stacks; anno-
tate and erase and revise the written world's histories.
Reshelve entire sections: anthropology into autobi-
ography, history into horror, philosophy into fiction.
Stand in line with books at the copier. Scan them
page by page, distribute them, remove them from
the shelves where they reside, awaiting institutional
affiliation and paid membership to be read. Valerie,
print these words as a pamphlet to insert into how-
to guides on entrepreneurship at the local Books-A-
Million. Make hundreds of copies and leave bundles
on top of coupon booklets at the Rite Aid, in piles of
newspapers at the bodega. Copy and paste passages
into Wikipedia entries. Write it as a script for subway
performers to sing.

Valerie, cease purchasing at once. No need for cheap-
ly sewn garments and advertisements, no need to
speak in hollow words. Withdraw from circulation.
Tear a hole the shape of your body in the fabric of the
global economy. You continue to exist. You still laugh
and your laughter spreads like contagion. Your hair
still shines, your teeth are white, and they, they, are
confused. There you are, but where is your money?
Your disappearance is one of feigned innocence, pretend ignorance—tools you know well. Only you can
sense that you've become a void. Step into the empty
space created in your own body, now purged of the
landfill of representations. Waste afternoons watching the passing of time. Grab hold of the scenery that

once was your world and drag it with you, changed, into the future. Cackle with glee as you remember the slogans that papered the walls of your suburban high school: *Rediscover the enchantments of life. You are already what you can be. It is only a matter of living all the way.*

3

So, said Ted, rubbing together gloved hands and blowing into cupped palms. *Who are we going to be today?*

You had been standing too long in the curbside slush outside the Tribeca Whole Foods. The skin beneath your fingernails was white. You considered the fate of Arctic explorers. You considered frozen, mummified prehistoric remains. You considered the clipped elegance of the townhouse-and-oak-tree lined streets. Shoppers jostled you as they made their way toward the store's windowed facade, lit by streetlights and glowing cool white fluorescence from inside. The automatic doors happily opened and closed to gulp up their bundled bodies.

How about San Francisco newlyweds with four weeks of vacation a year and absolutely no debt? They're here on holiday. Rented out a loft nearby. Having so much frenetic sex that they're starved, and they've rushed to the Whole Foods for sustenance.

Ted laughed and stuck out his hand for you to shake.

There were many ways to avoid detection: Your favorites involved aristocratic drag. The first time you'd gone stealing together (*my sister and I called it "getting,"* you told him), Ted feigned taking a call in front of Argentine wines, at first distracted and pacing, then frustrated, now worried, a bottle tucked into his raincoat. Phone to ear, he sailed past antipastos and soups, nodding, brusque, at the butcher, all the while assuring his fictional conversant he'd *be there soon.* Through floral, past checkout, he strode straight outside.

Ted, you had come to understand, liked to feel important, needed, under great external pressure: a medic required immediately at the hospital, a husband summoned quickly home, a department chair running to a forgotten meeting. You were ditzy and gullible, deeply in love with all the store's lies. You cooed at the products on the shelves, *so good, so necessary*. You wondered at labels, smiled at employees, stuffed novelties into your pockets, dawdling and sweet. Dumb girl, silly girl. It felt like an exorcism to wear her vacuous face as a disguise.

The automatic doors opened wide for the sex-crazed San Franciscans. It was wonderful to be rich. They could shop without thinking of prices at all. Stocking clerks nodded as you hooked a plastic basket around one elbow, weaving your unencumbered arm around Ted's waist. Yesterday's flowers were on sale today. In produce, a fine mist freshened the greens. *This week's deals—organic and cage-free eggs from a local farm; buy one dozen and get the second half-off*, announced a chalkboard beside sorted and sprayed stacks of rainbow chard. Your character, naïve, wondered about backyard chickens and rooftop farms in Chelsea.

A sales associate approached, offering samples of hot cider, suggesting that he might tour you around the store to deliver a prepared lecture on the products, the suppliers who provide them, the farmers and harvesters who lead simple, happy lives, who toil in the fields each day and return to their children at night. *We've got ethically raised beef from Hudson on sale this week*, the associate reported, and you checked his plastic nametag. JOE.

Oh, honey, did you hear that? Beef from Hudson, you enthused, and Joe joined in on the act, giving Ted a knowing nod. *Women*, the nod said, dragging along with it all that the word implied. *Shopping*.

Oh, Joey. Your banality was your disguise. *No one likes to be reminded that their personality is nothing but a habit*, Ted said after your first time shoplifting together. *The more you play a part, the more you'll lull them into a dreamy autopilot, or freak them out about their own lives so thoroughly that they look away*. Yes, Joe, your character said, she'd very much like to see the products, tour the store, hear the speech. You turned to bid farewell to an amused Ted, who had placed into his basket a bundle of parsley and a family-size bag of tortilla chips.

Darling, do we really need chips? you pantomimed, as Joe looked on, patiently.

I'm ravenous, Ted lied, placing a protective hand over the sombrero-clad figure on the bag. *Please.* You gave an exaggerated sigh. A health-conscious professional, his doting young wife.

Joe left you in dairy after a brief and uninspired tour of butters and meats. He had a pockmarked chin and flat tone, and you were under no illusion that his tour was anything other than compulsory, canned speech his boss required he recite throughout the day. You wanted to tell him your secrets: you were no newlywed; you'd waitressed forever; you, too, had debt. Instead, you stood before the refrigerator. The aisle was cool and unbusy. How could there be so many varieties of eggs? One carton cardboard, the next plastic, both claiming to rid the Earth of waste, to be ethical and green. *Cage-free organic eggs—better for the planet, better for you.* You, the shopper, were inclined to agree. The things within possessed mystical health benefits, were ethically superior, spoke to your moral compass and altruistic spirit. The story on the carton was trustworthy and true.

You consulted another row of the refrigerated shelf: these eggs did not tell their own story, did not disclose chickens' names or dietary habits or farm locations. They must originate from the supermarket itself, or maybe from nowhere, your shopper thought. If they didn't speak, they obviously had nothing to say. You checked the plastic-covered numbers wedged into the shelves, also frosty cold. The eggs with a history cost twice as much as the eggs without. Yes, this seemed reasonable. *Narratives, after all, are expensive*, your character rehearsed in your head. *Cooking up a believable story takes time and effort and lots of money. It's like Hollywood—although, I must say, I've never liked LA. Anyhow, fair is fair: these eggs are worth a quarter-hour's work at the consulting firm, and those only a daydreaming minute at my desk.*

Yes, the eggs whispered in agreement, speaking not in a human language but in the frosty ethers of refrigerator mist. *You're very wise. We're the best of the best, the top of the shelf. If you'd like to have us, you'll have to earn us. You'll have to work for it.*

This seemed coy and demanding of the eggs. Violent, even. But didn't they look so kind and unassuming in their carton, so healthy and helpful? You placed them in your basket. It felt right. You regarded yourself, arm crooked with your red plastic baby, small, strange treasures beaming at you from inside.

A salesclerk peered around the canned bean display, his face glowing with humility and dignity and kindness. An arbiter of taste. An educator, even, humbly offering judgments on products from his position of knowledge and connoisseurship, wanting only to assist, to help you make better choices. A ponytailed teenager approached, offering to bring a larger cart, wondering if you'd like more information about the dairy farmers whose yogurts were on view that day. *Yes, of course;* you'd never been one to pass up good service and more information. The teenager turned to the colossal refrigerator and Ted appeared beside you, sliding the basket from your elbow to his.

There you are, lovey. Where have you been?

You responded with some starry-eyed prose about harvesters eating the day's yield of strawberries. Ted grinned, walking you away from the eggs. *Oh really. Strawberries in the sun?* You passed creams and milks and cheeses and yogurts.

In Frozen Foods, a man stood surveying microwavable TV dinners. A bag of potato chips, two Band-Aid boxes, and a Women's Daily Multivitamin in his cart. He looked for a long time at the dinners. Condensation enveloped his body, concealing him, each time he opened and closed the freezer door. Ted positioned himself to regard frozen mangoes, pineapples, berry blends.

See that man, how he has only nonperishables in his cart? The man could stalk the aisles for hours, cart gliding noiselessly, load light.

He reminds me of Larry Povinelli, you said.

I was thinking that, too, Ted replied.

Mr. Povinelli, loss prevention officer, your uncle LP: code you'd invented with Ted. The man opened the freezer door again and again. Your well-heeled husband steered you past a display of cupcake tins and cream-cheese frostings and a sense of cold dread shot straight through you when Larry's eyes met yours: the feeling of standing exposed before the law.

In Aisle 14, you and Ted were again alone. Ted took a small artisanal olive oil from the shelf, tucked it underneath the corn chips in his basket. You selected a bottle of lavender balsamic, casually leaned toward your husband to brush your lips against his shoulder, and dropped it into your bag. This was better than pretend-play, better than dreaming. You placed a bag of dried porcini mushrooms in Ted's basket, finding that the olive oil was already gone.

By the time you stepped onto the escalator with Ted a few steps behind, his body was padded with dinner, a few friends' worth of gifts. Besides what Ted knew was in your bag, you had slipped three small tokens into your pockets—a Hawaiian-vanilla lip balm, a packet of roasted almonds, a box of herbal toothpicks. You had a secret even from Ted.

Round cameras installed in the supermarket's ceiling tracked your rise from lower floor to street level, and, as you ascended, you prattled in your husband's direction about the relative merits of soy milk versus almond milk versus hemp milk versus whole milk, the benefits and gustatory profiles of each. A chattering health nut, a consummate domestic, unable to shut up. Her annoyed husband, allergic to shopping, eager to return the two to their vacation bed. A tableau of heterosexual normalcy, terrifying enough to everyone around that you could glide past the checkout line and straight out the door.

Soon after he first revealed what he called his *habit* to you, Ted told you a story about the moment when stealing shifted, for him, from *I need* to *I want*. Now, he could barely tell the difference. But when first living in New York, he'd thieved only necessaries he couldn't afford: toothpaste, cleaning spray, deli meat. Sometimes an expensive pen or pair of gloves, just for the thrill. The occasional silky underwear or other treat for Virginia. All restraint faded away just a few months in. He and his friend Will were sitting on Prince Street in the pre-Christmas rush, trying to sell Will's paintings to tourists. *These dour portraits of his grandparents in Brighton,* Ted explained. *Two-hundred, two-fifty, max. A manicured man in a camel-hair coat came up—I remember how tall he was, that he had very long fingers—and stood there, cocking his head, appraising the paintings. He started negotiating with Will, really lowballing. All three of us knew he had money, and probably lots of it. But he had something to prove. He must have known he was negotiating over whether or not Will would eat that week. For sport. And I thought to myself, I could play that part better than him. I could have smooth hands and good taste. I could know about wine. I could walk around the city as if it were my store. And that's how it became a game. I wanted to see how rich I could look. And, you know, there's no limit to what can be stolen. Or, if there is, it gets higher and higher with all the world's excess. So, it's a game with no winner, and no end.*

4

Later that night, you sat alone on your mattress and emptied your canvas bag, spilling out vitamin bottles, dried fruits, chocolates, essential oils and skin toners and dried mushrooms and wildflower tinctures. You perched cross-legged and spread the products around you. They were a Dutch still life, baroque and internally lit, but instead of rotting like sixteenth-century flowers, they would either be used up completely, or would live forever with their plastic wrappings and preservatives. Unlike most immortal things, you could touch them, so you touched each precious one.

The products spoke their secrets to you, how they'd been carelessly tossed into cardboard boxes padded with Styrofoam, stacked among millions of cloned copies in ugly gray barges and set afloat on the sea, jostling the casings of impersonators, spilling and breaking when rolling waves set the barge askance. They'd been roughly handled, thrown into the backs of trucks by men who didn't care what they transported each day, who wanted only to listen to talk radio and who never thought to check on the products, to ask how they were feeling. They'd been unpacked by bored store clerks, surveyed, appraised, stickered with orange tags and arrayed neatly on shelves. They thought surely they'd be selected, scanned and inventoried, bagged in exchange for cash or card, transported from trunk of steel-blue SUV to middle shelf of Whirlpool Refrigerator. They would meet their ultimate refrigerated demise slowly, consumed sparingly, responsibly. You had intervened, though. You'd implicated them in something larger, more dangerous, more important. They had always had a sneaking suspicion they were bound for greatness. *You saved us; you'll love us*, they whispered. Your heart swelled. Yes, you would care for them, love them, be good to them always.

Thieving with Ted, you found that love had little to do with cookie-cutter domestic scenes, or with jealously guarding a possession. You tore the seal from a baggie of Black Mission figs and admired the way your bedroom light hit the packaging's aluminum underside. The figs could never again be transacted into ethanol-blend gasoline, or a duty-free Matisse, or a fraction of your time. They could no longer magically store all the world's greed. They were themselves and only themselves. You plucked a sticky lump from the mass and held it to your nose, letting its syrupy skin tickle the hairs above your upper lip. You squeezed the fig's plump little body, readying yourself for what awaited you inside. You no longer had to be careful and calculating. You no longer had to create spreadsheets and balance books, measuring what was possible against your remaining time. You could be ravenous. You bit.

5

The next morning, you called Leila to give her exciting news: you'd reached a new life stage by becoming expert in a skill cultivated in childhood. You walked toward the Broadway-Lafayette subway station, bought a coffee from the 7-Eleven, black and burned, and smuggled a grapefruit and packet of sunflower seeds into your bag as you explained:

> Valerie: _____ ...*and, like most of life, the trick to getting away with it is acting like you're not doing anything wrong. Acting completely natural. And soon, you figure out which employees are the minimum-wage workers and can't be bothered to chase you down the street, are probably cheering you on and doing the same when they stock the shelves, and which aging, red-faced guy is the store detective, the ex-cop.*

> Leila: *Well, in my opinion, you're basically putting your life at risk, your whole reputation, for a hunk of six-month manchego and a tube of rose day cream. The DSM says it's a combo of entitlement and fundamental lack of regard for your own personal value. If I was your therapist, I'd say you're struggling with impulse control, maybe a personality disorder—*

But Leila couldn't know how it felt. You were compelled to touch items on the shelf, to select those hungry ones among the hundreds that caused your fingers to vibrate, to draw close, to pull them into your pocket as your own. It was a relief to be stealing again. You took nonessentials, treats you could, hypothetically, afford: stuffed and salted olives, probiotic elixirs, brightening serums, worth a few hours' worth of gallery work. Pocketed, they became luxuries so precious, so unspeakably decadent, you'd never tarnish them by the mundane act of purchasing. Into the expanding pocket, one ounce of manuka honey and then another. A deli container of lobster salad from Maine, hair ties in three shades of blue. Trifles, you told Leila, all of them. Useless things that shouldn't exist.

Stealing

Valerie: _____ ...*and you discover that food tastes better when it's lifted. And then you can see no reason to pay, no reason to participate in the buying game when you can just elect to play a different game, a new one.*

Leila (skeptical): *Really? You think it's different? But can't you be arrested? So, you're not really opting out... and don't the stores plan for shoplifting losses? So, actually, you're just playing a different position in the same game. It's not like you're taking from the rich and giving to the poor, altruism and all that—*

Valerie (prickly): *Yes, I am. Taking from the rich and giving to the poor.*

Leila: *Who's the poor, then?*

Valerie: *Me, obviously. And you, when I gave you that silk scarf last week.*

Leila: *We're not poor, Valerie. You don't make me poor by stealing something for me.*

Valerie: *I'm sorry, I had no idea you'd paid off all your student debt and seized the means of psychology production.*

Leila: *Okay, convenience Marxism. Got it. Look, I'm just saying, stealing's not some big overthrow of the system. It's built into the existing order. The stores need to keep people in a perpetual state of wanting, and they anticipate that some nice white girls are going to want too much. You're basically under the spell of a manufactured neurosis.*

Valerie (pedantic, off topic): *Okay, but so what if it's neurotic? A neurosis is just a protective response to some-*

*thing fucked up in the environment. And aren't you the one
who told me that the body is* a social structure made up
of many souls?

Leila (irritated): *Don't intellectualize it. And don't use
my words against me. You just want to justify your absurd
capitulation to needing twelve different brands of tomato
paste and five hundred bobby pins et cetera on hand at
all times. If you want to get academic about it, sure; it's a
sublimation of the consumerist self; I'll grant you that. But
you're turning into a hoarder and you don't care. You just
want to satisfy the same urge we've all got in a different
way. You really think you can fill up some hole inside you
with a bunch of stuff?*

Valerie (defensive): *All I'm saying is that this way of
getting things shouldn't mean I'm bad, or impulsive, or
pathological, or whatever. I'm no worse than you. It's no
worse than buying.*

Leila was wrong. You weren't a hoarder. The revelation of getting
was that you no longer had to be frugal and moderate. You didn't
have to portion out or save up. No more skipping the single thread
of saffron in a recipe, no more off-brand *thank you* cards, dime-size
globs of drugstore conditioner for your split ends. If the things
were going to be made—and they were—the least you could do
was to help them live all the way up. You'd seen Leila ration her
pricy argan oil to last months, ordering cheap humidifiers and rug
pads and picture frames on Amazon, *treating herself* on a tired night
to an entire tray of tiramisu from Gristedes. Her favorite pair of
shock-pink Reeboks (bought) had been stocked in Bloomingda-
le's by the same minimum-wage hands as yours (stolen), flown
around the globe using the same amount of fuel on the same cargo
aircraft, dyed with the same neurotoxins that went on to scorch
the same plots of dirt, sewn from the same bloody hides peeled

from the same dripping carcasses, sun-starved cows branded by the same burning irons, knocked out with the same sedatives, electroshocked and metal-prodded and locked before slaughter in the same dark pens.

You stopped in front of a donut shop and stood looking through the glass. A classic American scene: awestruck consumer before transparent partition, sweet multicolored goods just beyond reach. The shop was not yet open. The sky was still purple, the air cold. Maybe it was Leila or maybe the cows laced to your feet, but you felt nauseated. You steadied yourself against the storefront and watched as a woman with cropped black hair and plastic gloves maneuvered behind the racks, counting out six donuts and placing them in a neat row, injecting their bodies with a jammy substance and glazing their tops, quickly transferring them to a tray to dust them with yellow and pink and blue and green sprinkles before setting them next to an oscillating fan to dry, to crust and harden, sugar and cream and fat congealing into a wonderfully soft yet solid form.

The baker was calm and industrious, and her methodical movements soothed you. Her hands worked as if they did not belong to her. You didn't want to eat the donuts. You wanted to know her, instead. Like you, she must yearn to touch forbidden things. She must have wanted to work in the donut shop to place herself in their proximity. The woman turned to face the pan rack, pale morning light lingering on her striped sweater. Probably she'd just been looking for part-time employment, had walked past the shop on her way into Manhattan, had noticed the *Help Wanted* sign and lied about having previous bakery experience and a deep passion for customer satisfaction. But maybe, you thought, she stole donuts while she made them, ate them for breakfast and lunch, took home the previous day's stale pastries to feed to her dogs, distributed donuts she'd glazed imperfectly to the panhandlers and pamphleteering zealots who stood outside the shop, waiting for nothing. Maybe she was practical and decisive. Maybe she was kind. Did she pack up donuts each morning for supermarket deliverymen? And, if she did, did she stand at the bakery's back door, waving goodbye to the trucks that arrived daily to carry her labor away?

The baker looked up from a Boston Cream, caught you staring. You realized you'd been so busy falling in love that you'd forgotten to listen to Leila, phone still pressed to your ear. The baker pointed to the shop's hours on the door, mouthing *we're closed*. Surely she knew about hunger and longing and loneliness. You turned from the window, continued up the stairs to the Manhattan-bound M train.

> Leila (extemporizing): _____ ... *might make you feel a certain way, but in actuality you're devaluing yourself, your own worth, by behaving like this. You're smart. You have an education. You're attractive and young and you've got a great job. And now you're telling me that you're willing to risk all that for the excitement of pocketing some breath mints, a bag of Cheetos, a USB flash drive you won't even use? You'll be unemployable if you get arrested. You won't be able to afford to live in New York, you'll have to move back in with your parents, and anyone who wants to date you will Google your name and find out you're a criminal. Don't laugh. A person with a healthy, productive attitude about their self-worth would never go around behaving so antisocially. Some people, people who didn't grow up in suburbia, people who can't smile at police and feel safe, get in big trouble for this thing you're doing just for kicks. If you can figure out how to value your own life, cultivate some self-worth, maybe you'll stop stealing, get your priorities straight, focus on your job* ...

6

Focus on your job, your narrator reprimanded you, borrowing Leila's voice. An influx of Fresh Direct deliveries and couriers and collectors and tourists made the gallery's reception desk, where you sat covering Sylvie's extended smoke break, as chilly as a restaurant walk-in cooler. *The waitress to receptionist pipeline,* you amused yourself. *Both jobs requiring goosepimpled arms and rock-hard nipples and a state of perpetual immune suppression from their female employees.*

Nic stopped by the gallery shortly after you took up Sylvie's position at the desk, the latest *Artforum* tucked into his tote. He moved as if on a stop-and-go conveyor belt to examine each painting in the exhibition, wire-rim glasses sliding down his nose as he took golf-pencil notes. When he had seen the show to his satisfaction, he stopped at the front desk to ask after Sylvie. *Sylvie's out today,* you reported, saving your friend from again having to reject Nic's offer to buy her lunch. He gave a pout, looked your outfit up and down, and asked if you were her replacement.

Just for the day, you said.

And what do you usually do around here?

Research and writing, you replied. *And I edit the catalog texts.* You indicated the wall of books behind Sylvie's desk, and Nic shifted to peer through the line of white orchids.

This is the current exhibition. You handed him a book, its hard cover embossed with the gallery's logo. No one actually bought the catalogs. Helene instructed Sylvie to evaluate visitors for relative financial and/or cultural capital and, if worthy, to give them a catalog for free. *To make our client base feel appreciated,* Helene said. *And to show that the gallery is passionate about fostering the intellectual and poetical aspects of the arts.*

Nic held the book as if it had been beamed down from outer space and was dripping alien goo, turning it over in his hands without opening it. *Research and writing?* He was skeptical. *You mean marketing. You write press releases?*

Among other things.

So, you're a copywriter.
I write lots of kinds of texts.
He paused, opening the catalog's cover and licking his fingers to unstick the pages. *If you'll bear with me, there's an important distinction.* He stepped back from the counter, the catalog in his hands, as if to get a better look at you. You were uninteresting. His unfixed gaze landed on the wall of catalogs. *I'll write a review of this show, for example. I'm going to write my own thoughts and opinions. That's the point of criticism, to present a singular, but unbiased, view. It's outside the realm of the transactional. It's a pure judgment. When you get paid to write a press release, or make one of these books, you're spinning a narrative to sell gallery inventory. You can dress it up in academic language all you like. But it's instrumental, at the end of the day. Like prostitution.*
You didn't respond. After another moment of wet-fingered flipping, he wedged the book between two orchids, tossed his scarf over his shoulder and, heaving himself against the heavy door, left.

When you returned to your desk in the afternoon, you stared at the catalogs for the next exhibition in their mute brown boxes, sealed and stamped in two languages from international travel. You had written these books, written the catalog texts, the introduction by Helene and the neatly laid-out and illustrated chronology of the artist. The main essay by Professor _____, who had been busy, much too busy to compile his notes into a proper text, *but perhaps you'd like to take a stab at it.* You took a stab at it, scrapping his notes and inventing anew, and he thanked you for being *a wonderful copy editor* and *barely touching my words at all,* and you sealed the envelope for his $7,000 fee and instructed the designer as to how large, precisely, the byline should be. You paid for image rights, checked captions and citations, organized the material in chronological order, situated the story you'd created into the larger story, the better story, the story of art. You wrote the press release, made up quotes about how pleased the gallery was, *so pleased,* to represent the artist, and how thrilled the estate was, *so thrilled,* to work with the gallery. You drafted sales pitches and highlights lists, conducted interviews from the gallery owner's email address with

[184   ]

reporters who addressed you as Helene. *Dear Helene.* The exhibition would be good. The work would sell. You hadn't seen any of the paintings in the book in person. You hadn't needed to—for you, language wrote itself.

The catalogs stared back at you, stupid lumps. You didn't need to open the boxes. They'd look like all the others: printed and bound in Milan by Massimo, their front covers a detail of the show's most expensive painting, the essay wearing Professor _____'s name careful to emphasize that the work *playfully subverted the rigid codes of body, identity, and representation.* You'd always liked to stand next to the subversive.

You gathered your belongings, avoiding the gaze of the boxes, not telling Sylvie or Helene or anyone. You left in the middle of the workday. The afternoon was cold and bright. You walked to a nearby bookstore and browsed the aisles with clear, unhurried intent. You texted Ted as a barrage of calls and emails from the gallery came through.

You should get out of there for a while, he wrote. *Tell them you need a break. Take a vacation.* The speech bubble next to his name paused, and then: *You have rent for the next few months?*

Sure, you had just enough.

Good, he responded. *You won't have to worry about money for anything else.*

7

That night, Nic appeared in your dreams, legs crossed on a conference table, big shoes, sharing his thoughts on how you might spend your idle hours. *You could take up writing,* he said, *and I mean real writing. You could write a story about your new friend. You know, seventy-five percent of the MFA students in this city are bankrolled by rich parents. Trust-fund patronage. You've got an interesting deal with this shoplifter. Different. But you'll have to find your voice, first. Your sentenc-*

es are too long. Adjectives all over the place. Lots of semicolons. Time to use your own words. But you hadn't realized that words could be owned.

In another dream, Nic sat in the dining car of a train, smoking at a small café table. Two women, their faces turned from you, sat across from him. Your manager had installed herself at a table nearby. You overheard Nic ask her about the recent exhibitions, reviews, reception from collectors and museums. She responded, mentioning you and Sylvie, and Nic said in French (you don't know French, and so of course dream-Nic said this in English, but you knew it to be French), *ah, yes, your underlings.* He turned and looked at you, the underling, and asked, *and what about you; on what are you working so hard?* You understood the importance of responding with a well-timed joke, a touch of your hand to your chin. You told him you were writing a sociological case study of yourself.

After ignoring you for a few minutes to chat, again, with your manager in French, refresh a round of drinks, Nic twisted to look at you and asked if the study might include fictional elements—records of dreams, for example, or fantasized figments. Perhaps a scene in which the main character encounters replicas of herself. A scene in which, in fact, she finds other women who share her face. *Of course* there was such a scene, you responded. In fact, you'd already written it.

The scene you told him you wrote in the dream:

> You, an art history graduate student, had been asked by the MFA students to visit their studios, critique their work. You were sitting alone with a painter whose gimmick was that he ironically replicated modernist paintings of women by Matisse, Manet, Picasso, Gauguin, the Surrealists, and so on; in his work, though, all the women were rendered with the same face, driving home that the artists had all been painting some universal *objet petit a*, a shared sub-conscious desire for the eternal feminine, which had been erased in reality by the demands and new sexual

distributions of Euromerican modernity. The student spoke eloquently. He had read his Lacan. You nodded, took notes, extemporized smartly about theories of representation, about how, today, it's considered impossible to ethically represent and so one must either mine old images to offer critiques or attempt to do away with representation altogether. *Precisely*, he agreed. *Representation is only ever a will to dominance or a return to some nonexistent innocence, and so, of course, the modernists' subjects are only ever a manifestation of their own wills. These women, they are ignored in themselves.* That hadn't been what you were saying, not exactly, but you didn't correct him. Perhaps, in sculpture, someone like Louise Bourgeois gets outside this, you suggested. He considered this, but decided he did not like Bourgeois's work. Too on-the-nose, he said. Or Adrian Piper, in performance, you offered. He scoffed. *I've heard she's difficult.* He wanted to show you his own canvases, which were leaning against the studio walls with their backsides to you, each stamped in ragged cursive with his full name and, underneath, date of completion. He turned the paintings one by one. The women were in disguise: in a bright skirt and cloche, hands squarely on armrests; in loose pants and a diaphanous silk tunic, transparent, her arms over her head; in a long dress, pastel pink, with flowers in her hair. Upon close examination, you noticed small flourishes, props and products and books lying on tables and paintings hanging on walls. The women lived inside agglomerations of everything that ever was, and yet they were fascinatingly empty. As he aimed each large painting toward you, you realized with concealed alarm that all the women shared your face. You'd never seen him before, but he'd seen you. He'd been painting you. And so, you realized, he was wrong—there *was* an eternal form without content, a body lacking interiority, and it was you.

Nic praised the scene. *Much better than that drivel in the exhibition catalog,* he said. You were pleased with yourself. You had invented the thing on the spot to make him happy, and it paid off. You could do good work. Good job, a good girl, a proficient writer. All the better if the critic lent his assistance. After all, you didn't have much to say.

You looked up to find a plate of chocolates before you on the table. *From the gentleman in the suit,* the waiter said, indicating Nic, who winked. Although he'd ordered them for you (*a treat,* he mouthed), you knew you shouldn't eat them. You were quite certain that Nic was the type of man who preferred women never eat, not even on their birthdays.

Your manager yammered on about the details of your assignments. The gallery would keep you very busy, she said. Even on sabbatical. You certainly wouldn't have time to fritter away composing outlines or doing formal research for your autoethnography.

The women at Nic's table turned to you, perhaps to ask about your plans to balance work and life, and you realized that they, too, shared your face. In fact, all the women on the train (save for your manager, gloating and large) shared your face. They were all writing the same sociological case study you were writing, Nic offering each one of them advice, sharing one's idea for a scene with another, entertaining a different-but-same woman every night. *Isn't it what you wanted?* Nic asked, surprised. *Getting rid of yourself. True exchangeability.* You pushed the chocolates away and tried to stand, but the chair stopped short, fixing you in position. You watched, half-standing, legs cramping, as the dining car filled with vibrant, well-groomed women all wearing the same pale face, the face you thought was your own, all investigating the same self, the self you thought was your own, all entertained and charmed by the brilliant Nic.

8

You two look exactly alike!

You had tried to make it clear to Ted over the course of several weeks that you were not jealous of Virginia, no, and although, yes, you agreed that it would be understandable if you were to feel that way, no, you were not particularly suspicious of their friendship, and no, did not want to meet her just to *confirm everything's kosher,* and yes, felt perfectly comfortable that his ex remain a nebulous figure in the back of your mind, and sure, while his concerns were kind, it wasn't as if the two of you were in an exclusive relationship, anyway. He made a startled little deer face at that last remark and said, simply, *all right.* Still, when you saw two thin arms attached to two pale hands clasping the steering wheel of a car he'd promised was *borrowed from a friend* for a day trip upstate, you knew he'd won.

The resemblance is uncanny! I can't believe I didn't notice it until just now. Ted opened the back door to Virginia's Corolla. He was delighted, ostensibly by your and Virginia's resemblance. Really, though, he seemed delighted with himself.

Valerie is a decade younger, said Virginia, tapping clean fingernails against the steering wheel.

You look like sisters, then! Ted replied, still satisfied.

Little sisters sit in the backseat. Virginia announced that she wanted to go to a museum in the Hudson Valley and, as she navigated the Bronx, Ted fiddled with the radio, switching between an evangelical sermon and a light rock station until Virginia pressed the thing off, stating flatly that she would tolerate no further mental colonization by either Chip Ingram or Phil Collins.

Did you look like Virginia? She hadn't yet turned around fully, but at the mention of *sisters* shot you a grin in the rearview mirror. Dark lipstick partitioned large teeth from white cheeks. You bared your own teeth at the car's window, checking yours against hers. Truth be told, you weren't sure what you looked like anymore. In the weeks before your sabbatical, the gallery's kitchen had overflowed with a glut of champagne truffles and cheese platters sent by clients for the holidays, and Françoise had routinely tempted you to stay late with offers of dinner from the bistro across the street. In your final week, unlimited Veal Bolognese in exchange for a Frank Stella sales note, pronto. *Arbeit Macht Frei*, the painting was called. *Work will set you free.* Françoise asked if you might please downplay the fact that Stella had lifted the title from the Nazi motto above the gate at Auschwitz. *Helene says it's too negative*, she reported, delivering the week's third Bolognese. In the morning, eyes weary and stomach heavy, you squinted into the bathroom mirror at your image, a ten-pounds heavier employee bloated from cranking out purple prose in exchange for calories. Or, it might have been all the palmier cookies and burrata Ted had deposited in your kitchen last week. You were having a hard time assimilating all these little luxuries, these minor coercions. Your face looked blurry.

Virginia drove the wooded highway in relaxed silence while Ted entertained you, inventing stories about the drivers of passing cars. You laughed on cue, studying Virginia, instead. She was slight and bony, with neatly cropped reddish hair and veiny wrists. She had a precise face. Your mind fed you the phrase *finely wrought*. This, you guessed, might be a still-further life stage, something you'd come into with age (or perhaps sooner, with significantly fewer opportunities, now, to dine on $50 pastas and *Arbeit Macht Frei*). According to your iPhone's health-tracking app, one's body was a personal possession to be guarded and cultivated. Really, though, your own felt entirely programmed, your cells ghostwriting a future in which you came to resemble Virginia more than your younger self. The perfectibility of a body's days (calories in, calories out; a Pilates class here, a colonic there), you thought, culminated only in its eventual death.

Ted tells me you work at a gallery, Virginia said. You replied that you were on an unpaid sabbatical, and she *mmm*-ed perfunctorily.

Virginia's a film scholar, Ted offered. *She's getting her PhD*, but Virginia announced she'd rather listen to religious loonies than talk about her degree.

Stealing

When Virginia slowed the car to pay a toll, Ted jumped out of the passenger seat and ran around the back of the car. *What the fuck is he doing?* you asked, but Virginia just smirked. Ted swept up plentiful coins from the pavement beside the toll machine with his hands, miming victory and pointing finger guns at you and Virginia through the car's windows. *We're rich*, he said, back in the passenger seat, laughing his strange, exclamation-point laugh. He spent the next mile counting coins into orderly piles on his lap before dumping them onto the car's floor. *Seven seventy-six, Valerie! Did you see that? We made money off of that toll!*

The museum's facade was squat and administrative, covered in a protective layer of snow. Inside, though, the space was huge and bright. Virginia's Corolla had neatly partitioned your three bodies, with driver, passenger, and backseat rider sorted into separate seats, discrete roles. The museum offered no such sanctioned places to stand or sit, no roadmaps guiding your way: only one massive, evenly lit room after another. You couldn't look at Ted without thinking about stealing or sex. You couldn't look at Virginia without thinking about the generic future you'd become. You fidgeted, nervous. You had to find some other way for your bodies to relate.

Virginia studied a laminated card, arms folded against her abdomen, slouching. She seemed like the kind of woman who was ambivalent about stealing and sex, or at least ambivalent about Ted. She wouldn't be caught wanting. *Most men prefer a woman who won't be caught wanting*, you told yourself, rationalizing that Ted, with his cowboy boots and frantic eyes and pretty mouth, was not *most men*. Still, a face like Virginia's was a judgment in itself. She made wanting seem vulgar. In the first gallery, John Chamberlain titled a mutilated automobile painted monochrome black *Norma Jean*. An effigy for a woman who wouldn't stop wanting. *I am a crashed car smushed to be neatly compact*, you thought. It was a lot of work, keeping your mind and body tightly wrapped up. Ted snuck behind you to pinch at your sides, making you squeal like a child, then stood with Virginia in front of the tallest sculpture, talking quietly as she waved her laminated card around. You trailed behind, watching. *Valerie, come on!* called Ted, and a museum guard made a shushing noise. Like a good child, you trotted their way.

In the next room, an old man tried to throw a crumpled water bottle into a polished metal box. Two guards rushed over, their Walkie-Talkies buzzing static and thumping against their sides. They whispered emphatically that patrons should *please not touch the art,* and the man scooped his water bottle from the box, again touching the art. *Not my fault that the art looks like a garbage can,* he mumbled, embarrassed. Ted strangled a laugh and checked your face, finding amusement. Virginia surveyed the scene, impassive. You decided that her silence was noble. She didn't judge the man for mistaking the sculpture for a trash bin, nor the artist for making sculptures that resembled trash bins. She was an anthropologist, detachedly observing what happens when two cultures collide. You put it together hours later that Ted must have learned the location of Donald Judd's studio from Virginia. You hadn't been seduced by him at all. He'd only been a ventriloquist proxy for this watchful statue of a woman, this academic ex.

Ted charted a route back to New York that hit all the major tolls; his victory dance grew lackluster after the sixth stop but, by the time you reached the Bronx, he'd made $24.53 in spare change and offered to buy a round of drinks. Virginia parked at a near-empty dive and Ted sprang out of the car and sprinted down the street, calling that he'd *be there in ten.* Nothing he did surprised Virginia. She watched him run in his cowboy boots as if he were a video installation. *It's because she spent the afternoon looking at art,* you justified. The eye gets trained to look in a certain way.

A TV hung above the bar's liquor rack, bathing Virginia's face in blue light. She ordered three pints and set her credit card on the bar, checked her phone, fixed her gaze upon the screen.

Do you think Ted's some kind of romantic? she asked you, eyes on a sallow billionaire's talking head. The billionaire explained that he was the victim of a years-long smear campaign. *I am the real tar-*

get, he repeated. His face was immobile save for a jaw that churned like that of a wooden puppet. *Change the channel*, another patron complained. *I see enough of this fucker on the posters at work.*

Did you think Ted was a romantic? You had no markers upon which to triangulate his social position: no job title, no stable residence to situate him in a neighborhood or scene, even his clothes stolen, selected for pocket size more than personal taste. It wasn't that he was unknowable. A cryptic backstory, an attractive and intermittently manic man who reveled in getting away with too much. Sure, then, a romantic.

Virginia dabbed a spot of beer from the bar. *Sorry*, she said. *You don't have to answer. That way we pass the Bechdel test.* She neatly folded her napkin and turned her attention, again, to the screen. Hurricanes had flooded a city thousands of miles away; people stood on their rooftops with signs spelling *HELP*. Elsewhere in the world, a river of protestors marched to a city square, where they burned candles, linked arms, chanted and swayed. *Later that day*, a severe, pink-lipped brunette reported, the same protesters ran, backs turned to cops in military gear with their guns pointed, safeties off. A factory collapsed; a man was elected. Fires, both natural and manmade, scorched the hills. Ted joined you at the bar, his torso bulky and emitting telltale clinks. He drank and rambled about the televised tragedies, used the words *innate evil*. Virginia got cross, told him there was *no such thing*, that he was an idiot to look for a higher power in the pendulum swings of history. Still, she said, she understood—really, she did—why Ted said *innate evil*. *It would be torture to watch this ongoing catastrophe and feel personally implicated, like its witness. Its perpetrator, even. Because it doesn't stop; does it? The blue glow just keeps going until I feel so sick or so stuffed that I turn it off or turn away.*

Right, said Ted, smirking. *Because you're innately evil.*

No. Virginia drummed her fingers, hard, against her pint glass. *Because I don't want to be locked into a technology-induced spin cycle of despair and apathy.*

Big sister and big brother are at it again, you told yourself, amused, sipping your beer and watching the television. The pink-lipped reporter gave you a conspiratorial look. *They're both right, you know*, she said.

Really? you asked.

Sure, she said. *He's right about the evil. Pending some massive upheaval of every existing fact of existence, it's basically preprogrammed. I can reliably expect at least fifteen reportable tragedies per week. But*, she continued, *she's right to want to turn me off.* She shuffled papers on her desk, glanced at a teleprompter over your head. *Don't tell my boss I said that. Bad for ratings, telling my own viewers to turn off their TVs. Anyway. Network performance metrics aside, doesn't it make you nervous? Ted and Virginia arguing like a married couple?*

I'm letting go of proprietary notions of romance, you responded.

She snorted, a string of brown hair falling from her hairsprayed shell. *You're kidding yourself*, she said, and you told her that you hadn't consented to an interview, so thank you, but goodbye.

During a commercial break, Virginia excused herself to *use the ladies' room* and Ted squeezed your knee, bit your earlobe, told you he thought it was *going very well.* You looked down at the bar to find that he'd had refilled your and Virginia's glasses to the brim from a bottle tucked into his jeans. The bartender's back was turned. He, too, watched the screen.

9

See? said Ted. You weren't sure what you were supposed to see. You hadn't yet had a cup of coffee or put in your contacts, and your internal dialogue and guts were jumbled from that morning's sex. Ted liked to fuck lazily before dawn, a sleepy, noiseless animal, rummaging nocturnal for comfort or food. You stared at a wren pecking the window of the Cobble Hill loft Ted was house-sitting that week. It stared back.

Like I told you, Ted continued, propping himself on an elbow.

There's nothing between Virginia and me. It's radio static. Finito. A dead line.
    When you recounted the day at the museum to Leila, though, she was skeptical. *In my professional opinion,* she said, ashing a cigarette into a succulent beside her bed, *they're still together, and you're the dash of spice they're adding to their...whatever. Soufflé. If you were my client, I'd say you were headed for a big, steaming mess.*

10

From: director@IWCgallery.com
Sent: Tuesday, April 28, 2015 4:04 PM
To: Valerie@IWCgallery.com
Subject: Your sabbatical

Dear Valerie,

I hope this email finds you.

We had absolute chaos today because Helene was unhappy with the latest press release. It was written by Sylvie, and very well, but Helene panicked and said it wasn't in the voice of the gallery. She asked me to write to you to see if you could kindly do us the favor of drafting press releases for the next few fairs and exhibitions. She's concerned that assigning gallery writing to Sylvie, or attempting to hire and train a new writer, will only result in hours of wasted time with no useable text to show for it. She feels that you are the gallery's voice, and I'm afraid she won't be pleased with content produced by anyone else.

As was articulated in your employment contract, Helene considers you an integral part of the IWC family.

She asked me to remind you that we've spent a lot of money and effort cultivating your voice and supporting you in your gallery writing. She'd like to offer the possibility of your name appearing on the colophon page of the next catalog on which you work, if you'd like. I know you said you'd be on sabbatical for a few months, and I know we agreed to a brief leave of absence, and I know—I know—that it's only been three weeks, but Helene will offer a dollar a word for you to produce a few brief texts for us while you're away. By the way—I ran into your Professor _____ last night at the Guggenheim opening. He told me about his new project, not sure if it's a novel or a memoir, maybe an autofiction type of thing about a young woman conning an aging intellectual. Juicy stuff. He confessed that you haven't been responding to his emails, either, and, frankly, expressed concern for your mental stability. We agreed that you are the most proficient copy editor we have ever had. Your interventions are so minimal and clean. You have a wonderful grasp of grammar and a real eye for typos. It seems that his work is going well. His book of interviews is just about ready for publication, but I'm sure you knew that already. He said you gave it a final look-over for him. He's such a brilliant critical mind. I bet the interviews are fascinating. You're lucky you got a sneak peek, so to speak.

Again, please do let me know as soon as possible if you'll kindly do us the favor of a few small writing assignments. Helene and I hope it might help you— and all of us here at the gallery—get back on track.

Yours,
Linda

Linda Schaffer
Senior Director
IWC Gallery
930 Park Avenue, New York, NY
www.IWCgallery.com

11

You and Julie played games after school until the summer she turned eleven. Fantastic games, elaborate and long, which could extend for days, roles and situations shifting without care for consistency. You both knew the basic outlines of a few available stories, and within their structure you could dose yourselves with entire worlds of feeling.

You set the roles, usually having to do with 1) who was the authority and who subservient; 2) who was the man and who the woman; 3) who was good and who evil; 4) who was normal and who was strange. Julie had to learn to quickly adapt. She was to be the *good daughter* of a thirteenth-century feudal serf, caught in a complex web of interactions with the estate's lord. She was to be the *evil witch* seducing young women away from unhappy marriages and domineering fathers to teach them herb growing and spell casting and the intoxicating pull of dancing round a fire, worshipping only that which they could feel within their own bodies. She was to be the *good wife* who rescued her politician husband's reputation, stood by his side in a horrible time of scandal when his image was threatened and his word was all he could own. (It was enough.) She was to be a *small deer frightened by evil coyotes*, and she paused and asked, *evil?* and you got annoyed, *yes, of course, evil.* She was to be *moss spreading on a rock upon which the other characters sat*, neither good nor evil this time, *of course.* But if the coyotes were evil, why wasn't the moss, oppressive as it spread to kill other plants in its path? The question was an important one: she couldn't play her character without knowing where it stood.

Julie was both what you created and herself at the same time. When she didn't like the games you set, she staged small insurrections: *I don't want to play by these stupid rules anymore.* And so you'd shift the rules, expand the game. Narratives were necessary only insofar as they demanded experiment. They collapsed into specificity and scenes and figures all too easily, and, luckily, it was quite conceivable that Julie would be a Ming-Dynasty aristocrat at the same time as a minnow in the pond who was then suddenly a milkmaid gathering flowers in feudal England who improbably loved a murderous fascist during World War II before coming to her senses, stabbing him at night.

You lay in bed after hours of playing and imagined the cosmos, imagined yourself a small speck on a small speck, each speck inconsequential and rapidly moving even then, even through you, despite all evidence that your body was solid and still. There could be no way, when you expanded the universe to the limits of your imagination, that it respected any law or moral system you could imagine. And so all you had, all you knew, must have, at some point, been made up.

In the games, you might breathlessly intone, *look, over there, did you see that,* and Julie would grow silent, fearful, glance around the woods for enemies behind every tree, just out of sight. There was no way to know if you remained in the same time and place as that of your house, your parents, the concrete walls of your school. In the game, there were no markers or clocks. Time didn't exist.

And then there were games you did not invent, but learned. You'd sit beside Julie on the driveway and ask: *truth or dare?* It was difficult to know which was more dangerous. Dares stretched the limits of what could be done with the body, while truths tested the borders of what could be spoken out loud. Neither could be taken back.

Another game you learned: Julie would hold her breath as long as possible while counting cars that passed. If seven cars passed, she would fall in love the following week. If more than ten cars passed, you would pass your science exam. If no cars passed, one of you would die. Your predictions banished the logic of cause and effect: Truth could be known all at once, like lightning, chains of chance linking one reality to the next.

Your grandmother caught you playing the chance game and scolded: *You're playing God, daring the future to change like that.* You squinted your eyes, making the outline of her permed hair, her birdlike hands and khaki slacks, skew and distort.

12

After a particularly successful trip to the midtown West Elm with Ted, you dropped a set of crystal champagne glasses, a ceramic planter, and a tiny gold-plated wall clock with no numbers on Julie's bed. *How can you afford all of this?* she asked. *You don't have money.*

I didn't buy it, Jules.

The next morning, over coffee, she told you that she'd stolen recently, too. A lime-green minidress from Anthropologie. *No one was looking,* she said. *There's no point in buying when you know you won't get caught.*

13

For Ted, it began with two rolls of toilet paper from the basement supply closet. The maintenance guy had left the door unlocked and it was cold outside and he'd had four or five beers. He didn't want to go to the CVS. It was late. He couldn't find his wallet. And his landlord had set the rent too high, anyway.

How old were you?

Probably seventeen or so, the first time I lived alone.

A half-empty bottle of Clorox All-Purpose Spray from a restaurant bathroom. He put it in his armpit and it leaked all over, turning the lining of his coat a kind of acid yellow and his pants, too, when it dripped, slow, the entire walk home.

Towels, hundreds of towels from the downtown YMCA. One day, he wrapped his track shorts and dirty T-shirt in a towel from the plastic-wrapped stack in the locker room, too small to cover his body but rough and absorbent and, best of all, free. He stuffed the damp bundle in his bag and took it home. He repeated the routine the next day, and the day after that, and then every time he went to the YMCA. By the end of the year, he had a waist-high stack, washed and folded and tottering beside his bed.

At some point, though, he stopped having a bed and stopped having an apartment. He returned the towels to the gym and gave his bookshelves to a friend and put the secondhand sofa, ripped, on the curb. He slept on his friend's couch next to the shelves that had once been his, and after a few weeks it was obvious to everyone that he'd been stuffing his dirty laundry behind the books. He didn't have enough cash to wash it. One morning, when his friend left for work, he threw out the old clothes and stole a four-pack of T-shirts from the Walgreens and, from then on, *laundry* meant a trip to the dumpster and the store.

And even when you got a little cash, you didn't stop throwing out shirts, added Virginia. *You don't have a maintenance sensibility.* Ted laughed. In his view, it was a habit. He liked having habits. He liked having T-shirts, too. Some were soft with designer labels, some cheap and starchy, some near-translucent, gossamer. He kept them at your house and let you wear whichever ones you wanted, even the nice ones.

If you don't have an apartment, you don't have to pay rent. If you don't pay rent, you don't have to work. If you don't work, you have a lot of free time for more creative pursuits. That's what Ted said. It turned out, though, that he spent most of his time stealing food and arranging a place to sleep for the night. Ted had lots of friends. He had friends he didn't want to have, friends with large couches who took long vacations and bought expensive knick-knacks. Ted was always available to talk, so they called him when they had dilemmas such as: Bacaro or Odeon for dinner? To splurge or not on the Saarinen chair? Would a $3,000 ashtray be gauche?

You're at the Design Within Reach on Greene? Ted asked. *I'll be there in five. We can take a look.*

Five always meant twenty-five or thirty, but Ted's friends didn't mind. People too rich or poor for jobs have a different relationship to time, an internal clock that isn't wound to the pulsing rhythm of the email alert, the cash register, the end-of-shift meeting. At the store, Ted helped his friends decide on the armchair, the floor lamp, the espresso machine. It was nice, yes, and he'd help them load it into the car, sure, stuffing his pants with novelties on the way. On the morning of the Crate and Barrel ottoman, he dropped two salt-and-pepper shakers, little ceramic birds on rocking-horse runners, into his pocket. He left them on your countertop the next day, useless but nice.

Other things Ted has stolen: a bottle of champagne, real champagne, in full view of the clerk at the wine store. He chatted with her about vintages and complimented her taste while you stumbled, distracted, your email pinging to announce a missing person, then *hot new restaurants in your area*, then the possibility of *Love Fraud! They're all around us; they look just like us, but they live to exploit us. Click here for a discount. Make your love life a safer place.* By the time you looked up from your screen, the Dom Perignon was tucked in Ted's coat. He tucked you under his other arm, waved at the clerk, and walked you and the champagne outside.

A fur coat on the day you cried about your student loans. The winter wind returned in late April to hurl itself against your windows and the heat in your apartment was broken all month. *And the bathroom floor is rotting*, Leila reminded you, but you told her to focus on the problem at hand. You sat in the kitchen with the oven at 450° and all four burners on and called the super over and over, but he didn't answer, and when your phone finally rang it was Sallie Mae reminding you to make a payment and you yelled at the woman who said her name was *Sheila* and you hung up, felt bad, dialed Ted, who said he'd *be there right away*. Four hours later, he and Virginia walked in and told you to close your eyes. You heard Ted's cowboy boots smack across the floor. He hung the coat, heavy, on your shoulders. It smelled like an animal. *It is an animal,* Virginia, still standing in the doorway, confirmed.

That evening, Leila cornered you to ask what Ted's mother looked like. *Ted's mom cleans hotel rooms in Vegas,* Virginia had told you the previous week, but you didn't know anything about her name or her face. *Why do you want to know?* you asked Leila. *Oedipal complex,* she said. *You and Virginia look suspiciously alike.*

Vitamins from Whole Foods: biotin, collagen, a canister labeled *Glow Matrix*. *If a burglar broke in, they'd think this stuff was mine,* you said when Ted asked to keep the stash under your bathroom sink. You were ashamed at that desire, the desire to be beautiful, to have beautiful hair and skin and teeth. Why did Ted take the supplements? No big surprise. He wasn't ashamed. He wanted to be beautiful while he was alive.

On a Tuesday trip to Dean & Deluca, you asked him, *are you afraid of being caught?*

He laughed. *I lie awake at night and sweat.* A two-pound bag of pistachios, eight crème de menthe truffles. *I'm serious, you know,* he said.

On a Thursday afternoon in early May before traipsing across the street to meet Virginia for a movie, rain numbing the dull gray sun: a bag of kettle corn, blue-cheese-stuffed peppers, two packets of curried chicken salad, and a hunk of salami. You stood at the olive bar behaving badly, skewering sundried tomatoes and drunken artichoke hearts with a toothpick and feeding them into your oily mouth. Virginia bought the movie tickets while Ted procured a bottle of wine. The trailers played and he poured three plastic cups, returned the previous day's question to you. *What about you; are you ever afraid?*

The golds and whites of an onscreen car crash collided with your face as you looked straight ahead. Fear or not, there was no way you could stop. How long had it been? Two and a half months? But, see, if you stopped now, there'd be no secret underneath your pristine surface, no precious awareness that, even as the managers nod and the security guards slouch, your pockets are stuffed, you're an insatiable thief. Plus, food goes bad and fashion moves quickly. If you stopped, your fridge would soon empty and your clothes would grow frumpy and, within a few months, you'd have to purchase, again, all the requisites required to fabricate a life. Can you imagine how much that would cost? The bank account necessary to stay *au courant*?

On an evening in mid-May, Virginia was sitting in your kitchen, painting her toes and talking absentmindedly about a different film, one you hadn't seen. The director played the main character, a wandering woman. Virginia thought she was *more real in her film than she was in her life*. You waited for her to pause before asking, *how much do you think you and Ted have stolen, cumulatively?*

She laughed. *You want to know our number?*

Yes, you told her, you did. You wanted to break it down, write it out, make it all add up. When you'd worked at the gallery, you often sat with two documents open on your computer: 1) an employment letter offering you thirty-eight grand a year for *approximately sixty hours a week, although the employee will be expected to attend evening and weekend events in accordance with the gallery's exhibition schedule, and will be expected to complete all unfinished tasks from home (please note that all work produced by the employee during their term of employment, whether during work hours or not, will be considered the property of the gallery)*; 2) the gallery's current inventory, titled *Price List*. The first time you'd played the add-it-up game, an exhibition of tiny marble sculptures—snowmen and Buddhas and fairyland animals and naked women sitting right on the polished concrete floor—was on view. You had to hop over them to get to your desk. Each one cost eight grand, ten grand, though some were upwards of eleven, twelve. The snowman with the protruding penis and jaunty hat. The rabbit whose every strand of fur was flawlessly carved. You picked a group of three or four sculptures from inventory and added them up to thirty-eight grand, gaggles of goblins equal to yourself. The next exhibition was *Warhol's Most Wanted Men*. You pulled up the price list, typed equations into Google, saw each silkscreened face worth eight-hundred of your life.

Virginia finished lacquering her left foot, blew on her toes. *I don't know our number*, she said. *Sorry. At a certain point, I lost count.* She set to work on her right foot. *Even if I knew, I wouldn't tell you. Can't have that information hanging around in your head if you ever get questioned by the cops.*

($150 × 75) + $723, you entered into Google the next day, accounting only for yourself. *Shit*, Leila said when you told her the sum. *In less than three months? Do you really need more? Don't you think you have enough?*

But who could say what *need* was in a world so overstuffed? You took two novels from a bookstore, only one of which you wanted. A tub of peanut butter, a set of wireless headphones, a bottle of Clinique exfoliator, $28.50, of which Ted used the bulk. You smelled it while he slept, synthetic jasmine, your face pressed to his dark, unkempt curls.

On a Sunday afternoon in Park Slope, the sky promising only rain, you: three avocados, a carton of raspberries, a packet of organic hamburger meat, a bag of specialty popcorn. Ted: three tall cans of beer, one jar of kimchi, a package of marshmallow cremes, a bag of pork rinds. Virginia: two tins of smoked trout, a jar of curry paste, a little bag of bath salts.

Did you know that babies take whatever they want, whenever they want? It's an innate human impulse. It's buying that's not natural. Do you think that's why we do it? Do you think it's in our genes to want all this stuff?

Virginia made a face. *Look around, Valerie. You think you're a Paleolithic woman picking berries off bushes? $32.99 for Madagascar vanilla extract; are you kidding me? You think you'd want this if it didn't exist?*

Hand-painted rice bowls from Williams Sonoma. *Did you know that one of Freud's students thought women shoplifted from department stores when, really, they wanted to grab penises? I read it yesterday. 'The women want to take hold of something forbidden, secretly.'*

Ted's grin bounced right through you. *Oh, really.* He steered your bodies from Virginia's view and slid a hand into your jeans. It was wonderful to be touched.

Sometimes, to atone for your sins, you were prudent and restrained. You stood before the filets mignons and strip steaks and ribeyes surveying prices: *$17.99/lb, $22.49/lb, $29.99/lb.* When you shopped with Ted and Virginia, prices didn't exist—or, if they did, it was only to advertise which among the things was the best, which item Ted would slip into his pants or Virginia her coat. Alone and saintly, you tucked a flank steak into your bag, *$12.99/lb.* No one could say you were the bad one. No one could accuse you of wanting too much.

On a smudgy, orange evening in late May, Virginia again asked if you thought Ted was a romantic. Before you could reply, she stated bluntly, *he's not.*

She was writing a dissertation on verité filmmakers of the seventies. *They refused to distinguish art from labor from life,* she said. *Their idea of filmmaking was so close to the everyday that ideas of work and art disappear.* Artists today could only ever achieve a hollow replica of what the seventies filmmakers had done. *Ted used to say he was interested in the "experiment" of living without a home, without money. Like poverty was a performance. But it's not possible to be a no-job bohemian anymore.*

Why? you asked.

Virginia shrugged. *Rising rent, for one.* She didn't feel like getting into it. She spent her time maintaining minimal credit-card debt and a one-room sublet and institutional credentials. It was tenuous, but it was enough. *That's why he keeps me around,* she stated, matter of fact. *For when shit gets tough.*

14

The weather turned in early June. It was a mild, windless night, and you walked toward the Chelsea apartment Ted was staying in.

A tall man in a newsstand made hissing noises at you from behind rows of bubblegum and roasted cashews and glossy magazines advertising gardens and motorboats and weightlifting and sex. *Why waste time trying to discover the truth when you can so easily create it?* a politician in a blue suit wondered on the front page of the daily. Elsewhere on the page, there were nighttime bombings. Funding was cut. Development continued. The protests had stopped. These problems, large and public. Should you buy the paper? Should you steal it, instead? You paid 75¢ for an apple. You'd become so cocooned in your rich life with Ted and Virginia that walking without them felt lonely. The people on the sidewalk continued onward through history. Sheets of narrative massed around you, pressing in.

Maybe Leila was right: you were only a minor player in Ted and Virginia's drama. Maybe you and Virginia were both minor players in Ted's drama with his mom. Freud offered only more narratives hidden from view, plots to unearth and bring to light. You were tired of paranoia. You wanted to live without the mental strain of connecting dots, splicing surfaces, discovering causes and effects. You bit into the apple, chewing something plasticky along with its waxy skin. *Argentina 4093*, a spit-mangled sticker announced. You flicked it to the curb and the tall news-seller scowled. You scowled back. The city scintillated around you, surreal. Why bother uncovering your actual role in Ted and Virginia's story when you could just invent one for yourself?

Making your way west, you studied balled-up fast-food containers and cigarette stubs and discarded coupon booklets at the sidewalk's edge. Each block a social microcosm, sortable by police presence and income bracket. Chicken bones and potholes on Ninth and 19th: the city didn't care, siphoned that block's budget off to baton-carrying cops. Streetlight filtering through crabapple trees lining Tenth and 21st, their pale green blossoms garnishing the sidewalk: the feel of money. You sat on the stoop of a red-doored townhouse and dialed Ted's number. The townhouse's owner, a museum curator, was returning from Beirut that evening, and you'd offered to help Ted wash sheets and scrub floors before she arrived. Across the street, a huge man, tanned and white-haired with a hard, heavy stomach, his gingham shorts showing off spindly legs, scooped a small dog's shit and glared your way.

You'd think someone rich enough to own a duplex in Chelsea would have a housekeeper, Ted said, letting you into the apartment. You remembered Helene's periodic panics and rationings at any sign of a stock-market drop. *Rich people are cheap*, you replied.

The curator had been away for three weeks, bouncing from Cape Town to Kolkata to Mexico City, collecting artists like post-cards for an upcoming show. You'd seen the previous iteration of her signature iterable exhibition, which recurred every three years. The curator curated a set of artworks concerned with ongoing humanitarian crises. Humanitarian crises made for the best art. Massive and visible suffering was outside the curator's realm of experience, and so acceptable for representing and theorizing. None of her blockbuster shows were concerned with the underlying issues that produced the sharp contrast between one city block and the next. None of the shows theorized the mundane problem of being a body that, daily, needed to feed itself, wear clothes. The actual conditions of the curator's life were off-limits for art.

Ted had already cleaned the bathrooms and ripped a stack of stolen gym towels into rags, which you took to the bedroom's parquet wood floors. You opened your phone and allowed YouTube to cycle through songs and videos, scrubbing your way past three elegantly framed photographs of drones and into the hallway. After three songs and five advertisements, you found yourself sitting near the living room's wide windows, having accidentally trapped your body in a tiny, dirty square of floor, no escape until the soapy liquid dried.

Ted had recently told you that *not buying* was the easiest way to *not exist*. It could be incidental, a condition of poverty, or strategic, or both. *Buy something; you leave a trace. Leave a trace; you exist.* Stealing was equivalent to not existing. You watched him as he cleaned. For someone who spoke so much about not existing, Ted sure existed a lot. He seemed to take real pleasure in scrubbing floors. He moved the dining room furniture to one side and stood, hands on hips and engrossed in his task, inspecting layers of accumulated dust where chairs and bar carts had stood. He poured soapy water and pushed it with a mop. He was wonderful to look at, like a painting when he was still and a dancer when he was moving. All at once, you realized how easy it was for him. Floating by on the surface, making other people want to help. You couldn't tell whether you resented him or felt envious. *Both, probably,* your narrator said.

The skin on your hands and face was coarse from cleaning products, and you told Ted that you were going to take a shower. He looked idly through the curator's fridge and selected a package of prosciutto, following you to the bathroom and peeling thin sheets from the plastic to fold into his mouth. He sat on the toilet and watched as you stripped your clothes and turned on the water extra-hot and examined the bath products, choosing the fanciest ones. He folded a piece of prosciutto into a neat square and fed it into your mouth, touching his fingers to your lips. He soaped your arms and your breasts and then kissed them, looking up at you with feverish eyes. *I am a precious object, I guess,* you thought.

You waited until your fingers were pink and swollen to towel yourself dry and put on your clothes. Ted was in the bedroom, sitting on the edge of the bare mattress, phone by his side. *She'll be home in an hour,* he said, and you collapsed onto the mattress and announced that you were too tired to do any more work. *That's fine,* he said. He picked up your shoe and began untying its laces. *You don't have to do a thing. You just lay right there.* He pulled at the shoe and you allowed your leg to bounce, heavy, against the mattress.

Look at that, Ted said, again picking up your leg to let it drop. *You'd be a great Method actor.*

Hm? You propped yourself up.

No, no, no. He knelt beside you on the mattress. *Back to sleep.* He pulled your other foot toward him and placed it in his lap, working out the sneaker's knot and loosening its laces. *You've never heard of the relaxation exercise?* You shook your head *no* with as minimal movement as possible, eyes still closed. You felt like a child. *It's one of the first things they teach you in acting school. But you don't get a thousand-dollar mattress to practice on. They give you a cheap metal chair. "If you can relax in the chair, you can relax anywhere."*

When did you go to acting school?

I didn't. I knew a woman who taught there. She let me sit in on a few classes. He wriggled the second shoe off and moved your leg in circles, clockwise, before allowing it to drop. You anticipated the drop this time and, wanting to do a good job, exaggerated its fall.

Nope, he said. No good. He picked the leg back up and dropped it again. Better. *There was one woman in the class; she was so good at the exercise that, by the end of her turn, she'd be drooling on her shirt.*

Really?

Yeah. He moved on to your arm, shaking your wrist until you felt only flesh flopping around the hard lines of your bones.

That's kind of hot.

You think so?

Sure, you said. *Being able to let go of your body to such a degree that it's an emptied-out shell. Becoming an object. Totally nonproductive.*

Hm. He pressed on your shoulder so that your torso rolled to the side and then fell, and then his hands were on your neck, fingers pressing lines over the base of your skull. You felt a sharp, almost hypnotic pain as the muscles began to surrender, heard yourself breathe a labored sigh.

I think it's stupid, the assumption that if someone's animate and blinking and nodding and doing whatever, there's a significant amount of agency involved, you said. *All action happens under some degree of coercion. I don't think you can tell from appearances how much choice is involved in a particular situation.*

He set your head on the mattress, adjusting it until you felt as still and complete as a stone effigy, and came to lay beside you, grinning and teasing at your theories. You smiled too and shut your eyes, flopping onto your back and lolling your head to the side. *You know, I am very tired. I'm not sure I can manage this conversation any longer.*

Perfect, he said. *You go right ahead and fall asleep.*

It took as much effort to affect sleep as it did, in your waking life, to affect attention: more, maybe, because this performance was new to you. You closed in on yourself and focused hard on making your body limp. How small of a space could *Valerie* take up, bound within this flesh? How tightly could you condense any will, any narrative voice, any sign of life or language? You folded yourself into a tiny compartment behind your eyes and allowed the rest of this body you called your own to be a lifeless lump. Ted, too, had transformed himself: his hands felt groping and young, a teen-ager almost sweet in his earnestness, but sweet in the way you'd learned men get when they transact that sweetness to get ahold of some part of you. The sweetness of your high-school boyfriend who repeatedly forgot not to come inside of you, performatively smacking his forehead and reminding himself out loud that you weren't on the pill only after your thighs were dripping and you were telling yourself and then him that it was okay, he'd gotten carried away, et cetera.

Ted pulled at your pants, his lips menacing and soft on your neck. He had turned himself fumbling so adeptly that it might as well have been another physical skill, the talent at feigning talent-lessness. Did you like it? You weren't sure that *liking* had much to do with it. Your mouth filled with saliva. Usually, after you'd let some guy take you way past the point of self-control, you surfaced afterward feeling a kind of superficial shame at being a girl. If you were honest with yourself, you hadn't let it happen very often, because having a body and being a girl was humiliating enough, or so you'd been told, and it seemed wise to cover yourself up with a hard exoskeleton. What had Gabby told you when you cried in the bathroom in middle school? *Turn into an armadillo. Nothing can hurt you that way.*

Emotions like shame, though—the kinds of emotions that make you cry in a bathroom—are tied up in meaning and cau-sality: *if* you do this thing or are treated this way, *then* a coherent and recognizable emotion will make itself visible. But emotions unhinged from words are simply the rising up of a certain force in your body, a swelling and tingling and compressing force. You had operated at a remove from this wordless body for so long. You had watched it on screens and in mirrors and within your own head, but you'd rarely fully submerged in it, a small animal lost and receding into the pits of your belly.

Ted rubbed himself against your hipbone in a series of short jerks and you slackened your tongue from your front teeth, taking measured and shallow, sleeplike breaths. He pressed his teeth to your neck and your eyelids fluttered like strobe lights and you caught sight of your limbs all sprawled and lolling and evacuated. You looked like a dead body, like you'd seen in photographs, bodies strewn by the bombings and shootings and drownings that marked calendar time in your world. The thought was repulsive and lacked perspective, but it felt true. You looked like the image of a corpse.

The only corpses you'd ever seen in the flesh had been painted with stage makeup, bled out and chemically recomposed: bodies hoping to fool mourners into believing they were only half dead. Their faces gave them away, though. Although they blushed artificial and serene with their silicone-pumped cheeks, the expressions they wore weren't animated by a structure or self. You knew how to do that with your own face: relaxing, unfocusing, voiding. You'd practiced in the bathroom mirror, growing up. To begin, you gave yourself a tight smile, which you slowly allowed to hollow until it was only muscle, no emotion, maniacal and false. You'd once read that smiling into a mirror tricks your brain, makes you think you're actually happy, and you become happy because of the faking. This game was nothing like that.

You'd tried for so long to be a shiny, perfect thing, to exercise or exfoliate away all the parts of you that didn't behave. But you'd never be totally healthy, nor totally plastic, and it was peculiar that the two ideals had merged into an ultimate goal in your mind. *Healthy plastic.* Ted rolled you roughly onto your stomach, and you limply complied. Television shows loved dead women, but you weren't sure if they wanted the women dead, or if they preferred them to have never been animate in the first place.

The same self-help articles that promoted *healthy plastic* advocated embracing whatever fantasies and desires you felt, pursuing them and calling it *liberation*, but this sex didn't feel like a rallying cry or an empowering march. You wanted to be debased, to be an object, a corpse. Maybe your desires were a symptom of the time in which you lived. Your need to be a murderous boomerang, to be dirty in the sense of wanting to return to the earth, to be wretched, to decompose. The only liberation you wanted was cellular liberation: to cease all productivity, to squander your energy, to slump like a carcass and rot.

Your legs twitched and hands fluttered and, all at once, the game shifted, you were alive: Ted picked your body up and set it on the floor, kneeling, and his fingers were inside you now, pressing into your guts. The object that was you reacted without your having to operate it at all.

You noticed it at first only as a pleasant sensation, a vague warmth, and then you realized that you were kneeling in liquid, your own liquid, and you felt it coursing between your thighs and soaking the fabric of your socks and pooling around your knees and he told you to spread your legs wider, said that you were soiling the floor, that you were dirty and you needed to clean it up and you wanted to, you wanted to taste it and he dipped his fingers in the liquid—maybe cum, maybe piss—and he fed his fingers into your mouth and you tasted it, and it was sharp and sweet, like brine. Then his fingers were in your mouth and you were allowing him to open your jaw and he was spitting, slow and precise, a globule from his mouth dripping down to meet yours and it was warm, very warm. It surprised you how warm it was, really. His spit didn't mix with yours, not immediately, and you couldn't say whether it had a taste of its own or if the difference was in texture, so you swished the glob around in your mouth until it had coated your teeth and gums and then you swallowed, proud, and opened your mouth to show him that you'd done it, that you wanted more. *Very good*, he said, *very good*, and his fingers were still beating a steady rhythm inside you and fluid, piss or something, you couldn't say, was sloshing from your insides in spurts. How could there be so much liquid? Where had you been storing it up?

Afterward, you lay happy and still by his side, fluid pooled now cool against your skin, and then Ted remembered the curator in a car back from the airport and the sheets still tumbling in the dryer and you mopped up your mess and sprayed some Lysol and put on your clothes, your shirt soiled from where it'd fallen on the floor, and the doorbell was ringing and Ted was pulling on pants, pushing you in the other direction, telling you to leave through the back. He'd figure out a way to help you out of the courtyard, was sure there'd be an exit and a place for you to hide, but no more questions; *please, Virginia, you really have to go.*

15

From: helene@IWCgallery.com
Sent: Monday, June 8, 2015 4:34 AM
To: valerie@IWCgallery.com
Subject: Re: Fw: Your sabbatical

valerie I see the email Linda sent last month and I see you did not respond. may I remind you that the gallery has given its all to you, and that you have a responsibility in turn to respond to emails and also do some very basic writing for me. the press releases by sylvie have been a disaster and all who read them know they are not in the voice of the gallery. i have very big interview with financial times upcoming this week and need you to conduct it for me please. call franciose urgently when you receive this message and we will work out a suitable payment for a few essays press releases interviews thank you

Helene Dupont
Founder and CEO
IWC Gallery
930 Park Avenue, New York, NY
www.IWCgallery.com

16

From: newsletter@powertactics.com
Sent: Tuesday, June 9, 2015 3:54 PM
To: valerie@IWCgallery.com
Subject: The power of a woman's natural authority

Valerie,

Do you ever feel that desire? You know what I'm talking about: the desire for direct, self-possessed, commanding presence. For the kind of authority before which men and diplomats and even their faithful dogs can't help but whimper, the type of power that angers oceans and sends herds scuttling and humbles the sky.

For many professional women, such power remains taboo. *Masculine* when wanted, *abrasive* when embodied, colleagues and combatants whisper behind the powerful woman's back that she can't possibly keep it up; she's a faker, a fraud.

Valerie, I know what that longing feels like. Eons ago, before I'd claimed my power, I felt the same longing you do. You long to know how to ask for a raise and be respected—no, *praised*—for asking. You want to persevere where others have succumbed to quivering numbness. You yearn to command the Monday meeting like a four-star general, to take no prisoners in the PowerPoint presentation, to forge ahead, battle on, fight the great and terrible where others have sat in corners, cowering, instead. You dream of staring your targets in the eye while you hit them in the heart. You thirst for the sound of missiles and bombs and explosions playing in the background, sure, whatever. You want to set impeccable, unencroachable boundaries with lovers and friends.

Valerie, you too can be a creature of war and fame. You can send a shock of fear through middle management. You can rise to the top. You need only wage war on those who would stand beside you, offering camaraderie, a balanced schedule, a helping hand. Wage war on what ails you, what fills you with wonder, fills you with doubt. You are a force of domination stalking the edges of the universe. You win at sports. Wage war on living itself.

Valerie, reclaim the authority you've abdicated since birth. Luxuriate in the unmistakable power that comes with a salary increase, a bejeweled finger, a hoard of followers who fall neatly in line. Once you've attended our latest workshop, none will stand in your way. They won't even try. Act now for an early-bird special and receive our exclusive three-day webinar, complete with daily lectures, journaling prompts, and role-playing exercises, for only $899.

xo Lisa
Founder and CEO
Power Tactics for Professional Women

17

Virginia recommended a psychic when you told her you were suffering from *depletion* or *demoralization* or *generalized malaise*. You did not want to rise to the top or claim your unshakable voice or wage war on whatever. You would prefer to be like one of her floating filmmakers. (*I warned you*, she said. *You want to be like Ted*.) She told you to renew the lease on your apartment and seek psychic guidance and texted you an East Village address, which you now checked against a sunken storefront crammed between a Planet Fitness and a laundromat. Flickering purple lights announced PSYCHIC READING * TAROT * CRYSTAL * PALM * AURA * MYSTIC VISIONS * $10 AND UP, and an eyeshadowed woman visible from the window played the part, lying on a patterned couch with a cigarette. She peered out through her smoke, raised a heavily lined eyebrow, and motioned you in. A moon-and-stars wind chime sounded when you opened the door.

How much for a basic tarot reading?

The psychic leaned against a plastic card table. It strained under her weight. *Depends on the problem you're trying to solve. Tell me, what is it you most want?*

What did you want? You thought for a moment and reported that you *wanted to find a way to inhabit the world*. The psychic asked you to be more specific. *Tell me again*, she said, shuffling her cards. *Tell me what it is you most want*. You had quit your job, you told her, and you'd broken laws and paid attention to your dreams and shoplifted a ton and had sex that could be described as *kinky* and *hot*, but it wasn't working. You didn't feel any further from money or closer to truth.

She nodded, shuffled again, cut the deck. *It's $10 to start, with extras along the way, depending on how many cards you want pulled, whether or not you want it recorded, et cetera.*

You agreed, signed your name at the bottom of a densely inked paper, situated yourself in a cheap metal chair.

Stealing

The reading, recorded for the querent for an additional $5 charge:

1. A secret has been revealed: there is no secret. There is only the long walk and sharp jolts of time and the folding in of matter upon itself. You find yourself a specific point in a whole you cannot see. From where you stand, reality appears as if born yesterday and delivered to your feet. You know this cannot be true.
2. Your imagination runs wild and you are deeply suspicious. Animals struggle to crawl forth from the watery recesses of your mind, hungry with paranoia and propelled by an uncertain longing. These animals—crustaceans, moths, howling dogs—toil with weak forearms, exhausted in downward currents, wet and shivering. The Moon does not issue its own light. It reflects the light of the Sun.
3. Some other world longs to crawl toward you, and signals to you in flashes of wondrous signs. Cups filled with laurel wreathes and baubles and snakes and spirits dance above you. Grasp them and they dissolve.

TRUE INTERPRETATION OF ADDITIONAL CARDS WILL COST $25 PER CARD. HALF INTERPRETATION WILL COST $15 PER CARD.

4. A perfidious Knight recedes, stealing swords. Please place three $5 bills on the table before you to continue.
5. You sit in a room of chairs covered in plastic. The plastic rustles and sticks to your skin, leaving red welts. Place fifteen $1 bills on the table to continue.
6. In a blinding flash, the contours of the room dissolve into your open palm. A $10 bill, please. And cross it with a $5 bill, folded in half.
7. I see pale flowers surrounding a pool in which you

swim without a body. Voices ring out around you. Are they yours? You pull yourself from the pool soaked in chlorine and copper. You feel more than you can express.

HALF INTERPRETATION OF ADDITIONAL CARDS WILL COST $50 PER CARD. TRUE INTERPRETATION IS NO LONGER AVAILABLE.

8. The Wheel of Fortune: *Interpretation not available at current price level*
9. The Seven of Coins: *Interpretation not available at current price level*
10. The Queen of Swords: *Interpretation not available at current price level*

Additional interpretations will remain available for fifteen days after your reading. Please fill out the evaluation form for fifteen percent off belated interpretations. We take your feedback seriously. Fortune telling is banned under New York City's penal code; your teller has taken great personal risk in revealing to you even a modicum of truth. Her work is punishable by 90 days in jail or a $500 fine. Please tip accordingly.

You or Valerie, fake-leather wallet nearing empty, bank account having dwindled toward extinction in recent months: *How many other cards can I have later, with the discount?*

The psychic: The first two cards tell the whole story. I could pull the entire deck, and that's the real reading, one card after another, looping back to transfigure the meaning of the first. So, you see, it's never complete. By the time the deck's laid out the correspondences are too convoluted to read. The first card is eternity, like god or nature or mystery, but even before I pull it, it's already pierced by the second card, the cross card, which cuts through eternity with time and death. If I pull all seventy-eight cards, they'll lay out the history of the present. But I'm not sure you can handle that. Here's what I can tell you: a poet once instructed me to eat a flake of my own dried blood, and I did. She told me to put a piece of my hair in honey and leave it under the moon and feed it to myself after it dissolved into sugar and dust, and I did. But these things didn't satisfy me. I simply digested myself and excreted myself and consumed myself again. The body is not a container. You are not meant to contain things, to be satisfied, to search for hidden meanings in what you've been. You are meant to ingest and incorporate, to tremble beyond the limits of your flesh, if only by a fraction of an inch. This is the only transcendence for which you can strive.

Your interpretations will remain available for fifteen days after your reading. All answers to questions asked after the reading will be priced at 25¢ per word. Please place two hundred and forty-three quarters on the table.

Wait, you said, *that last part was charged at a per-word rate?*
The psychic was both large-boned and plump. She looked like a vindictive housecat when she narrowed her eyes. *It's difficult to tell the truth. It's not cheap.*
But I don't have enough money, and you didn't tell me how much the final answer would cost until after you said it.
She seized the cards from the table, lining them up and tapping them against its surface horizontally, then vertically, until their edges aligned. *I can see why you're trying to get out of paying. You think that if you don't pay for something, you don't have to believe it.*
You did the math. *You're asking for over $60 in quarters, though.*
She shrugged, still shuffling and tapping. *As you wish. I know better than to demand honesty from a thief.*

18

Find a penny, pick it up, and all day long you'll have good luck. The rhyme was obviously slant and obviously American. Finders, keepers. A penny makes you richer. Wealth is equivalent to luck.

Ted was privately fanatical about loose change. You waited for him to scoop coins from fountains, to pick up quarters from sidewalks, check ATMs for forgotten bills. You waited, too, walking alongside him at supermarkets, department stores: waited for him to rummage the aisles and ceilings with his eyes, scanning for cameras and staking out blind spots, pausing for a beat to see if he'd been caught. Shoplifting, you came to realize, could be boring. There is no cultivation of a rich inner life while you're stealing from the grocery. There is only watching and dreading and calculation and fear. Willem de Kooning said *the trouble with being poor is that it takes up all your time.* Then again, he also said that the subject of women in art history could be reduced to *the idol, the Venus,* and *the nude.* Even misogynists have their moments of insight, you thought.

Each trip to the store began to remind you of the wave pool at the waterpark: your body packed tight with other bodies in a sea of chlorine and candy wrappers and urine, holding your breath and anticipating the rhythmic pulse of the next artificial wave. Swells predictably paced and reasonably sized, dangerous enough that you had to live entirely at your surface, a jumpy, strung-out animal, but not so dangerous that your mom didn't allow you to go in. Life lived in a wave pool is life without access to symbols or words. It is only watching and dreading and calculation and fear.

The nervous animal feeling, you attempted to convince yourself, was like taking drugs or writing or riding a bike, a sort of slack-jawed and flowing feeling. Being here now. After your trips, you recounted the stretches of boredom to yourself, painting them over with a layer of the symbolic, arranging blocks of time so they had a certain narrative drive. Still, more often than not, shoplifting had come to feel mundane, like drugs and writing and riding a bike can come to feel mundane. You stared into your fridge and made lists of necessaries, fretting over which items could be stolen and which would need to be bought. At the store, you dropped cans and bottles into your bag at designated spots and with habituated movements, pushing away the animal feeling so that you could continue riding another line of thought. Watch yourself. You'd forgotten how close you'd drifted with wings of wax toward the sun.

Ted and Virginia wanted a particular silk scarf and they wanted you to steal it. They didn't seem to want it for practical reasons. For them, luxury stores were sport. Ted had tried to get the thing twice before and had been forced to abandon ship each time, sensing detection. He wouldn't go into the store again. Too risky, he said. Virginia had accompanied him the first time, but her presence was unlikely to raise suspicions in the same way his would, so she and you would go in together. Ted claimed men were considered more prone to criminality by security guards and cops. Women were more agreeable and cautious and sociable, generally speaking. You did not appreciate generalities but conceded his point, if only because the mission sounded exciting. Sure, Ted could lump you in with the supposedly *more cautious*, if it meant you could take a risk. *I contain multitudes*, you thought, pleased at your own contradictions.

Ted outlined a plan. He would wait outside the store, scoping for security. Virginia would distract the sales staff. You would make the grab, and Ted would give a nod when the coast was clear. You and Virginia would waltz casually (*but briskly*, added Virginia) outside.

When to do it? Why not today? You took the subway to Spring Street and walked with Virginia into a room you'd seen before in a photograph, an advertisement. An advertisement for the clothing sold in the store. It felt strange to be inside the advertisement. The floor and walls and ceiling were shiny white, and the salespeople were gentle aliens, tall and with startled eyes and clad in head-to-toe black. They floated around the white store like survivors of the apocalypse, tending to their radioactive garden, their customers. Virginia tried on sunglasses and turned down a glass of water offered by one of the gentle aliens. You positioned yourself near a display of silk scarves. On second thought, Virginia would take that glass of water. Oh, thank you; she was so sorry for the bother, but might the alien dump out the ice cubes? Virginia much preferred room-temperature water. It was better for digestion. You moved one of the scarves underneath a sweater, out of the aliens' view. Perhaps Virginia might try on that dress hanging high on the wall. Let me see; yes, it was the correct size, but did it come in any other colors? Ah, well, this color was fine, was lovely, in fact. You held your breath. Yes, a dressing room, please. Only this one item, yes. By the time Virginia had changed back into her jeans and returned the dress to Alien No. 2, apologizing that it was beautiful but not right for her frame, you'd slipped the scarf up your sleeve. Ted gave a nod from the street. No, Virginia didn't want to try another dress just now. Perhaps another day. She had to run to an appointment. Thank you, thank you, goodbye. Another nod from Ted. It was time to go.

Casually, casually. You walked briskly but casually toward the exit. One of the gentle aliens stepped into your path.

Can I help you with anything? She assessed you and Virginia with alien eyes.

No, thank you, Virginia said, giving her a puzzled look. The woman focused her attention on you.

Can I help you with anything?

No, you said. *Just browsing today*. The alien stepped aside.

Again, casually. Briskly but casually. You reminded yourself that you were not quite yet caught. It would be unlikely, your narrator assured you. It would be absurd.

The unlikely always lurks too close: a guard emerged from the store's far entrance and apprehended you on the sidewalk, Virginia still walking ahead. You watched behind his shoulder as another guard, shorter than yours but red-faced and with a body exercised to test his uniform's seams, jogged toward Virginia and Ted.

Your guard wore an imperious expression, annoyed and bored.

You would have preferred to face the shareholders of the corporation, you thought. Or the suntanned CEO. It seemed unjust to stage a fight with these two men, one compact and angry and the other princely and tall, two men like parents or hall monitors, paid small-time salaries to enforce small-time rules. *Proxy war*, your mind offered.

Ted had broken from the well-exercised guard and was walking away. The guard followed. Ted yelled. *This guy's insane! Back off, man! Stop following me! I wasn't in the store!* He gestured toward you. *We don't even know that girl!* The guard continued to follow. Passersby stared.

A little-known secret: you do not have to be anywhere you do not want to be. If you find yourself in an unpleasant situation, you can easily resolve it by transporting yourself through space and time. Better yet, you can assign the body standing in your place a new name. For example, the bodies currently corralled by the two guards: not Valerie, Victoria, and Ted, but rather Rock, Paper, and Scissors. Or Thelma, Louise, and Brad Pitt.

Brad Pitt laughed maniacally. *Oh, really. Me? I'm the one who's in trouble? We'll see about that. Search me; go ahead; I dare you. I wasn't in that store.*

Cool it. He's just doing his job, warned Louise, testy.

Yeah, yeah, Brad Pitt said. *All in a day's work.* A crowd gathered. Brad Pitt was quite a spectacle, and he'd only just begun. He glared at the guard. *I'm sure you and I would be best buddies, if you hadn't picked a job as a second-rate cop.* The crowd grew excited.

Soap opera, your mind suggested. *Melodrama. Telenovela.* Brad expertly played his dual role as trickster (for you and Louise) and upstanding citizen, offended and outraged (for the crowd and the guards). The guards, for their part, puffed and strutted and shook their heads, protectors of all the world's stores.

You looked up at the tall guard with your shame eyes. Really, your entire surface was trembling with shame. You found yourself ideologically revolting. You wanted to be defiant. *I can see it under your sleeve*, the guard said, holding his hand open for the scarf. A

princely priest hoping to receive communion. Or was it the con-
gregants who opened their palms for the wafer. You were having
trouble keeping your stories straight. *When your time has come, your
time has come*, you told yourself, the phrase meaningless but reas-
suring. You handed over the scarf, and the guard shook it out, held
it up. You hadn't even looked at it before stuffing it into your shirt.
It was beautiful, painted with a serious-faced tiger, thin rainbow
leaves flanking its sides.

That it? your guard asked. *Nothing else?* You shook your head.
Six hundred and thirty, he called across the street to his partner. *Shit,*
the exercised guard replied. *Misdemeanor. Call 'em anyway?* Your
guard looked you over, nodded. You screened a mediation process
in your head. A fluorescent-lit room, some folding chairs, a gurgling
drip of weak coffee. Guards on one side of the table, and a rock,
a sheet of paper, and a pair of scissors on the other. *You see*, the
mediator explained to the guards, *your investment in the company is
completely misplaced. You're expendable. Where are your values? Do you
truly care about the provenance and proprietorship of a tiger-print scarf?*
She spoke deliberately, ankles crossed and face calm. *And you*, she
said, turning to the pair of scissors. *I assume your intended effect is
to be "subversive." Really, though: Do you feel brave? Do you feel anywhere close to free?* The mediator did not expect a pair of scissors to
respond. She clasped her hands and smiled mildly at both parties.

Brad Pitt sat on the curb, stewing. Your guard asked to see your
ID. Library passes and MetroCards and credit cards in your wallet
protested as you pulled out a worn plastic license wearing your six-
teen-year-old face. You heard a thin white sheet of copy paper ask
the short guard if he was a real cop, if she'd been seen taking anything, if she was being arrested. *No, no.* Well, then she wouldn't tell
him her name, and she didn't have any ID on her, sorry. Too late:
your own license was already gone. The tall guard punched letters
and numbers into a bulky black box attached to his hip by a cord.

Louise will resolve this situation, you thought. She usually exuded lawyerly management, shepherding you and Brad Pitt from
place to place. Now, though, she just stood stony. *She is neither Lou-*

ise nor paper but rock, you told yourself. *She is a sphinx.* The guards could yell and stalk and threaten to call the cops, and Brad Pitt could fuss and rage and pace, but the Sphinx would not allow this mess to go on for long. You felt a kind of pious devotion toward her, your savior. *Like he said, we don't know that girl*, the Sphinx repeated to the exercised guard.

Police do not care about sphinxes and movie stars. Like you, they play with a fictional language; unlike yours, theirs—the law— is a fiction backed up by force. Police do not listen to game-playing rocks or women named Thelma. When you speak, the voice they hear refers back only to the name on your state-issued ID.

The police arrived, ready, as always, for war. They asked which one of you was *Valerie* though you knew you were a smooth bluish pebble, a *Thelma*, a nervous horsefly hot and wild and trembling with flight. They recited sentences and slung handcuffs around your wrists although you were the sky, wristless, existing outside of any time that might be done, impossible to pull down. They sat you in the back of their cruiser although you were despair, a feeling, hiding your face from Virginia and Ted on the sidewalk as you were driven away.

IV.

ACCOUNTING

1

Artists who were not yet famous, but fancied themselves on the brink of fame—*emerging*, in art-world parlance, but emerging from where? from an MFA program? a Bushwick loft?—often gave me advice when I was covering for Sylvie at the reception desk or seated by their side at after-opening dinners (Helene hoping I'd drink too much and go home with them, for the next six months keep tabs on them, track whether or not they might fully *emerge*). One, a kid with a close shave and overly expressive hands, told me I should get in the habit of writing an account of all important happenings immediately after I got home. *No matter if you're tired or drunk or feeling sick*, he said. *It'll make the entry more authentic.* He thought he was part of some historical avant-garde, I could tell, and every avant-garde needs its watchful, quiet chronicler. He didn't want to fuck me that evening: he wanted me to go home and write about him. He was imagining his future archive, researchers and curators poring over his papers, piecing together his world for their books. Contemporary fiction writers debate the *ethics of stealing someone's story for one's work*, but painters and video artists don't worry so much about that. They want to steal, and they want to be stolen from. They want to circulate on the market alongside their work. Well, this account won't be useful to any of them—the artist, his imagined researchers in decades to come. I'll do as he told me, but not for him. For myself.

It's just before 4 A.M. and my eyes are glazed in the dull glow of the screen. Outside, the slow approach of the woman who makes her living collecting bottles and cans: the rustling of plastic bags and clink-clink of aluminum, the rattle of her shopping cart on the broken concrete. Perhaps getting arrested was the most important part of the weekend, the part to really get right. It doesn't feel that way now. Who can say in advance what the most important parts of a life will be? What accounting can hope to sort everything out?

Jail both was and was not what I expected. Fingerprints, mug-shots, questions about my name and address: I recognized these parts from movies and TV. Waiting in a hard chair, arms twisted behind my back. I do not know if the men in uniforms shuffling and scowling and condescending around me were police officers, corrections officers, guards, jail staff of indeterminate title. Certainly people of all genders can fill such roles, but these were men. I will call them men.

O-R release, one of the men muttered, jerking his head toward me. I asked him what that meant. He didn't reply.

Too bad, said another. *System's down. I can't process the identity check.*

Hear that? System's down, the first repeated to me. *You're out once we clear the identity check. Follow me.*

He led me through a door that looked fake, a movie-set door designed to be kicked down, and into a cell with no windows and no other occupants. Bright light cut across the floor from a room where more men huddled around an old Dell computer. One shuffled files and complained about his needy girlfriend. Another typed. The system didn't seem down. My cell's bars were rusty, but its walls were freshly painted in a sullen, indecisive gray. Maybe the bars were next up for renovation, I thought. The room was cold. A low moan from nearby. I watched the tips of my fingers whiten, and then my knuckles, my palms. *Can I have a blanket?* I called to the men in the bright room. The man whose girlfriend needed too much looked out at me, glared, and shut the door. All feeling flung itself away from me and into the corners of the dark, cold room.

Time passed; I was herded down a hallway, through several more fake doors, and into another cell, this one crowded and lively. A group of women sat on the concrete chatting amiably, as easy as if the cell were one of their living rooms or a bar. One had a glowing moon face and a chubby stomach and arms. After a few minutes, she crawled to the corner to sit on a stubby toilet, groaning periodically and continuing to chat. Another with long, lime green nails and shimmer dotting her eyes asked what I'd done. Shoplifting, I said. What about her? *Whoring!* she exclaimed, cackling. Her front tooth was chipped. It made her even prettier. I asked if she, too, was waiting for the computer system to get back online. *The system isn't down*, she said, talking loud enough for the man standing outside the cell to hear. *They say that to girls who've never been in before. It's how they make money.* I didn't understand how keeping me in a holding cell made them money. She didn't understand, either, but she recited a number and told me to call it. *They'll do the identity check for you. You'll be out in ten minutes.* I asked to use the phone and the cross-armed man obliged. I was out in twenty, slip of paper in hand for a court date in July.

Texts from Ted and Virginia: did I need help, need a lawyer, need bail? Was I okay? How long did I think I'd be in? I met them at a handsome Bed Stuy brownstone, its interior recently knocked out and rebuilt, lined with walls of books and decorative masks and hanging plants. We drank and they apologized and asked me to tell the story again and again until it turned into myth, at turns enraging and pathetic and dumb. The more I told it, the less it applied to what had happened. Ted laughed at my jokes but avoided my eyes. When it was time to sleep, he offered me the biggest bedroom and, after splashing water on his face, returned to the couch. If I hadn't woken to the unfamiliar room a sudden, nasty daylight, my stomach fitful and tender from alcohol, calves still twitching from fear, I wouldn't have known I'd slept at all.

In the morning, Virginia announced that we were going to have *a rare day*, the kind of day you allow yourself only after something goes very wrong. The kind of day I'd imagined every day would be in a world without work. Ted went to the store during the 9 A.M. rush to get provisions: food, water, more beer. Leila texted to ask when I was coming home. *I'm going to the beach with Virginia and Ted*, I replied. It felt like a lie. She and Julie didn't know about my arrest. They wanted to go to the beach, too. Would I mind if they tagged along? No, of course not. I stood under the shower a long time, but it never got fully hot. I toweled myself off and stared at a wall. By the time Ted met Virginia and me at the bus stop, his bag heavy with bottles and cans and jars, the sidewalks were ema-

nating thick heat and the sun was high. The bus shuddered to a
stop in front of us. When I stood to greet it, I found that the metal
bench had left angry red latticework on my thighs.

2

New York brownstones were not designed for this century's exces-
sive heat and, from Bed Stuy to Flatbush, I watched inhabitants
pour out of their homes and onto the hundred-degree sidewalks.
When the city is outside, in full view, it's impossible to maintain
the illusion of separation, despite all forms of distance between
neighbors. Kids with sparklers and melting popsicles congregated outside 99¢ stores, hands sugar-sticky and purple, voices loud.
Their grandmothers stood watch for the bus in elaborate polyester
dresses and orthopedic shoes; fathers gesticulated seriously to each
other, discussing neighborhood goings on beside rows of half-price
yucca and aloe vera leaves.

The bus passed Cricket Wireless, EZ Pawn, nameless clothing
stores, and I rocked my forehead against the window, projecting an
image of my narrator onto the street and watching her walk, elbow
crooked for plastic bags of shopping, picking up 50¢ mangos to
test their weight. Each misshapen fruit became momentarily real
in her hand only to withdraw again into the mass of matter when
she put it down. Around her, men bought booze for block parties
and barbecues, flowing in and out of bodegas, exchanging cash or
card through bulletproof glass. She'd never walk that street at that
moment, not really, and the mangos she held would be sold and
eaten before the day was done. She didn't have to shop for anything. She didn't exist. She was only a figment, my own lonely
imagination of myself, by myself, projected out into the general
order of things.

*More than three bus stops until I see another liquor store, and I'm
done with Virginia and Ted*, I decided. One stop: brownstones and
bodegas, a hair salon. Two stops: another hair salon, a hardware

store. Three stops: a Market Basket, two liquor stores. I wasn't done yet.

Virginia noticed me quiet and nudged my shoulder with hers, asked Ted to show us what he'd gotten at the store. He obliged, turning from the seat in front of ours to play magician to our steady supply of *oohs* and *aahs* at his haul. Still, though, he wouldn't meet my eyes. The anticipated bag of grapes, a container of hummus, a bag of tortilla chips. A few bottled smoothies. Individually wrapped brownies, a jar of pickles, salsa, a lonesome peach. The fanciest brand of bottled water, white wine, two six packs of Bud. I made the appropriate noises and Ted turned away. Virginia rested her coppery head against my shoulder for the remainder of the drive. Her hair, wispy strands tickling my skin, smelled like Ted.

3

The city bus expelled us, a few dozen dazed and anemic, publicly transported New Yorkers, onto the hard gravel and brambly lawn of Riis Beach with a loud exhalation of exhaust and old brakes; we trudged across the concrete parking lot and boardwalk to stand before the orgiastic repose of the sand below. *This is a rare day*, I told myself, thieving Virginia's words. *You're having a rare day.*

Julie and Leila reclined on a blanket in front of the boarded-up hospital building; they'd come before us and were just half-awake, with soft hangovers and reddening noontime skin. I dropped my bag near Julie, who woke to say hello before again closing her eyes. The sun was high and punishing, the waves easing, and the beach vibrated with anticipatory intensity. Headaches and dehydration could now be palliated with fresh drunkenness, cool alcohol soothing dull sunburned heat.

Virginia kicked off her pants holding a towel around her torso, revealing downy legs, visible ribs and gossamer armpit hair, until finally she emerged, bikini'd, into the sunlight. It was impossible not to stare. Ted stared, too, and a wild hatred gripped my guts. Seagulls flew overhead. *More than ten gulls before I have to take another breath, and I'll never speak to him again*, I told myself, sucking air in. Three gulls passed. I felt like a balloon. The sky exploded dark Rorschach blots at the edges of my vision. No more gulls. Fine. I released and breathed and resigned myself, nestling my body against Ted's on the blanket. He kissed my head, kind of.

A nap, a swim, a period of general acclimation to the crowded beach: Julie opened Ted's bag, helping herself to a red-and-white can, the well-bruised peach. *You always bring too much*, she said, and Ted shrugged. Julie threw a grape at him. He caught it in his mouth.

If she throws another grape, I'll ask him why he's being a jerk. Julie put her earbuds in. Grapes didn't want me to have answers. I unscrewed the wine's metal top and sat with my plastic cup, not watching anything, not speaking, only feeling myself carried along by the day.

When I woke, it was half past four. Julie was playing cards with Leila. Ted and Virginia were gone. Leila noticed me scanning the beach. *They're swimming*, she said, and there they were, torsos bobbing up and down with each oncoming wave. Leila and Julie wanted churros; they wanted rum punches; we all agreed it would be good to have more to eat. I was drunk and warm and aching. I offered to buy whatever food they wanted. After all, it was a rare day. I wasn't in jail. I felt rich.

I'd spotted a visor-wearing woman selling churros by the bathhouse earlier. When I arrived at the site, though, she had moved on. The bathhouse offered shade from the sun and its stone walls were cool, and I lingered there for a reprieve.

Squinting into the flat sun, I saw the woman across the parking lot. She was leaning against a Port-a-Potty, an umbrella propped overhead. Her churros were stacked, long and ridged and golden fried, one against another, wrapped several times in thin plastic and piled into a metal-wire grocery cart. Another woman stood next to her, speaking in Spanish and fanning herself with an MTA map, red Coleman cooler stuffed with rum punches and Ziploc bags of sliced mango on the ground by her side.

How much? I asked the woman with the churros.

Two for a dollar, she said.

I'll take twenty, I told her. She squinted at me, looked me up and down, assessing my capacity to consume.

They're for my friends, I said, and she seemed satisfied, began parceling pastries into grease-stained paper bags.

You moved? I asked, indicating the bathhouse from which I'd come.

The cops, she said.

I nodded. *They got you?*

She gave a little snort. *They didn't get me this time. Last summer, though, they got me five or six times. Always the same. They take me to the cell till one o'clock the next day, fine me $100, send me on my way. Today, they are out, yes. But I don't think for me.*

Who for, then?

She shrugged, neatly pressing the tops of the paper bags into precise folds. I asked her friend for ten punches and five bags of sliced mango and counted out $5 bills, soft and papery-thin from the heat. Though the churros had been out of the fryer for hours, their soft, oil-soaked bodies, coated in crunchy sugar and smelling of caramel and egg, were as hot as the pavement under my feet. The drinks and mangoes were heavy and cold, though, and, only halfway across the parking lot, my hands began to cramp from their weight.

Salt-hardened and wine-spilled sheet, hard-candy neon green rum punch, dull ache of cotton overshirt on sunburned skin. Ted chewed on a churro and threw a ball of wet sand in my direction. So, we were playing again. I rolled to avoid it and its form disintegrated, all at once, in midair, sand scattering across my skin. He laughed, I stood, and we were tripping over slime and seaweed and sand-filled beer cans and jumbles of shaved and pedicured and freckled and muscled-brown legs on our way into the surf. I held my breath and threw my body into the onslaught of the waves. *If he's nice, I'll stay.* Violent walls of ocean propelled me toward the shore.

4

The screen of my phone is, in fact, composed in part of rare metals extracted from nodules of manganese found thousands of feet below sea level. Multinational companies compete to quickly mine the ocean floor. The greatest concentrations of metals are found in volcanic fissures and ruptures in the seabed where sludge and water gush forth to form dense, glimmering mounds of gold, silver, copper, cobalt, zinc. It's likely that I touch this screen more than I touch any other thing, including my own skin. Stolen bits of deep-sea smudge against flesh, rub off onto my fingers.

Walking through the woods when I was young, I developed a strange infatuation with a tree in my path. I decided that I would touch the tree, make it the midpoint of my hike, and then turn around. I stood very close to the tree and tried to smell it; it had no perceptible smell. It was covered in exquisite, glowing moss, emerald spores extending in all directions. The moss was so cold, so delicate on my fingers, and I pulled my hand away from it at once. I'd touched something too precious for me. I felt clumsy, hot, oily, terribly embarrassed to have disturbed this inviolate thing. When I looked down, there was a wet, brownish smear across my palm. I turned away to find that the forest had a kind of snow globe feeling; everything was round and shaken and hyperreal.

Because the parts of the ocean floor disrupted by rare metal extraction are so remote, so unknown, it's nearly impossible to understand what the impact of seabed mining will be. Perhaps microorganisms will be disrupted, experience a violent outbreak. A contagion will spread, entire populations will die—it's hard to tell. The entirety of the moon is better known to us than is the ocean floor.

Unlike the moon, whose coordinates and surface are, by all measurable accounts, relatively stable, the perimeters of the ocean are in constant flux. The most expensive apartments in Miami and New York are sinking. Soon, residents will wade to work. Helene will ride a jet ski to the gallery. Linda from HR will hire a pedal-boat attendant to chauffeur clients to their favorite restaurants. Designer life preservers will come into vogue; Ted will steal one for Virginia, one for me. Countries jealously guard their boundaries, but the sea decides some borders for us. Swallowing up towns in hot waves and muddy beaches strewn with detritus, the ocean leaves port-city dwellers no choice but to pile into boats, to venture from their place of origin in hopes of making their home on other land. Such boats are greeted on foreign beaches by police with guns.

My most frequently recurring dream is of myself, seen from above, swimming in clear, sky-stained water, hair trailing like an electrified cape of diaphanous thread, feet turned amphibious, marine life undulating alongside me in clockwork circles. It's probably an image I saw in a luxury vacation magazine when I was young. Sometimes I trade bodies with the animals in the dream. Sometimes I know I am several animals at once; my dream mind does not see any reason why this should not be. Occasionally, an industrial highway or thick cable cuts through the seascape. Once, the scene was held within a crystalline globe, and an audience of strangers watched me through the glass. On bad nights, the dream-sea turns against me and large waves swallow me in a soup of drowned products. I crash into other bodies, reaching out to grab my wallet, my phone, a pair of sunglasses, all just out of reach.

In these violent dreams, the sea is slate gray or nearly black—in Hindi, *kala pani*, black water. In the nineteenth century, at the height of maritime trade, a rumor circulated among Brahmins that, should they enter the sea, they'd immediately lose their caste. British colonial merchants tried first with words and then with force to entreat—

And there, see, that's the limit of my knowledge. I have to open up a new browser window, type the word *Brahmin* into Google's search bar to check the word's spelling, figure out what tale

I'm trying to tell. But, for me, American girl, number-one consumer, a midrange accessories designer is the first search result.

Of course, Google tells me, *kala pani* has other meanings: Blackwater is the private military and security firm hired to murder dozens of Iraqi civilians during the Bush administration. The phrase is also Delhi jargon for life in jail without parole; *kala pani* was the colloquial name given to a British prison built on an island in 1857, where Indian revolutionaries were sent to be tortured and killed. Arriving on the island, sure of a looming death at the hands of their colonial captors, prisoners would look out toward the horizon one last time as they were marched inside. They could see no land in any direction, only endless ocean.

I don't know any of this, not really. But worlds of information await my tingling fingers, beckoning me to possess.

And what would happen if you could hold everything imaginable in your arms at once?

I guess I'd still be wondering after what I couldn't imagine.

Do you think you'd piece it all together to grasp the world as it is?

Well, no. If I could grasp it, I wouldn't be in it.

So, if you're stuck inside, what makes you think you can tell any story at all?

Stories aren't like objects. They're infinitely malleable. They can't be held or grasped or owned. I've been writing myself into being long enough that you'd think the story belonged to me. But that's not quite right, is it? Stories belong to no one.

Is that right? Stories can't be owned?

They can be consumed again and again. They can shape-shift and change. Anyone can invent one or grab another, make a few edits, spread it around.

They might be sneaky and promiscuous, sure, but that hardly means they're free. Stories are like anything else. Someone does the work to make them, someone pays the money to buy them, and someone else entirely reaps the profit.

5

Why am I typing all of this? Going on in an attempt to remind myself that there are larger tragedies in this world, causes I should dedicate myself to, people in trouble everywhere rather than only myself, here and now?

To avoid getting to the bad part, I guess.

6

In the ocean, cool saltwater buoyed my limbs and I bobbed in the surf, fixing my gaze at the horizon. I was hoping for the kind of large wave that I could watch form, several minutes and several hundred feet away, and track as it approached. *If a wave appears before I count to twenty, Ted and I are true lovers.* I counted to five, no wave. Twelve, no wave. Eighteen, the beginnings of a faraway swell. I filled my lungs to bursting, heart working hard within my ribcage, vicious as a small feral dog. I plunged myself beneath its crest. My body worked, it was real, was my own, and was lost, unclothed and unintelligible in the sea.

Held in mute suspension, I played my favorite game, *no context*, waiting for the critical moment of disintegration: *this will either result in an afternoon continued—wine and rum punches, magazines, sunburned stomach, Ted laughing and Virginia appraising—or will result in total loss, abdication of self, body swept out to sea and decomposed alongside military shipwrecks and undersea Internet cables and islands of industrial waste.* The undertow caught me, dragged me roughly, and my body was transformed into sheer matter under the spell of a force beyond my limited imagination. I pulled against the current. *You should have pulled with the current*, I heard my own voice in my head.

I surfaced and the sky convulsed into and out of view, as if the video camera that was my vision was being tossed hand to hand,

and the sun's brightness radiated blinding patterns upon the waves, violent white flashes, the glare of cheap fluorescence against aluminum packaging, and everything I could see was dissolving into light. I clawed for a surface to grasp, found none, was pulled again underwater, lungs shuddering sharp blazes in my chest. I couldn't get ahold of sensation. I couldn't make out a direction in which to aim my head. *You are drowning*, my narrator reported, her tone matter of fact. *You have lost all sense of perspective*, and it seemed laughable to hear her even then, at the moment of—what? my death? I sputtered into a gasp of air. *You're really being consumed*, I heard her say. *You should have made a better bet*, and another wave pushed me under. I hit something hard and opened my mouth, but there was nothing to say. All words were gone.

The feeling of drowning is incredibly lonely, the body powerless and alien and unable to be rescued: the lure of the inanimate, or else dispossession.

Whose body? my voice asked. *You're not drowning. Not yet.*

I extended my fingers and fiery nerves grazed a hard object, unintelligible, held onto it, an ankle, and I emerged soaked and sputtering and clawing at Ted's skin.

You okay? he asked, clearing hair from my mouth. I was not. He nodded, righted my bathing suit's straps, and pulled us toward shore. The water was shallow, and I felt the waves' tired remnants lick at my feet. *So, he's nice*, I heard myself think. *And you're true lovers. I guess that means you'll stay.*

On our blanket, I unfolded in Ted's arms, my body small and tired.

You okay? Virginia asked. *Waves look rough.*

A girl can weasel her way out of jail, Ted said, *but not out of drowning*, and Virginia was rolling her eyes, Ted was grabbing for her feet; they were amusing themselves again. *Watch out*, warned my narrator, but I turned her off.

Lifeguards waiting at the easternmost tower tracked their phones to watch the clock turn to 5 P.M., then blew their whistles, signaling their goodbye to intoxicated beachgoers. *You are no longer being protected* also means *you are no longer being watched,* and hundreds of bodies sprung forth from their blankets, thongs and shorts and bikini tops and sarongs shed onto the sand. A group of slender and unshaven men wore bright Speedos around their necks like jewels and, arms around each other, leaped into the frothy sea.

I watched a kite flying above, its bright primary colors flat and hard against formless clouds. The kite saw me, too, noticed the ordinariness of my body coupled with Ted's. Kites, though, don't know about categories like *criminal* and *innocent, faking it* or *true lovers,* don't know that the gentle repose of one body against another in one moment can be, in the next, exposed as farce. I curled against Ted, watching water droplets on our wine bottle tremble and slide down its side. I was very tired. Maybe I slurred a quiet word to him before I fell asleep, maybe I didn't: I can't remember any of that now. I remember only that, when I woke, Ted was gone, and Virginia was gone.

7

Julie and Leila were bare-breasted and drunk and playing a game that involved saying words very quickly and hitting each other's arms. Julie was the more nimble of the two, but also the more intoxicated, so her arms were splotched in angry, pink marks.

Where's Ted? I said. Pain in my eye sockets, debilitating headache. Rum punch.

Don't know, Julie said. *He mentioned going for a walk.*

He went to find a spot to take a piss, Leila added.

No, said Julie. *He was going to look for . . . what's her name? The pale one with the pixie cut.*

Virginia?

Yeah, her. She went to find a spot to take a piss.

Thirty minutes passed. Ted and Virginia didn't return. My drunk was fading and the sun was low in the sky. I paced the shoreline, scanning the waves. Virginia liked to swim. When we arrived, she'd stayed in the ocean for nearly an hour, *draining the evil spirits from her body*, she said, though I didn't know if she meant the previous night's alcohol or something more sinister. In any case, she wasn't in the water now, at least not that I could see.

By the time I returned to our blankets, Julie had packed her things and gone home. Leila was standing, scanning the shoreline, hand to her brow ridge. *There you are*, she said, spotting me only when I was nearly upon her. *I was looking for you. Did you all notice the commotion in the parking lot a few minutes ago?*

No, I said. *I haven't been back there since we arrived. What was it?*

I don't know. Leila settled onto the blanket. *There was a crowd standing around, just beginning to disperse. Jittery people, electricity in the air. Like something big had happened. A celebrity, maybe. Or a fight.*

Maybe Ted and Virginia went over to watch, I said.

I didn't notice them, Leila replied. *And Ted's tough to miss.*

I hadn't seen them in an hour, I replied. I had a bad feeling. Leila squinted into the water and lay down on her towel, only to push herself again onto her forearms, direct her squint at me. *You're right*, she said. *Something is off. Let's go look around.*

We walked the beach's perimeter; another hour gone. No cell service in this spot. What to do, what to do? We walked to the parking lot and sat on a picnic table, thighs touching, side-by-side. Silky black hairs covered Leila's legs. Sinking sun throwing neon-sign colors into the sky. Beautiful sunsets are banal like beautiful faces are banal. Ted's face. No cell service here, either.

Doesn't matter, Leila said. *If they leave the beach, they've got to come this way.*

A group of muscular men walked past us toward their car, hair slicked with water, tiny swim shorts clinging to hard-won thighs. Leila called after them and they turned, dazed, to stare at her. Stoned.

Have you seen a man in green swim trunks? Or maybe cowboy boots? she asked. *Tall, dark hair, good-looking guy? Might be with a skinny woman, kind of frail looking?*

No, one of the men shouted, *but let me know when you find the guy! Sounds like fun!* His friends laughed and slapped at his cheeks, his shoulders, his sides.

We sat for a long time. Sky a vivid, gaseous blue near land, a Whistler nocturne further out to sea.

Do you think they're okay? I asked.

No idea, Leila said. *Valerie, something's off with Ted. He acts kind of manic. And why does he always bring Virginia around? He wants something out of you, a love triangle, a free place to stay, whatever. I'm not going to wait around for him too much longer.*

Taxis circling now. *Last round!* they called. *Last round!* Leila hopped off of the picnic table and extended a hand.

Come on, she said. *Time to go home.*

8

Leila unlocked the apartment door and we entered to find Julie sitting at the kitchen table, computer open. *Did you find them?* She didn't look up from the screen.

No.

Weird. Do you think they're okay?

Not sure.

By the way, she said, *I figured out what happened at the beach. The commotion. Some guy's towel slipped while he was changing by the bath house. I guess he didn't have ID. The cops made a big deal of arresting him.* Leila shrugged, *typical NYPD*, and excused herself to shower. I sat beside Julie, shivering from sunburn, and wrapped myself in a sand-crusted towel.

There's a video, Julie continued. *Want to see?* Before I had answered, a stilled image, now moving, appeared on her MacBook screen. Five muscled cops, sunglasses resting atop thick skulls, light blue shirts and transmitter radios and guns tucked in belts, carried a man as slight and fiery as a bronze statue by his arms and legs. The man's face was hysterical with spit and tears. He was still naked. They hadn't let him get dressed. Four additional officers led the procession, talking among themselves, parting the growing crowd so that the group could pass. *Help me*, the man wailed, and a friend draped in gauzy red fabric, tattooed arms, headscarf blowing in the wind, followed, hurling abuses at the police, who, in turn, dropped the screaming man unceremoniously to the ground. He curled, momentarily, onto his side before their fleet of blue and white cars.

The crowd shuffled backward, phones out and filming, moving away from both man and cops. Two people, a tall man and a short woman, their backs to the camera, pushed toward the screaming man and the red-draped friend, the woman's pale arm snaked around her partner's waist, faces close and turned inward like two parrots murmuring seriously to each other. The man swiftly unhinged her embrace, closed one hand around the screaming man's ankle and urged her to stand back with the other. She covered her face with an elbow, shadowing the sun. He yelled something at the cops. *What's that guy doing*, shouted a voice close to the phone, maybe the person taking the video, I couldn't tell. Another voice, hoarse with excitement, replied, *I think he's trying to get the cops to let him go*. I didn't know why I was paying attention to the voices. The man who had held the screaming man's ankle was now forced against a cruiser, face twisted away, arms crossed behind his back. His partner dropped her elbow from her face and clasped her pretty hands at her pretty chest. He hadn't yet turned toward the camera. He hadn't needed to. I would have known it was Ted from any angle, at any resolution, image blurred, frame shaking.

Oh, my god, Valerie, I didn't get to this part the first time I watched. That's Ted—isn't it? Julie asked, and I nodded, heard my own voice saying *and Virginia*. My own voice, distant, asking Julie to turn the video off. *I think I've seen enough.*

9

Sound floated in from the sidewalk, a pair of drunks shouting about money. I rolled over to face the blank, white wall and pulled my sheet to my chest. Daylight cast imprecise lines over the wall's uneven surface: a century-old rental, its rooms roughly spackled and coated again in all-purpose white every year or two, each layer archiving past holes and trapping single, meandering hairs in time.

The previous day insisted itself into my present in splintered shards, an evening's humiliations riding the waves of emotion's hangover. Ted and Virginia together, arm in arm. Ted and Virginia courageous and justice-seeking, wanting to save the naked man from police, but not me. Ted arrested. Both gone. Or maybe not: it was morning, after all. Maybe it was all a horrible misunderstanding. There'd be missed calls and *God, we're so sorry, what a mess; did you see the video? can't believe it, two days in a row; lord knows what that looked like to you* texts waiting on my phone. I groped for the thing in my blanket. Seven messages from Leila, emails from the *New York Times* and a few galleries announcing summer shows, three calls from Julie, a voicemail from Susan. *Hi, Valerie, it's your mom. Haven't heard from you in a few weeks and wondering if you're okay. Hope you're finding time to have fun. Your uncle and the kids are going to be in town for the holiday, and we'd all love to hear from you. Okay. Well. Give me a call. Love you. Bye.* She forgot to hang up, and the last thirty seconds of the voicemail were marked by spastic rustles and rhythmic breathing. I listened all the way through.

I took my phone with me to the bathroom and sat on the toilet, cycling through the video on repeat. Ted and Virginia's faces turned inward and serious, inhabiting the same moment, their own inviolate world. Faces turned inward with such seriousness only ever belong to politicians or lovers. YouTube counted my views: I was the only one watching. Seventy-three views, seventy-four. After my eighth repetition, the number jumped by two, and a text notification cut YouTube's logo in half. Julie, messaging in quick succession:

hey, u awake?
i sound like a dude making a booty call, huh
imagine u got that text at 2am
sorry, not at all the right time for jokes
leila and i went for bagels, want one?
hope ur okay
we'll figure it out when we get home

The video's count continued to jump in multiples. I wasn't going to be able to shit; was I? I returned to my bed and turned notifications off and pressed *Replay, Replay, Replay.* Ted and Virginia, making life and death decisions to intervene in an arrest telepathic and together, but not for me. Virginia's eyes lucid, organizing the chaos before her, grasping at her shirt with pale, anxious hands. Ted straining to turn toward her as the cops pushed him away. An advertisement broke into the frame after a few dozen repetitions, splicing the scene with a staccato pop rhythm and fifteen seconds of models posing on their own, private beach. American Express wondered why I would go back to reality when I could, instead, get back on the sand. I brushed my teeth and wondered how YouTube's algorithm managed to pair videos of beach arrests with advertisements for a beach vacation. I pulled on some clothes and, propelled into mindless autopilot, set off walking the same path I'd previously walked daily toward work.

The summer air was rotten and heavy off the concrete; the sun blinding, like being born. I called Ted's phone. No answer. I called Virginia's, which went straight to voicemail. I didn't leave a message. Ted's again. I anticipated the first five searching rings, the same tempo that follows all neglected calls, but this time, the line kept ringing. Each ring after the fifth grew increasingly hollow and strange, like a question asked over and over until its content becomes irrelevant and its words point only to their asking. Eventually, even the line's lonely query drained from its sound. I grew accustomed to the rings. I walked without vision, matching each third step with the phone's searching toll. No one picked up.

It was only when I bumped into a khaki trousered man who glared from beneath his own phone and mouthed *watch out!* that I looked up to discover I'd arrived at the Williamsburg waterfront. Luxury glass condominiums blocked the gray river from view. It seemed impossible to believe that people, real people who breathed and fucked and felt pain, lived inside those poreless walls.

Ted's line continued to ring. I made concentric circles around a transparent building, counting my steps, until I'd reoriented myself in the direction of home. I'd been waiting so long that hanging up seemed like a coward's move, so I stayed on the line, listening to the phone recite litanies while I walked back to Ridgewood. In Bushwick, my ankles began to ache. Julie called and, in my haste to press *Decline*, I hung up both lines. I was very tired. The world around me spun static and silent without the ringing of the phone. I sat on a stoop until its inhabitants, two college-aged boys, opened the door, looking at me with doglike curiosity; but not saying a word. I walked the rest of the way home. I drank a glass of water and fell asleep.

10

What should I do today? Make Ted and Virginia pay for what they'd done? Find a way to somehow make my time with them pay off? Pay days, payoffs, payment plans, paychecks. Pay your dues. Pay attention. I hadn't been paying attention. Leila had seen the signs, had warned me them. I guess I'd known it, somewhere, too. I tried feeling badly about myself, but self-pity didn't suit either my rage or banality. I fixed a cup of coffee and mutely consumed the morning news. I sat on the toilet and stared like a zealot at the screen of my phone. It did not glow.

Julie's bedroom door was still closed by the time I left the apartment and set out again toward Manhattan, prepared this time with a water bottle and laptop and phone charger, my wallet, a few stray pieces of Ted's mail. Another relic of his having moved his life's monotonies and possessions, so slowly as to be imperceptible, into my home. I'd taken it as a sign he needed me; it seemed now he'd just needed the space. Still, I held out a small, reckless hope that perhaps Ted and Virginia had both been arrested and were sitting in a holding cell, that there were answers and explanations and apologies waiting for me, stuck behind bars. I'd go to Central Booking and ask after them. I'd need proof of address, full names and birthdates, something. I found a promotional offer for a credit card, a recent phone bill, an envelope from the Florida unemployment office, and a mailer from a nonprofit reminding Ted to do his part to *conserve the dying lands and waters upon which all life depends.* I wasn't sure, but I suspected Ted wasn't the type to *send $25 today to help create a future in which both people and nature thrive.*

Condensation from the elevated train's air conditioning dripped onto the street as a Queens-bound M pulled into the station. The block below was patrolled by the NYPD's most comically cop-like cops: six-foot-two men with broad shoulders and light-brown hair, bodies decorated in full military arsenal, bloated chests and exposed batons. I crossed the street to avoid getting caught in their gaze: past a Domino's and a line of display dummies sporting spandex bodysuits and inflated breasts outside a women's clothing store, past a 24-hour deli with slick linoleum tiles that sold snacks and rolling papers, though everyone in the neighborhood knew they made their money trafficking Spice in the back. Junkies stumbled and twitched and peed around the intersection all day, cars swerving and honking, careening by.

I stared, blankly, at a couple exiting the deli, a tall man with an easy gait and broad smile, his partner's body a neat outline. All at once, a vision of Ted and Virginia, or perhaps Ted and myself, sent the blood draining from my ears, then my fingers, my guts, until I was standing, weighed down and hollowed out, gray static occupying the space where I'd been. No, it wasn't them, wasn't us: only bodies cut to exhibit the same signs and symptoms. I felt a dull, hot fury at that rush of sentimentality, feeling cinematic feelings at generic replicas of my own little life.

The subway exhaled me out of the car and through the turnstile at Broadway-Lafayette. Outside, plastic chairs and checkered table-cloths and stringed lights had overtaken Mulberry Street, and bodies milled about, tense and anticipatory, preparing for a festival or feast. A cop car inched through the crowd, silent, its twirling red and blue lights passing over faces and hotdog carts, bouncing off of brick facades. No day is holy to police in New York. Not even the anniversary of some miracle or the death of some saint.

I trailed in the cruiser's wake, bodies jostling mine along the way. Soon, I knew, I'd be sorry to be so alone: this fresh ache a tired, daily disability, and I'd come to know only bland hate, the kind of hate that resembles more a word than a feeling, for Virginia and the sureness of her arm around Ted's waist, for Ted and his dumb heroism aimed at anyone but me. The sky was the rough, ominous black of an oncoming storm, and leaves rustled, nervous, along each tree-lined cross street. I couldn't remember why I'd come to Manhattan. Central Booking, sure, right. But why should I search for Ted and Virginia? Why had I stayed with them so long in the first place?

Central Booking or home. Answers or none. I looked into the sky, feeling ridiculous, and bid its angry, gray cloud blanket help me decide.

In grade school, preparing for standardized multiple-choice tests, I'd been taught to look out carefully for tricks hiding in a question's straightforward-sounding language. Real answers are never as simple as a neat line of alphabetized options would have you think.

Ah, but there's where you're wrong, a black-robed judge scolded from nowhere, his eyes small and unfeeling points in his head. *I'll bet you can locate the exact moment you went astray, selected the wrong option, veered off course.*

And that would have been?

Well, he said, consulting his records, *you made the choice to meet up—just a few blocks from here, even!—with a stranger you met in a grocery store. You continued to see him despite your friends' warnings. You made a choice, an informed, personal choice.*

But that wasn't how it happened at all, I protested. *I just went along with what presented itself. I followed the signs.* The judge had made it sound as though the chooser were a consumer, a rational agent of clear, sober mind. But choosing to be with Ted wasn't at all like standing in the supermarket bottled-water aisle or in front of a wall of T-shirts at the Gap. Real, non-purchasing decisions are slippery things, organized randomness disguised in the semblance of agency.

The judged sighed and shuffled his papers. *If that's how you feel, then you're foolish to live under a legal system that tells you you're free to choose,* he said, peering down. *Don't you know these laws will inevitably end up punishing you for your choices?*

A woman, heavy and stumbling and wearing tourist shorts, tripped into me, mumbled an apology, staggered off. The festival had entered its early afternoon stupor, with entire groups dissociating in pools of beer and vendors in white paper hats offering fried pork and spiked lemonade. My shirt snagged on a sandwichboard advertising sausages and cannoli. It was a shame to have to make my way through such a densely populated scene, I thought, hailed by screens and signs and foraging sweating bodies, all the while playing defendant and judge in the confines of my own heaving head.

I made my way to the corner of Mott and Prince to sit on the curb where Ted had once sat, waiting for me, readying his line about Donald Judd. I was readying myself for nothing, waiting for no one. A compact figure walked past in spandex, speaking rapidly into her phone, her dog nosing a discarded Twinkie wrapper on the street. I picked at a seam in my pants, imagining the spot on the curb where I sat as an eternal container. The pants' fabric was rough and cheap. If time moved backward, Ted's body and my own would be superimposed, and I wouldn't be so alone anymore, would I? And if I got up and someone else sat down, whoever they were would be added to the spot's collective mix. Time's passage was nothing but accumulation, and neither I nor the spot on the curb would ever accumulate enough to be complete. I looked up to find a fuchsia-faced man in a baseball cap watching me from the sea of pedestrians. He was promptly swallowed by the crowd, but his eyes had pierced me, wrenched me from myself, left their mark. I felt a small space open between the present and the thought in which I'd been, felt it dissipate, become banal, hard and separate. I could stage funerals for the passing of time. I didn't have to decide. I could simply get up and go.

11

Years ago, when Leila got a call that there had been an accident and no, it wasn't okay, no, her brother hadn't made it, I watched her shatter within her small frame, begin to sob, repeat that she had to get to Los Angeles. Not where her brother had died, but the last place they'd lived together. No reason to go there, really, besides the fact that a self is little more than a series of habits and a context, and so being the right self, or else getting rid of yourself, is often as simple as changing your context. I remember shepherding Leila to JFK, remember the woman behind the Delta counter, her polite tone and tidy hair and little pearl stud earrings, asking if *$566 for the next flight to LAX would be okay, honey?* I looked beside me to find that Leila had gone. Her body was there, crumpled against her suitcase and blinking, but she was gone. No one to steer her finances, her schedule, herself. *Yes, absolutely*, I told the woman, firm and implacable. I remember our pink martini glasses painted with sunsets and flamingos, stuck to cocktail napkins at the airport bar, remember its Tiki huts and tableside grills. I remember extending my Visa in a self-assured gesture at the Delta counter, the bar: the only form of love that seemed possible at the time.

At a midtown Enterprise Rent-A-Car, a middle-aged woman with long acrylic nails and weathered skin asked with genuine concern if I was sure I could drive. I looked tired. *I know that's what people say when a woman looks rough, but sweetie, you look like you could use some rest.*

I examined my reflection in the mirror behind her head. The person who stared back didn't read as particularly tragic: drained of color and a bit humorless, maybe, but no worse off than any other service worker pushed to an eighty-hour week. Yes, I told her, I could drive. I didn't know where Ted and Virginia had gone or where I was going. Maybe Virginia. My bank account had dwindled to the low triple digits, I had a court date in July, and my shirt stank with the sharp, vegetal smell of anxious sweat. But I could drive. I could obey the speed limit, follow the correct signals and signs, ferry myself safely toward an exit. She sighed, asked for my credit card, made photocopies of my license, and handed me the keys to an old Chrysler. I watched her face relax out of its *I value my customers* expression in the rearview mirror as I pulled out of the parking lot.

12

Electrical towers and construction vehicles abandoned for the evening flashed past my window before vanishing into the flat, brown New Jersey landscape. Driving alone felt like dissolving, hurtling along at eighty miles an hour held in the car's thin metal body, and I wondered if my body could sense its inhuman speed at a cellular level, if submitting time and again to the velocities of fossil fuels and satellite navigation and electronic markets had somehow scrambled my codes. The thought made me feel like a Luddite or maybe a conservative, praying I hadn't ingested too many images and chemicals to be redeemed. Still, there was something to it. A sort of complicity that couldn't be exorcised from my bloodstream or, like a tumor, excised away.

A storm had made its way up the east coast, throwing a dark, wet sheen on the road and leaving its bleak remains rumbling about the sky. It was getting late; my attention was fading with the day. That was fine. I should try to sleep. I should try to forget this body and what it had to think when it was awake. I had no idea where I was going. Maybe Virginia. I had only guesswork and speculation, knew only that Ted was gone, Virginia was gone. Ted was gone, Virginia was—I consulted Google Maps—two hundred and eleven miles away. Virginia, a woman, a warning, a target toward which I might aim myself. Virginia, the one name Professor _____ had never called me, though Ted, one time, had. I pulled into a rest stop, locked the doors, and hid myself in the backseat. I'd spent too much on a rental car, couldn't afford a hotel. *If my time comes, my time comes*, I told myself, pushing away thoughts of carjackers and horny truckers. The tired conspiracy of movie clichés, making anyone without a dick or a gun think it's suicide to navigate the world alone. I leaned my head against the window to feel the dull rush of highway traffic vibrate my skull as I slept.

When I woke, the sun was shooting long, soft rays of yellow light across the landscape, and the car's interior looked bright and new. Reality came back in scattered fragments. I felt like I'd been drugged. I closed my eyes to see spots of chlorine blue float against my lids. Virginia and Ted together, I remembered. Ted arrested, gone. Virginia two-hundred miles away.

Maybe she'd been dropping clues, warning me against men like Ted. Her casual references to Barbara Loden's film, *Wanda*, about a woman who falls, aimless, under a small-time criminal's pathetic sway. Her habit of quoting Chris Kraus novels, telling me *life isn't personal*, face serene and superior when I eagerly agreed. It wasn't personal; I wasn't personal; I shouldn't take what had happened personally. The gallery girl's purpose is to be condescended to and taken advantage of, to be pretty and to be revealed to herself as a pretty, little fool. It wasn't personal. Still, I hated myself for my vision of Ted's bare arms, the slender muscles lining his sides, as I recited Virginia's mantra, stolen from Kraus. If life wasn't personal, why couldn't I think of Ted as generic? Why did the three letters of his name transport me to the surface of his skin, give me the sense that what hid beneath was not only muscle and bone and fat but *him*, irrepressibly *him*?

He wasn't generic; he was generic. The drifter, the bank robber, the cowboy called Dick. Ted, whose handsome face might as well have been cut-and-pasted from *Warhol's Most Wanted Men*. I wanted to be close to him. If not to his body, then to his name, his image, a place he had been. I pulled out the pieces of junk mail I'd stuffed in my bag. Ted's name, my address. Domestic bliss. One envelope, though, was marked with a cheap yellow sticker. A forwarding address. The mail, some sort of unemployment document, had originally been sent to an address in Miami.

I opened my mouth wide to feel the skin of my face tighten and stretch, making my mandible pop into and out of its socket. Outside, only two strips of asphalt separated by a mud-spotted ditch and enclosed by dense, leafy trees. A yellow billboard tucked into the greenery announced AVAILABLE in sun-faded letters. I was available. I had nowhere to go, no one to be. I had a credit card and a rental car. I could pass through Virginia. I could go to Miami.

Two hundred miles later, I pulled into a rest stop straddling her state. My state. *Virginia*. Orange daffodils tangled in front of a squat, brick building wearing two American flags. Who cared for these flowers? Who weeded and watered this monstrously tidy plot of land?

I stepped out of the car to find my limbs like a borrowed sweater that had been folded in storage too long. Maybe, I realized, *life isn't personal* meant something more along the lines of what the artist Gino De Dominicis wanted to do, teaching himself to fly.

In a short black-and-white video, De Dominicis climbs onto an outcropping of rocks on a hill, pauses, and jumps several feet in the air, arms flapping wildly. He does not fly. Again he scrambles onto the rock and leaps; again he does not fly. *Probably I will never fly*, De Dominicis says to the camera, running once more up the rocks after once more having failed to fly. *But if I get my children and my children's children and their own children to repeat this exercise every day then perhaps, one day, a descendent of mine will suddenly know how to fly.* Repeated movements create muscular habits, cellular memories; these repetitions harden, solidify, become generic facts passed down through generations. De Dominicis's sad, earthbound state wasn't personal, but it wasn't destiny, either.

13

Early evening, Jacksonville. I'd been driving for ten hours, maybe eleven. Automated crop-watering systems hovered above the farmlands, projecting slow-moving rainbows into the air. The sky was a vivid purple dome pinning my car to the earth, and a neon glow pulsated under the surface of everything, beneath the green and orange grasses, old Coca Cola signs and reflective highway markers, behind chemtrails and underneath the oil-slicked pavement.

Chemtrails aren't real, I reminded myself. Where had I first learned that the mark left by an airplane should drudge up that particular string of letters, *chemtrail?* Certainly I'd begun to understand the term as a conspiracy only years after learning it as a simple fact. *Chemtrail.* The word had been, for so long, an untroubled surface, an easy means by which to refer to the live, white lines that occasionally slurred the sky.

Other words learned this way: *ravishment* and *Shanghai*, both encountered on lipstick tubes and meaning, simply, *different shades of red. Gap*, a store rather than an empty space. *Lackawanna*, a now-defunct quarry near my childhood home rather than a word meaning *a stream that forks* and invented not for my use, but by people who had, for centuries, inhabited the one-acre plot of land upon which my parents planted a neat yard, a bed of zinnias, an above-ground pool in which my flipper-clad sister and I splashed and swam.

Fourteen hours. I checked my phone. No calls from Virginia, no Ted, nothing. Julie wondered where I was. I didn't respond. Instead, I pulled up the video of Ted's arrest and watched it while hurtling down the highway. Time passed in a frictionless stream.

I watched the sun slink low in the sky, the edge of an ancient coin poking from the ground, and the scene was momentarily pregnant with warmth and light, and then a deep, sooty dark. The road was no longer endless highway, but rather one strip of pavement connected to other strips of pavement, all terminating in shopping centers and gated communities with names like *Hidden Holiday* and *Point Vista Villas*. Each house an oasis of glowing light. Comfortable people going about their comfortable lives. It was dinnertime for these people; for me, too, then. I'd taken the gnawing ache in my stomach to be the beginnings of loneliness, crushing and worried, at the thought of arriving in Miami and having no more driving to be done, no destination at which to arrive. Maybe I was just hungry, though. Was I really so gutted that it'd become impossible to distinguish between despair and a simple, repetitive bodily function? *Life isn't personal*, I told myself. I pulled over at an Indian-food deli and liquor store decked out in multicolored Christmas lights, which struck me as strange in this land of Anglo retirees and their golden retrievers, but maybe it wasn't. What did I, who'd thought *ravishment* meant only *red* for most of my life, know about Florida, anyway?

14

Seventeen hours, Miami. I'd reached that last, interminable leg of any road trip when the general destination has been reached but turns and side streets remain to be navigated, a precise address to be sought. Siri directed me absentmindedly, forgetting to mention turns before I was upon them, confusing this street for that. I tried to pay attention: identical blocks of low-slung, pastel houses. Dry lawns dotted with rusted-out cars and old refrigerators covered in tarps. Chain-link fences and palm trees. *You have arrived at your destination*, Siri announced before a squat, pink mobile home, electrical lines crossing over its roof. An old woman wearing slippers and a bathrobe sat in a white plastic chair in front of the house across the street, basking with moths in the stale glow of a lantern. She rose to peer into the car. I was no one she knew. She picked up a newspaper from her mailbox and waved it at me before allowing her door to slap closed behind her.

I investigated the mailbox beside hers, overflowing with envelopes and newspapers and bills, all addressed to Virginia. I looked at the pink house, its striped awnings, the single concrete step to its flimsy storm door. I couldn't make the outline of Virginia that lived in my head fit onto the home.

Grammatically speaking, some states of being assume a subject steering their course: *I'm thinking, he surrendered, she felt, they decide*. Insanity doesn't work this way: it either takes over the whole of its subject (*I was mad*) or else its subject is briefly possessed by it, and in turn possesses it in their grasp (*I had a moment of madness, had a crazy impulse, had an insane idea*). The force of insanity shoves grammatical culpability aside; this is why the accused claim it as their friend.

It could have been that I was tired; I might have been possessed. I walked up to the trailer and placed both hands and a cheek on its cold, metal door, feeling for who might be inside. I excised myself from history's forward march and hurtled, instead, into a moment when Ted still lived there with Virginia, when he'd at any instant pull aside the thin yellow curtains and see me, my face to his door. He wouldn't know me. He'd be the person he was when his mail arrived at this place, a person I'd never met, a man who wouldn't recognize me at all.

The door transmitted no signals. I walked around the outside of the house, peering into its windows. Its bed unoccupied, kitchen quiet, bathroom dark. No former incarnation of Ted, at least none that I could see, haunted this place. I rummaged for a spare key in the usual spots, and there it was, crusted with dirt from the under-side of a wilting gardenia. *Life isn't personal*, not even that most personal possession, a home. I unlocked the door and let myself in.

Inside, the house was quiet and dark, even after I'd turned on the lights. It made no apologies for its smallness. The bedroom was no larger than its mattress, which suited me fine. I opened the windows and lay down on the bed. My phone buzzed in my backpack and I rolled to grope for it in the dark, mouth suddenly tense and dry. It was only Yelp. I was in a new area: would I like to discover nearby restaurants? *Not now*, I selected. I was floating into outer space. No missed calls from Virginia. Nothing from Ted. I heard a car's horn sound, mournful and distant. A bird responded, repeating its cry.

15

I woke to a shadowless pale morning, the gurgling and hissing of a drip coffeemaker from a neighboring house. The day was already unfolding: sun beginning to unravel its heat, air floral and ripe. My tropical vacation, myself on a little vacation.

I dragged my body, limbs heavy, from mattress to kitchen. Coffee grounds in the freezer: that seemed like Virginia, respon-sibly suspending flavor in stasis for her return. Water in the coffee machine, switch turned *on*. I watched the pot sweat, steam curling from its lid to settle in a thin, dewy film on the window. I wouldn't watch the video again, I told myself. After all, what more was there to see? No possibility of pretending Ted was looking me in the eye rather than Virginia, asking my silent approval for what he was about to do. No fooling myself into believing they were sending secret messages, blinking in code about what should be done next. No, just as Ted had kept his name out of the search engines, he'd managed to keep his face hidden from me even in the evidence of his arrest.

Accounting

I checked the weather in New York: eighty-one degrees already at 9 A.M. I saw Ted's body in a jail cell, all smudgy and crumpled with heat and desperation. Well, no, I didn't know how Ted felt about being in jail, if that's where he was. I'd only read about the heat online. *If he cannot be forgiven, he cannot be forgiven,* I recited, scrubbing myself of projections and sympathies. Still, I Googled, *how long can you be held in jail NYC without trial?* Officially seventy-two hours, a lawyer's website told me. Unofficially, years. And the rules changed entirely if there was a bench warrant out for someone's arrest. Ted might easily have been the subject of a bench warrant, an ongoing investigation, something like that. *Inmate database NYC,* I typed, and entered Ted's name into the first site that came up. Nothing. I tried the local news for *Ted Smith arrest,* and still, nothing. My mind screened images of prison escapees, convicts running from the cops. More images borrowed from movies on prime-time TV. Ted on the lam. Ted taking flight.

Outside, a screen door's slap and the sound of slippers on concrete. The neighbor. I brought my coffee outside to greet her. She squinted and waved from across the street.

Ginny? Is that you? You here for Tara's stuff?

Ginny, Virginia. She'd mistaken me for Virginia, just like Ted.

No, I said. *It's not Virginia. I'm her friend.*

Her forehead creased between drawn-on eyebrows and shortly cropped, dyed hair. *Ginny's meeting you here?*

No, I told her. *I'm just visiting.*

Oh. I thought Ginny would come down to pack up her mom's stuff.

Maybe, I said. *I'm not sure.* I tried for a casual, off-handed tone. *Do you happen to know if Virginia's mom is coming back any time soon?*

She gave me a strange look, as if the girl she'd been speaking to had been suddenly replaced by a phantom or hologram. *No,* she said, slowly. *Tara's not coming back any time soon.*

16

Wells Fargo alerted me that my *balance was low*, and in an effort to cut my losses, I decided to return my rental car. I pulled into an Enterprise near the airport and was informed that a $40 charge had been added to the bill. *One-way trip surcharge*, the teenage boy behind the desk explained, *because you crossed state borders*. One abstraction atop another. I handed over keys and credit card. *We call it Enterprise Wars. It's a game we play on corporate. Pawning off our worst cars onto other locations by sending them on one-way trips. So, because of you, we've got this shitty car that'll just sit in the lot 'cause no one wants it. That means I gotta charge you the fee. Nothing I can do.*

I protested, feeling irked to discover my getaway trip had only been a move in an elaborate corporate chess game. The employee asked if, upon removing the fee, I'd give his location all tens when customer service emailed to solicit my review. Would I mention him by name, select *superb* for hospitality marks? Sure, no problem. He removed the fee with a flourish, and I felt vindicated, as if we'd conspired on the side of justice. *That's not how money works*, I reminded myself. There's no proportionality to this inescapable debt-credit-exchange-owing system, no cosmic scales subtracting $40 from my personal stock one moment only to add it back in the next.

I walked back toward Virginia's house through the downtown art district, watching the blocks turn antiseptic, the buildings modular and new. Somewhere beneath this pavement, I thought, magma hiccups and gulps and molten iron churns and wars roar between tectonic plates, but I couldn't hear it or feel it. How had I come to be so contained and alone?

White rectangularity and city-sanctioned graffiti exploded into round stucco and high palms and cursive scripts as the street numbers went up. Yes, sure, this part of the city was beautiful. It was beautiful in the way that neon signs off the highway are beautiful, in the way engraved shells at tourist shops are beautiful. A television-commercial sort of beauty, though such commercials have always worked upon the likes of me.

I took a table in the sun and ordered a daiquiri, justifying the expense by recasting the returned $40 fee as a form of grace. I'd been touched by divinity, and now I should imbibe. I didn't feel holy, though. I felt nothing: only a blank desire to punish myself by sitting outside in the day's hottest heat, staring at vacationing families lunching at the tables next to mine. Their linen shirts and sandals, their screaming children, their large plates of shrimp, blue-slushie drinks, volcano cakes. The families were generic: pink-faced Americans on vacation, much like me. I sat there feeling as they must have been feeling. The whole scene was designed so that we could feel no other way.

A balding man in a Cabana shirt gave me a strange look. I stared back; he looked away. I looked for signs of myself in his pink-faced daughter. I was a stray cat, a cat burglar, stalking about. What would I do if I caught her? Steal her away, make her my informant? Demand she confess how I'd become what I was?

Trudging back toward Little Haiti after two cocktails, *$28.09*, I stopped before a construction site bifurcating my path, forcing me out of my way. The site was wrapped entirely in plastic advertisements mimicking the facades of shops to come. *Luxury goods*, the signs announced. *Microboutiques*. A statement from the mayor announced his intentions to draw tourists, bolster the housing market, clean up the streets. A pair of police officers loitered beside a plastic simulation of a future Auntie Anne's. An advertisement for GUESS wrapped the site's southernmost corner.

GUESS, announced an automatonic blonde with clear skin and a gently parted mouth. I caught her gaze and she looked at me in fascination, touched parts of her own face and reached out toward me, but couldn't escape the surface of her advertisement.

Who put me outside myself? she intoned in pacified wonderment. We looked remarkably alike. *Like you and Virginia.* We even spoke in similar tones, were smooth and same in neuroses and phobias, identical in our desires and modes of self-control.

I'm not you, I replied. *You're not real.*

GUESS grew distressed, suddenly noticing the bird shit and dead insects collecting on the surface of her poreless arms, the sun-faded gradients traversing her GUESS-brand shirt, the small scribbles drawn just above her chin by graffitists the night before. To her relief, she found her hair still radiantly bright, smooth, supremely moisturized, composed of all the bits of sun the Gnostics thought had dispersed to create the world or mass hallucination as we know it.

I began walking away, and GUESS's provocations grew openly hostile, her exhortations and demands bitter and covetous. I mocked her with my movements, she complained. She didn't understand why I wouldn't join her. We looked like sisters. She'd always wanted a twin. She'd pluck me from obscurity, give me an unlimited wardrobe, offer me the security of plastic and police and general adoration. I could try to avoid her, but there were others like her. I'd soon learn she was impossible to escape.

A food stand on Sixty-Eighth Street, my ankles tiring and patience for this hellscape of cops and advertisements waning. The vendor packed me a Styrofoam box and I walked back to the trailer, warm saltfish roti and heat-wilted lettuce and coconut rice in hand. The slipper-wearing neighbor stared at me from her window. I waved to her; she did not wave back. I ate my dinner with Virginia's silverware, brushed my teeth in her sink. I used her toilet. I stood, feet bare, on her floor. Seventy-six degrees in New York, my phone reported. The sun now gone from the sky. A text from Julie, *wondering where u are.*

Took an impromptu vacation, I replied. *Don't worry. I'll be back.*

I removed my clothes and folded them; I cocooned myself in Virginia's bed. No mention of either Ted or Virginia's name in the New York dailies. Views slowing on the video of Ted's arrest. Outside, the streetlight buzzed a hesitant rhythm, willing itself to its nighttime duties. I waited for sleep to come so that I could forget.

17

Morning, a toilet flushing in the neighbor's house. A man's moans, low and pained, like a bellowing cow. Gentle, yellow sunlight through the windowpane. My little habits now, on this second day, already routine: coffee brewed in silence, daily papers searched for Ted and Virginia, weather consulted. It would be cooler in New York today.

Coffee poured into the sugar bowl rather than sugar scooped into the coffee mug. I stared, too long, at my mistake.

What would I do if I was with Ted? Clasp his hand in mine, sit by his side without speaking, allow him to rest. Press my lips to his forehead, which often gleamed with sweat even when the weather was mild. Curl my body beside his. I realized only several minutes into my fantasy that I'd imagined him as a hospital patient, terminally ill, in one of those tubed and collapsible twin beds.

What could I do? What should I actually do, in a practical sense? I needed money. I could push out a few thousand words, which would transform into a few thousand dollars, which could get me back to New York, rested and tanned, cash in hand for my court date, back on track. My vacation as a writing residency for Helene.

Virginia's kitchen table was small and circular, its legs gathered underneath its glass top like a bouquet of metal flowers. I opened my laptop (my *travel laptop*, a tiny, expensive thing given to me by the gallery so that I might work remotely), clicked on Microsoft Word. HR had requested a press release on Ana Mendieta. I had previously written—and the gallery's website now advertised—that her work *generates uncertainty to resist enclosure*.

A release. Enclosure.

The Word document, blank and white and only pretending to be a sheet of paper, stared at me. *Produce something*, its blinking cursor taunted. *Work your magic. Draw cash from thin air.* But any words I'd write for the gallery about Ana Mendieta would do nothing to describe those strange, luminous images she made, her vibrating, absent body inviting me, alive, to rot and vibrate and slime alongside. The words I'd write wouldn't mean anything at all: their worth was only a sadist's trick, my own life bound and strung up in front of me by Helene, forcing me to produce. To fabricate a dead woman's value so that her remains might sit in the same room as rich people. To draw some blood money for rent. I couldn't do it. I wouldn't write.

The sink was dirty with dishes; my clothes were in a heap on the bedroom floor. Practicalities. Small, simple tasks, easy to complete. But, when I took a sponge to a glass I'd used the night before, the thing slipped from my fingers and shattered in the sink. I grabbed for it, but it was in pieces, gone. A shard shaved a layer from my skin; thick red oozed out of my thumb. *My body should be much more solid than this*, I thought. And, what? Inside me, only more stuff.

Maybe this—clumsiness, fumbling with basic tasks—was what it meant, really, to empty a body of its self. Not a thrilling lay, not a new context. Just fingers forgetting the years of accumulated memory that had allowed them to wash dishes, for the most part, without error or thought.

Clothes and sheets were not as punishing as glass: I bandaged my finger and smoothed Virginia's comforter over her bed, folded the T-shirt and shorts I'd borrowed the day before, organized the scant belongings I'd brought with me by chance. My denim overshirt and sneakers. A makeup bag holding a lip balm, two tampons, and some hair ties. The four pieces of Ted's mail I'd grabbed before I left. My wallet, long devoid of cash.

The neighbor sat in her plastic chair, coughing, blowing shapeless clouds of cigarette smoke into the purple night. Was it her husband, her son, who had moaned in the morning? I hadn't yet seen a man emerge from her house. Maybe an illness kept him inside. Another Styrofoam clamshell stuffed with saltfish roti and wilted lettuce. Another evening awaiting a text from Virginia, a call from Ted. *I'm here, in your house*, I broadcast to them, wherever they were. Jail. Manhattan. Mars. *Come find me. Come kick me out.* Seventy-three degrees in New York at half past ten. I instructed Google to alert me to any mention of Ted's name in the news. I watched the moon make its way from one side of the window to the other.

18

It's a federal offense to open or destroy someone else's mail; I knew that. But I'd already broken into a house and been caught stuffing a silk scarf up my sleeve. And who kept watch over mail crimes, anyway? Which cop was assigned the *knocking door-to-door to investigate which envelopes have been torn today* beat?

Ted and I were, in many ways, unalike. Virginia commented upon it frequently. Ted, for example, was the kind of person whose voicemail inbox was always too full to accept a message. The little red circle floating above his message app usually contained a number in the two-hundreds; I never cast a sideways eye to find its count less than one-hundred seventy-six. He rarely responded to a text quickly, even if it was two forty-five and we'd planned to meet at three. At first, I'd considered this his way of injecting boring girl thoughts into my attention, like, *he'll never call*, or *he's with someone else.* I would fume as the clock hit 3:15, and then 4:00, 6:00, and, by the time he called at 6:45, I'd have exhausted myself from caring so much. Only later did I realize that, for Ted, time moved in fluid, warping laps. He wasn't stringing me along, messing with my head. Or, he was, but it was out of a sort of dazed myopia rather than a strategic attack. Ted didn't wait for anyone's calls. He didn't check the time. He was simply present when he was there and absent when he was not. Who could say what he was doing otherwise? Existing, it seemed. Being in the world, or else not.

Unlike Ted, I kept track of time. Because of this, I know that it was 7:34 P.M. on my third day in Miami when I decided to open his phone bill and begin my investigation. It was 7:42 P.M. when I made the first call.

A voice answered on the second ring. *Hello, Nancy's.* A woman, irritated, the shouts of a crowd engulfing her words.

Hello! My tone like a telemarketer's: bright and peppy, excited that someone had answered the line. *Hello! I'm looking for a man named Ted. Your number is in his call log. Do you know him? Do you know where he is?*

Ted? No. What's wrong, he dead or something? The voice covered its receiver, shouted something into the din.

No, I said, *he's not dead*, as far as I knew. Something, a hand, continued to muffle the other end of the line; I had no idea if the voice was listening to what I said.

Okay! Well! Tell him I need him to work this weekend!

To work?

Yeah, to count the money!

You're talking about Ted?

Ted? She was, again, interrupted by a shout rising from the noise. *Who did you say you were?*

I'm a friend of his.

I don't know any Ted.

But you just said—

Listen, honey, can you come into the bar if you want to talk?

No, I replied, *I'm sorry. I can't.*

Look, I'm sorry, too, she said. Noises, voices. *But it's a busy night.* She hung up.

Maybe, I reasoned, I should consider it lucky that that first call was a fluke. A trial run with a distracted bartender, no need to parse her garbled response. Likely Ted had phoned to check if the place was open—when? I consulted his phone bill: the first of June, 4:12 P.M., four or five times after that. He'd stayed on the line only a minute, minute and a half each time.

I opened a browser window and searched, again, for the video of his arrest. My computer knew its location by heart, found it before I'd finished typing *y-o-u*, that streaming site's strange arrogation of the direct address. *Play*, I selected. Virginia's image clasped its hands. Ted's did not once look at the camera. *Replay*. It did not look at the camera. *Replay*, an advertisement. *Skip advertisement*. It did not look at the camera. Another advertisement. This time, though, YouTube would not allow me to *skip*. A disembodied male voice told me about an app that would help me write; a small red button linked to Grammarly's website. I poured myself a mug of peach schnapps from a bottle I'd found in the cabinet, the kind of booze I'd only ever poured for another underage girl. I downloaded the app.

Cool evening air carried the sounds of traffic from a nearby highway inside; I allowed it to lull me into a calm, droning tedium as I fed old Word documents from graduate seminars and gallery catalogs through Grammarly. *Thesaurus mode*, I selected, and Grammarly complied. *Meditative* minimalist paintings became *quiet* and *contemplative* performances. An Impressionist's *fresh interrogation of color* turned, for Ana Mendieta, into *a radiant exploration of light*.

Any basic academic integrity contract will include a stipulation that the writer must not plagiarize themselves, their already accomplished labor. This means, of course, that a writer *can* plagiarize themselves, or rather, that a writer can plagiarize a former self. Copyright laws bundle any mark or scribble bearing an imprint of personality under a single, sovereign authorial name, but the university hesitates, pauses, concedes a self not so stable over time. I barely remembered writing the words I now gathered and assembled into one-inch margins, twelve-point font. I imagined stuffing all the sentences I'd ever written back into my body like babies, scolding my offspring for being born, telling each one as I repossessed it that it was *mine*; *you're mine*; *you're me*; *you're mine*.

Me, mine, myself as the gallery, the gallery's voice. A voice is supposed to emanate from a person; isn't it? Thought assumes a subject, a thinker. *I am conscious. I think. I am.* A voice mumbling words is how humans distinguish themselves from animals and machines. But here I was, language seamstress for the voice of a bodiless brand. You can't plagiarize from a subject who doesn't exist, I thought, shaping words into paragraphs, an effort authored by the gallery, by me. I patched paragraphs together, pairing introductory remarks from a curator's MoMA lecture with a sales note on Robert Morris. Command+F, and Mendieta replaced Morris. *You betrayed Ana Mendieta for a paycheck*, I told myself. We've all done things like that, I guess. I took another swig of schnapps. The release was complete. Eight hundred and twenty-three words into eight hundred and twenty-three dollars; I emailed HR both document and invoice.

I had shut the windows earlier that evening, hoping to muffle the neighbor's morning cries, but I opened them again before bed, thinking that it would do me good to allow another voice (if the sounds of madness, of pain, could be called a voice) in. In the morning, I'd continue to piece Ted together through his calls, reassemble him into something I could know, could hold. Meanwhile, the app would conjure dollars from discarded words, make enough money to keep me here, free from myself, from New York. I closed my computer and shut off the lights. I was, if only briefly, happy. It'd taken the industrialists centuries to automate workers' bodies, but, for me and an algorithm, only twenty minutes to automate the voice.

19

From: alerts@WellsFargo.com
Sent: Tuesday, July 5, 2015 5:38 PM
To: valerie@IWCgallery.com
Subject: Wells Fargo Account Alert

This is an automated message with important information regarding your Wells Fargo account. A one-

time fee of $50 has been charged to your credit card
and a spending freeze has been placed on your account. It appears, Valerie, that something quite suspicious indeed is going on with your finances. Your
checking and savings accounts have progressively
dwindled, and your credit card has been used for
various purchases in and around LITTLE HAITI,
MIAMI 33127. Since you didn't report any upcoming
travel to your friendly local Wells Fargo representative, we're certain this activity is not your doing. More
likely than not, your finances have fallen prey to an
identity thief. We hate to say it, Valerie: we warned
you. We suggested identity protection insurance for
the low cost of $10 per month. You have a high-appre-
ciation-probability identity, although you're currently in the less-than-profitable phase of Initial Earning and Debt Repayment. Protecting your identity
would have been—in your current life stage—quite
affordable. You refused to take the necessary steps,
though. How could you have been so careless? Your
entire personhood is, after all, dependent on several random strings of numbers—your Social Security
card, which you promptly misplaced after your mother mailed it to you in your second year of undergrad;
your Wells Fargo Rewards Debit Card and Visa Platinum Credit Card, both stamped with numerical
codes across which you like to run your thumb when
they're tucked in your jacket pocket, eroding white
paint from their raised surfaces; your ZIP code and
ATM PIN number; your date of birth. Valerie, how
could you have been so foolish as to leave your identity uninsured? Now, your self has been appropriated
by another. Who knows to what use your identity will
be put? Who can say what might happen next? We,
your bankers, can no longer help you. Consider this

an official cutting of ties. All that remains for you now is your physical body.

20

My physical body. *Inventory: one body*, I recited. *Considered by its occupant mostly as a fleshy vessel for shifting contents, a walking surface, an animate image.* Guts a sluggish jumble, more or less swollen according to the time of day. Hands sometimes shaky and bird-boned, fingertips twitchy and pulsing with nervous blood, and other times as stiffly bloated as water-ballooned latex gloves. A regularly aching left knee, origin of complaint unknown. Tongue usually pressed hard and insistent against the ridged roof of its mouth. Eye sockets sore from tensing. I didn't want to produce a new self to inhabit this body. I didn't want to be productive at all.

I spent the first forty-five minutes of the day convincing Wells Fargo that a rogue retiree had not, in fact, stolen my identity, and the next hour corresponding with HR about minor edits to the press release. I'd now had more intimate contact with my job and my bank than anyone else since I'd arrived in Miami. Wasn't that how it usually was, though? Most of one's life allocated to being a sieve for money to pass through. The only time my life hadn't been like that was the few months of sabbatical I'd spent thieving with Virginia and Ted.

A morning rainstorm delayed my walk to the bank. *To authorize the unfreezing of your account*, the customer service representative had said, by which she meant, of course, me handing over my ID, maybe a check or some cash. *Authorization*, a funny word for it. Paying my way into having a name, becoming an author of account. I had often wondered if Ted had a bank account. I suspected he didn't. He kept a curled and pockmarked credit card in his wallet, though I never saw him use it. There had to be some way in which he paid his phone bill. Virginia, probably. Aside from that, I couldn't think of any other costs he'd have. Debts, maybe, but he hid those from me.

The storm was brief but, while it lasted, relentless. I couldn't see a thing outside the window. Aside from the gray indications of houses in the distance, the outlines of powerlines in the neighbor's yard whipping about, everything was a streaked and streaming blur. Afterward, the sun emerged beatific, as if apologizing for the downpour. Pools of water on the pavement doubled its image, and the world was, briefly, fine.

Walking out of the trailer park, I heard an insistent, dry coughing from another neighbor, a woman who lived in a white-shuttered, turquoise home, sharp yuccas and hibiscus growing around the telephone poles alongside. I'd seen her dragging a bucket of cleaning supplies from her car to her doorstep in the evenings. Was this the type of woman Ted's mother was: tired, coughing, in thick-soled clogs, cleaning beachside mansions and five-star hotels and tending to her own garden, still? Would I ever know him again so that I might find out?

21

An afternoon wasted with useless calls to numbers on Ted's phone bill. No answer, no identifying details on the answering machine. A disconnected line. A confused, elderly woman with a thick Polish accent who swore she didn't know Ted, had never received a call from his number. I insisted that she think harder. She got angry with me and threatened to hang up. I told her that, if she did, I'd call right back. Eventually, we agreed that a telemarketer must be routing calls through her line. Her attitude toward me changed and she called me *girlie* when she said goodbye.

Good luck, girlie, she said. I caught sight of myself in the mirror when I used the bathroom after our call. I didn't much look like a *girlie* anymore. I hadn't showered since I'd left New York. My hair was braided in stringy clumps at the base of my neck, and my scalp ached to be washed. Much less than makeup—of which I hadn't bothered to steal any, though I could have, since I passed both a CVS and a Walgreens on my evening walks—I hadn't soaped my skin in days, and it stretched tight and dry over a newly angular face. It was as though a different person had come to live in my body. As though my face no longer knew me. It wasn't that I disliked the person who had replaced me in the mirror. I simply did not recognize her.

I forced an expression onto her face to see what she'd do: this woman did not want to smile. She was faking it, her smile bitter and thin. This was not the face of a girl who could easily get away with shoplifting from stores. This face was too tired, too preoccupied, to mime all my old tricks. The white teeth and freshly washed hair. The bouncing ponytail. All the little inanities that had allowed me to get away with it.

But, if my former self had been only an animate symptom of some much larger, nebulous evil—its symptom and its excuse—then my having gotten rid of her face wouldn't do much, would it? Attacking her face was like waging war on a shield of marshmallow fluff. At least the voice I heard on my calls, that practiced *hello*, was still my own. *My own*. Funny that a voice or a face should be something to own. I never bought this body. I never bought these words. I'd stolen into the house in which I was sitting; I'd been loaned the computer into which I wrote.

22

I crossed out each number as I called: so far, twelve blue lines hatched the phone bill. This call would be my thirteenth. 917, a New York number Ted had first called on June 4th, and then shared brief, periodic exchanges with until the 18th. A woman answered in an affected tone: someone, I guessed, who was accustomed to thinking that others were desperately awaiting her *hello*. I told her I was looking for a friend, hadn't heard from him in a few days. Found her number in his call log. I didn't see any reason to fabricate an involved lie.

Ted, Ted, she said. *Racking my brain. I'm sorry, could you tell me, again, what you're looking to know?* I imagined her parted lips disclosing movie-star teeth, lightly coffee stained and wide-set.

I'm a friend of his, I repeated. *Haven't heard from him in a few days. Wondered if you knew anything.*

Oh, sweetie. She was enjoying this; I could tell. *You're in deep, huh? Snooping through his phone. Sure, yeah, Ted. I slept with him for a month, probably a year ago now. We went our separate ways, just like you two will. But we kept in touch. Friendly, you could say. I let him stay in my apartment when I went to Venice for a few weeks this summer. We met up to exchange keys, and that's probably when he called. Nice guy, good fuck. Hoped he'd fuck me again in exchange for the place to stay, but no luck.* She paused. *That's it, the one-hundred-percent truth. Sorry if it's not what you wanted to hear.*

I felt something vague and sinister, a sort of rage, stirring in my chest. What was it Virginia had said? *It's not possible to be a no-job bohemian anymore.* When I'd asked why, she'd said *rent*. If I was a symptom, so was Ted. But I hated him. Hated him for skimming off the surface, collecting me like a piece of Monopoly property, another house at which to stay. Who cared if Ted was in jail?

Smells of burning, a fire pit or charcoal grill, blew across the air. A group of three scrawny dogs nosed at the garbage cans and geraniums lining the sidewalk, lazily chased tiny lizards scuttling by. Somewhere, though I couldn't see her, a woman sang freely. *A woman's only human. You should understand.* I cared if Ted was in jail. I still cared. I consulted his phone bill and made another call.

Hello, New York Presbyterian.

Hello. I'm calling on behalf of my husband, Ted Smith, to check in on his outstanding account.

Smith, Smith. Mr. Ted Smith. Okay, one sec. The line crackled with static. *Yes, Mr. Smith owes the hospital $15,486.*

Thank you. I wrote the sum down on Ted's bill, seven meaningless symbols, as if I really were a checkbook-balancing wife. *And what was that for, again?*

I'm sorry; I can't give out that information on the phone, the voice said. *Not unless you can confirm his Social Security number and you're listed in the release form.* Fingers on a keyboard, droning electric hum in the background. *Nope, you're not. Sorry.*

An email from the gallery. *hello valérie, thank you for the Mendieta release. Helene was v pleased. we have a big David Smith that needs a sales packet. think you can have it by tomorrow EOD?* Of course, Françoise. I'll have it by the morning.

23

Outside the kitchen windows, an early haze. Neon sun and pink sky. Heaving coughs from the woman in the turquoise trailer; the metallic rattle of a shopping cart. I looked onto the street: each short driveway was punctuated by a recycling bin, and a shirtless man was collecting cans. 81 degrees in New York.

Man escapes police custody New York, I entered into Google, selecting include results from the past week. A woman, but not Virginia, had tried to escape from a burning car. No one had escaped the police. *Include results: all time,* I amended. Two months ago, a man, cuffed and charged for armed robbery, took off running down Atlantic Avenue while he was being walked into Central Booking, Google reported. In 2013, a federal prisoner snuck away while being transported to another detention center; he was found breaking into a house in Sunset Park in the late afternoon. A nineteen-year-old named Johnny, hands still shackled, hid underneath a contractor's van before being hunted down by dogs. A suspect slipped out of his handcuffs after being arrested for larceny. A twenty-one-year-old in an olive-green jacket walked straight out of the precinct. A man, thirty-one, bolted from police. All these different ways of getting free. The stories had one thing in common, though. I followed each one through to its end. Every man who'd escaped either ended up dead, or was caught.

24

Hello. Soft voice, Caribbean accent. I asked about Ted. *Describe this man for me*, the voice instructed. Easy enough: good-looking and tall, black hair, gray spot in his eyebrow, cowboy boots.

Ah, yes, the voice said. *The one who used to sleep at night on the bench at Tompkins.*

Excuse me?

The tall one, with the silver bike, who locked it to the bench at Tompkins while he slept. I know him from playing cards. A high roller. Big bettor. He slept sometimes in the stairwell when it was cold. The voice moved fluidly up and down the scale as it spoke.

With whose money could Ted have been betting? And why would he have slept on park benches and in stairwells rather than in my bed, with me?

And who are you? the voice asked. *A girlfriend?*

Yes, I said, *a girlfriend.* A girlfriend, a void. A voice with questions.

He's probably gone drinking, my friend. He'll come back eventually; don't worry. If I see him at the park, I'll tell him one of his girls is calling around.

Ted's girls. Me, one of Ted's plural-form *girls*. One, that basic unit of individuality. One doesn't want to be a *girl*.

When I went away to college, my first boyfriend cheated on me with a girl named June. I tried to make myself jealous of June, but this required thinking of her so frequently that I started to admire her, to like her, even. Her nervous prudishness and her lazy diction. Her tight jeans, the way she dotted the i's on the notes she wrote my boyfriend with hollow circles. I wanted to be nice to her, to do nice things for her, to love her how a boy might love her. I wanted to have her as my girl. It was as if the only way to get out of the position of being the girl, of being adored and humiliated and belittled, was to have a girl of one's own. Maybe this was how Virginia felt about me. Maybe she was making herself into a subject by turning other women into her and Ted's objects. Their collective, collectable girls.

HELLO? The greeting screamed like a sacrificial plea; I held the phone from my ear and decided to get straight to the point.
     Hello, I'm calling to ask if you've heard from Ted Smith recently?
     Smith, that fucker.
     You know him?
     That fucker owes me money, big time. Listen up, lady. How about you tell me if you hear from Ted Smith? You tell me where he's hiding out, huh? One-hundred percent chance he avoids me like the plague. Weasel-ass sneak.

Hi, can you hear me?
     Yes, I can hear you just fine.
     Okay, good. I've got terrible service. Who's this?
     I'm so sorry to bother you, but I'm calling about my friend, Ted. I haven't heard from him, and your number is listed in his recent calls. I'm wondering if you might know anything.
     Ted, Ted. Oh! Ted. The guy who found my mom wandering in Crown Heights.
     Wandering?
     Yeah, wandering. It was nighttime, a few weeks ago. He got her out of the road and bought her some shoes, I think. Must have gotten her to talk, I don't know how, but somehow got an address out of her. Brought her home.

She'd forgotten her meds. He said he knew how it was, schizophrenics. Told me his ex's mom was one, too.

    Oh.

    I tried calling a few times to thank him, but he never picked up. A shuffling, shifting sound. *Hey, why are you calling about him? He's okay? He went missing? You need help finding him? I can ask around, you know. I can ask some guys to keep a lookout. I know how to find people. Comes with the territory, as they say. And this kid—this guy, man, whatever—I owe him a favor, is what I'm trying to say. You want me to ask around?*

    No, thank you, I said.

Wind billowing the kitchen curtains, the smell of oranges, street-light flickering against the twilight. Virginia's mother, Tara, schizo-phrenic. I remembered the neighbor's strained tone, how she'd pronounced every syllable when she'd told me *Tara's not coming back.* Ted and Virginia had lived closer to paralysis and immensi-ty and truth and death than I did. I hadn't even known it. What would I lose by being locked up? Only the daily shuttling of myself between a job and a bank.

Hello, Anton Kern Gallery. An abrupt, high-pitched staccato answer-ing a gallery's phone after 9 P.M.: a sales assistant working late, I guessed.

    Hello, I said, inventing quickly. *I'm calling on behalf of Mr. Ted Smith. He had an appointment with your gallery a few weeks ago, and I believe he left his jacket there. Could you kindly let me know if you have any notes in your system as to whether or not it was returned to him?* It wasn't a great lie, but, given that this voice had answered a nighttime call, I hoped the assistant was green enough that the story might pass.

    Let me check. Just a minute. The click of a button; I was placed on a silent hold. When the voice returned, it had changed. *I don't believe your employer had an appointment with the gallery. Our gallery has an ongoing complaint against Mr. Smith, upon which I'm not autho-*

rized to comment further. It's unlikely he'd be allowed on premises. The
assistant paused. *Who did you say you were?*
I apologize, I said. *My boss's name is Tod Smythe, S-m-y-t-h-e.*
The clicking of a keyboard, breath close to the phone. *We don't
have a Tod Smythe in our system.*
Ah, well, must have been Hauser & Wirth, then, I said. *Thank you.
Goodnight.*

25

The morning spent writing an announcement. The gallery now
represented another fifty-something abstract painter. Texts from
Julie sharing encouragingly indignant opinions about *the militariza-
tion of the NYPD* and the *unjust exclusivity of the heteronormative couple
form.* I made little hearts in response. I agreed with what she said in
theory, but I couldn't make myself feel anything about it. My mind
wouldn't perform its usual telescoping function, mapping general
onto specific, abstract onto concrete.

Outside, a solemn nod from the neighbor. I sat on the trailer's
metal step, feeling as if I'd been slamming my body, with all my
energy and for days without pause, against a brick wall. The sound
of a plane overhead. I looked up and saw nothing.

I sent a text to Ted's number, *hey, where are you, are you okay.* It
didn't go through. None of my recent messages to him or Virginia
had gone through.

Ted, T-e-d. That word, that string of letters, no longer held
together any coherent form. The void I messaged was not the
person about whom the voices on the phone spoke, was not the
body whose presence had given me such pleasure, was not the man
whose tricks and habits had filled me with frustration and joy. I
couldn't blame him, though, for his incoherence. His lies.

Another airplane, its roar a violent interruption against the
electric blue sky. Still, I couldn't see the source of the sound.

Lies. That word didn't really apply to the situation, did it? A lie gives way to a corresponding truth. Here, though, behind the series of letters spelling Ted's name, I could find only shifting fragments of fiction, each discrete and as true as it could be in itself, but none linking up with the others to form anything resembling a narrative, a life.

Evening air anticipatory and buzzing: something ominous floating about. A few calls before bed, then, to chase away the feeling. I decided to try a new game, and aimed my phone at my laptop, playing one device off the other, making Ted speak from my voicemail box after clicking *record.*

Hi, it's me. Ted. Just calling to say hi.

I dialed a number who'd called his phone three times between June 13th and 15th. I played my recording for the man who said *hello.*

Hi, it's me. Ted. Just calling to say hi.

Ah, Ted. Hello. The voice was low and eager. I imagined another man like the one whose voice I'd stolen, a man beamed in from the seventies standing beside a wooden table and landline, restricted to pacing a five-foot radius by his phone's coiled cord.

It's good of you to call, Ted. Haven't heard from you in a bit, and Angie's been wondering if you'd be up for another round.

Outside, a light rain, the slur of tires against wet pavement. I was lying on Virginia's mattress, phone to my ribs, breathing as little as possible.

Is that Ted? A woman's voice from another room, or else muffled by a receiver pressed against palm or shirt. *Tell him he can come over any time. Tell him I'm ready for him. Tell him you'd love to watch.*

You hear that, Ted?

The droning hum of a generator. Distant, rhythmic tapping. One, two, three, four in quick succession, and then again, more emphatically, one, two, three.

I think you've got bad reception, Ted. I can't hear much of anything from your end.

The window sucked in its curtain until the fabric was flush with the screen and then released it, round, into the room.

Hello? You there?

I remained still.

Ted, I'm going to hang up. I can't hear you. Check your reception and call back.

Pacing Virginia's kitchen, her bedroom. Unsatisfying pacing. The house was too small. My hands and legs a jittery mess. I shook them, wild little shakes, counted my breaths. Eyelids opened and closed, lungs expanded and contracted, heart beating. I opened my computer, checking for emails from the gallery. Nothing since the announcement I'd sent at 11 A.M. The neighbor's coughs into a cavernous night. Seventy-five degrees in New York. I was too excited for my bedtime routine. I decided to make one last call to calm myself. I wouldn't use Ted's voice this time. I recited my usual introduction into the receiver.

Who is this? A voice like a tomb, hostile and cold. *I said, who is this? Why do you want to know how I know Ted Smith?*

This voice, I realized, wouldn't give me any information. It would only eat up my time, get me to say things I shouldn't say. I was afraid of voices like this one. Too afraid to wonder why Ted had been on its line for two hours and thirty-two minutes, June 18th, 4:12 P.M.

Never mind, I said. *Forget it. I'm sorry.*

Do you know where he is?

No, I said. *No, I'm just a girl he slept with a few times. I'm being stupid and going through his phone.*

You're with him? You have his phone?

As soon as I hung up, the number called back. I let it go to voicemail. It called again and again. I'd done something very wrong. I wouldn't make any more calls tonight. I turned my phone off and lay on the mattress. I burrowed my face into a pillow and let myself cry.

26

From: director@IWCgallery.com
Sent: Monday, July 13, 2015 11:09 PM
To: Valerie@IWCgallery.com
Subject: Your position at the gallery

Dear Valerie,

I hope this email finds you well. I'm writing on behalf of Helene to check in about your continued commitment to the gallery, and to discuss the documents you've sent in recent days. As you know, Helene has been thrilled with them, and we are, of course, grateful for your help in producing them. We've always considered you a talented writer.

When you asked for a sabbatical, we agreed that we'd keep your position unfilled and allow you to write remotely for a per-word rate. Our expectation, of course, was that you'd produce new material during this time; although this was not outlined specifically in your contract, we considered it an unspoken, and tacitly understood, agreement. However, in reviewing the latest Ana Mendieta release, we noticed a striking similarity between the second paragraph and a passage from last year's *Radical Sixties* catalog, which you worked on.

Indeed, upon further examination, it appears that a majority, if not all, of the material you've sent in the past week reiterates themes and passages in already-written texts produced during your tenure at the gallery. While we cannot confirm direct plagiarism, and are not accusing you of such, we hope that, if it's the case that you put less than your full, original efforts into the recent documents, you'll work with us to find a way to remedy the situation. I have attached a document outlining the legal process guiding your return of the per-word loss (on the order of $5,792). I hope you understand we mean no ill will and are not interested in becoming involved in a trivial financial battle; however, Helene feels strongly that, if you did not do the work, you should neither wish nor need to keep the disbursed money. I'm certain that, as a professional who has, in my experience, always kept her word, you'll agree.

With very best wishes,
Linda

Linda Schaffer
Senior Director
IWC Gallery
930 Park Avenue, New York, NY
www.IWCgallery.com

27

Hello?
 Valerie, hi.
 Virginia. You're alive.
 Yeah.
 You're with Ted?
 No. Listen, I'm sorry to call you like this. But are you living in my mom's house in Miami?

The neighbor's cries, almost delirious tonight, cut through the low hum of the highway from beyond the trailer's walls. Something—a plastic tarp, maybe, I didn't know—slapped against the siding of a nearby house. I waited for the sounds to stop.

Valerie?

No.

Valerie, the neighbor told me you're there. She sent a picture.

Another cry, louder, and then silence. Breathing sounds. My own, I guessed. Breathing could be another way to mark the passage of time, I thought. The measure of a body's static against the droning darkness.

Valerie?

I'm sorry. Yeah, I'm at the house in Miami. You and Ted disappeared. I was trying to find you.

Listen. Get out of there. Now. That place is private. As in secret. As in it's for my sick mother. You have no right to be there. And that's not all. Shifting, rustling. *Are you going around calling Ted's friends, asking where he is?*

A mosquito, huge and delicate, beat itself against the window screen, humming with desire. Did mosquitoes breathe? Its body felt so near and so far from my own.

You know what? I don't need an answer. I've heard from three people that they got calls from your number. Some girl calling around, won't say her name, tells them that Ted is missing, have they heard from him, et cetera. I know it's you. What the fuck kind of game are you playing?

I was trying to find him. I saw he got arrested. I was trying to help.

You saw he got arrested.

Yeah. The video. You two are together, huh?

The line was as still as a live wire. I rustled around in the dark with my eyes, waiting for the neighbor's moans to break the mute air.

Yes, she said. *I figured you knew. What did you expect?*

What did I expect? Something more difficult and true and redeeming than what little of his life Ted had revealed to me when we were together. Or else nothing, I guess.

Listen, Valerie. I'm sorry. But how did you get those numbers? The numbers you're calling?

From Ted's call log.

And how did you get Ted's call log?

A car's headlights tracked a line across the bedroom wall.

He was getting his mail sent to my house, I said. *I found his phone bill. And your Miami address.*

Goddamnit, Valerie. You've got to get rid of that bill, okay? Everything of Ted's you have, all of his shit, you've got to get rid of it. Destroy it, eat it, whatever you want to do.

Why?

Virginia paused. I heard nothing, not even silence, from her end of the line. *Valerie,* she said, *have you heard from Ted? Seen his name in the arrest reports? Found him in any of the criminal databases? Because I haven't. I call Central Booking, all four locations in the city, every day, and they still don't have anyone by his name.*

I can help find him, I said. *I'm trying to help.* That voice, my breaking-apart voice, ugly and hopeful and scorned and small. I felt sick.

Help? Help? You're helping to leave a trail for whoever else might be looking. You're helping to put everyone in his life on red alert, to let them know he's gone. What I'm trying to say is, if Ted is on the run, you don't want to be able to find him. Because, if you can find him, anyone can find him. Including the cops.

My eyes had still not adjusted to the night: they fed me only the velvety inside of a closed curtain. I waited for another set of headlights to search their way across the wall. None came.

Don't you get it? Virginia's tone was now truly cold. I remembered my earlier call, with its voice like a tomb. *When you live like Ted does, you have to string one day to the next, and sometimes it doesn't work out. Sometimes the thread breaks. No more narrative. Ted's gone. Doesn't matter if he's gone in general, or just gone from your life. Not every question has an answer. There are some things you can't know.*

I don't want to know everything, I said. And I didn't. I really didn't. But I did want to know about Ted. I did want to know this.

You don't? You really believe that? Because that's why Ted wanted to get to know you. He said your eyes narrowed when you looked around a room. He said you were sharp. But the last thing he needs right now is someone who's sharp. Got it? Time to drop the search. Leave it alone.

Still, no headlights. No mosquitoes, no more cries.

You there?

I was, I wasn't. Virginia's room was quiet and very dark.

Valerie, please. Tell me you hear me. Tell me you'll cut it out. It's over now. Done.

V.

BACK TO WORK

1

Sometimes the only thing one can do is drag oneself back to work. Back to the grind, back on the clock. Back to the job begun when the first angry microbe grew a skin to distinguish itself from the primordial slush, that multiplying, spiraling, borrowing, replicating, reckless and extravagant former friend. Back to the work of hardening one's fragile microbial edges against every crush and crash, the work of storing bruised memories and tucking one's insides back inside. Back to the work of cells differentiating. Back to the work of swatting horseflies away from one's exposed fleshy edges while attempting to find some clothes, to grow a skin. Back to the work of rioting and roiling and stewing inside one's new purple body, the work of being alone.

Back to the work of growing a voice with which to overlay a vision of, for example, a wooden four-legged thing with a word, let's say, *chair*. Back to the work of vomiting oneself out as an image, a gender, a race, a name. Back to the work of gasping and spitting, fusing and dying, to the work of the tweezer, the powder, the loofah, the brush. Back to tasks, to scrubbing dried crusts from ceramic bowls and flecks of shit from porcelain bowls. Back to forming one's face into a pleasant expression when interrupted by one's lover, a passing thought, a wasp, a wrong number dialed on the phone. Back to the work of fielding and filtering the electronic transmissions pulsed ceaselessly, for profit, into one's skin.

Back to the work of sitting in one's *chair* and typing words into that vague, hulking sentience, the computer, its screen. Words like, for example, *to enthusiastically apply*, *to have the appropriate skills*, *to apologize for the delay*. Back to the particular interest. To the application, the proposal, the questionnaire. Back to the work of buffing and shining one's face into a girl's face, the work of pushing words out of a girl's mouth about *art*, meaning *buy*. Back to the work of signing checks, the John Hancock, of creasing the envelope, giving a lick. *August rent*, one might write on the check. Back to that work,

the cruel work, the old work.
    Or, perhaps, not.

Acknowledgments

This book began its life when a man, then still a near-stranger, encouraged me to lie. *If you want to write a book, you should tell your boss you got some prestigious writing residency and ask for a sabbatical,* he instructed, and I did.

I had received no such residency. To Dominique Lévy, the woman and the corporate body: I am not sorry for my lie, but I am grateful that you permitted me to take leave of my work as your voice so that I might invent the one that speaks here. To Sylvia Gorelick, Karin Schneider, Aliza Shvarts, and Begum Yasar, my brilliant friends and teachers: our conversations during this time were this book's beginnings. Thank you.

Sarah Strange generously loaned me her car and pointed me toward Dowelltown, Tennessee, where Benjy Russell's cabin proved a far superior writing studio, I imagine, than those offered by even the swankiest residencies. During my time there, I wrote the first draft of this book accompanied by the words of Anne Carson, Chris Kraus, Ben Lerner, Dolly Parton, Marcel Proust, Ariana Reines, Lynne Tillman, the anonymous Google reviewers who awarded New York's jails zero stars, and the many shoplifters (or imaginative wannabes) who recounted their escapades on Reddit and Quora.

I am immensely grateful to have found in Claire Messud a mentor and advisor whose literary genius is matched only by her kindness and wit. I am also deeply indebted to Keisha Knight for showing me how to pull the emergency break so that I might dig deeper; Thomas Corbani, for the conversation that led to this book's closing; and Robin Treadwell, for tending to these pages with a close eye and sharp intelligence.

It is rare to find an interlocutor whose vision both matches and exceeds one's own, and rarer still for this person to be one's editor. Rebecca Wolff, this manuscript would have existed forever only as a 1.1 MB PDF on my external hard drive were it not for you. Thank you for your faith, your patience, and your impeccable editorial guidance. My thanks, also, to Marilyn Silverman for her fastidious copy edits, and to Jason Zuzga, Emily Wallis Hughes, and Carolyn Latino, whose savvy and thoughtfulness paved the way for this book's appearance in the world.

I completed a final revision in Sarah Wyman's cabin in New Paltz, New York, accompanied by the voice of Aretha Franklin and a small, nameless being who, I imagine, wanted to see it done before taking final leave of my flesh. My deep thanks to Amie Worley for sitting beside me, and for reminding me that a novel is also a form of life. And, if this book's beginnings demanded I invent a fake residency, its end birthed a real one: Sarah, I am honored to have been the Trout Lily Initiative's inaugural writer in residence.

To my parents, Brian and Linda Werder: Dad, your bedtime stories first taught me that words enchant this world. Mom, I consider your willingness to share episodes from my childhood and your own—and to see them represented, however imperfectly, here—an act of great vulnerability. Thank you.

Kai Werder, I'd like to say that you didn't know what you were starting when you first dared me to steal a lip gloss from the CVS when we were small, but I suspect that you did, because you haven't stopped daring me to find ever greater amounts of courage since.

To the man who encouraged me to lie so that *Thieves* might have its start: Christopher Cramer, you have been this book's best reader, most incisive critic, foxiest muse, and most steadfast advocate. To say that I am grateful could never be enough. You know I'm not one for systems of ownership and possession, but: this book and my love are yours.